Praise for *USA TODAY* bestselling author

KASEY MICHAELS

"{A} hilarious spoof of society wedding rituals wrapped around a sensual romance filled with crackling dialogue reminiscent of *The Philadelphia Story*."
–*Booklist* on *Everything's Coming Up Rosie*

"A cheerful, lighthearted read."
–*Publishers Weekly* on *Everything's Coming Up Rosie*

"Michaels continues to entertain readers with the verve of her appealing characters and their exciting predicaments."
–*Booklist* on *Beware of Virtuous Women*

"Lively dialogue and characters make the plot's suspense and pathos resonate."
–*Publishers Weekly* on *Beware of Virtuous Women*

"A must-read for fans of historical romance and all who appreciate Michaels' witty and sensuous style."
–*Booklist* on *The Dangerous Debutante*

"Michaels is in her element in her latest historical romance, a tale filled with mystery, sexual tension, and steamy encounters, making this a gem from a true master of the genre."
–*Booklist* on *A Gentleman by Any Other Name*

"Michaels can write everything from a lighthearted romp to a far more serious-themed romance. {Kasey} Michaels has outdone herself."
–*Romantic Times BOOKreviews*, Top Pick, on *A Gentleman by Any Other Name*

KASEY MICHAELS

The Bride of the Unicorn

HQN™

ISBN-13: 978-0-373-77271-1
ISBN-10:   0-373-77271-8

THE BRIDE OF THE UNICORN

HQN Books August 2007

First published by Pocket Books

www.HQNBooks.com

Printed in U.S.A.

More newly released classics from

KASEY MICHAELS

and HQN Books

The Secrets of the Heart
The Passion of an Angel

Other books from Kasey Michaels

A Most Unsuitable Groom
Everything's Coming Up Rosie
Beware of Virtuous Women
The Dangerous Debutante
A Gentleman by Any Other Name
Stuck in Shangri-la
Shall We Dance?
The Butler Did It

And coming in September

A Reckless Beauty

**The next installment in
The Beckets of Romney Marsh series**

The Bride of the Unicorn

PROLOGUE

1801

Evil is easy, and has infinite forms.

Blaise Pascal

And doom'd to death, though fated not to die.

John Dryden

"CAROLINE, DO SIT STILL, CHILD. It's enough that this coach is rocking as if John Coachman were blind as well as deaf and can not see the ruts, without your bouncing to add to the jostle."

"Felling ill again, pet?" Henry Wilburton, seventh earl of Witham, and soon to become a father again at the advanced age of forty-six, looked adoringly at his young wife, who was still dealing with the fractious three-year-old. "We shouldn't have stayed so long. Silly children's party."

Lady Gwendolyn pulled Caroline closer to her on the wide velvet seat, tucking the carriage blanket around the colorfully embroidered hem of the child's gown and the chubby legs that refused to remain still, then hastened to reassure her husband. "Nonsense, Henry. It was a delightful evening. I'm much improved now. It was ill-advised of me to have sampled the syllabub, that's all. At least not until I am past this third month. My reaction to sweet creams was much the same with Caroline, remember?"

"Vividly, my dear, vividly," Lord Witham answered, stretching forward from the facing seat to pat her hand. "I suppose I will simply have to cosset you outrageously for these next months, a chore I admit I look forward to with great delight."

"You are the very best of husbands, Henry—and I vow to hold you at your word. I rather enjoy being cosseted." She reached across her daughter to lift the leather flap over the window and peered out into the darkness brightened only by the coach lamps riding high on either side of the driver's box, then frowned. She hadn't been entirely truthful with Henry about the state of her stomach. A lingering queasiness was still giving her fits, and she could barely wait to be out of the swaying coach and on solid ground again. "Are we nearly home? I believe I see raindrops on the pane."

"Very nearly, pet. Caro, my rambunctious little lamb, why don't you sing us the song your mama has just taught you? You remember—'Now Is the Month of Maying.'"

"No, Papa," Caroline answered with a mulish pout squeezing her small, perfect features. "Caro's tired," she said as she burrowed her blond curls against her mother's breast.

Lady Gwendolyn chuckled at this not uncommon display of temper. "Willful little beast, isn't she, darling? We can only hope our unborn son will have half Caroline's starch. Boys should be— What's that? Henry? That was a shot, I'm sure of it!"

She watched as the earl immediately cocked his head toward the window to his left, then frowned at the unmistakable report of a second pistol shot. He opened his mouth to warn her to take hold of the strap, but it was already too late for her to have time to obey him.

A heartbeat later all three occupants of the coach tumbled to the floor when John Coachman, whose deafness might not have alerted him to the noise, hauled mightily on the traces, then put on the brake as two dark-cloaked riders plunged out of the trees and directly onto the roadway in front of the horses, calling: "Stand and deliver!"

Caroline immediately began to wail, sounding not hurt but angry, as if overcome by a mighty indignation born of finding herself sprawled inelegantly on the floor, wedged partially beneath her mother's body. Lady Gwendolyn couldn't blame her, for she too was feeling the effects of being tossed about like so much flotsam.

"Are you all right? Good. Quiet her, Gwen," Lord Witham ordered as he helped his wife back onto the seat, then reached into his pocket and withdrew a small purse that contained ten or twelve gold pieces. "I have enough on my plate being robbed, without Caro's bawling to add to the chaos. Damned depressing, you know. I was told this road was clear of high-toby men. I'd give half my fortune to be able to turn my pistols on them, but it's best not to put up a struggle. Give me your jewels, sweetheart, and I'll step outside and deal with the wretches. We'll be out of this and home safe and dry in a trice, I promise you."

Lady Gwendolyn, forgetting her nausea and fatigue, fumbled to remove her diamond earrings and the matching bracelet the earl had given her just that past Christmas. She handed them over, then laid a hand on her husband's arm. "Filthy beasts. I won't give them my rings, Henry," she told him firmly, "nor shall they have my beautiful pendant. There are some things that simply cannot be replaced."

Lord Witham's smile was eloquent with love, so much so that Lady Gwendolyn felt herself dangerously near to tears. "Anything can be replaced, my sweet," she heard him say, "except you and our dearest Caroline. Now hurry, my pet," he added, frowning. "We can't have the rascals catching more than a glimpse of either you or the child. You are both too beautiful by far, and I don't wish to tempt them."

Tamping down what she considered to be a reasonable rise of hysteria, Lady Gwendolyn slipped the rings from her finger for the first time since her husband had placed them there on their wedding day, and laid them in his hand. She was just raising her hands to her throat to slip the pendant up and over her head when the off door was flung open and a man wearing a full face mask gruffly ordered Lord Henry to leave the coach.

"Henry, no! For the love of heaven, don't leave us." Lady Gwendolyn felt her bravado desert her, and she clung fiercely to his arm, but he gently shook himself free of her grip, smiled reassuringly yet again, and stepped down into the road.

Left alone with her child, who was now wide-eyed and quiet, Lady Gwendolyn willed herself not to fall to pieces. People were robbed every day on the king's highways. The lack of safety in these enlightened times was a national disgrace, as she had heard when the subject was discussed earlier, at Sir Stephen's party for his youngest son's birthday.

But people weren't just robbed of their valuables, Lady Gwendolyn remembered. Sometimes, if they resisted, they were shot—killed! A man had met that terrible fate trying to defend himself just last month, somewhere near to London. Shot dead, he had been, and scarcely a mile from his estate.

Not that anything so terrible would happen to them. After all, this wasn't London. This was Sussex. This was a civilized countryside. And her dearest, bravest Henry was cooperating with the highwaymen.

And yet...

Lady Gwendolyn was so frightened, no matter how reassuring her husband's smile had been, and longed to do something to help him. Her hands went to her throat and the gold chain that still hung there. It wouldn't do to have the highwaymen discover her wearing it and believe they had tried to hide some of their valuables. She quickly removed the pendant and chain and hung it around Caroline's throat, prudently stuffing its length inside the collar of the child's dress. No one, not even a highwayman, would be so basely cruel, so dastardly, as to search an infant!

But it wasn't enough. There had to be something else— some other way to help. Henry had asked her to do something, something about Caroline. Yes, yes. She remembered now. He had wanted her kept quiet and concealed; he had distinctly said so. She looked down at the child, to see that Caroline's little chin was quivering, as if she were about to burst into tears once more.

That wouldn't do. That wouldn't do at all!

And then Lady Gwendolyn was struck by an inspiration that would both keep her daughter quiet and hide the pendant from the highwaymen. Henry would be so proud of her for thinking of it! Why, at the next party they attended, Henry would hold court at the dinner table, recounting their brush with highwaymen and his wife's brilliance.

Leaning forward, she raised the velvet-covered seat her husband had just vacated and surveyed the small, roughly lined compartment usually reserved for extra luggage. "Here, my darling," she whispered, lifting Caroline and placing her small body in the compartment. "You hide in here for now, until Papa comes back. Be very quiet, please, so you can surprise him when I tell you to come out again. Can you do that, Caroline? Can you be a big girl and play this game for Mama?"

"A game, Mama?" Caroline repeated, visibly brightening. "Caro play a game?"

"Yes, darling! What a good girl you are. You are my sweet, darling Caro. Now give Mama a kiss."

She hugged the child, clinging to her desperately, fearfully, for a moment before motioning for Caroline to bow her head so that the seat could be lowered back into position. Then Lady Gwendolyn sat down on the seat, daintily spread out the satin skirt of her gown, took a deep breath, and dared to push aside the leather curtain and peek outside.

It was raining steadily now, a drenching downpour, but the flickering light from the coach lamps provided her with a vague, distorted view of what was transpiring in the roadway.

She saw Henry standing no more than three feet from the door to the coach, his back to her, his hands raised, as one of the highwayman held a pistol leveled at his chest.

A second robber stood nearby, and she could see her jewels glinting in one gloved hand as he aimed a pistol up at the box, at John Coachman, an old man so timid and defenseless that Lady Gwendolyn had more than once suggested to her husband that the man was getting past it. And it was true. If John had only had the ears to hear the first shots he might have sprung the horses and they would be home and dry now, as her dearest Henry had promised, instead of sitting stranded on the roadway, in the clutches of these nefarious highwaymen.

Lady Gwendolyn shuddered, her feelings of helplessness returning. What was taking so long? Surely it was almost over now. Or were they planning to search the coach anyway? But why would they do that? They already had her jewels. They already had all of Henry's money.

She pressed her fingers against the cold pane, wishing she could touch her husband, wishing she could hear what was being said, wishing she were stronger or smarter or braver.

And then the robber holding her jewels raised his pistol slightly and fired, the flash of powder visible a heartbeat before the earsplitting report that caused her entire body to flinch uncontrollably.

She heard rather than saw John Coachman's body tumble into the roadway, for she was already looking toward her husband, who had dropped his hands and turned toward the coach, toward her.

"Gwen!" she heard him shout as he took a single step in her direction, his beloved face pale and frightened in the dim light. "Get out the other side. Run! Run into the trees!"

Run? Take Caro and leave him? Never! And yet, even if she had wanted to obey him, she could not have done so.

She couldn't move.

She couldn't breathe.

All she could do was watch, horrified, paralyzed, her fingers still locked behind the windowpane, as another shot rang out and Henry was flung forward heavily, to fall against the side of the coach, then slide away from her, to the ground.

"Henry—no!" Lady Gwendolyn reached for the latch, disregarding the earl's warning, forgetting her child, not caring for her own safety. She threw open the door her husband, her protector, had closed behind him a minute earlier—a lifetime ago.

Her hands braced on either side of the opening, she struggled with the damning reality of seeing her husband lying just below her feet, his body facedown in the mud, a dark, ominous stain spreading on the back of his jacket. "Henry. Oh, my dear God—*Henry!*"

She raised her head and screamed at the highwaymen, her voice high-pitched with mounting hysteria. "We gave you all our money—all our jewelry. We gave you *everything!* And you *killed* him. There was no reason, no need. *Why?* Why did you do this?"

The man who had discharged his second pistol into the seventh earl of Witham stripped away his dark mask, revealing wickedly grinning features as he advanced in Lady Gwendolyn's direction. "Good evening, Gwen. Beastly weather, isn't it?"

She stared at the man as his face was revealed in the flickering light of the coach lamps, unable to understand either his presence or his actions. She then looked down at her husband's body and shuddered convulsively before turning uncomprehending eyes back to Lord Henry's killer. "But why? *Why?*"

She continued to watch as the man—this man she knew, this man she had trusted—took another step forward and slowly pulled a third long-barreled weapon from his belt....

BOOK ONE

A QUESTION OF HONOR
October 1815

Chance is a nickname for Providence.
Sébastien R. N. Chamfort

CHAPTER ONE

We die only once, and for such a long time!

Molière

LORD JAMES BLAKELY trusted his nephew did not view the scene now unfolding for his benefit as particularly jolly. Such interludes were by right supposed to be off-putting, damn it, deadly solemn and hung heavy with foreboding. Later—once the body had grown stiff and cold—there would be ample time for Morgan Blakely to perform a jig on his grave.

If he could.

For now, however, Lord James, in his own way, and in his own good time, would dance.

He had set up the particulars for this occasion with infinite care—planned his starring role down to the last detail. The gloomy, barnlike bedchamber suited his purpose perfectly, for he knew it had never been the most advantageous stage setting for any save moribund frolic.

Lord James had long ago opted to take his physical pleasures in somewhat less inhibiting surroundings, the more baseborn his partner the better. That sort of female did not take exception when the play turned rough. At least they had never shown their distaste—not for the heavy blunt he'd paid down to indulge his appetites.

And if he'd ruined one or two of the round-heeled bitches for the business, well, what of it? Nothing lasted. Nothing lived forever.

And he should know. He could see the demons gathering now, hovering in a far corner, high against the ceiling, rubbing their clawlike hands together and licking slimy, reptilian lips; eager to snatch him up, slash out his soul, and pitch it down, down, into the very bowels of the earth.

But not yet. No. He still had time. He still had something he had to do; a last, perfect mischief that would render his damnation tolerable.

Lord James moistened his parched, fever-cracked lips and looked about the room, searching out his audience of one.

The chamber was particularly musty this October evening, its bog-water green velvet draperies shut tight, its heavy Tudor furniture hulking ponderously against the tapestry-hung walls, the wretchedly ineffectual fire in the oversized grate hissing rather than crackling.

The price of good wood could beggar a man. The smoke and sizzle of green wood might make living plaguey uncomfortable, but it was more than good enough to die by.

The world outside the drafty windows couldn't have been any more appropriate, nature helping him with his scene-setting. It had been raining all day; a heavy, drenching, reminiscent downpour that had set all the usual damp patches on the ceiling to showing themselves to disadvantage while lending to the stale, musty air another aroma to ponder: mildew.

The only sound Lord James heard was that of rainwater splashing tinnily into a half dozen pails set at irregular intervals on the threadbare carpet—along with his own decidedly evil chuckling and intermittent coughing, as he had just completed entertaining his guest with a little tale about a liaison he'd once had with the local rat catcher's daughter.

Vulgarity was so comforting, such a glaringly human vice in the midst of this tawdry business of dying. He, Lord James Blakely, rapidly fading but still cheerfully malevolent, would do his damnedest to make his passing as miserable for his guest as possible. He might be only a few days or hours away from being put to bed with a shovel, but was that any reason to alter by so much as a hair the habits of a lifetime?

"The rat catcher's daughter. My congratulations, Uncle, for you are nothing if not consistent," Morgan Blakely said now, as Lord James went off in another paroxysm of high-pitched giggles. "I have always so enjoyed your feeble attempts at humor. You really should have written them all down somewhere, for the sake of posterity, you understand. But then, you did write some things down, didn't you, some little tidbits of information—and then forwarded them directly to France via one of the less discriminating smuggling gangs that frequent the coast."

Lord James's face blanched, his enjoyment decimated, and he looked furtively at his nephew. "You know about that?" he asked, his handkerchief still pressed to his mouth, a string of spittle dribbling from his chin.

Morgan spoke in a deadly sweet drawl, his distaste for his uncle maddeningly obvious in the relaxed stance of his long, leanly muscled body. "Dear me, yes," he answered, smiling for the first time since he'd entered the bedchamber.

Lord James gritted his teeth, shaking with fury. "When? How?"

"Must I really indulge you? Oh, very well. I have known since before Waterloo, since shortly after my return from France. As for the how of it—you do remember my mission during the war, don't you, my area of operation? Tell me, Uncle—was the money you received for selling secrets all the sweeter for the thought that the information you forwarded to Bonaparte could have meant the end of your brother's son? I've occasionally wondered about that possibility—in idle moments, you understand."

Morgan knew. Cold-hearted bastard! *If only I had my pistol, I'd shoot him square between those mocking devil-black eyes, and consign him to hell before me!*

But Lord James didn't have his pistol. He was dying; defenseless in front of the man he had planned to bring low, now with more reason than simple hate to goad him. Was there no justice? No justice at all?

Lord James's eyes slid away from his nephew's face. He felt himself growing weaker by the moment, and still he had not begun to tell Morgan the reason he had summoned him. Instead, Morgan had taken center stage, had muddled the plot with a last-minute alteration to the script. Lord James had wondered why his contacts on the Continent had dried up three years ago—and with them nearly his sole source of income. Morgan had done it. His own nephew!

Yet why was he surprised? Shouldn't he have known that Morgan was behind it—his maddeningly secretive nephew with the heart of stone and ice water in his veins?

Suddenly it became important to Lord James that his nephew understand the horrors he had been through, the very valid reasons for his treason. "This house took all my money, always has. Decrepit pile, the bane of every younger son! Why else do you think I agreed to work with Bonaparte? But my contact stopped asking for my help, stopped sending all that lovely money." He tried to lift himself onto his elbows. "Because of you. All because of *you!*"

Morgan raised a perfectly manicured finger to stroke at one ebony eyebrow. "Ah, your *contact,* at the War Office. Thorndyke, wasn't it? Yes, that was his name. George Thorndyke. He became very useful, once we were able to supply him with secrets we wished passed along—through other channels, of course. I could not have the family name involved. Having one's own uncle hanging from a gibbet could be a tad embarrassing, you understand. I did tell you that poor Thorndyke is dead these past two months or more, didn't I? I know you've been out of touch here in Sussex, dying and all."

"Thorndyke's dead?" Lord James narrowed his eyes as he glared at Morgan. "What did you do?"

"Uncle—how you wound me. You know I am not a man of violence. Thorndyke died suddenly. Hanged himself in his study only hours after I left him, as a matter of fact. And we'd had such a lovely visit, too. It was a most depressing funeral. You can count yourself lucky to have missed it."

Lord James's once large frame, now ravaged by illness, seemed to shrink even more under his nephew's casually spoken words. It didn't matter now. He couldn't be hurt now, carted away for treason. Yet he had to know. "Who else? Who else knows?"

"Actually," Morgan answered, "nobody." He pulled over a chair and positioned it at his uncle's bedside before sitting down. "I thought it prudent to keep your dirty linen in the cupboard."

"Your father," Lord James spat grudgingly, his ravaged face pinched into a condescending sneer. "Your endlessly ungrateful idiot of a father. You did it for him."

"For my father, yes," Morgan answered shortly. "I discovered that, at the time, I wasn't willing to sacrifice his good name in order to exercise a paltry justice on you. But that is neither here nor there now, as your sadly wasted body has saved me from suffering through another interview such as the one I had with Thorndyke—just to tie up all the loose ends now that the war is over, you understand. Dearest Uncle James—and I trust I have deduced correctly: that *is* a death rattle I hear in your throat, isn't it?"

Lord James looked at his nephew, seeing the dangerous facade the world saw, the darkly handsome, impeccably dressed gentleman of fashion whose sartorial splendor could never quite disguise the fact that Morgan Blakely could be a very, very dangerous man.

"I've always hated you, Morgan. If it weren't for you, I would have inherited all my brother's wealth. I had so counted on that. Instead, all my plans have come to naught. And now I am dying, while my holy brother still lives, mumbling his prayers on his makeshift altar while you live high on the Blakely money. There is no justice in this world."

"I see no need to make my father any major part of this discussion."

Lord James's temper flared. "Of course you don't! I thought I had summoned you—but you were coming anyway, weren't you? To be sure of my death? And you're here to watch me die, not to discuss my hypocrite brother. My brother! Loves his God more as each new dawn brings him closer to his own day of reckoning. Funny. Don't remember Willy spouting scripture when we were young and tumbling everything in sight. Even shared a couple of 'em."

"That will be enough."

Lord James ignored his nephew's warning and continued: "Hung like a stallion, your sainted father, just like you. Hypocrite! That's what our Willy is. You don't like his praying and penance any better than I, do you, nevvy? Serves no purpose, does it, when we both know there is no God. You and me, we know. Only the devil, nevvy, only the devil. Believe it, nevvy. There *is* a devil. It's him or nothing. He's sent some of his fellows on ahead to welcome me. See 'em? Over there—hanging from the ceiling like bloody bats. The sight would set Willy straight on his knees for sure, bargaining for angels."

A muscle twitched spasmodically in Morgan's cheek. "Your mind is going, Uncle, otherwise I would have to take you to task for your obscenity. However, I see no crushing need to remain here and listen to your ramblings. If you wanted me here for some purpose other than to allow me the faint titillation of watching you shuffle off this mortal coil I suggest you organize your thoughts and get on with it."

"Ah, yes. Indeed, let us return to the reason for your presence, and hang this distasteful business about spies and Thorndyke and your so damnable, so *patient* revenges. Poor nevvy—this is one death scene you cannot manipulate to your own designs. Morgan Blakely is not omnipotent this night!"

Morgan inclined his head, not in acquiescence but in obvious condescension.

Nevertheless, the smile was back on Lord James's face, not that it was an improvement, for years of dissipation had taken a permanent toll even before this last illness struck him down. But all was not lost. His darts had begun to hit home. His adversary was attempting to leave the field—although not before telling him about Thorndyke, not before indulging himself with at least one surgically precise parting shot. Well, he had taken that shot, and now it was time to get to the real crux of this bizarre meeting.

"All in good time, nevvy. You had me worried there for a

moment, admitting that you had allowed sentiment to keep you from turning me over to the government, but you're still the same, all right! Cold to the bone. No wonder we hate each other so—we're two peas in a pod. Killed your share and more, haven't you? And liked it, too, didn't you, boy? The devil's deep in you, just as he is in me."

His smile faded and he became intense, for he knew he was about to close in for the kill. "But you've got bits of your mother stuck in you, too. A soft side, a silly, worthless part of you that actually *cares*. That's why I sent for you. You're vulnerable, and I like that. I can use that. Listen closely, nevvy. You think you know me, but you don't. Selling secrets to Boney was child's play, something to do to pass the time. How do you think I've survived all these years? I ran through my wife's money in less time than it took to bury her along with the puling brat she'd died trying to birth—good riddance to bad rubbish—and I had to poke about, looking for another, more reliable source of income."

Morgan held out his left hand and inspected his fingertips, frowning over a small cut at the tip of his index finger. "How utterly fascinating, Uncle. I am, of course, hanging breathless on your every word," he drawled with patently deliberate nonchalance.

"Damned impertinent bastard!" Lord James accused hotly, struggling to rise from his pillows. "Never have I met your like! *Never!*"

"No, no," Morgan corrected, his tone insultingly amiable. "I'm your image, Uncle, remember? 'Cold to the bone,' as I believe you said. Oh, dear. Is that the gong calling me to dinner? What a fortunate escape. Never fear that I shall find my meal inadequate. I took the precaution of bringing a basket with me from Clayhill." He rose slowly, pushing the chair back to its former position, the cool precision of his movements galling Lord James. "If you should chance to expire while I'm dining, please consider this our last tender farewell. Good evening, Uncle."

Morgan was nearly at the door before Lord James spoke again, for it took him that long to regain his breath after his last outburst. He had to say this now—say what he wanted to say, what had to be said—or else Morgan would be gone for good, and James would have died for nothing. If he could not leave behind some festering evidence of his malevolence, the only legacy of a childless, bitter man, it would be as if he had never lived….

"That's it. Run away. No one can capture the Unicorn!" he called out, his voice loud in the quiet room. He lay back against the pillows, listening to the drops of rainwater splash into the pan nearest the bed, waiting for Morgan's response, but not really expecting any.

"I've always thought it the height of irony that *you* were the Unicorn," he continued when he felt enough time had elapsed to build the suspense he desired. "England's greatest spy. My nemesis. And so modest about it. If I had not broken the codes that made up the messages I delivered to the smugglers, I might never have guessed. Even Wellington never figured out which was which, did he? Pompous, posturing dolt! But I recognized you immediately, recognized myself as I could have been—*would* have been if Saint Willy hadn't been born first. So, yes. Yes! I *did* know my treason could mean the death of you. It was part of the joy of the moment! Jeremy's death was no more than an accident of good fortune. But the war is over. Napoleon is banished. And still you cling to your secrecy, still you stand quietly and allow another to claim all your glory."

Lord James paused for a moment, then smiled. "I hold the key to that man's destruction, nevvy," he continued quietly, liking the hint of menace in his voice. "Would you like it? What would you and your patient revenge do with the perfect tool for that man's destruction? Shall that key be my parting gift to you, your legacy?" He lifted one skeletal hand, indicating the bedchamber and all of the house. "Along with this decrepit pile, of course."

"You're lying," Morgan said, his hand on the door latch, his back still turned toward the bed. "You have nothing I want. You were a most deplorable traitor, Uncle, barely worth the effort it took to ferret you out. You say you knew my identity, yet you seemed surprised to learn that I, in turn, had caught *you* out. But I will admit your dramatics are interesting, if a trifle lacking in style—especially that little bit about Jeremy. Perhaps you should have devoted yourself instead to penny press fiction."

His nephew didn't believe him! He was going to leave!

Sudden panic lent Lord James new strength. "I'm not lying, damn you! Think, nevvy. As the twig is bent! Willy can tell you. I was always what I am now, capable of anything for the sake of a few gold pieces. Trading in secrets was my only mistake, a miscalculation of old age and greed, but not my only source of income. I was better when I was younger, sharper."

"Hence this splendor in which you live, Uncle," Morgan taunted, spreading his hands as if to encompass the faded ugliness of the bedchamber before opening the door. "I'll ask one of the servants to come sit with you. Obviously you are now slipping toward delirium."

"No! I'm telling the truth. I swear it." James clawed his way to the side of the bed, the better to see his nephew, the better to allow his nephew to see him. "You cannot know all the things I've done, the vile, dastardly crimes I've committed."

"Cannot and do not care to know."

Lord James sneered. "Oh, nevvy, how far you have to fall from that perfidious pinnacle of indifference you perch on. You *do* care. You *will* care, because I hold all the cards now, all the answers to your schemes that you still do not admit to, even to yourself. You want revenge, nevvy. Damnation, man, you may even deserve it!"

"Perhaps you're right. But it will be in my own time, Uncle, and in my own way."

"Of course. I should have realized that you wouldn't wish my help, even if I am trying, in this feeble way, to atone for any indirect connection I might have had with dear Jeremy's death. I understand, nevvy." Lord James began to pick at the coverlet, his eyes averted from Morgan. "But then, there is still the matter of the child."

Lord James held his breath as Morgan let go of the latch and turned, his dark eyes narrowed as he stared straight into his uncle's grinning face. "Child? What child?"

"What? Did you say something, nevvy? I cannot hear you very well, and the room grows dim. Come closer, nevvy. Come close so that I can give you my last confession."

He heard Morgan's footsteps and smiled into the frayed collar of his nightshirt. He counted to ten, slowly, then began to speak once more. "Once upon a time," he began, then chuckled at his own wit, the laughter turning into a wet cough that left bits of blood on his already soiled handkerchief.

"Once upon a time, nevvy," he continued, "there was a man like me, a man who found himself where he should not be, while another man, a lesser man, usurped his rightful place.

We met, this man and I, no more than once or twice, and we bemoaned our fate together over several bottles of wine. Perhaps more than several bottles."

"Go on," Morgan urged, pulling the chair back over beside the bed. "Continue your fairy tale."

Lord James shot his nephew a searing look, reveling in the lack of necessity to hood his dislike for the younger man. "I have every intention of continuing," he said shortly. "We chatted idly, without real purpose—until the day the man's circumstances changed and it became imperative for him to take steps to protect himself. He tried to enlist my help, but I refused. Why should I do for him what I might have done for myself?" He shook his head. "I only wonder why I never did it for myself when I was younger…when we all were younger. I only wonder…."

Morgan stood. "And I can only wonder, Uncle, why I am allowing a perfectly good roasted chicken to continue to lie downstairs untasted in my dinner basket."

"No! Don't go! You must hear the rest. I did not help the man, but I know what he did." Lord James lowered his voice conspiratorially. "I followed after and watched—then fired my pistol to scare them off before they'd finished. He was even so stupid as to lift his mask and show his face, to crow about his success, so that he knew I saw him plain. That was a great help to me, almost as great a help as the child. After all, nevvy, what good is it to know something if you cannot turn a profit from it, hmm?"

"Uncle, I haven't the faintest notion what you're talking about."

"Of course you don't," Lord James agreed, feeling very satisfied with himself. "As one of those Greeks scribbled so long ago, nevvy, 'The fox knows many things, but the hedgehog knows one great thing.' You look surprised. Did you think I was a total barbarian? I know something of the classics. *You,* nevvy, are like the fox, but *I* am the hedgehog. Blackmail, which depends on knowing a single great thing, would never occur to you. But it occurred to me."

Lord James rubbed his palms together, gleefully remembering the long-ago night of his greatest brilliance. He could see it as clearly as he could see his nephew's strained features. Maybe more clearly. "I waited until after the shot that silenced the woman before I fired my own pistol, frightening them off. And then I waited longer still, until I was sure they had gone, before riding in. I found the child on the ground—muddy, her mother's blood mixing with the mud and rainwater on her face and little dress. The father was half sunk in the mud— back shot! But I digress. Bit me, the little hellion did, when I pulled her away from the bodies just as her mother breathed her last. I could have killed the child then—snapped her neck like a dried goose bone—but I didn't. I needed her, you see."

"The child?" Morgan's voice was hushed, as if he wished to ask the question but did not want to interrupt. Which was as it should have been. It was time the boy paid his uncle a little respect.

"Yes, of course, the child. I put her in a safe place. Not a very nice place, I suppose, but you must remember—I could just as easily have disposed of her. Suddenly I had all the money I needed, although the fool never knew it was his occasional drinking companion who was taking a share of his new wealth. All the money I could ever want, delivered to a safe address at the beginning of each new quarter. Such a gentlemanly, civilized arrangement—for a time."

He stopped his story once more, to cough, and to contemplate the injustices of his life.

"The payments stopped a few years ago," he continued swiftly, not caring for this part of the story, "when the man demanded more proof and ordered me to produce her. I couldn't, for they told me she had reached her teens and left the orphanage where I had so gladly deposited her that first night. That was careless of me, wasn't it, nevvy? Misplacing the brat like that, if in truth she had left the orphanage. Luckily I already had Thorndyke—or unluckily, depending upon how you consider the thing. But this is the chit's house by rights, not yours as is stated in my will, considering that the blunt I got from blackmailing her parents' killer is what kept this place going for so long. This hulking money-eater and several grand estates scattered all over England that were deeded in her name by her father—all are hers. She's a rich orphan, this missing heiress I spared in my generosity."

"You have proof of this dastardly crime, I imagine?"

"Proof? Imbecile! You demand proof from a dying man?" Lord James could not hide his elation, sure all his hooks had sunk home with deadly accuracy. Now, at last, his little play was falling out as he had planned. It almost made his dying worthwhile, to be able to leave the noble Morgan behind to ruin his life trying desperately to right his uncle's wrong.

Now it was time to reel out the line a few feet before hauling his newly caught fish in once more. "Never mind, Morgan. I shouldn't have mentioned it," he said, pressing back against the pillows. "Obviously you're not interested in my heartfelt confession. Why would you want to help me atone, in this the house of my death?"

Morgan rose from the chair, his cool composure discarded, his eyes flashing fire. Grabbing hold of his uncle's nightshirt with both hands, he half dragged him up from the bed so that Lord James had to turn his head to hide a triumphant smile.

"Enough of this nonsense! This is no game we're playing, not anymore. No more dancing around the facts, Uncle. I need to hear you say the name. I need to hear the proof from your own lips. Damn you, man, answer me!"

Now, Lord James thought. *Now is the time to take my exit—now, while he believes me.* He began to cough, racking coughs that had him spitting small specks of blood that tasted of rust and maybe even the dirt that would soon cover his mortal shell. There were two Morgans hovering above him, menacing him with their flashing dark eyes. Defiance flashed in Lord James's own eyes. "You—you're the smart one, nevvy. You already *know* the names!"

Morgan's desire to kill was apparent, but Lord James knew his nephew's need for information would take priority, leashing his bloodlust, at least for the moment. "The child? Is she still alive? Surely you must know something. Where could she have gone?"

"A whorehouse, if she was smart," Lord James answered, feebly trying to push his nephew's hands away. "Chopping turnips in someone's kitchen if she was stupid. Unless she's dead. You know the way of orphanages. It's a hard life. Even harder than mine has been. Maybe that's why I lost touch. Or maybe I was lied to. Maybe the little brat is feeding worms. What were you hoping for, Unicorn—to lay your head in the lap of a virgin? I'd like that too, for you'd have to die to do it."

Morgan released his grip on the nightshirt, which allowed James to slump back against the pillows, gasping for breath. "You're lying, old man. Your story is full of holes. I don't believe a word you're saying. You've just taken bits of well-known truth and conveniently twisted them around for your own evil motives."

Was he lying? Lord James couldn't remember. He had told so many lies. Was this the truth? Yes. Yes, of course it was the truth. He hadn't made this story up, designed it from bits of truth woven together with clever lies, to fashion a tapestry of revenge against his brother's son. Had he? Oh, Christ—*had he?*

But wait. He remembered now. He had proof!

Lord James dragged himself to the edge of the bed, knocking over a candlestick as he groped on the nightstand for the proof that would seal his nephew's fate, the one piece of evidence that would start him on what Lord James sincerely hoped would prove to be the path to his destruction. The path to destruction for all of them—and the revenge Lord James longed to see, if only from the other side of the grave.

His fingers closed over the pendant, and he fell back against the pillows, holding it out so that the long gold chain swung free. "Here! Here is your proof! I found it around the child's throat. Take it, nevvy. And then think, damn you. *Think!*"

Morgan ripped the pendant from his uncle's hand and held it up so that its gold chain twinkled dully in the candlelight. "It can't be. I won't believe it. You could have commissioned a copy. It would be just like you, for you've never done one genuine thing in your life. Uncle. Uncle? Do you hear me?"

Lord James was scarcely able to speak. Everything was suddenly moving too fast. Morgan was confusing him. He had wanted to enjoy this moment, draw it out, savor Morgan's frustration, then leave him with the Gordian knot of the puzzle he had set him. But now he could barely think clearly, and his ears were full of the sound of rushing water.

Fear invaded his senses, washing away the elation, the thirst for revenge. This was real. His death—so long contemplated but never really believed in, never before comprehended for what it represented—was upon him. The pain in his chest was suffocating, pushing him down into a yawning blackness, a total nothingness that terrified him by its absence of recognizable reality.

This was all wrong. He had been wrong. Nothing was playing out as it should. The play was not the thing. Revenge wasn't sweet. Not at this cost. Never at such a cost. He wanted to live. Longer. A second more. A minute more. Forever. Why? Why should he die?

Oh, God, but he was frightened. More frightened than he had ever been in his life. God? Why had he thought of God? Why had that well-hated name popped into his head? Could there really be a God? Could there be an alternative to nothingness, a substitute for hell? No wonder they had cried, those people he'd killed over the years. It was the terror that had made them cry! The terror of the unknown, the fear of the God he had sworn did not exist.

It was all so real now.

He had been wrong. His revenge against his brother and Morgan wasn't worth this agony. He didn't want to go to hell. If there was a hell there had to be a heaven. Why hadn't he seen that? Morgan was the smart one. Why hadn't *he* seen that?

Lord James didn't want to spend the rest of eternity burning, burning, burning....

Morgan had to find the girl for him! He had to seek redemption for his poor uncle's most terrible sin, save him from the demons. He'd tell Morgan everything he wanted to hear, tell him now. Tell him the chit's name; tell him everything he wanted to know; hold nothing back. Confession. He'd give his genuine confession. Confession was good for the soul.

He grabbed at his nephew's sleeve, trying to anchor himself to life for just a while longer. "Morgan? Could we be wrong? Is there a God? Oh, what if Willy's right? What if there is a God? What if there is? What if I'm telling the truth? Am I lying? I can't remember anymore. Help me, Morgan! I can't remember the truth!"

"Not now, old man," Morgan said, his voice tight. "Truth or lie, you have to tell me the rest of it, and then I'll judge for myself."

"Judge? We'll all be judged! Save me, Morgan! Save my immortal soul! You already know the name. Check—check the orphanage in Glynde," Lord James rasped, vainly trying to pull Morgan closer. "In Glynde," he repeated, his eyes growing wider and wider as he stared up at the ceiling in horror. The demons had migrated, to circle just above him. They were grinning in avid expectation, their long, pointed fangs glinting in the candlelight, the unearthly *whoop-whoop-whoop* of their black bat wings sucking the air from his lungs.

Lord James heard a sound coming to him as if from a distance. What was it? Oh, yes. Morgan. His dear nevvy was yelling, still asking for proof, his carefully constructed facade of civilization stripped away just as Lord James had foreseen it—yet he could not take pleasure in the sight. For one of the demons was on his chest now, resting on its bony, emaciated haunches, its birdlike legs folded at the knee as it dug razor-sharp talons into him, letting all the remaining air bubble out his mouth, to be followed by a rising river of blood.

"You know. You...must only *remember*," Lord James whispered, his voice clogged with blood, with mounting terror. "The murders...our neighbors...the missing child... the searching..."

The play couldn't be over; the finale had to be rewritten.

Yet the curtain had come crashing down…too soon. Too soon. He couldn't do anything right, even die.

"No one ever told me! I didn't know!" Lord James shrieked, his voice suddenly strong in his last agony. He felt himself beginning to choke, drowning in the hot liquid that rushed from his ears, from the tin pots—from everywhere in the universe—to pour into his lungs. He clutched at Morgan with a strength born of impossible panic, tearing at the fine white linen of his shirtfront. It had to be the truth. There was a girl—there was! *Wasn't there?* "Find her, nevvy—or I'm damned…or we're both forever damned! Willy…*brother… pray for me!*"

CHAPTER TWO

Men use thought only to justify their wrongdoings,
and speech only to conceal their thoughts.

Voltaire

THE SUN SHONE BRIGHT as Morgan Blakely and his father, William, duke of Glynde, walked away from the family mausoleum at The Acres, the duke's ancestral Sussex home. Each man was dressed in funereal black with an ebony satin armband, and each carried his hat while following behind the young minister who had conducted a mercifully short ceremony in the village church.

The duke appeared more than usually frail and wiped at his eyes with a large white handkerchief already banded on all four sides with a thin ribbon of black satin, as if his wardrobe was perpetually prepared for mourning—which, in a way, Morgan realized, it probably was. His father had buried his wife, both his sisters, one of his sons—and now his twin, James—in somewhat less than fifteen years.

Morgan though it must be a depressing way to live, surrounded by all that dying.

He sighed silently and glanced back up the hill at the impressive Italian marble structure that held all his relatives save the one at his side. How long would it be before he took this walk alone, leaving his father's mortal remains locked behind those airless walls of veined pink stone?

Would his father forgive him—truly forgive him—before he died?

Would he, Morgan, forgive himself? Could he live with himself? Why did he live at all, with Jeremy dead? Were thoughts of revenge enough to keep a man alive? They hadn't been enough for Uncle James.

But his father was speaking, and for once his tone held no censure, no pity. "It was quite a lovely service, wasn't it? I had never supposed that the Reverend Mr. Sampson could discover so many pleasant things to say about our dearest brother James."

"Indeed. I find it remarkable that anyone could summon up a single kind thing to say about the man, Father. And hauling his carcass here to The Acres for interment in the mausoleum is decidedly unnerving, as we have only succeeded in walling him up. Frankly, I would have much preferred to snuggle the bastard twelve or more feet belowground with a boulder or two piled atop his chest, on the off chance he should try to rise again."

"Morgan! Keep a civil tongue in your head, if you please. We have just buried a man. My brother. My twin. The man with whom I shared our mother's womb. Had it not been for the vagaries of the birth order, we might well have buried the duke this day."

"Now, there's an intriguing thought," Morgan responded, putting on his hat even as he nodded his goodbye to the minister, who had earlier begged release from any refreshments being served to the mourners after the interment, citing the necessity of attending at the bedside of an ailing villager. "I can only wonder how The Acres would have fared once

Uncle James reached his majority and transformed the place into a brothel."

The duke looked at his son with rheumy blue eyes that had faded over the course of his three and sixty years, like curtains hung too long in the sun. "I will pray for you, Morgan," he said, his voice tinged with sadness liberally mixed with resignation.

Morgan bristled, then swallowed down any hint of anger at his father's words. Anger did no good in battle or when trying to reason with the unreasonable. That did not mean that Morgan Blakely, Marquis of Clayton, was not conversant with the tumultuous emotion. He simply chose to ignore it. "You do that, Father," he said, deliberately stripping the black satin ribbon from his sleeve and stuffing it in his pocket. "You pray for me. Pray for Uncle James. Pray for Jeremy."

"Do not make a mockery of your brother's immortal soul!" The duke's thin cheeks flushed with unhealthy color. Or righteous indignation. Or possibly even religious fervor. Morgan could never be sure. "Not when you were partially the instrument of his death."

Morgan took one step backward, stung as sharply as he would have been if his father had just slapped his face. "You never tire of that song, do you, Father?" he asked after a moment. "Do you sing it every morning as you wake? Does its accusatory melody lull you to a dreamless sleep at night?"

"Now you're being impertinent, Morgan," The duke countered quickly, laying a hand on his son's forearm. "I have forgiven you. In my heart I have forgiven you. My God demands it of me."

"Really?" Morgan smoothly removed his arm from his father's grasp even as he allowed his full lips to curve into an amused sneer. "*Your* God. Wasn't that exceedingly accommodating of him? Promise me, Father, when next you speak with him—and I am quite convinced that you will—thank him for me. And pray don't insult the fellow by reminding him of how damnably cold his charitable forgiveness is to us poor sinners. Ah, here is one of the grooms with your pony cart, Father. How thoughtful of the boy. I shall forgo a ride back to The Acres myself, as I wish to be alone a while longer—to mourn Uncle James, of course. I wouldn't wish to distress you with my tears."

The duke shook his head and sighed deeply, as if to acknowledge the impossibility of finding a way to communicate with his son. "If you wish it, Morgan. I will see you at the dinner table, I hope. And in time to help me lend a blessing to the meal, please. I do not ask much of you while you are at The Acres, but I must ask that you follow my wishes in such matters. Coming to table with a glass of Burgundy in your hand is offensive."

Morgan assisted his father up onto the seat of the pony cart, then stepped back and bowed to the man. "I would rather cut off my own arm than offend you, sir," he drawled softly, then motioned for the groom to drive on, leaving him behind to contemplate his uncle's passing.

And to wonder why the sun was shining while Jeremy, and all of Jeremy's older brother's hopes for happiness, lay moldering in that pink marble mausoleum on the top of the hill.

THE SMALL ORPHANAGE at Glynde, a foundling home of indeterminate age and antiquated drains, was situated just outside the village proper, sunk in a small cutout of land and hidden behind a stout wall and a stand of trees. Good ladies and gentlemen riding in their carriages, farmers on their carts, and even people on foot could pass by the orphanage without fear of having their sensibilities offended by the sight of too-thin legs, too-large eyes, or the many tiny graves that lined a plot at the bottom of the kitchen garden.

The world, Morgan knew, was a hard, unforgiving place for an orphan in this land where wealth was too rare, where poverty and hunger already hung too close to home to be reminded of it daily, and where sympathy was reserved for the alms box at Christmas and Eastertide.

For all his newly discovered religion, even the very Christian duke of Glynde had not as yet extended his largesse past repairing the steeple of the Reverend Mr. Sampson's church, to bestow his bounty on the unwanted, unloved children whose very existence cried out for compassion.

He should bring the duke here, Morgan thought. He should shake him out of his self-imposed religious limbo and back to the world of the living. Hell and damnation, just the smell emanating from the place should be enough to do that.

Or perhaps, like the rest of the county, his father simply hadn't looked, hadn't chosen to see past the walls and the trees.

Morgan knew he hadn't seen past them either, except for a few times when, as a young, adventurous child, he had talked Jeremy into climbing over the high walls of the orphanage to steal apples from the single tree within the packed-dirt courtyard.

It wasn't that there were not ample trees at The Acres or that the one within the orphanage wall was of a tastier variety. It was the thrill of the adventure itself that had intrigued Morgan. Just as the risk of the thing had led him to ride his father's best hunter bareback at midnight, to steal away to watch a hanging in the village square, and to visit the local barmaid at the Spotted Pony at the tender age of fourteen.

Always dragging Jeremy, who was three years younger, along with him, of course, although he had allowed his brother to remain outside the first night he visited the Spotted Pony. There were limits, even to the debaucheries of headstrong youth.

No, he wouldn't bring his father here. He couldn't do that, any more than he could confide in the man about Uncle James's unbelievable deathbed confession. William Blakely's religious fervor—now doubled, thanks to his grief over Jeremy's death—could not be corrupted by orphans and tales of foul murder.

After all, if the duke lost his devotion to religion, his only talisman in a world gone mad, there would be nothing left for him to live for, and Morgan would soon after be forced to make that solitary journey back from the mausoleum.

Now, unfashionably early in the morning the day after Lord James's funeral, as the marquis alighted from his mount at the gates to the orphanage, gates that hung drunkenly from leather straps stretched long past their best effectiveness, he dismissed depressing thoughts of his father and of the lack of one single person in the world to whom he could confide his deepest hopes and thoughts. Instead, Morgan wondered silently if he had ever stolen food from the mouths of any of the foundlings, who must have viewed a ripe red apple as a prize beyond price.

But he didn't wonder for long. There was no sense in condemning himself for the follies of his misspent youth, for he had long since outgrown them for the follies he had indulged himself in since becoming—in the eyes of the world, at least—a man grown.

He approached the gates purposefully, refusing to regard what he was doing as anything more than hunting mares' nests because of a dying man's insane blatherings, and pulled on the rope that set a bell to sounding tinnily on the other side of the wall. And then he waited, slowly realizing that, although there had to be at least thirty orphans in residence, he had not heard a single sound since the bell stopped ringing. Not a laugh. Not a cry. Nothing. He might as well have been standing outside a graveyard.

"Well, lookee here. Glory be ta God, and ain't ye a fine-lookin' creature ta see so early in the mornin'? And rigged out just loik a Lunnon gennelmun with it all, ain't ye?"

Morgan turned about slowly to see a small, slight woman well past her youth—and most definitely years beyond any lingering hint of beauty she might ever have possessed—standing just behind him, a large bundle of freshly cut, still damp rushes tucked beneath her left arm.

He removed his curly-brimmed beaver and swept the woman an elegant leg, the distasteful aroma of unwashed female flesh assaulting his nostrils. "Good day, madam," he said politely as he straightened, suppressing an urge to take out his scented handkerchief and press it to his nostrils. "Allow me to introduce myself. I am the Marquis of Clayton, here to see the person in charge of this charming institution."

The small woman cackled—like an ancient hen with a sore throat, Morgan thought—then smiled, exposing her sad lack of teeth. She had some, for certain, but they were stuck into her gums at irregular intervals, as if she had stood at some distance while Mother Nature tossed them at her one by one, and she'd had to open her mouth to catch them as best she could.

"Mrs. Rivers? And what would ye be wantin' with the likes of her, boyo? Drunk as a wheelbarrow the besom is, and has been ever since the quarter's funds showed up here a fortnight ago, don't ye know. Bring yerself back next month, when she's murdered all the gin and can see ye straight. She's always been one fer a well-turned leg."

"I'm afraid my business can't wait that long," Morgan said as the woman moved to brush past him as if he—and his impressive title—didn't exist. She was the rudest individual he had ever met—and yet she intrigued him. She had a look of cunning intelligence about her, well hidden by the grime on her face, but still noticeable.

He decided to give it another try. He'd use the name his uncle had not given him, a name he already knew. "I've come with a mission—to locate a child, a young lady by now, I suppose. Her name is Caroline. Blond hair, or at least it was when she was little. She would be about eighteen."

The woman stopped abruptly, looking back at him slyly across one bony shoulder. "And is that a fact, boyo? And what, I'm askin', would a fine upstandin' gentrymort like yerself be doin' pokin' about for Caroline? Plenty of willin' bodies at the Spotted Pony—iffen ye don't mind a dose of the clap. Go there, why don't ye? I'm past such tumblin's now, even with a pretty un like yerself."

Until the woman spoke the name aloud as if familiar with it, Morgan had been willing to believe that his uncle's story was just as he had presented it—a fairy tale meant to send his nephew off to chase his own tail. Until this very moment he had refused to believe there was a grain of truth in James Blakely's words, or a single reason to hope that he, Morgan Blakely, had at last found a fitting instrument of revenge against his enemy.

"Surely you jest. You are the very picture of feminine beauty. What's your name, madam?" he asked now, extracting a single gold piece from his pocket and offering it to her.

"And that's a golden tongue ye have, don't ye, boyo? My name is Mary Magdalene O'Hanlan, seein' as how ye asked so nice like, but I've been Peaches since m'salad days in Dublin and then in Piccadilly." The woman smiled, then quickly snatched the coin from his fingers, biting on it to ascertain whether or not it was real before stuffing it inside the low bodice of her filthy gown. "M'cronies dubbed me with the name 'cause I was so good at stealin' sweet things from the stalls. I was the best—once. But that's a long time past, and best forgotten."

Her smile vanished as she leveled narrowed eyes at Morgan. "Now take yerself off, pretty boy. I ain't got nothin' more ta say. Just like I told that other fella all those years back—a mean-lookin' mort with a smile that wide, but that still couldn't hide the old divil what was peekin' out between his two eyes—there ain't no Caroline here. Not no more."

Morgan shook his head, disgusted with himself that he should feel so discouraged. He should have known. "She's dead, then?"

Peaches cocked her head to one side, blowing a greasy lock of graying red hair out of her eyes. "And did ye hear that from me? Ye got a mind what leaps ahead fast as a horse can trot. Mayhap she is, boyo, and mayhap she ain't. It depends, don't ye know. What would the loiks of ye be wantin' with Caroline Monday anyhows?"

"Caroline Monday?" Morgan repeated the name questioningly. "Then this particular orphan we're speaking of has a surname—a last name? Perhaps she isn't the one I'm seeking after all."

Peaches snorted. "Don't know a lot, do ye, boyo? It's me what named her Monday. That's the day I found the creature on the doorstep, just like I find so many of 'em, cryin' her little heart out fer her ma. She told me her other name all by herself," she continued, smiling reminiscently. "No higher than m'knee, she was, but she told me her name plain. Just afore she bit m'hand as I was offerin' it ta her. The divil's own rogue, she was, and no mistake. Then she caught the fever, like so many of them do, and I wouldna gived a plugged pennypiece fer her. But she didn't cock up her toes, not that un, even if she was poorly for ever so long. Too stubborn ta know she should be dyin', I said then ta anyone who'd listen, and I say it again now. Too simple mean stubborn by half! Think she was the bloody queen o' England herself!"

Morgan was elated by this information, but he deliberately tamped down his enthusiasm, saying only, "Yet you told me, as you told this other man you spoke of, that Miss Caroline is gone."

Peaches allowed the bundle of rushes to fall to the ground. "Miss Caroline, is it, now? And don't that sound grand fer a foundlin' brat?" She peered at him again, as if assessing him for flaws. "Now I'm thinkin' mayhap it's time some more of your worship's lovely gold passed over *Miss* Mary Magdalene O'Hanlan's palm?"

"Perhaps," Morgan replied tightly, and then for the first time spoke aloud of the memory his uncle's patently false, contrived confession had brought crashing to the forefront of his mind. "Or perhaps it's time I rode to the village to summon the constable, so that you can tell him that Mary Magdalene O'Hanlan is a member of the gang of nefarious and long-sought kidnappers of one Lady Caroline Wilburton, daughter of the earl and countess of Witham, who were cruelly murdered on a roadway not thirty miles from here some fifteen years ago?"

Peaches plunked herself down atop the bundle of rushes,

her skinny calves sticking out from beneath the hem of her gown. "The divil you say, boyo," she responded as she looked up at him, her voice tinged with wondrous awe but not a trace of fear or guilt. "And would ye be knowin' if there's a reward in the offin' for the safe return of this poor little darlin'? After all is said and done, it's me what kept her little heart beatin'—what with m'lovin' good care of the tot, don't ye know."

Morgan knew he could either dole out a coin for each piece of information or shorten the process by some minutes by acknowledging how important the woman's answers were to him. Deciding to leave subterfuge for another day and for someone less sharp than Peaches O'Hanlan, he pulled a small leather purse from his pocket and dropped it in the Irish-woman's lap. "Where is she?"

The purse followed the gold coin before Peaches answered him. "That's what I like, boyo—a fella who comes right to the heart of the thing. She's not here, nor has she been in this stinkin' hole fer this year or more. But I knows where she be, and it's more than a good ride from here. Ye'll be needin' me ta get ta her, don't ye know. Needin' me to point her out ta ye, ta get her ta trust ye. And it's the only real mither she's ever known or remembered since the fever struck that I am, the only one she loves. I'm her dearest Peaches, that's what I am."

"How commendable of you. You'll be well rewarded if you continue to cooperate. That purse is only a pittance, one that could be trebled. Gather whatever belongings you have and meet me outside these gates in an hour. I'll return with my carriage."

Morgan felt very tired as he turned to mount his horse. What was he doing? The Irishwoman could be lying to him. His uncle James most probably had been lying to him. And yet some of the puzzle pieces were already beginning to fit. He had to continue the search for his instrument of revenge against Richard Wilburton. He had been patient for three long years. It was time to act. "An hour, Miss O'Hanlan, and no more. And don't breathe a word to anyone."

"Me?" Peaches responded, scrambling to her feet. "It's close as an oyster I'll be, and ye can take that as m'word."

"I'd prefer not to take either your word or your person anywhere, Miss O'Hanlan, but as you Irish say, 'Needs must when the devil drives'."

Morgan swung himself up into the saddle. "Oh, and one more thing. Kindly bathe before I come back. You reek of the sewers, *Miss* O'Hanlan."

Peaches gave a flirtatious flip of her bony hand as Morgan guided his horse toward the path. "Dip m'self in parson's ale? Well, all right—but only a little bit, and only 'cause ye're a such pretty thing, boyo."

CHAPTER THREE

Beware, as long as you live, of judging people by appearances.

Jean de La Fontaine

"DULCINEA? DULCINEA! You sweet, wretched angel, I see you skulking out there. Come in here to me at once! I have just now had the most splendiferous notion!"

Caroline Monday lifted her small chin from her chest, where she had let it drop while she indulged herself in a moment of exhaustion not unlike all her waking moments, and tiredly hauled herself up from the slatted wooden bench pressed against the wall of the hallway outside one of the small rooms reserved for affluent patients.

"Aunt Leticia, *all* of your notions are splendiferous," she soothed kindly as she walked toward the open doorway, "and as you have these notions at least three times daily, I see no need to rush lickety-split to hear the latest one."

"Oh, pooh," Leticia Twittingdon, who would never see the sunny side of fifty again, complained from her cross-legged perch on the wide cushioned window seat, thrusting her lower lip forward in a pout as Caroline entered the room. Miss Twittingdon's long, angular body was dressed from head to toe in brightest scarlet, and a crimson silk turban perched primly on her childlike curls. "And I was so certain you'd want to have me teach you the names and various titles of all of good King George's royal princes and princesses. All accomplished young ladies should know these things by rote, Dulcinea. It isn't enough merely to be beautiful. We must complete your education. Let's see, is Princess Amelia still alive? I seem to remember some tragedy about that dear little thing."

Caroline bent to pick up Miss Twittingdon's wool shawl, which had somehow found its way to the threadbare carpet, and laid it over the back of a wooden chair. "Another time, dear lady," she said, smiling wanly as she pushed her palms against her arched back at the waist, trying to ease her aching muscles. She was so tired. But then, she was always tired. "This particular well-informed debutante is woefully late emptying the chamber pots today."

"Dulcinea! How many times must I remind you that genteel ladies such as yourself do not speak of such base mortal necessities? Chamber pots, indeed! Don Quixote de la Mancha, that dearest and bravest of knights—a veritable saint!—would have deemed them golden chalices. Oh, dear. Should I have said that? Have I been sacrilegious?"

"I really wouldn't know. If I understand the meaning of the word correctly as you have taught it to me, life itself is sacrilegious. Perhaps you should call me Aldonza, as in Mr. Cervantes's book?"

"Never!" Miss Twittingdon lifted one index finger and jabbed it into the air, as if to punctuate her denial. "I may not be a man, and thus forbidden the splendiferous adventures of Don Quixote de la Mancha, but I will *not* be denied my Dulcinea!"

"Of course you will not be denied her. Please forgive me,

Aunt Leticia. I must be overtired to have forgotten my high station so far as to mention the pots. I spent most of the morning peeling potatoes in the kitchens and half the afternoon on the public side attempting to convince Mr. Jenkins of the folly inherent in his wish to bite off Mr. Easton's left ear as he held the little fellow tight in a stranglehold."

Miss Twittingdon shivered delicately as she leaned forward, her long, needle-sharp nose all but twitching, to hear the latest gossip. "The horror of it! And did you succeed?"

"I'm not quite sure," Caroline told her before sinking into the chair and leaning back against the shawl, which smelled of dust and the old lady's rose water. "Mr. Jenkins ended by biting off the bottom half of Mr. Easton's *right* ear—although Mr. Easton didn't appear to mind. But then, Mr. Easton doesn't mind much of anything, not even his lice. Tell me, should I consider a change of ears a success?"

Leticia tipped her head to one side, pressing a finger to her thin lips. "I shall have to ponder that a moment…. No, I don't believe so, Dulcinea. I thought you told me that Mr. Jenkins confined himself to the occasional proboscis. But truthfully, my dear, I don't know why you bother going over to the public side at all." She lowered her voice conspiratorially as she added in a near whisper, "A lady shouldn't say this, I suppose, but they're all as mad as bedlamites over there, you know. As mad as bedlamites."

Caroline turned her head away from Miss Twittingdon who, after five years in the private side of the asylum, had yet to recognize that she, too, was an inmate and not a pampered visitor. Perhaps if she visited the public side she might begin to understand the precariousness of her position, for if her brother—"the Infernal Laurence"—ever chose to stop sending quarterly payments to the proprietors of the asylum, Leticia would soon find herself in one of those narrow, unheated cells. But then, what good would frightening such a dear, harmless old lady do?

The only wonder was why she, Caroline Monday, hadn't been reduced to madness herself in the year she had worked as a servant of all work at the Woodwere Asylum for Lunatics and Incorrigibles. From her first day there, when one of the inmates had flung his own excrement at her, Caroline had known that her move from the Glynde orphanage had provided no great stepping stone up to a better life.

But Caroline had survived.

She had survived because the only alternative to survival was the unthinkable failure of death. Or, as Peaches had suggested, she could travel to London and join the ranks of the impure who hovered around Covent Garden hoping to make a passable living at "a fiver a flip"—at least until her teeth loosened from a bad diet, her body showed the ravages of one or more of the many venereal diseases rampant in the area, or her love of blue ruin, one of Peaches O'Hanlan's many colorful names for gin, left her "workin' the cribs for a penny a poke."

Peaches hadn't really wanted Caroline to become one of the soiled doves of Covent Garden. Caroline knew that now. She had simply intended to frighten her into realizing that a life spent as general dogsbody in an asylum full of raving maniacs was preferable to following in the footsteps of so many of the orphans who were pushed out of the foundling home to make their way as best they could.

"Will you have time for lessons this afternoon, Dulcinea?"

Caroline shook herself from her reverie and looked to the older woman, smiling as she saw the apprehension in her face.

Miss Twittingdon hated to be alone and in charge of filling her own hours, for she often found them stuffed with unlady-like thoughts concerning her brother, thoughts that fright-ened her. "And of course I do, Aunt Leticia, don't you know," she answered. "Don't I do my best to make time for you every day?"

Miss Twittingdon frowned, shaking an accusatory finger in Caroline's direction. "No, you don't—or else I wouldn't be hearing snippets of heathen Irishisms slipping back into your voice. We do not begin our sentences with 'and' and then tack a 'don't you know' on the end of them. Both are appall-ing examples of Irish cant. To speak so is a sure sign of low breeding. You will remember that, won't you? You must! Or how will you be able to show yourself to your best next Season when you make your come-out?"

Caroline rolled her eyes. She had been listening to this insane business of her come-out ever since first meeting Miss Twittingdon, who had immediately demanded that Caroline address her as "Aunt." She hadn't been very impressed with the notion at the beginning and complied with the daily lessons only because Miss Twittingdon seemed to have an endless supply of sugar comfits in a painted tin she hid under her bed.

But over time she had grown fond of the woman and enamored of the lessons and the books her "aunt" read to her as well. Not that improving her speech, memorizing simple history lessons, and learning the correct way to attack a turbot with knife and fork—and Caroline had never so much as *seen* a turbot—were of much use to her here at Woodwere.

But Leticia Twittingdon's room was warm in the winter and there was always a fresh pitcher of water for Caroline to use to wash herself, and there was something vaguely comforting about having someone to call "Aunt," so that it now seemed natural for Caroline to listen to Leticia's grand plans for her "niece" without stopping to wonder at the futility of the thing.

Or even of the pain Leticia Twittingdon's grand schemes for Caroline's future caused, late at night, when Caroline lay on her thin cot in the attic, knowing in her heart of hearts that Caroline Monday, unlike Dick Whittington's cat, would never look at a king.

"Caroline! Caroline! Come quickly! There are people here to see you. Downstairs, in old Woodwere's office. Have you done something wrong? Did you filch another orange while you were in the village? Woodwere may keep Boxer and the other attendants away from you, but even he can't pluck you from a jail cell."

Caroline watched as Leticia uncrossed her legs and rose to her full height to stare across the carpeted floor at the doorway, where Frederick Haswit, a remarkably homely dwarf standing no more than three feet high, was jumping up and down on his stubby legs in a veritable frenzy of apprehension. "Is that any way to enter a lady's chamber, sirrah?" she asked, arching one thin eyebrow. "Really, Ferdie, the disintegration of manners instigated in this modern age by hey-go-mad gentlemen such as you is appalling. Simply appalling! Furthermore, there is no Caroline here, but only Dulcinea and myself."

Caroline smiled at Ferdie, another of her friends at Woodwere, who had been installed at the asylum six or seven years previously, when he was no more than thirteen. He had been placed there by his father once the boy's doting mother had died, as the man did not appreciate having "a bloody freak" cluttering up either his impeccable lineage or his Mayfair town house.

Ferdie stamped one small, fat foot. "Not Dulcinea, you ridiculous twit! Caroline! *Caroline!* Oh, never mind. You're too addlepated to know chalk from cheese."

"At least I can see over the top of the dinner table to *find* the cheese, you abbreviated little snot," Miss Twittingdon responded, looking down her long nose at the dwarf.

"Who is asking for me, Ferdie?" Caroline inquired quickly as the dwarf stuck his small hands in his pockets and struck a belligerent pose, obviously ready to go into battle with the woman, a move that would do Caroline no good at all. "Do I know these persons?"

"Of course you don't, Dulcinea," Mrs. Twittingdon pointed out in her usual reasonable tone, a tone that had played accompaniment to many an outrageously splendiferous notion. "You are not yet Out, and so you know nobody. I wouldn't allow it. Why, as your guardian, I haven't as yet even given you leave to put up your hair!"

"Of course," Caroline echoed meekly, refusing to snap at the woman. Besides, she had enough to do wondering whom she might have offended lately with her sometimes sharp tongue, or what sleight of hand she had indulged in while visiting the village—picking pockets was one of the skills her first mentor, Peaches, had taught her—that might now have some back to haunt her. "You will forgive me, I hope."

But Miss Twittingdon was speaking again, and Caroline tamped down any niggling fears in order to listen. "Did these persons leave their cards, Ferdie? You know we receive only on Tuesday mornings from ten until two. There is nothing else for it—they shall have to leave calling cards, as civilized people know they ought, with the corner bent down to show we did not receive them. As *you* should have known, Ferdie, if you were civilized, which we all are aware you are not.

Then, if we so choose, we will condescend to receive them next week. Do toddle off downstairs now and pass on this information, if you please, and don't hesitate to remind these people, whoever they may be, that certain basic rules of civilization must be maintained, even here in this benighted countryside."

"Heavens yes, Ferdie," Caroline seconded, caught between apprehension and a real enjoyment of Miss Twittingdon's strict rules for receiving visitors in a madhouse. "Do tell them that Miss Caroline Dulcinea Monday regrets that she is not receiving today. She receives only on Tuesdays, and this, after all"—she began to giggle—"is already *Wednesday.* Can you do that for me, Ferdie—with so many *days* to remember?"

"Levity is not called for at this dark hour, Caroline, even if that loony red crow over there can't see it," Ferdie told her portentously, slowly shaking his too-large head. "Your visitors are an odd pair—an Irish drab and a great, large gentleman dressed in London clothes. Has eyes black as pokers and talks like he's used to being listened to. Maybe you didn't steal another orange. Maybe you've broken a *big* law this time. Maybe he's come to take you away and brought a keeper with him to tie you up. Maybe—"

"Maybe I'll *hang,* Ferdie," Caroline snapped, her usual good humor evaporating under the uncomfortable heat of the dwarf's melancholy suppositions. "Well, Aunt Leticia," she proposed airily, turning to look at the older woman, "shall I trip off downstairs and do my best to stare down this well-dressed hangman, or will you stand firm beside me here while I… Ferdie! Did you say an *Irishwoman?*"

Frederick Haswit nodded with some vigor, then puffed up his barrel chest, folded both his hands over his heart, and recited importantly:

"A winsome damsel she is not,
with scrawny breast and lackluster hair,
her teeth numbering little more than a pair.
I saw her there, and must tell you true;
She peered at me, and laughed—hoo, hoo!
The man, he silenced her mirth with a look,
showing she's naught but this black king's rook.
It is in him I see the menace, the danger,
deep in the eyes of this intimidating stranger.
So come now, sweet child, we'll hie away to
the sea,
the ridiculous Miss Twittingdon, Caroline—
and me."

"Your meter worsens with each new, excruciatingly uneven couplet, Ferdie, and I for one wouldn't cross the street with you, let alone run off to sea in your company," Miss Twittingdon told him flatly, reaching into the sleeve of her scarlet gown to extract a lace-edged handkerchief and lift it to her lips. "Red crow, indeed! It's no wonder you've been locked up. I would have had you put in chains and fetters myself. But enough of this nonsense. There is nothing else for it—show the gentleman upstairs."

"And the Irishwoman as well, Ferdie," Caroline instructed, sure that the dwarf had described Peaches. She hadn't seen her in over a year, since the day the woman had left her, weeping uncontrollably, behind the locked gates of Woodwere.

Caroline frowned. What could Peaches be about? Certainly she hadn't found a protector for her, some London swell who would, according to Peaches, set her up in a discreet apartment on the fringes of Mayfair, then use her for his convenience until he tired of her. Peaches had always thought such an arrangement to be the pinnacle of success—especially if the woman was smart enough to ask for diamonds at regular intervals and talented enough to lift coins from the man's purse each night after he'd taken his pleasure on her and fallen to snoring into his pillow.

"Come sit here, Dulcinea," Miss Twittingdon commanded, indicating the best chair in the room which, as there were only two chairs in the room, both of them as hard as the bread served in the servants' hall, was not much of a recommendation. "And don't cross your legs, even at the ankle. It is a deplorable habit. And pull this brush through your hair. You look as if you've been tugged backward through a hedge. And—"

"I thought no woman of breeding began her sentences with 'and,' Aunt Leticia," Caroline interrupted, hating the fuss the woman was making over her. She had no time to think of her ankles, her hair, or even her grammar. She had to rack her brain for a way to rid herself of this London gentleman and not injure her friendship with Peaches, who the good Lord knew probably only meant well.

"A woman of breeding is also never impertinent, Dulcinea," Miss Twittingdon intoned solemnly, arranging her own skirts neatly after depositing her lean frame in the other chair. "Now hold your chin high—ah, just so—and fold your hands in your lap. It wouldn't do for anyone to see how you've gnawed your nails to the quick. And don't say a word, my dear. I, as chaperon, will be in charge of this interview. Do you think our London gentleman likes red? I do hope so. I'm considering dyeing my hair to match my turban. His reaction, the opinion of a man of the world, a man who moves in the first circles, will be most helpful, don't you think?"

"Ferdie says he's a hangman," Caroline pointed out,

curling her hands together so that her bitten nails were hidden against her palms. "He probably would like you to dye your hair black."

"Oh, pooh!" Miss Twittingdon said, shaking her head so that the scarlet satin turban slid forward, to hang suspended drunkenly over one eye.

Caroline bit her bottom lip, fearful that if she laughed, her giggles might easily turn to tears.

MORGAN WAS HAVING MORE than a little difficulty believing himself to be where he already knew he was—in the small, stuffy office of the owner of the Woodwere Asylum for Lunatics and Incorrigibles. He was having even more trouble reconciling himself to the fact that he was accompanied by a wizened, foul-mouthed Irishwoman named Peaches—for the love of Christ, *Peaches!*—who had eaten with her hands when they stopped for nuncheon at a nearby inn, and then strolled outside to the innyard, moved her skirts to one side, spread her feet wide apart, and relieved herself beside the closed coach, like some stray dog lifting its leg against a tree trunk.

"Coo! Not bad for a loony bin, is it, yer worship? Bet ye a bit of this would be like a torchlight procession goin' down m'throat."

Morgan, shaken from his reverie by this rude interruption, looked to where Peaches was standing beside a well-supplied drinks table, fondling a lead-crystal container filled with an amber liquid he supposed to be brandy. "You will oblige me by removing your grimy paws from that decanter at once, Miss O'Hanlan."

Peaches pulled a face at him, but moved away from the drinks table. "No need to put yerself in a pucker, yer worship. And it was just a little nip I was after, don't you know. That beefsteak at the inn was tough as the divil and left m'gullet dry as a bleached bone."

Morgan sat very straight, his right calf propped on his left thigh. The woman had been trying his patience all day, but he refused to be baited. "I'm sure there is a pump out in the yard, if you're in need of liquid refreshment. I believe I can handle things from here without your assistance."

Peaches swaggered across the room to stand in front of him. "Oh, and is that so, yer high-and-mighty worship? Like I keep tellin' ye, Caroline won't give ye the time o'day without me here to vouch fer ye. Not that it's much of that I'll be doin', still not knowin' what ye're about and all." She marginally relaxed her threatening pose. "Is our Caroline really rich? Always thought there was somethin' special about the wee darlin'. Raised her up m'self, I did—raised her up proper—and fed her outta me own bowl. Wouldna had a whisker of a chance without me, and don't you know. Now, yer worship, if we could talk a little mite more about that reward?"

Morgan ignored her questions and asked one of his own, not of Peaches, but merely rhetorically. "Where is this fellow Woodwere? That dwarf said I should wait here for him. I doubt I should tarry too long, for this is such an insane quest that it would be no great wonder if I ended the day locked inside this madhouse myself." He turned to look at Peaches, still unable to believe the woman was proud of what she had done. "A madhouse. How could you have steered Caroline—any child—into employment in such a pesthole?"

"Because there weren't no better openin's hereabouts for earls' daughters, I suppose," Peaches shot back, jamming her fists on her hips. "Ye beat Banaghan for fanciful notions, yer worship, do ye know that? And where else was I apposed ta put her, I ask ye? The local workhouse? Caroline wouldna lasted a fortnight there."

"*A-hem.*"

Morgan wheeled about in the chair to see the dwarf standing just at the edge of the threadbare carpet. "What is it? Didn't you locate Woodwere?"

"No, I didn't, which isn't surprising, because I didn't go looking for him," the dwarf answered solemnly, then grinned. "But I did tell Miss Monday about you and the Irishwoman. You can come upstairs, if she comes with you," he said, indicating Peaches with a slight inclination of his large head. His smile disappeared as he added, "What did Caroline do wrong, sir? Is this about the oranges?"

Morgan stood, then retrieved his hat, gloves, and greatcoat from a nearby table. "No. Oranges do not enter into any business I have to discuss with Miss Monday, although you have piqued my interest, Mr.—"

"Haswit. Frederick Haswit. But you can call me Ferdie, since you're not here about the oranges. Unless you've come about that bolt of cloth, of course. But you don't look any more like a draper than you do a greengrocer. What crime of Caroline's are you here to punish?"

"Ah, and it's keepin' her hand in, our Caroline is," Peaches said happily, walking over to pat Ferdie's misshapen head. "Taught her all she knows, I did, and it's a pretty fair teacher I am, too, even if I've lost the touch a mite. The rheumatism, ye know. Else why would I be workin' with foundlin' brats, only the good saints could say. It sure an' isn't because Mary Magdalene O'Hanlan cares a clip about the creatures. A roof over me head and a dry cot, that's all I cares about now—and mayhap a little reward for doin' a good turn now and again. Come on, little fella, fetch me ta Caroline."

Morgan lifted his eyes to the chipped paint of the ceiling and silently cursed his dead uncle who, he believed, was probably grinning up at him from the bowels of hell at the moment, enjoying his nephew's predicament immensely, then followed after Peaches and Ferdie as they left the room and walked toward a wide flight of stairs.

As the marquis walked along, he took out his pocket watch, glanced at its face, and was faintly surprised to see that it was only a few minutes past five. It should have been later, considering all he had been through already this day, since encountering Peaches that morning at the orphanage fifteen miles away in Glynde.

But now, at last, the moment had arrived, and he was about to come face-to-face with one Caroline Monday, who might or might not be Lady Caroline Wilburton, who as a child of three had disappeared without trace from the scene of her parents' brutal and still unsolved murder.

Morgan had been only fifteen when he saw young Lady Caroline for the first and last time. He had very little remembrance of her beyond a hazy impression of blond hair and very sharp elbows, one of which she dug into his ribs when, at his mother's orders, he attempted to pick her up as she teetered precariously at the edge of the fish pond while Morgan, Jeremy, and their parents were at Witham for a visit.

He remembered the earl and his beautiful young wife much better, having suffered an impressionable youth's wild infatuation with the countess, Lady Gwendolyn, that hadn't lived out the summer. News of her horrific death that October had reached him at school, and he had immediately remembered his supposed deathless passion for the woman, which caused him to sink into months of melancholy, during which he produced the only poems he had ever penned in the name of Grand Romance.

As he climbed the stairs, Morgan conjured up a mental picture of Lady Gwendolyn, sure that the real Caroline, whom everyone had searched for, then presumed dead all these long years, would be the picture of her beautiful, sweet-smelling mother. That was all that this visit to madness would take, he was sure, one quick, assessing look—and then he would be on his way back to Clayhill and sanity and, of course, his solitary thoughts of revenge.

"This way, sir," Ferdie called back to Morgan. The dwarf was already dancing down the long hallway in the direction of the single open door at the end of the passage. "Miss Twittingdon is waiting for you. But don't mind her—she's an inmate, if you take my meaning."

"She's one of the loonies, ye mean," Peaches—whose steps had slowed as she gained the hallway—said, her usually booming voice lowered to a whisper. "And what would ye be, Ferdie, iffen ye don't mind me askin'?"

Ferdie pulled himself up to his full height, which brought him just past the bottom button of Morgan's waistcoat, and announced:

"All men are measured alike in the eyes of God;
but a father's vanity gauges with a different rule.
A mother's love protects while she has life,
but once she is gone, naked hatred runs rife.
Hide him away, secrete the embarrassing Haswit.
Remove him, forget him, brand him a half-wit!"

Morgan looked down at Frederick Haswit, *really* looked at him for the first time, and felt a twinge of guilt. He had dismissed the youth, who looked to be at least in his late teens, as being faintly feebleminded merely because of his size, assuming that Ferdie was incarcerated at Woodwere because that was where he should be. Granted, the fellow was vaguely eccentric, spouting bad poetry at the drop of a hint, but did he really need to be hidden from the world, locked away from a normal life?

"Haswit. You can't be Sir Joseph's son, can you, Ferdie?" Morgan heard himself inquiring, not realizing that he had come to that conclusion until he spoke the question aloud. "Sir Joseph Haswit. As I recall, he resides in London year-round and is known to be a childless widower."

Ferdie's expression was painful to see. "As he sees it."

"I'm sorry," Morgan said sincerely. "We English can be remarkably cold bastards."

Ferdie tipped his great head to one side, and his painful grimace became a smile in earnest. "Not to worry. The world will come to an end in eight months anyway. Eight months, three weeks, and four days, to be completely precise about the thing. Nobody can stop it. Everything has to balance out."

Peaches backed up until she was pressed against Morgan's side. "More'n a few slates offa this one's roof, yer worship, and don't ye know," she whispered to him out of the corner of her mouth. "If it's wantin' me ye'll be, I'll be in the coach, m'shiverin' body stuffed under the lap rug, and mumblin' a prayer ta the Virgin—iffen I can call one ta mind."

Morgan grabbed hold of Peaches's elbow as she attempted to back toward the staircase. "In eight months, you say, Ferdie," he said calmly. "You seem very precise about that. I wonder why."

"Eight months, three weeks, and four days. And why not?" Ferdie answered, evading Morgan's searching look. "June 7, 1816. It's as good a day as any to die."

"I imagine you might have a point there, Ferdie," Morgan said consideringly, remembering the horror in his uncle James's eyes as that man had gasped for his last breath. "I doubt the day matters much to a dying man. It's only what that man may have done while alive that puts the fear of the Hereafter into him."

"The dear Christ preserve us, and it's as queer as Dick's hatband ye are, the both of ye!" Peaches exclaimed in high hysterics, pulling against Morgan's grip on her arm, her eyes wide with fear. "Caroline! *Caroline!* Where be ye, gel? And it's a pair of bleedin' madmen ye should be savin' yer dear Peaches from, don't ye know! Where are ye, Caro?"

"Peaches! Is that you? Oh, Peaches—I can't believe it!"

Morgan looked down the hallway, following the sound of the female voice calling out the Irishwoman's name, to see a thin snip of a girl dressed in little more than rags barreling at him full tilt, her well-shaped legs bare nearly to the knee.

Behind her, standing tall in the doorway, appeared a woman dressed from head to foot in brightest scarlet. "Dulcinea!" she cried, bracing her hands against either side of the door frame as if an invisible Something were keeping her from taking so much as a single step into the hallway.

"Caroline, you bacon-brained besom!" Ferdie shouted, beginning to jump up and down in obvious fury. "Her name is *Caroline!*"

"Silence, you doomsday Lilliputian! *Dulcinea!* Come back to me at once, you impulsive child! How many times must I tell you that well-bred young ladies don't— Oh, pooh!"

As Ferdie unleashed a badly metered poem pointing out

the flaws inherent in "batty biddies" who believed themselves better than they should be, and as the lady in scarlet stared owlishly at Morgan, then took a single step backward, to begin adjusting her slipping turban as if suddenly realizing she was in the presence of Somebody Important, and as the little blond waif and the weeping Irishwoman fell on each other's necks, Morgan Blakely, Marquis of Clayton, searched in his pockets for a cheroot, which he stuck, unlit, into his mouth before leaning against the wall, an island of contemplative calm in the middle of the raging storm.

CHAPTER FOUR

Her wit was more than man, her innocence a child.
John Dryden

CAROLINE SAT perched on the window seat, the index finger of her left hand to her mouth as she absentmindedly worried at the already badly chewed nail, watching the handsome, impeccably dressed Marquis of Clayton as a bird might watch a snake sliding through the tall grass.

His hair was as dark and glossy as the bottom of a wet wooden bucket, and his heavily hooded eyes were blacker than a stormy night. He had the smooth, tanned complexion of a man who saw the sun much more often than she did, and she removed her finger from her mouth to gaze down at her own too pale skin, whose only color stemmed from the chilblains spiderwebbing her hands and fingers.

Her intensive scrutiny, which had also taken in the vertical slashes in his high-boned cheeks—lines that spoke of a man who kept a tight rein on his emotions—his aristocratic nose, his beautiful, clean white teeth, and even the fact that his shoulders were as wide as his long legs were straight, concluded with a visual inspection of his clothing.

He was dressed all in midnight-blue, his linen snowy and exquisitely starched, and the ruby winking in the folds of his cravat tempted her to mentally cipher how many pairs of wooden clogs the stone would fetch for the inmates on the public side if she could just lift it from his person and take it to Seth Bosley, a storekeeper in the village who was not averse to dealing in such questionable transactions.

Not that she'd ever try such a thing. Peaches had taught her well, and Caroline had needed no more than one look to conclude that the Marquis of Clayton was no easy mark. The smartest way to deal with a man like him was not to deal with him at all.

"More tea, my lord?"

Caroline smiled as she watched Miss Twittingdon lift the crude jug and pretend to pour tea into the chipped tooth glass she had pressed on the marquis once the commotion in the hallway had fizzled to a stop and they had all adjourned to the old woman's room.

"Thank you, no," the man who had introduced himself as Morgan Blakely, Marquis of Clayton, replied, setting the glass on the tabletop. "I've had quite enough. And I must say, the cucumber sandwiches were extremely pleasing. It is always pleasant to indulge oneself in a hearty repast after a day's journey, especially at this time of year."

"And it's clear as day that the man's ta let in his attic," Peaches whispered to Caroline, as the Irishwoman was sitting close beside her on the window seat. "I ain't seen hide nor hair of any sandwiches—just them plates with spools of thread plopped on 'em."

"It's how we practice serving tea," Caroline whispered back at her. "Sometimes Aunt Leticia gets confused. What I fail to understand is why our gentleman caller is going along with the sham. Kindness doesn't seem to set easily upon his shoulders."

"Don't let the cove fool ye, Caro. If he's bein' kind, it's only 'cause he's loonier than her, that's the why of it, and don't ye know!" Peaches shot back at her. "I'll tell you true. It was just leadin' him on, I was, hopin' ta gets a chance to see ye again, my dear darlin' girl. Never believed his fairy tale fer a minute, I didn't. Callin' ye the lady Caroline and sayin' ye was the daughter of an earl. Flippin' batty, that's what he is!"

"But he tells a plausible story," Caroline said, tilting her head to one side and watching while the marquis appeared to listen intently as Miss Twittingdon told him of her plans for "Dulcinea's Come-out."

Peaches pushed a faintly disgusting sound through her pursed lips. "Plausibibble, is it now? And what sort of high-falutin word is that, Caro, I'm wantin' ye ta tell me? I hardly know ye anymore, girl, and that's a fact. Where did all m'good teachin' take ye, if yer gonna be spoutin' jawbreaker words no one can figure out?"

Caroline dipped her head forward slightly, then turned to wink at Peaches. "Ah, and it's a glory to hear ye in a snit, don't ye know," she said, easily falling back into the lilting Irish brogue. "But it's not ta go puttin' yer hair in a twist ye should be, Peaches, m'love—yer Caro can still curse a fuckin' hole in a copper pot at ten paces."

"Ah, isn't that lovely? Utterly charming."

Caroline's head snapped up. The marquis was now standing directly in front of her—and she hadn't even heard the scrape of the chair as he stood. "Your veneer of civilized speech, as touted to me by Miss Twittingdon, slips with alacrity, Miss Monday, when you are confronted with the equally articulate—in her own way, of course—Miss O'Hanlan."

"How did you do that?" Caroline demanded of him, not

caring that the marquis had overheard her. "How did you get across the room without my hearing you?"

Morgan looked at her curiously for a moment, then smiled. "A veritable sponge, aren't you, little girl? Sopping up the vernacular of the gutter, and the clipped accents of the gentry—and now planning to enlarge your education by requesting lessons in silent, economical movement from me. What new thievery are you planning, Miss Monday? Or am I incorrect in suspecting that our young miss of the pilfered oranges and stolen yard goods is at this very moment considering the benefits to be derived from being able to sneak up on unwary persons and filch their purses?"

Caroline pushed aside his words and his accusations with a wave of her hand as she concentrated on examining his feet—feet clad in high-top, hard-soled Hessians that certainly should have made *some* noise as he walked toward the window seat. "No, no," she said dismissingly. "I was only thinking how wonderful it would be if I could learn to move so silently as I pass by the Leopard Man's cell each morning. He always hears me coming, you understand, no matter how hard I try to be quiet, and it's a considerable feat trying to race past before he can...um, before he can..."

"Yes? Please continue, as you have piqued my interest. Just what does this Leopard Man—is he spotty, to have earned such a name?—do as you pass by his cell each morning?"

"Dulcinea! You are not to speak of such things," Miss Twittingdon warned her direly, although she did not rise from her chair, seemingly preferring to continue sipping her "tea."

"Ah, go ahead, dearie," Peaches prodded, giving Caroline a short poke in the ribs. "About time his worship got hisself a peek at the world most of us live in, and no mistake."

Caroline looked past the marquis to see Ferdie Haswit, who

was sitting cross-legged on Miss Twittingdon's bed, his mouth stuffed with sugar comfits, nodding his agreement with Peaches.

"Very well," she said at last, lifting her chin and glaring straight into Morgan's bottomless-pit black eyes. She'd tell him the truth, and watch for him to flinch, to turn away in disgust. That would give her a true measure of the man. "His name is really George Ustings, but we call him the Leopard Man because he refuses to wear clothing, either summer or winter, and decorates himself by drawing circles on his bare body with his own excrement. Not that it matters, for everyone knows—or so they say—that lunatics can't feel the cold or the heat. But to answer your question, in the mornings, when I am passing down the corridor in order to get through to the women's side, George waits for me, then grabs hold of his—" She hesitated only momentarily, then swallowed hard, and continued, "He grabs hold of his cock, my lord, and speeds me on my way past his cell by chasing me with a spray of hot urine. I know it is hot, my lord, because George has very good aim."

Her "party piece"—as Miss Twittingdon had once dubbed any public recital—completed, Caroline suddenly realized that she was embarrassed, not by what she had said but because she had used an innocent person, George Ustings, to her own purposes. No longer wishing to observe the marquis's reaction, she lowered her eyes to stare at the ruby stickpin and asked, "Do you still wish to believe that *I* am the long lost daughter of these people, the earl and countess of Witham? Or perhaps you've changed your mind."

She watched as Morgan lifted one well-manicured hand and removed the stickpin, twirling it between his thumb and forefinger as if the shiny bauble were some small treat he was about to offer her. "I do not recall putting forth the theory that I believe you to be Lady Caroline Wilburton, young lady. I've only said that Lady Caroline—an innocent child orphaned by the brutal murder of her parents fifteen years ago, to then disappear from the face of the earth and be presumed dead after an extensive search that undoubtedly included the countryside around Glynde proved fruitless—should be returned to the bosom of her still grieving family if at all possible. And, for my sins, I've decided that you should be that innocent child."

Peaches pushed against Caroline's shoulder and whispered none too softly, "Mad, his bloody worship is, Caro. Mad and bad. He don't care a flip who ye are. It's usin' ye he's after, and no mistake. Listen ta me, darlin'. Tell him it'll cost him— tell him it'll cost him dear."

Caroline looked at Morgan Blakely's clean well-shaped nails and at his strong hands that were free of chilblains.

He was so clean. And he smelled good. She felt certain he had never gone to bed hungry or been forced to tie down a screaming inmate while other, beefier servants administered emetics and purgatives to cleanse her system of ill humors.

Caroline's gaze traveled from Morgan's hands, past the glittering ruby stickpin, to his handsome, expressionless face. No, it was not completely without expression. She was certain that there was a hint of disappointment deep in his eyes. "You say you don't care whether or not you have discovered the real Caroline Wilburton. But that's a lie. You do wish to find her. I can see the longing in your face. So why are you still here, since you are already convinced that I am not she?"

The marquis lifted one expressive eyebrow, a movement that fascinated Caroline against her better judgement. He spoke quietly, so that only she and Peaches could hear him.

"Why? That is a very good question. Perhaps I am terminally afflicted with an undeniable affection for happy endings. Perhaps I am no more than a bored English dandy out to enliven his life by stirring up a fifteen-year-old hornet's nest. Or, just perhaps, my reasons are my own. If you wish to ask questions, Miss Monday, ask them of yourself. Which would you rather do—live as a rich heiress with the world at your feet, or continue to spend your mornings dancing out of the way of George Ustings's squirting cock?"

MORGAN SAT ALONE in the private dining parlor he had ordered for himself at the Spread Eagle, the inn where he had decreed he and his odd party would spend the night before continuing on to Clayhill. As he sat nursing the snifter of warmed brandy he had requested of his host, he remembered Peaches's declaration at Woodwere.

"Mad. Mad and bad," she had said, and maybe the crusty Irishwoman was right. It was mad, what he was about to do, and he must be bad clear through to the marrow of his bones to be contemplating doing it. He felt dirty, soiled with a filth ten times fouler than anything to be found in the sweepings of the cells at Woodwere. But then, he had been to the depths before....

What he really could not justify to himself was the great length to which he had already traveled in his effort to revenge himself on his enemy. It was one thing to have saddled himself with a foul-mouthed, thieving foundling-home brat turned servant at a lunatic asylum. But to have agreed to drag along the insufferable, too insightful Peaches, as well as the sadly confused Miss Leticia Twittingdon and the morose (and quite easily remembered) dwarf, Frederick Haswit, was stretching the boundaries of credulity.

And yet, it was the only way he could persuade Caroline

Monday to leave Woodwere—by agreeing to her demand to be accompanied by her friends and, lest he forget it, by turning over to her the ruby stickpin that had so lately adorned his cravat.

"Excuse me, my lord, but might I come in for a minute?"

Morgan, who'd had his back to the door, lifted his booted feet from the wooden table top and turned in his chair to see Caroline Monday standing directly behind him.

"I'm a quick learner, my lord," she said, grinning, as his reaction to her quiet breaching of his private domain showed in his eyes before he could hide his surprise. "All it needs is to walk balanced on the balls of one's feet. That, and to rid myself of my wooden clogs—something I would not do at Woodwere even if it meant risking a wetting from the Leopard Man. I cannot begin to tell you of the filth that is on the floors all over the public side."

"Yes, I can imagine—and already have, as a matter of fact. And for the small indulgence of sparing me a cataloging of that assorted filth, Miss Monday, I vow you will have my undying gratitude," Morgan drawled, moving his hand to indicate that she should sit down in the chair beside his. It did not occur to him to rise, as a gentleman should, until she was seated. "Now, what might I do for you? Are you having trouble sleeping? Shall I ring for our host to bring you some warmed milk, which you surely must be accustomed to having before you are tucked up in your comfortable four-poster bed? Or perhaps, if you merely find yourself at loose ends, you might like to mingle downstairs in the common room for a space, separating some of the local farmers who patronize the place from their purses. Anything I can suggest to ease your way to your rest. In other words, which Caroline Monday are you this evening?"

He watched as Caroline took her seat, a small smile flitting at the corners of her mouth. "You truly enjoy listening to the sound of your own voice, don't you, your lordship? I had a terrible time calming Aunt Leticia so that she would agree to go to bed. She believes you are Don Quixote come to life, and we are setting off on a glorious quest. Ferdie is at this very moment composing an ode to your determination. But I believe Peaches has the right of it. She thinks you're plotting something much deeper than rescuing an earl's daughter and returning her to her family."

Morgan took a sip of his brandy. "You know, Miss Monday, with more teeth and less dirt, Miss O'Hanlan might just consider making her living as a soothsayer. Yes, my motives run deeper than altruism. But they are no concern of yours. You are to be exceptionally well recompensed for being Caroline Wilburton."

"But you don't believe that I really am Lady Caroline."

"Do you?"

Caroline sighed, the sadness in her tone not lost on Morgan. "No. No, I don't. Lady Caroline Wilburton has to be dead. You said there was a wide search, a search that continued for a long time. They couldn't have missed me, if I were she, now, could they, considering that these murders you spoke of were committed not twenty miles from the orphanage?"

"If there really was a thorough search," Morgan heard himself say, then frowned as he wondered when his mind had given birth to that particular thought. After all, if the murderer *had* discovered a living Caroline, the child might then have identified him as the man who shot her parents. The idea lent more credence to the murderer's seeming willingness to be blackmailed—and likewise provided additional weight to Uncle James's rambling confession. "Miss Monday," he continued smoothly, relegating that supposition to the more private regions of his brain, "as I've told you, you are to be well paid for participating in my plan to present you to the Wilburton family. I have already agreed to ride herd on your coterie of misfits as part of my payment for your cooperation. However, there is a limit to my patience, and your questions are pushing toward it."

He watched as Caroline leaned forward and took an apple from the wooden bowl that sat on the table, rubbed it against her thigh, then took a healthy bite of it with her small white teeth. Talking around a mouthful of the juicy—and somewhat loud—fruit, she said, "That's a pity, because I have several more questions for you to answer. How, for instance, do you explain the fact that my name is Caroline? Peaches told me that I supplied that name myself the same morning she found me sprawled in the mud outside the orphanage kitchens."

Morgan lifted a cheroot from his pocket, stuck it in his mouth, and leaned forward, sticking its tip into the candle flame. "That's simple enough," he said, exhaling a cloud of blue smoke. "Our dearest Prince Regent married Caroline of Brunswick in 1795, shortly after which this entire island became knee deep in Carolines, with everyone from dukes to chimney sweeps naming their offspring after the new Princess of Wales. Do you have any more questions, or will you leave me in peace to contemplate the absurdity of this day's events?"

He had to wait for his answer until Caroline had finished taking another bite of the apple, the sight of her small, well-shaped, yet badly chafed hands against the red skin of the apple and her obvious delight in the taste of the fruit making him believe he might possibly be slightly ashamed of himself.

Caroline nodded, chewing furiously, then wiped the back

of her hand across her lips, where small droplets of juice had made them glisten. "I want you to tell me the story again, please," she told him, her wide green eyes alive with interest. "I only listened with half an ear earlier at Woodwere. To tell you the God's truth, for the most part I was lost to anything except the thought of escaping the place, once you said I might leave with you. *Please.*"

Morgan inhaled deeply on the cheroot once more, then blew out the smoke with a resigned sigh. "Don't wheedle, Caroline. The role of supplicant doesn't suit you."

She shrugged her shoulders. "Arrogance suits you," she said, grinning at him. 'Peaches says you're as proud as Paddy's pig. You're probably bursting at the seams with pride that Aunt Leticia puts you on a pedestal alongside her hero, Don Quixote. And Ferdie, he—"

"Oh, very well, brat," Morgan interrupted wearily, "if it will shut you up and hasten your departure, I will tell you the story again."

She stood up, depositing the apple core on the table, then sat down once more, her legs tucked up under her. "Start with the murders. Were they very gory?"

"The earl was shot in the back, if that makes you happy, brat, and the countess took a bullet in the chest, close by her heart. Oh, yes, the coachman was also killed. Did I neglect to mention that?"

Caroline leaned forward eagerly. "You did, but never mind. How were the bodies found?"

"The coach horses bolted, most probably thrown into a frenzy by the bark of the pistols. Also, the coachman seemed to have neglected to put on the brake."

"He may have been too busy dying to think of it," she interrupted, her eyes sparkling with interest and, Morgan decided unhappily, the keen basic intelligence he had already suspected, an unlooked for aptitude for deduction that might hinder as much as help him in the coming months.

"Possibly. Unless the person or persons who kidnapped young Lady Caroline deliberately set the coach rampaging down the dark road. Whatever, it lurched into the next small village along the roadway, two of the horses so injured by their mad dash that they had to be destroyed while still in the traces, and the villagers rode back down the road to make the grisly discovery."

"Poor horses. None of it was their fault," Caroline said, her small heart-shaped face wearing a woeful expression for a moment before she rallied. "Go on. There was no sign of the child, Lady Caroline?"

"None," Morgan agreed, looking at Caroline curiously. She could listen, unmoved, to a description of the terrible murder of three human beings without batting an eye, yet was bothered by the destruction of animals. Was human death so commonplace in her life? He felt a faint stirring of pity toward her—it had to be no more than pity—then quickly, prudently, squelched it. "The woods lining both sides of the roadway were searched, on the off chance she was thrown from the coach when the horses bolted, but there was no sign of her. I was away at school—both my brother, Jeremy, and I—and we only heard about most of it in letters from our parents. But the late earl's brother, Thomas, now the eighth Earl of Witham, spared no expense in searching for her."

"Or so you heard," Caroline broke in, pointing a finger at him, so that he noticed, not for the first time, that the nail was badly bitten. For all her show of bravado, for all her seemingly thick hide, the girl must have some vulnerability to fall prey to such a nervous habit. "Continue," she ordered imperiously, so that he had to struggle to suppress a smile. "How long did the new earl search? Did he soon call it off so that he could enjoy his new position?"

Yes, the girl was smart, perhaps too much so for her own good—most certainly for his. "The new earl and his wife and son were devastated by the tragedy, and had the full sympathy of the neighborhood. There was a rash of arrests in the succeeding months, and many a highwayman hung in chains from gibbets up and down the roadway, although not one of them would admit to having taken Lady Caroline. But the murders had been committed in October, and with the coming of winter and several heavy falls of snow, hope for finding the child began to fade. In the end, there was nothing to do but assume that she was dead."

"For fifteen years," Caroline said, as if speaking to herself. "Yet you came searching for her—and found me. Why?"

Morgan abandoned his chair to move to the window and look out over the darkened inn yard. How much of the truth would he have to reveal in order to put an end to her questions?

He turned to face her, wishing her rather exotically tilted green eyes weren't looking at him so closely, wishing that she didn't look so vulnerable beneath her atrocious clothing and overlong mop of unruly dark blond hair. She was little more than a child, yet she had seen more in her few years than most old men. Could he, too, now use her and then discard her, as society discarded its orphans, and still live with himself?

"I met a man recently," he began, deliberately tamping down any further misgivings about what he planned to do. "He was dying and made his last confession to me, including the admission that he had been involved in the disappearance of Lady Caroline. His last wish was for me to find her and return her to the bosom of her family, in expiation of his sin." He smiled, spreading his hands wide as if to bestow a blessing on this dead sinner. "How could I, as a God-fearing Christian, refuse?"

Caroline looked at him levelly for some time from across the dimly lit room, then shook her head. "You're lying," she pronounced flatly. "Or, at the very least, you are not telling me all of the truth. But it doesn't really matter, I suppose. I'm out of Woodwere, and Aunt Leticia, Ferdie, and Peaches are with me. I don't need to know why you want to use me, as long as you keep your promise to take care of my friends."

"Oh, so you noticed my reluctance to adopt those three sterling characters, did you?"

"I would have had to be blind as a cave bat not to," Caroline returned, grinning. "They'll be nothing but trouble, you know, even if they mean well. Except for Peaches, of course. She'll be after your silver, bless her heart. So why did you? Adopt them, that is."

That was a good question. Morgan, smiling thinly, squashed the cheroot into the tin dish holding a small candle. It had cost him a good deal of blunt to convince Woodwere that he could deal without Haswit and Miss Twittingdon, and he felt certain—as their relatives never visited anyway—that the director planned to continue to collect fees for housing them. "As soon as I have an answer for you, imp, I shall race hotfoot to report it to you."

She uncurled herself from the chair and stood, tilting her chin at him defiantly. "You just do that, my lord. We made a bargain, you and me, and I'll see that you stick to your end of it."

Morgan stood and executed an elegant leg. "I am your servant, Lady Caroline," he said mockingly, then added as he straightened, "although there has been one small alteration to my plans. I had not really counted on finding you—for from this moment on you are to consider yourself the true Lady Caroline—and my plans were more slapdash than well thought out. I cannot take you and the rest of our traveling freak show to Clayhill. It's too dangerous, as I wish to keep your discovery private until I have groomed you sufficiently to take your place in London society."

Caroline pulled a face, her mobile features turning mulish. "Aunt Leticia has been preparing me for my come-out for over a year. I know how to behave. I even know how to eat turbot."

"My felicitations, Lady Caroline," Morgan returned affably, watching as she scratched an itch on her stomach—an itch that probably signaled the existence of a family of fleas that had taken up residence in her gown. "However, Miss Twittingdon's undoubtedly comprehensive instructions to one side, I fear I must insist upon some further education in the ways of the *ton*. To that end, and because my father no longer moves in society, either in London or here in Sussex, I have decided to move directly to The Acres, his estate. There we can prepare you for your reunion with your relatives without them immediately locking you up somewhere as a disgrace to the family name. Now, are there any more questions, or may I bid you a good night, my lady?"

Caroline looked at him through narrowed eyes, then quickly snatched up another apple from the wooden bowl. "I think I understand everything now," she said, her grin once more turning her into a scruffy wood sprite. "Good night, my lord. I look forward to seeing your father's house. Is Mr. Clayton as arrogant as his son?"

"There is no Mr. Clayton, my lady," Morgan told her,

deciding to begin her education. "My name is Morgan Blakely, and I am the Marquis of Clayton, among other, lesser titles. My father's name is William Blakely, and his most senior title is that of his grace, Duke of Glynde. Do you think you can remember that?"

"If I'm 'well recompensed,' I suspect I can remember anything—and *forget* anything just as easily. Miss Twittingdon didn't teach me that, but Peaches did," Caroline said, then skipped out of the room, closing the door behind her, leaving Morgan to wonder if, this time, his revenge, his planned retribution for an unpardonable sin, was truly worth the bother.

And to wonder why Caroline Monday's intelligent green eyes pleased him so—on a level much more personal than thoughts of revenge.

CHAPTER FIVE

It is impossible to please all the world and one's father.
Jean de La Fontaine

CAROLINE SAT COMFORTABLY on the soft leather seat of Morgan's closed coach, enjoying the unfamiliar feeling of having her stomach filled with good food. She had been eating almost constantly since driving away from Woodwere, and warranted that no single ambition in this life could be loftier than to continue filling her belly at regular intervals until she was as immense as a wheelbarrow and rocked from side to side as she walked.

Not that she believed she would get that chance, certain that she would soon be sent on her way. She had seen the marquis briefly this morning as they all exited the inn, before he climbed on his beautiful bay horse, vowing he would not ride inside with the four none-too-sweet-smelling additions to his entourage while he retained a single sane bone in his body. He had said much the same yesterday, Peaches had told Caroline, while the two of them were traveling to Woodwere, a statement that just proved that the marquis was "too high in the instep by half."

But it wasn't his desertion, riding ahead to The Acres and leaving the coach to follow along as best it could, that had forced Caroline to conclude that her introduction to polite society was still no closer to becoming a reality than it had been in Miss Twittingdon's room as that lady taught her the correct way to curtsy to the Prince Regent. No, it was more than that.

Morgan Blakely, Caroline had decided, had spent the night adding up one side of his personal ledger with the benefits to be had from declaring Caroline Monday to be Lady Caroline Wilburton, then deducting the drawbacks to such a scheme on the other side. Peaches, Aunt Leticia, and Ferdie—who had taught her all she knew about ledgers—had to number on the minus side, as she probably did herself. He certainly had not gone to any great lengths to hide his contempt for them all.

The only thing that could make the ledger amounts tilt in her favor would be if the marquis had some very personal reason for wanting to have her declared the missing heiress. He hadn't labored very long claiming that he was just an Englishman doing what was right. He had his own reasons for finding Lady Caroline, she was convinced, and his own plans for using her to his advantage. And, most probably, to someone else's disadvantage.

But Caroline would leave off all this heavy thinking for a while, she decided, and enjoy her second ride in a coach in as many days. She had never before traveled in such style, having rarely left the orphanage for more than an occasional trip into the village, and had been transported to her position at Woodwere on the back of an open wagon. To be surrounded by luxury such as that provided by the marquis's crested coach was an adventure that nearly outstripped last night's treat of sleeping in a bed with only two other people, Peaches and Miss Twittingdon, sharing it with her.

Unwilling to miss a single moment more of the trip due to fruitless introspection concerning Lord Clayton's motives for seeking out a plausible Lady Caroline Wilburton, she lifted the leather flap and looked out at the scenery that was flying by at a dizzying pace. According to the marquis, they were now traveling the same roadway the earl and his countess had ridden along that fateful night.

She squinted out at the trees, bare of their greenery in anticipation of the coming winter, and tried to imagine how they had looked that night fifteen years earlier, with the bare branches illuminated only by the light from coach lamps, like those on the marquis's coach that had lit their way to the inn last evening. They would have been traveling quickly, the earl and his lady, in order to reach the warmth and comfort of their home, but not too quickly, because it would have been difficult for the coachman to see the road unless there was a full moon that night.

Did highwaymen ply their trade only during a full moon, or did they confine their activities to moonless nights? Peaches would know, Caroline felt sure, but did not bother to ask. It was enough to let her imagination set the scene.

Caroline sat back and closed her eyes, deliberately using that imagination to conjure up two well-dressed people and the child who was traveling with them. She had seen detailed drawings of society people in the dog-eared fashion plates she'd often pored over in Miss Twittingdon's room, so it wasn't hard to picture what that doomed trio must have looked like, with their fancy clothes and curling feathers and elaborate jewels.

It had been late at night, so the child was probably sleeping—or crying. It was either the one thing or the other with children, Caroline knew, thanks to her years at the orphanage.

For the moment she'd pretend that the child was quiet, determined to stay awake past her bedtime, but on the edge of sleep, her head nodding wearily against her mother. And then, just as they all thought they were nearing their home, they heard shots, and a threatening, highwaymanlike voice called out the well-known words: "Stand and deliver!"

Caroline shivered, tensing as if she had actually heard the man's command. She could clearly imagine the pandemonium that must have been unleashed inside the doomed coach at that terrible sound!

In her mind's eye she could almost see the horses plunging to a halt, hear the coachman yelling, understand the countess's plight as she was caught between fear for her husband and child and a reluctance to part with all her beautiful jewelry. And the earl. Poor man. Caroline could feel his frustration. How he must have wished to take up the pistols hidden in the pockets of the coach—like those she had earlier discovered in the marquis's coach—and leap to the ground, shoot down the highwaymen, and protect his women.

Why hadn't he done that? Caroline frowned, her eyes still squeezed closed, her palms damp. Why was she supposing that he hadn't? Perhaps that was why he and his wife had been shot. Perhaps if he had stayed where he was, even hidden himself—hidden himself? and where could he have hidden inside a small coach?—the highwaymen wouldn't have blown a hole in him, and his lady wife wouldn't have had to scream and scream and scream....

"Caro, m'darlin'. It's bored to flinders I am, and that's a fact, what with these two loonies snoring louder than hens can cackle. Why don't ye give us a song?"

"*No!*" Caroline's green eyes shot wide open, her mouth suddenly dry, her heart pounding furiously. "Caro's tired!"

Peaches crossed her arms beneath her flat breast and snorted. "Well, aren't we cross as two sticks this mornin'? Tired, is it, with the sun climbin' high in the sky and not a single turnip chopped or nary a chamber pot emptied? It's a fine lady ye'll make, little gel, and that's fer certain—fer ye surely has the temper fer it."

Caroline pressed trembling hands to her cheeks for a moment, then sighed. For a moment, just a moment, it had all seemed so real. Perhaps a single year was still too long for an imaginative person such as she to work in a madhouse. "I'm sorry, Peaches. I was just trying to suppose what it was like to be robbed and murdered. Do you think the real Lady Caroline saw what happened? Do you think they carried her off and sold her to the Gypsies, or did they just kill her and leave her body for the animals?"

Peaches waggled her head from side to side, chuckling softly. "Better not ever let his worship hear ye askin' such questions, and don't ye know. But since ye're askin', the way I figure the thing, the high-toby men planned ta sell the bairn ta the Gypsies—seein' as how we all know how Gypsies like boilin' up and eatin' little kiddies—but she proved ta be such a trial that they got rid of her at the orphanage, sayin' good riddance ta bad rubbish."

"At the orphanage? In Glynde?" Caroline leaned forward and peered at Peaches intently. "Then you're saying that I *am* Lady Caroline?"

"As long as his worship feeds me I'll be sayin' anythin' he says, little gel, and so should ye," Peaches told her, then closed her more than usually shifting, secretive eyes. "Say it, think it, and swear on m'mither's grave ta the truth of it, don't ye know. Now go ta sleep, iffen ye're so tired, and so will I. We won't be gettin' ta his worship's da's place fer a while yet."

Caroline, who knew Peaches was right—hadn't she said almost the same thing to the marquis last night?—leaned back against the soft leather, knowing it would be impossible for her to close her eyes again without immediately conjuring up the horrific scene that had played behind her eyelids only a few moments earlier.

Instead, as Miss Twittingdon's head nodded onto her shoulder and the snores of Ferdie and Peaches competed with the sound of the coach wheels as they rolled on and on along the roadway, Caroline Monday peered out at the passing scenery, gnawing on the tip of her left index finger until she had drawn blood.

THE ACRES MIGHT HAVE BEEN Morgan's birthplace, but he had ceased many a long year ago to consider it his home. As he rode along the wide, tree-lined avenue that led to the four-story mellowed pink stone structure, he wondered why he felt that way and why it had been so impossible for his father to love him.

Perhaps, he considered thoughtfully, they had been too different or, as Uncle James had hinted, too much the same.

According to his uncle, Morgan's father had seen his share of adventure in his salad days, before he ascended to the dukedom. Then, in short order, he had taken a wife, fathered two sons, buried that wife, and become so bloody *responsible* that laughter and frolic seemed to be foreign words, unable to be understood by the man.

Along with many other of his uncle James's deathbed assertions, Morgan was still having more than a little difficulty believing that his father had ever been a carefree youth. William Blakely, as far as Morgan could see, had been born full grown, with no notion of what it was like to be young, to career around the countryside with some of the tenant farmers' sons, changing signposts and liberating chickens from their coops, or cutting a lark in the village—or even laughing out loud at the dinner table.

When he couldn't talk Morgan into seeing his point of view, or sermonize him into sensibility, William had taken to whipping the "frivolous frolic" out of his son, punishing Morgan for setting an unsavory example for his young brother, Jeremy. Those whippings had come to an abrupt halt when, at the age of thirteen, Morgan pulled the switch from his father's hand and flung it across the room, daring the man to come at him with his fists.

The next day, over his weeping mother's protests, Morgan had been packed off to boarding school for most of each year, where he instantly became an outstanding, if not outstandingly well behaved, student. Two summers later his mother died peacefully in her sleep, and William buried his grief by way of a closer association with religion, a turning point that Morgan now saw as the worst possible catastrophe to strike the Blakely sons.

Jeremy, three years Morgan's junior, was not allowed to rejoin his brother at school once the year of mourning was over, as William had decided to continue tutoring his younger, more beloved—more tractable—son at home, preparing him for a life among the clergy. After all, as the duke had said at the time, heaven only knew boarding school was not proving capable of knocking any sort of sense of responsibility into his older son.

But the duke hadn't counted on Morgan's compelling personality or Jeremy's near worship of his hey-go-mad, neck-or-nothing older brother, who appeared in his orbit for only a few months a year. In the end, Morgan was sure, it was that love, that devotion, that misplaced adoration, which had led Jeremy to follow that older brother into war—and to his death.

And William Blakely, devastated by this additional loss, had turned even more devotedly to his God, and away from his remaining son.

Morgan pushed aside his memories as the wide front doors of The Acres opened and a footman raced to offer his assistance. Morgan dismounted, patted the bay's rump, and instructed the boy to make sure a groom rubbed the horse down well before he fed and watered him. And then, knowing the coach carrying his oddly assorted entourage would not arrive for at least another hour, he took a deep breath, squared his shoulders, and walked up the steps to enter his father's house.

"Good day, m'lord," Grisham, the family butler—who had more than once hidden a filthy, bruised, much younger Morgan so that his father would not see that he had been fighting with one of the village boys again—inclined his balding gray head stiffly and held out his hands to take the marquis's riding crop, hat, many-caped greatcoat, and gloves. "We had thought when you left yesterday morning that it was for a return to Clayhill. Is his grace expecting you?"

Morgan laid a hand on the man's shoulder. "Now, Grisham, what do you suppose?"

The butler lowered his eyelids and pressed his chin toward his chest. "Forgive me, m'lord." Then he raised his head once more and smiled. "But, if I may be allowed to say so, sir, I am extremely pleased to see you again."

"You are most definitely allowed to say that, old friend, and thank you." Morgan looked around the high-ceilinged entrance hall, then toward the closed doors to the main drawing room. "Is my father in there?"

"No, m'lord," Grisham answered, his voice rather sad. "He's where he is every day at this time. In young Master Jeremy's rooms."

"Sweet Jesus, Grisham, does the man enjoy suffering?" Morgan shook his head. "Well, there's nothing else for it—I'll have to go upstairs. Do you have any sackcloth and ashes about, old friend, or do you think this road dirt I'm wearing is enough to make me look the penitent?"

The butler didn't answer, but only stood back, bowing, so that Morgan had nothing else to do but walk toward the wide, winding staircase. He reached the bottom step before he turned. "My coach will be arriving within the hour, Grisham. Inside it will be three women—I cannot bring myself to call them ladies, I fear, at least not until they are all bathed—and a young, smallish gentleman. Please see that three rooms are prepared in the guest wing, and one in the servants' quarters. I believe you'll have no great difficulty ascertaining which of our new residents belongs under the eaves. Simmons—my valet, as you might remember—is riding atop the coach with my driver. He'll see to the unpacking of my things. Tomorrow will be soon enough for him to ride to Clayhill to collect more of my wardrobe, for I am planning an extensive stay here at The Acres."

"Yes, m'lord," Grisham said, bowing yet again, his face expressionless. "That is wonderful news. And should I order three extra places set for supper, for your guests?"

Morgan scratched at a spot just behind his right ear. "I don't think so, Grisham. Our guests can bathe, then dine in their rooms. I don't wish to push my luck."

"Very good, sir. I'll see that your instructions are carried out to the letter."

Smiling, Morgan returned the butler's formal bow. He

could always count on Grisham to stick to business, without turning a hair at what the marquis knew was an outrageous set of instructions. "You do that, Grisham," he said, turning to head up the stairs two at a time. "Oh," he added, looking back over his shoulder, "and you might want to hide any valuables that may be lying around in the bedchambers. Just on the off chance any of our guests decide to cut short their stay with us in the middle of the night."

Morgan's smile faded as he climbed the stairs to the first floor of the forty-year-old house. The original estate house had burned to the ground ten years before Morgan's birth, and the duke and his lady wife had perished in the blaze. The new H-shaped building, although fashioned very much like its predecessor on the outside, had been divided in the new, modern way, with the public rooms on the ground floor and extensive family chambers on the first floor.

Jeremy's rooms were located to the left of the top of the staircase, through a door at the end of a wide hallway lined with oil paintings depicting bucolic country scenes found nowhere on this particular estate, several doors beyond Morgan's former bedchamber. The duke's chambers occupied a large area in the middle of the house, with the guest rooms taking up the wing to the right of the staircase. The nursery was on the third floor, half of which was also devoted to quartering the upper servants. The kitchen servants and, for tonight at least, Mary Magdalene O'Hanlan, had their beds in small cubicles under the eaves in a section of the attics.

Morgan's mother had been in charge of furnishing the house, for nothing save a few portraits and several sticks of furniture had survived the blaze, and her good taste could be clearly seen in the light colors and delicately carved furniture that would make any outsider believe that The Acres was a well-loved, happy home.

Only it wasn't. It was a shrine, or at least a part of it had been turned into a shrine, one dedicated to the memory of Lord Jeremy Blakely, dead these past two years, four months, three weeks, and five days.

Morgan pulled a face as he realized what he had been thinking. He was no better than Ferdie Haswit, ticking off the days from the termination of his personal world, his personal happiness, in much the same way that Ferdie was counting down the days until, if his prediction proved correct, the entire world would end.

Should he, Morgan, be locked up alongside Haswit in a place like Woodwere? Should his father the duke be incarcerated there with him? Or was Ferdie Haswit the sane one? How did the world make these judgments? And why, Morgan wondered briefly before dismissing his random thoughts, did any of it matter in the first place?

He approached the door at the end of the hallway, hesitating only slightly before depressing the latch and stepping into the small antechamber that led directly to his brother's bedroom. "Father?"

There was no answer, which Morgan considered to be a great pity, for it meant he would have to go searching the three large rooms of the apartment for the man. It wasn't an expedition he looked forward to with any great anticipation. Steeling himself to blank-faced neutrality, he advanced into the apartment, deliberately refusing to look to his left, where Jeremy's life-size portrait hung against the wall, or to his right, where his brother's collections of bird's nests, oddly shaped stones, and ragtag velveteen stuffed animals were displayed on table tops.

Morgan knew without looking that every piece of clothing Jeremy had worn in the last months he'd been at home still hung in the wardrobe in the far corner.

Jeremy's silver-backed brushes gleamed dully in the half-light, as this wing was on the shady side of the house and the sun had already made its circuit past its many windows.

His brother's riding crop, a birthday gift from Morgan, was curled on the coverlet on his bed.

The lopsided birdhouse Jeremy had hammered together at the age of six was displayed on the night table.

A pair of mittens knitted by their mother for his fifth birthday lay on a chest at the bottom of the bed.

And a Bible, opened to the Twenty-third Psalm, rested on the desk where Jeremy had written his farewell note to his father before riding away in the middle of the night to seek out the adventure he would never have found at The Acres.

Jeremy's rooms were exactly as they had been before he went off to war, to join his brother, his idol, and eventually to die a terrible death in that brother's arms.

"You say you have forgiven me, Father," Morgan said softly, giving in, only momentarily, to the pain. "Yet this room is still here, still the same. How can you truly forgive if you refuse to forget?"

"Who's there? Grisham? How many times must I tell you that I do not wish to be disturbed when I am in here? Is there no peace to be found anywhere in this world? No compassion?"

Morgan took another step into the room, to stand just at the edge of the carpet. "No, Father, as a matter of fact, I don't believe either of those things does exist," he said, espying the duke standing just beside the windows, his thin face eloquent with pain. "Just as there is no real forgiveness, no entirely selfless charity, and precious little understanding."

He took two more steps, turning to peer into the smiling blue eyes of his brother, brilliantly captured in the painting that was done on his seventeenth birthday, then slanted a look full of meaning at his father. "There is, however, revenge. The Old Testament, I believe, is chock full of it. An eye for an eye, a tooth for a tooth—and, in admittedly a rather backhanded, perverse way, a child for a child. Tell me, Father, are you at all interested in winning some revenge of your own?"

CHAPTER SIX

With how much ease believe we what we wish!
Whatever is, is in its causes just.

John Dryden

CAROLINE LOOKED DOWN at her fingertips and the skin that was still soft and puckered from her bath, the first she had ever taken in a tub. She lifted her wrists to her nose, sniffing at the delicate scent of rose hip soap, a smile coming to her face as she raised her shoulders and rubbed her cheek against the collar of the soft pink terry wrapper the maid, Betts, had provided her with after helping her dry herself with huge white towels that had been warmed beside the fireplace.

Beneath the wrapper was a miles-too-long white cotton nightgown, old and mended, but with touches of lace at the hem, high collar, and cuffs. It had been one of Lord Clayton's mother's nightgowns, Betts had told Caroline, long since passed on to the servants' quarters and well worn. Caroline thought it to be the most beautiful nightgown in creation.

She had told Betts, smiling at the girl, who was no more than a few years older than she—and who appeared to be shocked speechless at the admission—that she had slept in her shift in the summer and in the same clothes she worked in during the colder months. Betts's possible disapproval had kept Caroline silent about the fact that, during the hottest nights, tucked up under the eaves in her narrow cot, she had dared to sleep with no clothing covering her at all.

Clucking her tongue over the sad state of Caroline's bitten nails, Betts had nevertheless taken care to rub a perfumed ointment of crushed strawberries and cream into her new mistress's hands, vowing that it would soon heal the dry, chapped skin, then solemnly repeated these ministrations on Caroline's roughened feet and heels, an embarrassing and somewhat ticklish process that had made Caroline giggle nervously.

Betts had also helped her to wash her hair, then exclaimed that it was three shades lighter than it had been before the determined scrubbing that brought tears to Caroline's eyes. Now, hanging halfway down her back, each strand free of tangles, Caroline's hair was only faintly damp, for Betts had brushed it dry as the two of them sat on the hearthrug, warmed by the fire.

Now, lying back against the pillows as she sat cross-legged in the middle of the large tester bed, Caroline placed a hand on her stomach, enjoying the unfamiliar feeling of fullness that lingered a full two hours after her meal, which had been served on a silver platter—nothing like the wooden trencher she had used at Woodwere or the chipped bowl that was dipped into the common gruel pot at the orphanage. She was so full, in fact, that she didn't believe she could eat above two of the half-dozen soft, crusty rolls she had stuffed into her bodice while Betts's back was turned and later hidden behind one of the cushions on the chair in the corner.

Betts, before she left, had put forth the hope that "Lady Caroline" would have a restful night, and she had watched proprietarily as a footman slipped a warming pan between the

KASEY MICHAELS   101

sheets. Once the door closed behind the maid, Caroline had investigated every drawer and cabinet in the room, lifted each exquisitely formed figurine, inspected every small decoratively carved wooden chest and dainty porcelain box, sniffed at the contents of the crystal bottles on the dressing table, then whirled around in a circle in the middle of the room, arms outflung, laughing aloud at her good fortune.

All in all, Caroline decided happily now, looking around the candlelit room, she truly must have died—and this was heaven.

She had just stifled an unexpected yawn and was about to slip her toes beneath the coverlet, reluctantly giving in to sleep, when the door to the hallway opened once more and Miss Twittingdon—dressed in her ridiculous blue and purple plaid woolen wrapper and pink knitted slippers—entered, to stand beaming at Caroline.

"I've just come to check on my charge, my lady Dulcinea," she said, approaching the bed. "I do hope you've been treated in accordance with your exalted rank. Otherwise there is nothing else for it but to sack the servants. Every last lazy one of them. Although I must say they have been extremely cooperative thus far, even going to the trouble to cut my meat for me when I found the chore beyond my strength."

Caroline giggled and threw her entire upper body forward, pressing her forehead against the mattress, then rolled onto her back, her arms and legs spread wide as her sleek curtain of hair splayed out on the coverlet. She began sliding her limbs back and forth across the coverlet, in much the same way she could remember making angels in the snow at the orphanage when she was a child.

Then, looking up at Miss Twittingdon, her green eyes twinkling with mischief, she exclaimed, "Aunt Leticia! Can you believe this? Can you honestly believe any of this? Look at me! I'm reaching as far as I can in every direction, and still I'm miles and miles from the edge. We could fit six other people in this bed. Maybe eight!"

"My lady! To think such a thing! You are virginal," Miss Twittingdon pointed out.

"Oh, pooh!" Caroline exclaimed, deliberately teasing the old woman with her own saying. She scrambled from the bed, not even noticing that her bare feet might be chilled by the cold floor, and began racing around the room. A generous amount of the material of her overlong nightdress bunched in one hand so that she wouldn't trip, she pointed out one treasure after another to Miss Twittingdon until she happened to catch sight of herself in the tall freestanding mirror placed in front of one of the curtained windows. She released her grip on the material and stood rigidly still, looking at the stranger who grinned back at her. "Oh, my!"

Her smile slowly faded as she approached the mirror, one hand to her cheek as the other pressed against the cool glass, to confirm the evidence of her eyes. "Is this me, Aunt Leticia? Is this really *me?*"

"Of course it is you, my lady," Miss Twittingdon stated firmly, if only slightly deferentially. "Surely you have seen yourself before this. You look as you have always looked every day of our acquaintance. Beautiful. Sweetly, heart-breakingly beautiful. However, you are barefoot, which I cannot approve, any more than I can like the notion of you remaining under this bachelor roof. I would be shirking my responsibility as your chaperon if I did not admit that. Have you had any of the apricot soufflé I was served earlier, my dear? It was supremely satisfying."

Caroline began to gnaw on one side of the tip of her little

finger, then abruptly dropped her hand, whirling to face the old lady she had cared for, the dear woman who had shared her comfits and her clean water and her faintly scrambled knowledge with her. "Aunt Leticia, you—you've *always* seen me as looking like this?"

Miss Twittingdon smiled, looking almost motherly. "Always, my dear. My beautiful Lady Dulcinea."

"Lady *Caroline*," Caroline corrected apologetically, turning back to the mirror. She took her disheveled hair in her hands, twisting it around and around itself, and pulled up the long blond coil against the back of her head so that it looked vaguely like one of the styles she had seen depicted on Miss Twittingdon's fashion plates, then tilted her small chin and looked down her nose at her own reflection. "You must remember to call me Lady Caroline, Aunt Leticia. It is very important to the marquis's plans."

And then she crossed her eyes and grinned.

"Sons and fathers, fathers and sons;
Do you e'er wonder which are the ones
Who, siring, or born through transient lust,
First turn family love and honor to dust?
Father and son, son and father;
Living and lying are such a bother.
The days keep turning, the hate burns bright,
And the only peace is in endless night."

MORGAN CAREFULLY PLACED his wineglass on the table beside him and looked at Ferdie Haswit, who was perched elflike on the center cushion of the overstuffed couch. "Maudlin little beast, aren't you?" he inquired casually while idly wondering why he had thought to pour himself a glass of wine when it had only gone eleven—he, who never drank before three.

Ferdie grinned, showing even but widely spaced small teeth that reminded Morgan of a monkey he had seen once at a local fair. "Not really, my lord. I encountered your father this morning at breakfast. You had just finished and gone, although I noticed that you had left your plate all but untouched. The duke promised to say a prayer for me. Do you think he believes he can ask the good Lord to make me grow?"

"Now, why do I find it difficult to believe you expect me to answer that particular question?" Morgan put forth, feeling vaguely embarrassed for his father.

Ferdie waved one short arm as if in dismissal of Morgan's words, his pudgy fingers spread wide. "You're right. Never mind that last bit. His grace was most solicitous, offering to have one of the servants fetch me a pillow so that I might be more comfortable at table. A very agreeable man, your father. So tell me, if a confirmed although recently liberated lunatic might be allowed to inquire—why do you two dislike each other?"

"I have always considered it a mistake in judgment to overeducate infants," Morgan said, staring piercingly at Ferdie. "They ask such impertinent questions."

"Sorry," the dwarf apologized quickly, holding up his hands as if the marquis had just produced a pistol from behind his back and leveled it at him. "At least your father acknowledges you. I imagine I'm just jealous, when I should be grateful that you allowed Caro to convince you that she couldn't bear to leave her dear friends behind if she tossed in her lot with you. You aren't going to hurt her, are you? I'd have to kill you if you did, and I rather like you."

"Maudlin, impertinent, *and* bloodthirsty. You have quite a lot of vices stuffed into that small body, don't you, Ferdie?"

"See? I told you I liked you!" Ferdie maneuvered his body forward and hopped down off the couch. "You couldn't care less whether or not you insult me, when most people either stare at me like they're seeing something that just climbed out from beneath a rock or look at me with pity in their eyes—like your father. And yet you treat me like I have a mind—as if I can *think!* You can't imagine what it is like to have people talk above you, as if you can't understand plain English, or yell at you, as if you're deaf as well as stunted, or hate you—call you names or throw stones at you—because you scare them, because your very existence reminds them that God still makes mistakes. But you—you don't hate me or pity me or look down on me." He shook his large head, tears standing in his eyes. "You treat me like I was just *anybody.*"

"Which is not the same as saying I like you," Morgan pointed out, beginning to smile. "You can be as obnoxious as all hell, you know."

Ferdie clambered back up onto the sofa cushions, then turned to wink at Morgan. "Yes, my lord. I know. I've had considerable practice at it. But I'm not short of a sheet. I'm just short."

Morgan threw back his head and laughed out loud, enjoying the joke. His smile faded seconds later as he sensed someone hovering in the doorway leading from the entrance hall, and he turned to see Caroline Monday standing there.

Or at least his mind told him that he was seeing Caroline Monday, he acknowledged as he rose automatically, as he would do any time a lady entered the room. His eyes told him something entirely different, for he barely recognized the girl.

She was dressed in one of the housemaids' Sunday best, he supposed, for he had asked Grisham to apply to the servants for assistance in clothing his guests. The soft blue gown, which fit remarkably better than the atrocious rig-out she had been wearing since he met her, was very flattering to her petite, slim body. He noticed with almost affectionate amusement that she had stuck the ruby stickpin through the round white collar of the gown and wondered briefly if she had done it for adornment or only to keep the jewel close to her, in case he should think to retrieve it.

Her hair surprised him, for it looked paler than he remembered, a soft white-blond, and it was neatly held back from her forehead by a wide ribbon, to hang straight as a poker halfway to her waist. But it was her face that took and held his interest, for he hadn't realized what a pretty child she was, how finely her straight, faintly upturned nose fitted her piquant, heart-shaped face, nor had he noticed the finely sculpted lines of her small chin and her long, graceful neck. And her eyes. They weren't just green; they were emerald, and long lashed below winglike brows. And they were rather exotic, turning up just marginally at the outer corners, like a cat's. He had already decided that he liked her eyes. Very much.

In short, Caroline Monday, cleaned of the grime and rags that were nearly all he had seen of her until now, was quite a revelation, and for the first time Morgan began to believe he might just be able to pull this off—he might be able to present this orphan brat to London Society. Even though she looked nothing like the tall, graceful, heartbreakingly beautiful, endlessly memorable Lady Gwendolyn.

"Good morning, my lord," he heard Caroline say as she advanced farther into the room, then grinned as she saw

Frederick Haswit. "And don't you look fine as ninepence this morning, Ferdie!" she exclaimed, skipping over to stand behind the couch before bending down to drop a kiss on the top of the dwarf's head.

"Good morning yourself, Caro. You're looking more than well, you're looking brand-new. Where's the splendiferous scatter-wit?"

"Don't be naughty, Ferdie. Aunt Leticia will be down soon. She's having some trouble deciding if she should wear her purple turban this early in the day. They feeding you?" she asked, lowering her voice conspiratorially. "I've got some rolls from last night hidden upstairs, and I saved some lovely pink ham from my breakfast tray. Betts wouldn't let me come downstairs until now, or I would have searched you out and fed you long before this, just like always. You know I'd never forget."

Morgan coughed, he hoped with discretion. Clearly Caroline and Ferdie had some long-standing arrangement that dated from their days at Woodwere. "It will not be necessary to save scraps for Ferdie, Lady Caroline," he told her, motioning her to a seat. "He breakfasted earlier with my father. Isn't that right, Ferdie?"

Caroline walked around to the front of the couch and sat down beside her friend, taking his hand between both of hers. "Is that true, Ferdie?"

Morgan resumed his own seat, his full lips thinning as he heard her ask for confirmation of his statement. Impudent chit! Did he look so very untrustworthy? "Why would I lie, Lady Caroline?"

She turned to look at him for some moments, then smiled. He was thankful to see that she still had all of her front teeth—and they were straight and nicely pearly. "Why would you tell the truth, my lord? After all, lies have been taking us all a long stretch in the past day and night. You and Betts and Aunt Leticia and that butler person I saw in the other room just now are calling me Lady Caroline, Ferdie is sitting big as life in this fancy room just as if he wasn't used to being chained to a wall two weeks out of every four for tossing a stone at somebody or biting someone's shins. And I saw Peaches upstairs a few minutes ago. She told me she doesn't have to do a lick of work to keep this roof over her head. Lies, truth— I don't think I know the difference anymore."

"I suppose you have a point, imp," Morgan said, considering her words, "although I find myself feeling faintly insulted by your lack of trust. Perhaps you'd feel more comfortable if I wrote down a full listing of what I am and am not prepared to offer to you and your friends, and then signed it."

Caroline shrugged. "That wouldn't do much good, my lord. I can't read any jawbreaker words, you know. Ferdie has taught me some, and Aunt Leticia taught me to read from the magazines." She grinned at him. "I can cipher a little and spell some, and I could tell you that Rome is in some boot-place called Italy, if you were to ask me—and I know how to eat turbot."

"Yes," Morgan replied, sighing. Her English was so much better than he had expected that he hadn't considered the possibility that she could not read. She was such an odd mixture, part servant, part lady, part runny-nosed urchin. "I believe you have mentioned the turbot. It's a good thing we don't have to be in London until the end of March. We have our work cut out for us."

"Why?" The question came from Ferdie, who had hopped down from the couch yet again, to perch cross-legged on the low table that stood between the couch and the chair on which Morgan was sitting.

"Why? God's teeth, Haswit, the chit's damn near illiterate," Morgan told him, seeing the answer as simple. He looked at Caroline, who had crossed her legs at the knee as she sat, craning her neck to look up at the ornately painted ceiling, her mouth open in a small *O* of admiration, and shook his head. "Among her other sadly glaring failures in what is expected of a young woman of her station. I've already discussed this with her."

"Yes. What of it? You said the real Lady Caroline has been missing for fifteen years. Do you really suppose that Society will expect her to act like just another debutante making her come-out? Orphans aren't taught to read. And that's another thing. Why haven't you taken Caro directly to this earl who's supposed to be her uncle? Why are you keeping her here—keeping us all here—until we go to London?"

"I'll explain, Morgan, if I might, as long as I have reluctantly agreed to lend my consequence to this dubious enterprise."

"Father. Good day to you. I thought you'd be upstairs performing your morning penance." Morgan closed his eyes for a moment, wishing back the words. His father had agreed to his plan. What else did he want from the man? His love? Gaining the difficult, was he now going to be foolish enough to hope for the impossible?

All eyes were directed toward the doorway as the duke of Glynde entered, his steps measured and slow as he approached Caroline. "Turn your heart to God, my son," the duke said, not looking at Morgan, "and your life to good works, and you will be a more contented man."

Morgan reached for his wineglass, not trusting himself to speak, and decided to be "contented" with watching silently as his father bowed to Caroline and introduced himself.

"Frederick has raised reasonable questions, Miss Monday," the duke told her, then walked around the table to sit in the chair beside Morgan's. "But I have reasonable answers. You see, it is above everything wonderful that my son has found you, but it will not be a simple matter to prove to the world that you are indeed Lady Caroline Wilburton."

Morgan sliced a quick look at his father from beneath hooded lids. For a man so in tune with his God, he lied with smooth, credible brilliance. Perhaps Uncle James had been correct and William Blakely was once more than he now appeared.

"You can't prove it at all," Caroline pointed out quickly, sticking out her chin. "But then, no one can prove that I'm *not,* can they, my lord—I mean, your grace?"

The duke looked toward Morgan. "Learns quickly, I see, just as you said. A veritable sponge. And her speech is remarkably good, much better than either of us should have any reason to hope. I find it difficult to believe you found this child in a madhouse."

"And her hair is conveniently blond, Father. I remember Lady Caroline as a small child, and her hair was so blond it was nearly white. Her name is Caroline—not an uncommon appellation, I must acknowledge, but helpful. For all we know she could actually be the true Lady Caroline."

The duke shook his head. "No, that's impossible, I'm afraid. I was one of the many who took part in the search for the poor child. The blanket from the coach was located a good mile away, one small slipper wrapped inside it, but we never found another trace of the child. Both the blanket and the slipper were smeared with blood. It has been and remains my opinion that the child wandered away after the murders and was carried off by foxes or some such thing."

"Then you don't believe Un—the man who told me he had delivered the child to the orphanage in Glynde to have been telling the truth?"

Morgan watched as his father clearly struggled to find the correct words to say what he felt. "I believe the man who told you this to have been sunk in delirium and despair, his mind warped by years of misfortune. No Christian could have known what that man said he knew, seen what he vowed he had seen, and then done what he said he did. It is inhuman, barbaric, and totally unacceptable to me."

"Really?" Morgan took another sip of wine, to find it bitter on his tongue. "It's curious you should say so, Father, when you seem to find it simple enough to believe the worst of some people."

"Sons and fathers, fathers and sons; Do you e'er wonder which are the ones who—"

"Stubble it, Haswit," Morgan interrupted quietly, skewering the man with a look. "You are not indispensable to my plans."

"Morgan! I will ask you to not be rude to Frederick," the duke exclaimed, disappointment in his son's failings evident on his careworn face.

"Ah, that's all right, your grace," Ferdie put in, grinning at Morgan. "I like him."

William smiled at the dwarf, his expression a benediction. "What kindness in the face of adversity such as you must suffer. What charity. I am humbled, sir, by your humanity."

Ferdie grinned back at him. "Yes, your grace. I know you didn't expect me to exhibit any really *human* traits. I am only sorry I can't juggle little red balls or do somersaults or any of those things we dwarfs are supposed to do, so that you might feel more comfortable around me."

Morgan drained the contents of his glass in one long gulp, beginning to feel as if he had made a major blunder in bringing Caroline Monday and her bizarre entourage to The Acres. "Could we possibly get back to the matter at hand—unless you'd like us all to join hands in prayer for a moment, Father? Lady Caroline has a right to know what is expected of her over the coming months. I suggest we tell her."

The duke, his lips drawn thin, nodded in acquiescence, and Morgan stood and began to pace the length of carpet beside his chair. "Caroline, Haswit here has asked an important question, one that my father has attempted to answer by putting forth the argument that Society—a fickle beast, as you shall discover—will not accept you if you do not fit their notion of what Lady Caroline Wilburton should be. This is correct, but only partially."

"You have your own reasons for wanting Society to accept me," Caroline said, shifting on the couch so that he could not avoid looking directly into her intelligent green eyes. "You've already hinted at that enough. I'm not so empty in my upper stories that I don't know you want me around—me, Ferdie, and Aunt Leticia—as much as you'd want the Leopard Man hiding behind one of your doors as you went walking by of a morning. But I don't really care about that, as long as we can stay here. Truly I don't."

"How terribly discreet of you." Morgan smiled thinly. "But please don't forget to list Peaches in your catalog of undesirables, imp. I am, I must tell you, even less enamored of her than I am of you. Grisham had her room searched this morning and discovered that she had supplemented the stuffing in her mattress with a quite lovely, quite irreplaceable silver bowl belonging to my deceased mother."

Caroline's unexpected grin of real pleasure caused a knot to form in the pit of Morgan's stomach as she poked one pointed elbow in Ferdie's ribs. "Swears she's off the bite, Peaches does, but she was an arch dell in her grass time and needs must keep her dabblers alive."

Morgan stopped pacing to stare at Caroline, whose newly washed and clothed body, she had just reminded him, still housed the mind and vocabulary of the streets. "If by that announcement, *Lady* Caroline, you have attempted to convey to me the knowledge that Peaches was once a master thief who feels the need to keep her hands quick, I'm afraid I must inform you that I will not countenance another midnight foray through the lower floors in search of booty. Or, if you need a further explanation, the cove's fly, and if the arch doxy gets herself snapped with her daddles grabbin' another bit of rum quid, she'll be boned and clapped for a Newgate bird."

Caroline's grin became, if anything, even wider than before. "That was wonderful! You're a swell, and you know the canting lingo! Ferdie, did you hear that? See? I *do* know some things that I should."

Morgan longed to bite on his fist in frustration, but restrained himself. "No, imp. You know pitifully little of what you should know and entirely too much of what you shouldn't, which is why these next months will be busy ones. It is not enough to clean you up. We shall have to begin as we would with the three-year-old Lady Caroline."

"Wash her, brush her, cut her hair,
Clothe her in what she ought to wear.
Train her, teach her, give her a name,
And then, my lord, you'll play your *game*."

His latest poetic effort delivered in forbidding tones, Ferdie directed a long stare in Morgan's direction before turning to Caroline. "Think hard and long before you agree to this, Caro. His lordship and his sainted father had deep doings here, whether you want to believe it or not. They're going to use you, then toss you aside when they're through with you. Woodwere ain't so bad, you know. We can still go back."

Caroline's full bottom lip came forward in a pout. "I am not a baby, Ferdie," she said mulishly. "And I'm not Lady Caroline Wilburton, and I'm never going to be rich. But you're right. His lordship picked us up, and when he's done with us he's going to put us down faster than he can spit. But if I'm going to be used, as you say, I intend to be well rewarded for it." She looked up at Morgan, her expression so sweet it was as if she was about to request his opinion on the chances of it coming on to rain before noon. "Have I mentioned that yet, my lord?"

"You mentioned that you've been talking to Peaches," Morgan answered, remembering the enterprising Irish-woman's frequent hints in that direction, "which, I suppose, is much the same thing. Very well, infant, what sort of reward do you have in mind?"

"Nothing much, for a rich man like you," she told him, although he noticed that she was no longer looking at him. It was as if she felt slightly ashamed to be put in the position of bargaining. She had a good bit of pride for a foundling brat. "I would like a small cottage, just large enough for the four of us. Here in Sussex, because I like Sussex. I haven't ever been anywhere else, but this way I won't be disappointed, you see. I shall have a yellow dog and some fluffy white cats and a bed of my very own. Maybe even a room of my own. And— and an allowance. I would definitely need an allowance—

that's money paid to me every year, so that I will never have to empty another chamber pot."

She wasn't avoiding his gaze now, he noticed, as she stared up at him, her faintly pointed chin tilted defiantly, her high-boned cheeks flushed with becoming color. "Ferdie only says Woodwere 'isn't so bad.' It's worse! I'll not go back, my lord. None of us will go back. So you can teach me and dress me and use me to make trouble in London, because I'm sure as I can be that you're up to some mischief. I'll do exactly as you want without asking any questions—just as long as we get that cottage."

"Morgan, perhaps we should reconsider before this goes any further. Perhaps this child would be better off if we abandoned this scheme of yours and…" The duke's voice trailed off and he spread his hands as if seeking the proper words for what he wanted to say, but then he closed his mouth and let his hands fall into his lap.

"Agreed!" Morgan said forcefully to Caroline before his father could open his mouth again and ruin everything with a belated attack of Christian conscience. Stepping in front of Ferdie, his hand extended to seal the bargain, he said, "One cottage, four bedrooms, one yellow dog, and several fluffy white cats. They are yours, no matter how this ends, Lady Caroline."

"And the allowance!" Ferdie piped up, standing on the cushions so that the top of his head nearly came level with Morgan's chin. "If we're about to be damned, at least let us take full pockets along to hell."

Still holding Caroline's hand and still looking straight into her wide green eyes, Morgan said solemnly, "And an allowance, Caroline. You have my word."

BOOK TWO

A QUESTION OF TRUST
February 1816

Alas, regardless of their doom,
The little victims play!
No sense have they of ills to come,
Nor care beyond today.

Thomas Gray

CHAPTER SEVEN

Lord, I wonder what fool it was that first invented kissing!

Jonathan Swift

"'THERE IS A STRANGE CHARM in the thoughts of a good legacy, or the hopes of an estate, which wondrously alleviates the sorrow that men would otherwise feel for the death of friends.'" Caroline looked up from the book, her fingertip still pressed against the page, holding her place, to smile at Morgan. "Peaches would appreciate that, if she could hear it put in terms she'd understand, wouldn't she, my lord? Mr. Cervantes may dress it up in clean linen, but all he's saying is that pity is short-lived when there is the chance to make money from someone else's death. The king is dead, my lord—long live the king!"

"You are sometimes more truthful than tactful, Caroline. Don't interpret—just resume reading. You are nearly done." Morgan felt the corners of his mouth twitching in an involuntary smile as she bowed her head once more and the story of Don Quixote de la Mancha's death continued toward its sad, uplifting conclusion.

He had little patience with romantic novels, but Miss Twittingdon had proved relentlessly insistent that Caroline test her new proficiency in reading with this particular book, and he had decided not to argue the point with the well-meaning if faintly single-minded woman.

Within a few days of settling into The Acres in October Morgan had announced that he desired exclusive control over the tutoring of Caroline. He had proclaimed this directly after he had found the two women huddled together in the music room, Miss Twittingdon encouraging Caroline to "remember that *real* ladies have their hair powdered at all times, not that I have been able to do so thanks to that Infernal Laurence and his wretchedly closefisted way with money"—and Miss Twittingdon had been grudgingly restricted to the role of chaperon.

She performed admirably in that position, riding herd on Caroline's table manners and always making sure that the child did not walk about the grounds unaccompanied, but Morgan was grateful that she'd been abed with a cold these past few days, for her constant presence during Caroline's lessons could at times prove distracting.

Especially when the late winter sun shone brightly through the windows of his father's study, as it was doing now, to light small golden fires in Caroline's long blond hair and he longed to push his fingers through the sleek, shining mass, to experience its warmth. Or when, as he taught her dance steps in the music room, Miss Twittingdon's clucking tongue made it nearly impossible for him to hold Caroline's slim waist as he ought while he directed her through the maneuvers of the waltz.

Of course, being without Miss Twittingdon was not the same as being unchaperoned, for Frederick Haswit had developed the most annoying habit of bursting into the room without asking permission, to stand beside Caroline's chair and glare at Morgan as if he knew just what he was thinking.

Yet how could he help what he was thinking now, what he had been thinking from almost that first full day at The Acres? Caroline was a child, yes, but a most winning child, with none of the artifice other young women her age were taught to employ in their dealings with gentlemen.

She did not know how to lie, possessed not a hint of guile, and seemed to find no pleasure in the usual feminine wiles such as coy smiles, lowered lashes, or even the occasional ladylike simper. Caroline Monday was genuine. What he saw was what she was, shortcomings and all.

And she was so very, very bright! In a little over three months she had gone from runny-nosed urchin to appealing woman-child, full of questions and curiosity and brimming over with delight in the world around her. For a little over three months Morgan had, in order to teach her, been forced to see the world through Caroline's eyes, and he knew deep in his heart that she was not the only person gaining an education.

He listened now with half an ear as Caroline continued to read, stumbling slightly over some of the longer words, but in general giving a remarkable performance, for which he, as her teacher, permitted himself to take a modicum of credit.

From his position, leaning back against the edge of his father's desk, he watched her mouth move, watched as varying emotions played across her mobile, pixieish features, and smiled yet again as she continued to use the index finger of her small, white hand to keep her place as she read. If only there were some way to train her away from gnawing on her fingernails...

His gaze reluctantly left Caroline's face and the soft curve of her cheek and chin to take in her rigidly correct posture and the sprigged muslin morning gown that was only one representative of her new, extensive wardrobe. He smiled again as he remembered her constant delight in the pretty materials of her gowns and the soft leather of her slippers, and he only wished he could feel avuncular about the child who had impetuously hugged his father when the duke presented her with a large ermine muff at Christmas. According to Betts, who had grown quite fond of her new mistress, the silly child had for weeks slept with the luxuriant fur pressed against her nose.

He would have to be the world's greatest fool to lie to himself and vow that he had not wondered how Caroline's mouth tasted, how her small, high breasts might feel cupped in his large hands, what it would be like to teach her of the joys of the flesh as well as the correct way to cross a room or to thank someone for an offer to dance or to dip her fingers into a bowl of scented rose water between dinner courses. He knew, without knowing why, that she would once more prove herself an apt, eager pupil.

Whenever he had these traitorous thoughts—and they were traitorous, both to Caroline's trust in him and to his intended use of her once they were in London—Morgan did his best to remember how Caroline had been when he found her at Woodwere, to remember that it would be a dangerous folly to lose sight of the fact that he was doing nothing more than attempting to fashion a silk purse from a sow's ear.

Or was he? Was it the height of ludicrousness to believe— when he was alone, lying in his empty bed, remembering her laughter at one of Ferdie's poems or recalling her as she sat with her legs tucked up beneath her, her bottom lip caught between her teeth, doing her best to embroider small stitches on a sampler—that he might possibly have actually stumbled across the real Lady Caroline Wilburton? Or was it more ludicrous to be planning to take this innocent anonymous child, who just happened to suit his purposes, and use her to seek his revenge?

How could he salve his conscience by telling himself that he had lifted not a single person but three from the stinking sty of poverty and the horrors of a madhouse, when he had cold-bloodedly planned to use the most innocent, the most trusting of them all for his own ends?

And to desire her? To trade shamelessly on her trust, her innocence, her joy of living this new, worry-free life, to take advantage of her by seducing her, using her sweet body as he had used so many women, and then fobbing her off with some bauble and a few empty promises—how could he live with himself if he did such a thing?

Peaches and her ilk understood such matters. Actresses and the members of the demimonde expected to be used; they encouraged mutually satisfying associations. Many married women in the *ton* dabbled in affairs, picking and choosing their lovers in much the same way as gentlemen of the *ton* amused themselves by bedding the wife of the man they had just played cards with at Boodle's that evening.

And yet, remembering that Caroline Monday was naught but a foundling-home orphan, a child with no family, no real protectors, no standing in society, Morgan knew he could not bargain with her as he would with any woman of the world. He felt the same reluctance to deal with her as he had always experienced when presented with the latest crop of debutantes being served up on the marriage mart every April. With these young, virginal women it was marriage or nothing, with no kisses stolen in secluded gardens, no tumbling in dark, discreet rooms on the fringes of Mayfair, no jewels in exchange for favors extended.

With one major difference. The debutantes had bored him to flinders. Caroline excited him beyond measure.

He needed a woman. A willing woman. Any willing woman. That was all he needed. He had been too long in Sussex, too long under his father's strict, crushingly religious and moral roof. To close his eyes at night and see visions of Caroline's long blond hair spread out on his pillow, her smiling face looking up at him in welcome anticipation, was a firm indication that he was losing his grip and it was time he moved on.

But he couldn't move on, not until late March, when Caroline would be moving with him, as he and the rest of this strange entourage were transported to the duke's mansion in Portman Square—and the game, as Haswit had called it, began.

Until then he would just have to be careful. He would have to turn his mind away from thoughts of Caroline's appealing honesty, her open, beguiling personality, and her increasingly attractive appearance. He would take out his horse, no matter how high the snow was piled against the windows, and ride the fields, burning off this incredible energy he felt whenever he was in her presence, use physical exertion to tire himself so that he dragged himself to bed at night too exhausted to dream.

He would concentrate on the reason he had sought out Caroline Monday in the first place. Perhaps it was time he joined his father for his morning penance in Jeremy's rooms. That should be sufficient to remind him of Uncle James's hints of the perfect revenge, the purpose behind this mad scheme upon which he had so hastily embarked three short months ago.

And, mostly, he would work to convince himself that what

he was feeling for Caroline was merely lust and had nothing to do with any growing affection for the absurd woman-child.

"'For if he like a madman lived, at least he like a wise one died.' Oh, Morgan, isn't that wonderful? Aunt Leticia is right to hold him in such esteem. I'm so proud now that she wished to call me Dulcinea. And to think, in this modern age, Don Quixote de la Mancha would have been locked up in a place like Woodwere, right alongside the Leopard Man, to be purged and chained and hidden away from the world."

Morgan sliced a look at Caroline, seeing that tears were running freely down her cheeks even as she smiled wistfully, like one still caught in a dream. No wonder it had never occurred to him to doubt her virginity. He had never encountered such blindingly bright and shiny innocence in his entire life. He turned his head, cursing under his breath, and wondered if the most honorable thing he could do would be to leave her immediately, walk out into his father's home wood, and fall on his sword.

Only a few moments ago he had thought himself *glad* that Miss Twittingdon was abed, leaving him and Caroline alone? He must be mad, just as Peaches had declared him to be! And what had another Caroline, Lady Caroline Lamb, once whispered to him about Byron? Oh, yes. She had termed him "mad, bad, and dangerous to know."

It was true. Man, any man, at his worst, at his most selfish, would have to be considered mad—and most definitely bad. And he certainly knew he was dangerous to Caroline Monday. Her very presence with him now, unchaperoned in his father's study, proved her gullibility, her misplaced trust in his gentlemanly honor—if she even knew that she shouldn't be alone with him, although he had to believe Leticia Twittingdon had taught her that much. Of course Miss Twittingdon had taught her that most basic of rules.

And yet, Caroline Monday, who had not so long ago been witness to sights that would have made a grown man faint, who had been the target of a naked man armed only with his madness and the one thing he could control—his bodily functions—probably thought society's strictures about men and women being alone in each other's company were ridiculous in the extreme.

Besides, as he already knew, she trusted him. She called him Morgan, and he called her Caroline, as if they were cousins, or brother and sister. She might even have grown to like him, to feel comfortable in his presence. Safe. Unthreatened.

But then, she didn't know what he was thinking, did she?

He pushed himself away from the desk. She had closed the book and was now lovingly stroking its front cover, the way she would probably stroke the head of that yellow dog she wanted. "It's only a story, Caroline," he reminded her coldly, walking across the room to take the book from her hands and replace it on the shelf. "You would be better served to read Bacon. 'Hope is a good breakfast, but it is a bad supper.' Remember that, imp, and learn to rely on yourself, and not fanciful dreams."

"Oh, pooh!" Caroline wiped at her tears with the backs of her hands and stood up, to smile at him, the action reminding him that she was deliciously small, the top of her head reaching no higher than his shoulder. "Bacon also said, if I remember it correctly, 'Some books are to be tasted, others to be swallowed, and some few to be chewed and digested.' My belly, my lord, is at the moment most happily replete with Cervantes's mad, wonderful, *wise* Don Quixote de la Mancha!"

Morgan tightly intertwined his hands behind his back,

refusing to give in to the nearly overwhelming impulse to drag this unbelievably bright, unreasonably optimistic, and most maddeningly naive, *quixotic* creature into his arms and kiss her senseless. "Young ladies of quality do not say 'belly,' Caroline," he said tersely, not unaware that he had been moments earlier judging himself in danger of turning into a lecher, but he was now wondering if he perhaps should be more concerned that he might be turning into a high stickler of no humor, like his father.

She wrinkled her nose at him—which he considered a miraculous leap upward from her previous habit of descending into low cant and accusing him of being a "beetle-headed prig"—and retorted, "I don't see why not. I've got one, you know—a belly, that is. I've got a belly, and I've got feet, and I've got ankles, and I've even got *legs*—see?" She lifted her skirts, exposing those legs, those long, perfectly formed legs and shapely ankles, to his surprised gaze.

"You will oblige me by remembering that you are being trained to be a lady. There are times when I believe I would have encountered less trouble if I had sought to break a Russian bear to the bridle."

"Don't interrupt me, Morgan," she retorted, surprising him with the cool command in her tone—as if she had been born issuing orders. "I have a belly, and I have legs. Indeed, I have an entire body beneath these clothes. A body of which Aunt Leticia and you tell me I'm supposed to behave as if I am unaware, which is stupid as well as impossible, for I have to eat, don't I, and I have to walk. I like being a lady, Morgan, when I can eat whenever I'm hungry and wear pretty clothes that I don't have to share with a host of biting fleas and read all these lovely books and dance to the music Ferdie plays and listen while your father proses on over dinner about God and

Creation and how wonderful heaven must be—but I must tell you, Morgan, I'll be damned for a tinker if I can like pretending I don't know I have an arse!"

"Yes, imp, you do," Morgan replied carefully, refusing to allow himself to display anger at her descent into the vernacular of the lower classes. "And quite a lovely one, too, I imagine."

Caroline had raised one hand threateningly as he began to speak, her chewed-nail index finger pointed up at his face, her mouth open as if to hotly debate whatever he said. That hand abruptly fell as she tipped her head to one side, openly flirting, boldly employing one of those winning feminine wiles of which he had believed her innocent. "La, sir, I believe you are being far too forward for a gentleman of your station, a gentleman who is dealing with a young woman of quality." She raised her hand once more, to begin fretfully fanning her cheek. "I fear I am all but overcome, my lord Clayton, and needs must sit down."

"On your arse, brat?" Morgan asked, laying his hands on her shoulders as she laughed out loud.

Little witch! She was testing him past all endurance with her quick mind—and those teasing emerald eyes. And those full, smiling lips. And the provocative stance of her small, yet lush body. Yes, her body. Her long legs. Her shapely ankles. The small, intriguing indentation his fingers had found just above her waist as he had held her during those maddening waltz lessons. And the slight swell of her breasts rising above the bodice of her—

"Oh, the hell with it. The bloody hell with it!" he exploded, pulling her close against him and bringing his mouth down on hers.

Her lips tasted slightly of the sweet Acres honey he had

watched her drizzle clumsily onto her toast that morning at breakfast, licking the stickiness off her fingers with the tip of her pink tongue, innocently sending him into an agony of frustrated desire.

She kept those delicious lips tightly closed and almost puckered, the untutored action reminding him that she had no experience with kissing.

But he did.

He slid his hands along her slender shoulder blades and up either side of her slim throat, cupping her face gently, then used his thumbs to lightly massage her full bottom lip, delicately tugging it downward, until he could feel the soft exhalation of her honey-perfumed breath.

Capturing that same bottom lip lightly between his teeth, he ran his tongue slowly across the soft, sensitized skin. When she did not resist him, he repeated the action with her upper lip before, slanting his own lips slightly, he slid his tongue along her smooth teeth and into her mouth.

Willing his hands to remain where they were, he allowed his tongue the intimacy of running across hers, deliberately engaging her in a duel in which he, the experienced man, already knew the outcome. And just as in a duel, he employed all the winning moves of the exercise, thrusting, then retreating, advancing unexpectedly, withdrawing slightly to change position, and then attack again.

But then, as always, Caroline surprised him. Expecting capitulation, he was unprepared for her stunning riposte.

He felt her small hands slide up his chest, momentarily tangling in the intricate folds of his neckcloth before reaching his face, where her thumbs repeated the action he had employed moments earlier. Small teeth nipped at his bottom lip. A tongue tip glided along his upper lip, gently probing the corners of his mouth. And then that tongue, that honey-scented, untutored yet eager little tongue, slid past his teeth to flutter against the roof of his mouth like a butterfly beating its wings against the bars of its gilded cage.

Morgan's world rocked, curiously, unexpectedly tilted on its axis, and he had to wrap his arms around Caroline's small body or else spin away from the earth, to float, lost and alone, among the stars that already blazed so brightly behind his closed eyelids. So sweet. So precious. So very lovable. Caro. His own sweet Caro.

"A crafty animal is friend rat,
Who turns the tables and chases our cat.
He speaks one way and acts another,
Is this the way of a gentleman's honor?"

Haswit! Of all the stupid bad luck! Morgan snapped back to his senses, quickly putting Caroline away from him, refusing to wince as she raised trembling fingers to trace the lines of her moist, faintly swollen mouth, looking up at him as if she had just now awakened from a dream and could not quite understand how she had come to be standing in the duke's study.

"It's all right, Caroline," he said quietly, knowing he was lying. *It* wasn't all right. And *it* would never be all right again. "Ferdie, please don't feel you have to stand on ceremony and knock before entering a room," he then said, wheeling about to confront the frowning dwarf. "After all, my dear father has given you the run of the house."

Ferdie stomped—and for a little man, he stomped quite convincingly, Morgan thought idly—across the room, stopping only to grab hold of a straight-backed wooden chair, which he then dragged to within a foot of Morgan before hopping onto it, to stand chest to chin against him. "I do not have a glove, sirrah, so this will have to do." And then, before Morgan could react, Ferdie slapped him hard on both cheeks.

Surprised into reacting, Morgan raised a hand to rub one stinging cheek. "You're challenging me to a duel, Ferdie?" he asked, not knowing whether to be amused or ashamed. He knew how loyal Haswit was to Caroline, and it wasn't as if the little man hadn't already issued several warnings—all couched in atrocious verse—that warned of this protective devotion.

"A duel?" Caroline tugged on Morgan's sleeve, reminding him of her presence, for he was finding himself growing increasingly awed by Ferdie's impressive show of bravery. "You can't fight a duel with Ferdie. He's half the size of you."

Morgan looked down to where Caroline's hand pressed against the material of his coat, then turned his head back to stare at Frederick Haswit's frightened yet determined features for another long moment. "Half my size, Caroline? You've learned much these last months, but I'd say that you are sadly mistaken in this case. Mr. Haswit here is twice the man I'll ever be—in every way. But you are right in one thing: I will not fight him. I don't have to, for I've already lost."

Morgan continued to watch as Ferdie's eyes filled, so that the homely little man of the stunted body, this giant among men, had to blink furiously to keep tears from spilling onto his cheeks. "I won't be entering this room again without knocking, my lord," the dwarf said finally, allowing Caroline to assist him down from the chair. He smiled up at Morgan, adding, "I know now that I can trust you."

And then, still hand in hand with Caroline, who looked back over her shoulder only once as they walked away, her brow furrowed in conspicuous confusion, Ferdie Haswit, his steps light and carefree, his barrel chest puffed out importantly, escorted his best friend in the whole world, the beautiful young woman he had offered to die for, from the room.

Leaving Morgan Blakely, Marquis of Clayton and self-declared Supreme Idiot of the Realm, behind, to struggle with the sudden envy he felt for a young man who owned nothing yet possessed everything of value.

CHAPTER EIGHT

I am like the unicorn
astonished as he gazes,
beholding the virgin.

Thibaut de Champagne

OF ALL THE PALATIAL chambers in the duke of Glynde's fine mansion, Caroline had soon decided she liked the octagonal music room best.

She delighted in the way the entrance to the room had been cut across the far corner of a small groundfloor drawing room, its ceiling-high wooden double doors painted a thick, creamy white—rather reminding her of warm, frothy cow's milk as it looked in the pail.

When she stepped through the doors, as she had been doing religiously every afternoon since her first week at The Acres, her hands lingered on the golden handles, and she surveyed the room as she had done that first day.

Her eyes were first greeted by the winter sunlight that shone through the pairs of slim, many-paned floor-to-ceiling windows that marked each of the eight sides of the fairy-castle room. There were no dark heavy draperies here, but only sheer, airy curtains topped by rose satin flounces—like the fancy turbans perched on Aunt Leticia's infant-fine hair.

Sweeping into the room, she looked up to pay homage to the painted angels and cherubs that graced the intricately decorated domed ceiling, their most private parts prudently concealed by portions of a trailing rose satin streamer that had been painted on the ceiling, its twining length gathered up here and there by painted bows and floral bouquets.

After practicing her newest accomplishment—the demure curtsy—on the chubby creatures, Caroline cast her gaze appreciatively around the remainder of the room.

A large harp stood near one of the pairs of windows, and a piano adorned with gilt and pastels was positioned beneath the center of the dome. Rose-striped satin chairs and highly imaginative chaise longues upholstered in green-as-spring-grass velvet littered the flowered carpet whose shape mimicked the eight sides of the room.

It was a fairy-tale sort of place. The sort of room where Caroline could dream that she was only one of twenty or more guests gathered to hear fine music, to listen, enraptured, as a lovely woman dressed all in white stood beside the piano and sang unfamiliar yet beautiful words in a voice like liquid silver, her hands clasped together at her bosom, her expression otherworldly, her audience moved to tears.

Caroline adored it.

Another reason she liked the music room had to do not with its beauty but with a man who did *not* visit here. Its owner, Morgan's sad-faced, rather forbidding father, never crossed its threshold—which was a good thing, as far as Caroline was concerned, for she had never before seen a man so capable of robbing the world of joy simply by showing his face and ever-present Bible at the dinner table.

Caroline felt guilty that she could not quite like the duke, especially since it was so apparent that Morgan fairly worshiped the man, but there was nothing else for it—the man was a doomsday merchant! Why, she'd felt more cheer from the undertaker who came to Glynde to bury the orphans, more warmth from a fireplace full of cold ashes. In short, the Duke of Glynde, in Caroline's firm opinion, was the sort of fellow who could light up a room simply by leaving it.

She walked to the piano and timidly touched a fingertip to one of the keys, still pleasantly startled whenever she heard the small, tinkling sound the action precipitated.

"Such a beautiful smile, my most truant Lady Caroline," she heard Morgan say from somewhere behind her. "Anyone would think you were hearing a symphony. Have you forgotten that we were to have a lesson in globes before dinner?"

"Oh, pooh," Caroline responded, again employing Miss Twittingdon's favorite expression of frustration. She could have said many other things, but had learned that gentlewomen as a rule did not, when displeased, insult a person's antecedents or colorfully describe possible alternate uses for their intestinal organs. Which was a great pity for, thanks to Peaches O'Hanlan, Caroline Monday had become very much the mistress of such basely eloquent rejoinders. "I detest globes, Morgan," she added, turning to face him, hoping her smile was sufficiently sweet to divert him. "They're—they're so *round*. Almost as round as poor Mr. Woodwere's bald head—and nearly as littered with bumps."

Morgan tilted his head slightly to one side, his eyes narrowed as if examining her, which was one of his most disconcerting habits. She longed to cover herself, as she would if he had walked into the room just as she was rising from her bath and Betts had yet to wrap her in one of the fluffy white towels. How had one kiss affected her so much? "Very well, imp," he said at last, so that she relaxed fractionally. He seated himself in one of the rose chairs, his long legs crossed at the ankle as he continued to look at her. "I am not quite in the mood to look at anything that resembles Mr. Woodwere's pate. You like this room, don't you, Caroline?"

"It's better than most I've been in, I suppose." Her eyes slid away from him, to concentrate on admiring the way the sunlight danced along the taut strings of the harp. She never truly felt at her ease anymore around Morgan. It was difficult to feel only friendship toward a man who had the ability to set her heart fluttering just by saying her name.

He gave a sharp bark of laughter. "Damning with faint praise, are you? This is a beautiful room, Caroline, my mother's favorite. I like it well enough myself, or at least I did until my father had me wash all the windows, inside and out. There are sixteen of the bloody things in all, with an even one hundred panes per window. Do you know how many panes that makes, Caroline?"

She moved away from the piano to seat herself on the edge of one of the chaise longues, directly across from Morgan. "Enough to make you hate your father very much by the time you were done, I'd reckon," she answered honestly. "I know I would. You, with a houseful of servants at your beck and call who could wash them for you. I would never lift my finger to scratch my own head if I had half so many people scurrying about to do my bidding. The way I see it, my lord, there's no sense in keeping a dog and barking myself!"

"You misunderstood, imp. I was ordered to wash the windows as a punishment," Morgan told her. "Although, as I remember it, I did have some help. Once my father went out riding, and I was left alone to do my penance, I saw the tip of a second ladder appearing around the corner of the building, and...well, never mind." His eyes clouded, as if the memory pained him, and Caroline hastened to change the subject.

"Would you like me to tell you about Mr. Woodwere, Morgan?" she asked brightly. "You barely had time to meet him that day we all left the asylum, and I know you cannot think too highly of him, but he is really a wonderful man. Or at least he was kind to me."

"Really? How so? I admit to being intrigued at your notion of kindness. Did he only have you walk past the Leopard Man on alternate Tuesdays? But, no. He would have been 'kinder' than that. I know! You were allowed to don gloves before holding down inmates for their purges. My, my. When you have mastered the art of embroidery, I suggest you do a sampler for the man, in gratitude for his great 'kindness.'"

Caroline sighed, rolling her eyes as she lost patience with him. "You don't understand. I guess I shouldn't blame you. How can you understand? For you, punishment was having to wash a few windows. For me, punishment was delivered with a stick or a belt or the flat of someone's hand. Sometimes a fist. And sometimes for *nothing!* Sometimes I was punished just for *being,* just for living instead of dying like I was supposed to do, just for having a belly to feed as well as two hands to work with, just for needing clothes on my back, so that same back could help hoist a water pail or chop a turnip or clean the goat shed, because the goats were necessary, and I wasn't. There were always more than enough orphans to go around, but we only had two goats. You may not like Peaches overmuch, but she was all that stood between me and Mrs. Rivers, and I owe her my gratitude." *So there,* she added silently, knowing she was being childish and not giving a tinker's dam.

"And then, shortly after I went to work at the asylum," Caroline continued, as Morgan raised one dark eyebrow, "I met Mr. Woodwere, who became my new Peaches." She closed her eyes for a moment, reliving the night she had cannoned into the man as she fled the common room. No, she wouldn't think about that now. If there was a God, if the duke's Supreme Being really existed, she would never have to think about that night again. "Mr. Woodwere didn't like that I was so young, for the rest of the servants were much older. It was his idea to put me mostly on the private side, so that I only had to go over to the public side one or two days a week. And never at night." She shook her head. "Never, never *ever* at night."

She brightened, smiling. "That's how I met Miss Twittingdon and Ferdie, working on the private side. Mr. Woodwere was never my friend, at least not in the way Peaches and Miss Twittingdon and Ferdie are, but he was a nice man. I would have washed his windows twice a day if he'd asked me, and I wouldn't have spit on them when he wasn't looking, either."

Morgan leaned forward, his elbows on his knees, his hands steepled as he pressed his fingertips together. "You live in an entirely different world from me, don't you, imp?" he asked, although she was fairly certain he did not require that she answer. "Your values, your priorities—everything is so real to you, so easily recognized for what it is and what it isn't. It wouldn't take you years and years to avenge yourself on someone who had done you wrong, would it? You'd just curse him out on the spot, give him a good kick in the shins for emphasis, and then get on with your life."

Was he insulting her? Or was that a hint of sadness she heard in his tone? It must be terribly oppressive, being so wealthy and educated. Complicated, too. Caroline shifted uncomfortably in her chair. "Is that so bad? If I were to sit and think on things that go wrong, like some silly, broody hen," she said earnestly, a hint of Irish brogue entering her voice, "I should think that I would never have a moment to do anything else but hatch sorrows. What's the sense of walking about with m'head down, like a cold rain was drenchin' me? I'd much rather be looking up, don't you know, peekin' out for rainbows."

"I see. And do you consider this place another of your rainbows? After Peaches and Mr. Woodwere and Miss Twittingdon and Ferdie, I mean," Morgan asked, spreading his arms as if to indicate the music room, the entire estate.

Caroline relaxed her guard and smiled broadly as she stood, holding her hands in front of her as if waving away his words. "Ah, Morgan, m'lad, I consider this to be more than just a paltry rainbow. Dry sheets, a full belly, a roof to keep the snow off my blanket. *This* time I'm thinkin' our Caro has stumbled straight over a pot o' gold!"

Morgan laughed out loud, rose to take hold of her wrists, then bowed to kiss her right hand. "Someday, Miss Monday, when all this is over, I believe I should like to apply to you for lessons. Not in globes, you understand, but in life. I believe you could open whole new worlds to me."

And then he left. He just turned and left.

Caroline watched as the marquis strode from the room, his rigid posture yet again reminding her of a faintly reluctant yet resolute solder marching off to war. What private war was he fighting? How could she help him fight?

For there was a battle coming. She couldn't be sure what this battle was or where it would take place, but she was not so silly as to be unaware that—whether or not she knew the why or where of it—she had already wholeheartedly enlisted on Morgan's side.

However, she wouldn't think of that right now, she decided as she sat herself down on the brocade piano bench, her knees not as steady as they should have been. Right now she would be content to press the back of her right hand against her left cheek, holding Morgan's kiss as close to her as she could.

CAROLINE STOOD in a small puddle of golden light radiating from two carefully arranged candelabra, looking into the long mirror, shivering slightly in the chill night air. She held the velvety white towel against her protectively a moment longer, then slowly let it slip to the floor. Her body, warm and rosy from her totally unnecessary yet longed-for second bath of the day, didn't look any different than it had two days ago. Two arms. Two legs. Two breasts...

Two arms that had ached to hold Morgan Blakely close to her, so close that nothing and no one could ever separate them. Two legs that had gone as warm and fluid as bathwater when his lips met hers, leaving her unable to stand without his support. Two breasts, that had pressed against his broad, hard chest, tingling with vaguely frightening sensations totally alien to anything in her experience.

She frowned worriedly as she continued to look into the mirror, unable to understand. Why couldn't she see any difference? There was a new awareness now, when she moved, when she felt Morgan's eyes on her as they sat across from each other at the dinner table, when the soft silk of her most intimate undergarment slid past her hips as she stepped out of it in order to bathe.

The human body held no great mystery for her, after being raised in an orphanage and forced to share her quarters, and often her bed, with dozens of other bodies of all shapes, sizes and sexes.

To Caroline, a body was merely something that was either too hungry or too cold or too hot or too tired—and too prone to expelling various offensive liquids and solids that she, as a dependent orphan and, later, as the lowliest servant, had been forced to deal with and dispose of as quickly as possible. A body was a shell that had to be fed and clothed and only caused its owner trouble by getting sick or breaking one of its bones or getting in the way of Mrs. Rivers's stinging birch switch or one of the attendant's well-aimed kicks.

That her body—or anyone else's body, for that matter—could become so important had simply never occurred to her.

She picked up the towel once more and turned away from the mirror, truly chilled now, and hastened to slip into her nightgown before Betts returned from the kitchens with the warm milk Caroline had begged her to fetch, saying she needed it in order to sleep. Then she carefully replaced the candelabra where they had been and folded the towel before hanging it on the warming rack, saving Betts a step or two.

Ignoring the small stepping stool, she hopped lightly onto the high mattress and snuggled down beneath the satin counterpane, holding the lace-edged hem of the soft cotton sheet close against her chin. Three months of sleeping in outrageous luxury had not been enough to keep her from experiencing a delicious, almost decadent delight in the exercise. She reached under the pillows to extract the ermine muff, smiling as she touched the black-edged tassels, then rubbed the long-haired fur against her nose in much the way she had rubbed a small, tattered scrap of blanket against her nose as a child, sucking her thumb and rubbing the blanket until she fell asleep.

She looked up at the ceiling and the shadows that danced there thanks to the flickering flames from the candles. The bit of blanket had long since fallen into nothingness, and she didn't suck on her thumb anymore, and hadn't for years and years. But the fur was so soft, and she was alone, so no one could see her. There was no harm in one small bad habit. Hadn't Peaches made her feel better about biting her nails by telling her that bad habits were "the single thing that lifts us up above the critters, and don't ye know? Ever once see our old nanny goat pickin' her nose, did ye, or that bloodless biddy Rivers's dog fuzz the cards or nick the dice—not that that's such a bad thing, mind ye, iffen ye does it right. But did ye ever hear a little birdie fart in a church? O'course ye didn't! We be the only ones with bad habits, which is how we can tell we're people. Ye have ta walk on yer hind legs, little girlie, afore ye can drink yerself under a table!"

Peaches. Caroline caught her bottom lip between her teeth, thinking about her dear friend and mentor—who had reluctantly cooled her heels at The Acres for less than a week before loping off in the middle of the night, taking three china bowls and a pair of silver candlesticks with her. If only she were still here... Peaches would know how to answer her questions—if Caroline could only think how to ask them.

Caroline frowned and slid deeper under the covers, knowing that it would take a lot more than warm milk to help her to sleep tonight. Closing her eyes, she fought back the disturbing mental image of what happened between a man and a woman—what Peaches had called "the dirty deed" when she first broached the subject of Caroline's traveling to London to turn her hand to "the business," since she was not eager to work at Woodwere.

She could still recall the Irishwoman's blunt, no-nonsense

description of the act that, if a girl wasn't careful, led to disease, injury, and unwanted children. According to Peaches, men paid down good money to perform this deed, and women had been allowing them to do so ever since Adam and Eve—who for years did nothing more than have everything handed to them without having to work for it and ran around that place called Paradise like brainless twits, not wearing a stitch and talking to snakes—first discovered "the beast with two backs."

The Irishwoman's revelations had not quite the same appeal as the duke's smiling-faced description of Eden before Eve's "great sin" served to have both her and Adam thrown out into the world to suffer, and yet, Caroline knew, when you got right down to it, the stories were pretty much alike. Adam, the "innocent," got to enjoy the dirty deed, while Eve only got to suffer a monthly flux and the pain of childbirth. But then, Caroline also knew, men always did get the best of everything while women were left to pick up the blame and the filthy end of the stick.

But she couldn't think of that now. She had to get back to the dirty deed. Boys and girls at the orphanage were separated at the age of seven, so she certainly had no knowledge to draw on in that quarter, but she had seen the public side of Woodwere and she had long had a very clear knowledge of the physical differences between men and women.

She had even seen the dirty deed itself, as performed by several of the inmates. One night shortly after arriving at the asylum, after Woodwere had retired to his apartments, one of the attendants had come to Caroline's cot, to invite her to a party. And what a party it was, taking place in the filthy common room where the least violent inmates were allowed to gather during the day, the women on Mondays, Wednesdays, and Fridays, and the men on the remaining days— except Sundays, of course. On that day all of the inmates on the public side were chained in their cells so that visitors, many stopping off at Woodwere on their way home from church, could pay a penny apiece to walk down the halls laughing, poking fun, and throwing coins so that the poor wretches might perform for them. It was the Leopard Man's happiest day of the week—having all those lovely targets.

Caroline had walked into the common room with happy anticipation, having already heard the laughing voices as she approached along the hallway, carefully tiptoeing past the sleeping Leopard Man. A smile on her lips and the attendant's promise of some food and drink uppermost in her mind, she was hardly prepared for the sight of more than two dozen filthy, naked bodies rolling about on the urine-soaked straw.

Everywhere she looked men and women were twined together, some hip to hip, some mouth to mouth, some hip to mouth. Two men kissed and fondled each other at the urging of the attendants, while three women attacked a fourth, their hands and mouths everywhere, biting her until they had drawn blood. The woman they were attacking only laughed, screaming instructions at the top of her high, cockney-accented voice.

A young girl no more than sixteen cowered in a corner whimpering, clutching a rag doll to her face until, as Caroline watched, one of the senior attendants—a big, mean fellow Caroline knew only as Boxer, advanced toward her, fumbling with the buttons on his breeches. The young girl began to scream and scream and scream....

Of everything she witnessed, the girl's earsplitting screams had haunted Caroline most. She pushed the soft white fur of the muff against her mouth now as she had pressed her hands against her lips then, trying to force back the same bitter bile that had risen into her mouth at the time, until she was able to tear her horrified gaze away and run, run as fast as she could, until she barreled, weeping hysterically, into the broad chest of Mr. Woodwere, who quickly shooed her toward the private side of the asylum. Dear Mr. Woodwere. For all his inability to control either the inmates or most of his staff, he had somehow been able to protect Caroline from Boxer's basest instincts. She had providentially found herself another guardian to succeed Peaches, who had protected her during her years at the orphanage.

Why wasn't Peaches here now? Why couldn't she ask her if those poor demented creatures had felt as if they wanted to hold on to each other forever, as if their limbs had turned to water, as if their breasts and all of their most intimate bodily parts had tingled and sent vague yet shocking messages to their jumbled brains? Had those feelings led them beyond kisses—to perform the dirty deed? Was this varied and gross act, which seemed closer to violence than to any expression of affection, truly rooted in something as beautiful as a kiss?

Was this dirty deed born of the same sort of longing Don Quixote de la Mancha felt for his Dulcinea?

Or was there another sort of deed, another way for this business of men and women to be played out? She certainly couldn't ask those questions of Aunt Leticia or Betts or the duke. And she most assuredly would never ask them of Morgan Blakely.

But there had to be. For she hadn't felt dirty two days before, when Morgan held her and kissed her. She had felt wonderful. Not guilty, like Eve. Not wretched, like those inmates and attendants at Woodwere. Just wonderful. Completely, perfectly wonderful.

Hearing a slight sound at the door to the hallway, Caroline sat up quickly, then wiped at her cheeks as she realized that she had been crying. "Betts? Is that you? Do you need help with the tray?"

No answer came, but only more sounds, almost as if someone or something was scratching at the wood. Throwing back the covers, she slipped out of bed, taking up the long white dressing gown and shoving her arms into it as she approached the door, eyeing it warily, as if a monster—like the ones Peaches had told her ate up little children who harbored bad thoughts—might be lurking on the other side. "Who's there?" she asked, pressing her ear against the wood. "Betts?"

There was another slight clicking sound, and she looked down to see the latch moving upward. Swallowing down hard on her fear, for she had believed herself safe in the duke's household, she stepped back and watched the door slowly swing open wide.

No great bugbear appeared in the door frame, fangs dripping with saliva, red eyes glowing, ready to burn her to a cinder where she stood. Nobody was there at all. For a moment she believed that she must have imagined the noise and the door had somehow come unlatched by itself. She had been frightened for no good reason.

It served her right, thinking about the dirty deed.

And then she looked down at the floor and saw the small covered basket, a large pink bow tied to its handle. She stared at it for some moments, unable to believe that someone had left her a gift and then crept away, not waiting to be thanked.

It must have been Ferdie, she decided, remembering how he had spent the last two days apologizing for having burst into the duke's study to challenge the marquis to a duel. But he didn't have to bring her a gift. She had been rather glad of his interference at a moment when she had begun to wonder what on earth she was about, kissing the Marquis of Clayton like some cheeky guttersnipe, even if she had been more than a little worried that the dwarf might have lived to regret his reckless bravery.

She stepped into the hallway to look up and down, just to see if Ferdie was hiding behind one of the large chests or potted plants that hugged the wainscoted walls, then picked up the basket and hurried back into her chamber, closing the door behind her.

Climbing back into bed, her gift already tenderly deposited in the middle of the jumbled coverlet, Caroline noticed a neatly rolled sheet of paper tucked up in the pink bow and pulled it out, unrolling it and holding it close to her bedside candle, prepared to read Ferdie's poetic apology.

She hadn't even really looked at the paper before the basket tipped over on the bed, its lid falling open even as something inside the basket hissed and spit as if angry at its rough treatment. A moment later, as Caroline prudently inched back against the headboard, sure she had been gifted with a snake, a small pink nose was visible, pushing its way past the cracked-open lid, to be quickly followed by long white whiskers, two large yellow-green eyes that overwhelmed a sweet, white furry face, and two black-tipped, pointy ears.

"*Meow,*" the small kitten said, as if bidding Caroline a good evening, then, with a toss of its head, pushed aside the lid completely and tumbled headfirst onto the coverlet. "*Meow!*" it repeated, this time indignantly, before righting itself and licking one snow-white paw, as if cleaning up after its harrowing experience.

"Oh! You sweet darling!" Caroline abandoned her defensive pose at the headboard and scooped up the animal in one hand, rubbing its moist pink nose with her own before hugging the kitten to her, stroking its soft white fur, then laughing out loud when she noticed that the tip of the kitten's tail, like it ears, was tipped with inky black fur. "You look like my muff!" she exclaimed as she laid the kitten on her crossed legs and began tickling its fat pink belly. "Only you're warmer and much the prettier by half, aren't you, my little Muff, my sweet Muffie? You are a female, you know," she told the cat, pushing up its tail. "I can tell these things."

Muffie took immediate exception—either to her new name or to Caroline's inspection of her sex—and sank her small pointy teeth into her new mistresses's index finger, pushing her back paws out to inflict long scratches along Caroline's inner wrist, drawing blood.

Caroline didn't care about the scratches. Muffie had spirit. She might be small, and female into the bargain, but she was a fearless little imp. "Betts will be here soon, Muffie," she told the kitten who, having defended her honor, had sunk down in Caroline's lap, purring quite loudly as she kneaded a small ridge in the coverlet with her front paws. "I'll ask her to please fetch some more milk from the kitchens—and a box with dirt in it, as you're too young by far to go outside to relieve yourself. Would you like some milk, Muffie? Of course you would. Oh, Ferdie! What a wonderful gift!"

Saying the dwarf's name reminded Caroline that she had yet to read his note. Careful not to disturb Muffie, who had already closed her eyes and was sound asleep, she leaned over to pick up the paper once more, uncurling it from the bottom and holding it up to the candlelight, to read:

My dear Lady Caroline,
Miguel de Cervantes, creator of your esteemed Don

Quixote de la Mancha, has written, "Every man is as Heaven made him, and sometimes a great deal worse." I fear that, as Don Quixote is an example of man at his best, I am representative of that same creature at his worst. I will not stoop even lower, to ask you to forgive my recent unpardonable conduct. I can only offer you this small gift and my promise not to repeat my offense.
Morgan.

Caroline read the note straight through three times, her hand trembling as she held the paper open, then laid it carefully on the night table.

His "unpardonable conduct."

What did that mean?

He had kissed her. She had kissed him. Nothing more. Nothing less. But to call that kiss an act of "unpardonable conduct," an *"offense?"*

Why? He hadn't touched her, not really, and he hadn't hurt her. They hadn't done the dirty deed.

Hadn't he enjoyed their kiss? Hadn't his arms ached? Had he remained rock solid and unmoved by their sudden closeness, unaffected by the strange yet immensely pleasing sensations that had coursed through her own body, leaving her to spend these last two days furtively looking into every mirror she passed, wondering why she still looked the same when she knew Morgan's kiss had changed her irrevocably?

Caroline looked down at Muffie, tears stinging her eyes as she realized what she had to do now. She could have accepted this apology from Ferdie, who had barged in unwanted to protect her and to rescue her from herself. She could have accepted Muffie from Ferdie.

But she could not accept the kitten from Morgan any more than she could accept his apology.

Because she couldn't be sorry that he had kissed her. And she would never be sorry that she had kissed him back.

MORGAN HAD DISMISSED Simmons more than an hour earlier, telling the valet he felt confident he could undress himself this evening, so he was not well pleased to hear a knock at his door.

He remained slouched down in the large chair in front of the fireplace, staring into the dying flames, a half-empty brandy snifter dangling from his fingertips. Taking a deep, disgusted breath, he called out, "Enter!" in a tone that he was sure would dissuade any but a fool or a very brave man from doing as he had bid, and took another long drink of the brandy.

So sunk in his own disturbing thoughts was he that he immediately forgot he had a visitor, and the hand holding the snifter froze in midair when, a few seconds later, Caroline Monday's voice came from somewhere behind him, saying, "Good evening, my lord."

He looked down at himself—at his white shirt, which was minus a neckcloth, the upturned collar open at the throat; at his buckskin-clad legs and his stockinged feet, which were stretched out, resting on one of a pair of decorative brass andirons.

He placed the snifter on the table beside him and pulled himself to his feet, running a hand through his hair, only to have one errant dark lock fall forward once more onto his forehead. Then he turned around slowly, hoping he had heard incorrectly, that his brandy-befuddled brain had played a trick on him. "Caro," he said softly, seeing her standing not three feet from him, her bare toes sticking out from beneath the hem of her dressing gown, her long blond hair unbound and hanging to her waist, the wicker basket he had left at her door earlier held in front of her, tightly grasped in both her small white hands.

"I—I'm sorry to disturb you, Mor— I mean, my lord," she said, her eyes averted, as if possibly, just possibly, she knew how excruciatingly stupid it had been for her to come to his rooms.

Alone. Unescorted. Barely clothed. At midnight.

Disturb him? When had she begun to disturb him? When had he not been disturbed by her? When had her incredible innocence and her unselfconscious beauty and her indomitable spirit not disturbed him, heated his blood, driving him to impetuous acts and impossible dreams? Dear God. Did she have to come to his rooms to taunt him with her piquant little face and her tip-tilted green eyes that seemed to smile even when she was sad and her pathetic bitten nails and her lively, inquisitive mind? Hadn't he suffered enough?

"Lady Caroline," he responded coldly, protectively, when he realized that she had stumbled over his name and then addressed him formally. "Haven't you learned anything these past three months? You are not to be in a man's private rooms. Not in the daytime, and most especially not at night—and dressed as you are, as we both are. Leticia Twittingdon might be an addlepated romantic, but she is not so short of wit as to have neglected to impress you with those pertinent facts."

Caroline took a single step backward and lifted one hand from the handle of the basket to begin biting on the side of her fingertip, then just as quickly drew her fingers into a tight fist and moved her hand to her side, but not before he saw the long scratches on the delicate flesh on the inside of her wrist. "I know, my lord. I'm not going to stay above a minute. I—

I just wished to return your basket. Muffie is a most exceedingly wonderful kitten—perhaps even the most wonderful kitten in all of Sussex, all of England—but I can't keep her. I—I just can't."

"Muffie?" He looked at her curiously for a few moments, then smiled as he understood. "That's an exceptionally pretty name, Lady Caroline, and most fitting. But I don't understand. Is it because she scratched you? Why can't you keep her?"

She bowed her head, and her blond hair glowed from the light emanating from the fireplace, the faint hint of a halo reminding Morgan of a painting he had once seen of a guardian angel hovering over a small child as it attempted to cross a rickety bridge above a raging river. "Because," she said quietly, almost too quietly for him to hear her.

"'Because?'" What in living hell was that supposed to mean? "I believe you're going to have to be more explicit than that, imp, for I spent the majority of the afternoon combing the countryside on horseback in the snow, looking for just the right kitten. I had thought to gift you with a yellow dog, but the farmers told me it is too early in the year for a litter."

She raised her head, and he could see tears standing in her eyes. He felt as if someone had just plunged a dagger into his chest. "A dog? Really, Morgan? And a yellow one, too. You are so kind to have remembered. But I really couldn't—"

"Couldn't accept a dog. Yes. Yes, I know." He rubbed at the back of his neck, suddenly very weary. "Look, Caro, sit down for a moment, won't you?" He indicated the chair he had just vacated. "It was cowardly of me to have left you the basket and a note, then run away like some green youth afraid to face up to what he's done. We really should talk."

He stepped back and she walked past him, to seat herself primly at the very edge of the burgundy leather cushion, the wicker basket balanced in her lap. She looked like a scolded child or a penitent novice—and so damnably virginal that he longed to toss her onto the hearthrug and make love to her until she looked rumpled, touched, and alive, more human—the way she had looked that first night when she had come to his private dining room at the inn and taken such lusty bites of that apple. Only cleaner, he reminded himself, smiling ruefully at his own thoughts.

He went down on his knees in front of her, holding on to the arms of the chair. "Caroline," he began, not really knowing what he would say. "Caroline, I brought you here to The Acres because I wanted to prepare you to be presented in London as the seventh Earl of Witham's long lost daughter. I didn't tell you why, and you've been kind enough not to ask questions."

"You're paying me very well not to ask questions, Morgan," she pointed out, lifting Muffie from the basket, for the kitten had begun to express her outrage at being so long confined. "And you're taking care of Aunt Leticia and Ferdie and even Peaches—or you would have if she hadn't worried about going soft, living in such luxury, and taken a flit. Besides, your father has been so very kind to me, to all of us. If the duke, with all his Bible reading, believes what you are doing is right, then I know it's right, too."

Innocence. It radiated from her, even though he knew that she could have few illusions after her time at Woodwere. He watched as she held the madly purring kitten against her cheek, rubbing the soft fur against her skin. It was clear she already felt a deep affection for the animal. As a matter of fact, he was beginning to feel jealous of the cat's ability to get so close to her. "Then I don't understand, Caroline. You've accepted clothing from me, food and shelter from my father.

So why can't you accept that damn— I mean, why won't you allow yourself to keep Muffie?"

She tucked the kitten just below her chin, where the animal lay curled against her, like a living ruff, one small paw batting at an errant lock of her long hair. "I want to, Morgan. Truly I do. I've never had anything of my own before—anything alive and real. But—but you said it was unpardonable conduct. You said it was an *offense*. You seem so sorry that you did it, while I…while I…"

Morgan leaned back on his heels as Caroline's voice faded and she buried her face in Muffie's fur. What a child she was. What an adorable, honest, lovable child. "You rather liked our kiss the other afternoon, didn't you, imp?" he asked teasingly, beginning to enjoy himself, beginning to feel that maybe he wasn't the worst cad on earth after all. "Is that what you're trying and failing to say—that you can't accept the kitten because you didn't consider what we did to be unpardonable conduct?"

"Don't you laugh at me! Don't you dare laugh at me!"

Before he could react, Caroline had leapt to her feet, still holding a now hissing, spitting Muffie, the basket tumbling unheeded to the floor. She took two steps in his direction, then glared down at him through narrowly slitted eyelids. "I didn't do anything wrong. I may have kissed you, but I didn't let you do the dirty deed. I would *never* do that, not with you, not with *anyone.* So don't you dare call it an offense and then try to make everything right by fobbing me off with Muffie. I won't feel guilty just because you do. I won't feel bad and dirty now on account of how good I felt before. I won't be sorry that I kissed you, or even sorry if I liked it very much—even if you are the most arrogant, *stupid* man from here to John o'Groats. *I won't!*"

Morgan looked up at her in bemusement, wondering just what in hell she was talking about. Then, slowly, and not without some pain, he waded through her torrent of words, settling on "dirty deed." What had this frightened, confused child heard? What horrors had she seen? Damn Peaches O'Hanlan for sticking her in a place like Woodwere, exposing her to God only knew what sort of behavior!

No, Caro wasn't really Lady Caroline, but that didn't mean she was any less innocent or any more prepared to deal with the vile, licentious, and even deviant conduct that was probably commonplace in an asylum like Woodwere. Morgan had toured the Hospital of Saint Mary of Bethlehem during his first visit to London, gone with some of his new friends who had received a special pass to view the inmates, the bedlamites, caged like wild creatures at some bizarre human menagerie, and been sickened both by his companions' obvious delight and by the sights he had seen.

He had tried to tell himself that Caroline hadn't been exposed to more than the Leopard Man's occasional obscenity, although he knew in his heart that he was being ridiculously optimistic. But still he had reassured himself with the comfortable illusion that she had served mostly on the private side of the asylum, dealing with amiable eccentrics like Leticia Twittingdon and protected by that courageous dwarf, Frederick Haswit.

So much for wishful notions.

Morgan stood, placing his hands on Caroline's shoulders, feeling the nervous tremors that rocked her slim body. "I've really done it this time, haven't I, imp? I've confused you into believing that you should feel guilty for enjoying our kiss two days ago, that you are now in danger of committing the 'dirty deed.' And, perhaps worst of all, I have given you the impression that I am ashamed and sorry that I kissed *you*."

She lifted her chin in a challenging way and charged, "Well, aren't you?"

"No, imp, I am not," Morgan answered honestly. "I am most very definitely not sorry. It *was* a most enjoyable experience. I am, however, more than slightly ashamed of my behavior, for, as Ferdie so eloquently pointed out, I had no right to take advantage of your innocence, your trust. For that I am very, very ashamed, and cannot even begin to ask for forgiveness."

Muffie began to protest at being held, and Caroline stooped down, placing the kitten on the seat of the chair before turning to Morgan once more. "I think I understand now. You liked kissing me, but you are angry with yourself for having done so. But you did enjoy it? I mean, did your stomach get all funny inside, and your legs go all weak and water, and—and you wanted to hold me and hold me?"

God's teeth! Why didn't the girl simply shoot him and have done with it? Even being boiled in oil had to be less of a torture than listening to her describe how she had felt when he kissed her. "I believe you have drawn a fairly accurate description of my reaction."

Her slight, tentative smile was like a heavy body blow, robbing him of his breath. "So, Morgan, you enjoyed the kiss as much as I did. It is only the thought that you shouldn't have been so ungentlemanly, so forward, so very naughty as to have done so that you find unpardonable?"

"Exactly." He believed he had suffered less during the worst days of the war. Caroline's words held up a mirror to the workings of his mind, and he could not like what he saw. "May we abandon this subject now, or do you wish me to write it all down for you, now that you read so well?"

"No, silly. You don't have to do that. I understand now."

Caroline's smile broadened, and her green eyes twinkled mischievously in the firelight. "And now I can keep Muffie! Oh, Morgan, thank you! Thank you so very much! Now we can be friends again!" She grasped his arms, standing on tiptoe, and planted an enthusiastic kiss somewhere near his mouth before turning to scoop up the napping kitten and race from the room, her dressing gown held high, exposing her bare feet and perfectly formed ankles to his bemused stare.

He stood very still for a long time, looking at the closed door, then seated himself in the chair once more, taking up his snifter of brandy.

"'Friends,'" he muttered, giving the wicker basket a kick. "The ridiculous chit thinks she wants us to be friends. God's teeth, I must be mad." And then, draining the snifter of its contents, he began mentally marking off the days until they removed to London, and wondering if the end still justified the means.

CHAPTER NINE

Rich the treasure,
Sweet the pleasure—
Sweet is pleasure after pain.

John Dryden

CAROLINE SPUN AROUND in front of the mirror, admiring the cut of her new riding habit, then grinned. She felt sure she had never been so happy, not that there had been many happy days in her life to compare to the warm feeling of contentment she carried with her through the days now that she and Morgan had become such good friends.

February had faded into March almost without her notice, for she had been too busy with Morgan, doing her best to please him as he continued his tutoring of her—while sometimes disappointing him by making him repeat what he had said, because she had been too busy staring at the way his increasingly intriguing mouth alternately puckered and smoothed when he spoke simple French.

Aunt Leticia, bless her dear scattered self, was once more feeling "fit as a fiddle," and had only yesterday had the splendiferous notion to enlist Betts's assistance in cutting and restyling her hair to mimic that of a drawing she had seen in the latest edition of *La Belle Assemblée* that had arrived in the morning mail pouch. Unfortunately, this particular splendiferous notion had left Aunt Leticia's hair a mere two inches long all over her head, immediately prompting Ferdie to concoct one of his most scathing poems, which had something to do with shorn sheep and ancient addlepated muttonheads.

Aunt Leticia had confined herself to her rooms once more, not unduly upset by what that "evil Lilliputian" had said but heartbroken over the fact that, much as she couldn't understand how it had happened, all her turbans were suddenly too big.

His grace, the Duke of Glynde, had been for the most part keeping to himself for the past weeks, but as he had assured them all that he was only preparing himself for his first excursion away from The Acres in almost three years, she supposed he must be extremely busy, packing his trunks and that sort of thing.

Besides, Caroline doubted she could be made unhappy by anything now that she and Morgan understood each other so well. He was such a dear, Morgan was, letting her read all the novels she wanted rather than forcing only dry history and ciphering on her, having explained that she might better understand Society if she were to read Jane Austen's lovely works—none of which, Caroline was grateful to learn, contained a single mention of the dirty deed.

This discovery added to her happiness. She had been right all along. There were other ways to go about the business, and the Society in which people like Morgan and the duke moved had found them. Devotion from afar, for one, like Don Quixote's chaste adoration of his Dulcinea. And kisses—indulged in while in an upright position and with both participants fully clothed—were at least hinted at in Miss

Austen's books. Caroline had been right to feel sure that the duke and that lovely lady whose portrait hung above the fireplace in the main drawing room had never rolled around on the floor like wild beasts, touching each other in places a person probably shouldn't even touch herself.

But reading the novels was not without its pitfalls. According to Miss Austen, Caroline had not only behaved badly in allowing Morgan to kiss her but had been compromised completely. Caroline had giggled out loud when she read that part, wondering what terrible punishment Miss Austen would have declared necessary for two people caught out doing the dirty deed. But no matter what the lady might have said on that head, by rights, again according to Miss Austen, she and Morgan should have been marched directly to the altar simply for kissing each other—which was just about the silliest thing Caroline could ever imagine.

Marry Morgan Blakely? Why, that would make her the Marchioness of Clayton—Lady Clayton. She, Caroline Dulcinea Monday—her string of names deriving from a child's babblings, a confused old lady's wishful thinking, and a day of the week—a marchioness? It was above everything ludicrous. Morgan had most certainly thought so when she dared to teasingly broach the subject with him last week. Why, he had turned so deadly white that she had laughed until her sides hurt.

Yes, it was such fun being Morgan's friend. Except that he didn't kiss her anymore, and he was very rarely ever alone with her, and he hadn't put her through her paces, practicing the waltz and other dances in the music room, in almost a month.

What he had done was begin teaching her to ride, which she enjoyed very much now that she had learned not to be so afraid when she looked down at the ground from atop her very high horse. And she was becoming a considerably good rider, or so Morgan had told her, possessing a tolerable seat and a light hand on the reins.

She smiled again at the thought and turned away from the mirror, wondering what to do with herself for the next hour. They would go riding again later this afternoon, she and her good friend the marquis, once Morgan returned from checking on one of the duke's tenant farmers who had been injured in a fall from a wagon. That man, it seemed, had served with Morgan on the Peninsula.

The Peninsula. She had read about the war during her lessons in history and had heard about the war even while at Woodwere, but it was only today that she'd learned that Morgan had been a part of it. She had learned this, not from Morgan, who rarely told her anything about himself, but from Betts, who had whispered the information as if it was some sort of secret.

"The duke don't like no one talkin' about it," Betts had told her before being called away to help turn mattresses in the family wing. "His other son, Master Jeremy, died in that heathen place. You been to Master Jeremy's rooms, my lady? They're creepy. None of us maids like goin' in there to clean. It's like Master Jeremy could show up any minute, even iffen we know he's locked up tight with the rest of the Blakely bones."

Jeremy. Caroline had been surprised to hear that Morgan had once had a younger brother. She had asked Betts as much as she could before the maid was called away, and now knew the location of Jeremy's bedchamber, although she was still left with more questions than answers. But then, she knew that it never paid to be too inquisitive. Hadn't she gotten in trouble time and again at the orphanage for poking her nose into places it didn't belong?

And yet, Betts's description of Jeremy's rooms had piqued more than a casual interest on Caroline's part. Why hadn't anyone told her about Jeremy before this? Why were there no portraits of the dead youth in the family gallery? Why did his name never seem to come up in conversation? Had he done something wrong? Were the rest of the Blakelys ashamed of him? Why was everything that had ever belonged to Jeremy locked up in his rooms?

Caroline nearly gnawed on a fingernail before remembering that Betts had painted her nails with that foul tasting stuff Morgan had ordered prepared to break her of the habit. She glanced at the mantel clock, to see that Morgan probably wouldn't be back at The Acres for at *least* another hour. She was dressed, fed, and ready for her riding lesson. The duke was probably just sitting down to his usual solitary luncheon. There was time enough and more to satisfy her curiosity if she really wanted to.

But she wouldn't, of course. The duke and Morgan had taken her up, taken her in, and she owed them her loyalty and their privacy. So what did it matter to her if Morgan had not chosen to tell her he'd had a brother, that they were both in the war? He didn't owe her anything.

She sat on the edge of the bed, careful not to wrinkle the divided skirt of her lovely forest green riding habit.

Morgan didn't owe her anything; she owed him everything.

He had told her nothing about his plans to use her in London; she had kept barely any secrets from him.

She had been born, she had grown up in the orphanage, and he had found her at Woodwere. What great secrets could she tell him? That she had no idea who she really was? He already knew that. Would he like to know that she had wet her cot until she was nearly ten, earning her more than a few beatings until Peaches had taken to waking her in the middle of the night to visit the privy? She'd rather crawl away alone and die than tell him that secret. Or could she tell him that she still sometimes dreamed of canopied beds and pretty houses and soft, scented female bodies and satin-clad men, and that in her dreams everyone laughed a lot and they all had lovely piles of curled white hair? No, she hadn't ever told anybody that secret, not even Peaches.

So let Morgan keep his own secrets, and she would keep hers. She had twice promised not to question him on his motives, and she would keep those promises.

But not to tell her that he'd once had a brother? That she simply could not understand. Caroline would have given everything she'd ever hoped to have just to know that maybe, a long time ago, she too might have had a brother. Or a sister. Or a mother and father who'd cared about her. To date, her idea of a caring mother had only gone so far as to be grateful to the unknown woman who had taken her to the orphanage and not sold her to the Gypsies or left her to starve under the hedgerows.

Her hand traveled to her mouth again, and she grimaced at the sour taste that met her tongue when she tried to bite one of the short rounded nails. What was she doing, sitting here alone in her chamber, asking herself silly, unanswerable questions? She knew what really, *really* bothered her. It wasn't that Morgan had chosen to keep secrets from her. It wasn't that the duke had never mentioned his dead son.

What upset her most, what had pushed her to biting at her nails after being so very good about not doing so for nearly a week, was that the duke scarcely seemed to notice that he had a *living* son. Caroline knew she had received more care and attention from Peaches, Aunt Leticia, Ferdie Haswit, and even Mr. Woodmere than Morgan ever got from his father. It was a strange sensation, feeling sorry for Morgan because he had a father but didn't really have a father. She might be an orphan, but at least she was loved.

Caroline hopped down from the bed, looking toward the closed door to the hallway...which led to the larger center hallway at the top of the staircase...which led to the other wing...which led to Jeremy's rooms. Perhaps, if she traveled down that hallway, if she looked inside Jeremy's rooms, she might discover something, some clue to the duke's behavior.

And perhaps not, she thought, pulling a face. But at least it would help to pass the time until Morgan's return.

MORGAN TUGGED BACK on the reins to allow Caroline's horse to pull slightly ahead of his along the path leading to the fields where they usually rode. He admired her erect posture as she sat the sidesaddle, and the way her spine seemed to curve lovingly as her body shifted with each up-and-down movement of her mount's slow canter.

He must be an admirable teacher, he thought proudly, for her to have come so far in such a short time. But then, she was an unusually apt pupil. A sponge, or so he had termed her in the beginning, although he had altered his description since coming to know her better. She was not merely eager to learn but possessed the hunger, almost the need, to know all that she could about something, and then pass judgment on it as well.

She questioned everything, from why Napoleon wasn't simply shot the first time he was caught—"which certainly would have eliminated the need for all that mess this past summer at Waterloo"—to why people who had enough food and money to eat any time they wished to would confine themselves to rigid hours for dining. Unfortunately, he hadn't been able to answer either of those questions to her satisfaction, but she had told him she didn't mind, that no one could ever seem to answer some of her questions. At least Morgan didn't "cuff my ears for asking them."

They reached the unplowed field and Morgan drew his horse abreast of hers, only to laugh as he saw that the feather on her green velvet hat was giving her fits as the breeze blew it across her eyes.

"Dratted thing!" Caroline exclaimed, pushing the feather back where it belonged. "You know, Morgan, it's one thing to be fashionably rigged out, something Aunt Leticia puts great store by, but it is another kettle of fish entirely to have to deal with all these fripperies."

"Your new hat is very fetching. The annoyance is the price you must pay to be considered all the crack."

The stiff breeze caught at the long feather once more just as Caroline opened her mouth to answer him, and she was forced to push it away with the tip of her tongue "Oh, pooh!" she shot back quickly. "Morgan, you cannot make me believe I look 'all the crack' with a silly feather stuffed in my chops."

"You may have a point, imp. Why don't you tuck the feather behind your ear for now?" Morgan suggested, refusing to spoil the afternoon by telling her she should not use the word "chops." The way things had been going since he had climbed out of bed this morning, he had a feeling this ride over the fields with Caroline might be the only enjoyment he would have out of the day. "Then we can indulge ourselves in a little race—from here to that tree on the far corner of the field?"

He watched as Caroline mentally assessed the distance, then turned to him, her green eyes twinkling. "Lady cannot possibly beat your Thor without at least a small head start," she said. "Say 'go,' Morgan, and then give Lady and me to the count of five before you unleash your great beast."

"Done," Morgan told her, and a moment later Caroline was off, her head bent low over the mare's neck, asking Lady to give it her best. Morgan had given Caroline a riding crop, but she had steadfastly refused to use it, telling him that beatings had never gained the one wielding the whip anything but resentful service, and nary a drop of loyalty. And Morgan thought she was probably right. Lady had been just that, a complete lady, to Caroline ever since their first meeting in the stable yard.

Morgan deliberately counted to seven before urging his own mount forward into an immediate gallop, and it didn't take him long to pass Lady, so that he was already dismounted when Caroline reined in her horse beneath the budding limbs of the old tree. "Do you know what I like best about our contests, Morgan?" she asked as he helped her to alight from the mare. "You never let me win. I'm going to beat you one of these days, but I would hate it if you didn't give it your best. But next time, perhaps I will ask you for a count of ten before we begin. For Lady's sake, you understand. She is beginning to feel slightly ashamed of her poor showings."

"Did she tell you that, imp?" Morgan asked without expecting an answer as he took a rolled-up blanket from behind his saddle. These daily rides had been combined with small lessons, given while the horses grazed and rested, and Caroline now knew the names of most of the flowers and trees that grew at The Acres. She waited until he had spread the blanket on the ground, then sat down, carefully arranging the skirt of her riding habit as if at last aware that her ankles, even covered by boots, should not be put on display. "What should our lesson be about today, Caroline? Or do you want to review the proper way to go down a receiving line?"

She shook her head, dislodging the errant feather yet again, so that she sighed and pulled the hat from her head, leaving him to admire the way Betts had braided the long locks and wrapped the thick blond coil tightly around Caroline's small head like a coronet. "Can't we simply talk today, Morgan? I'm so weary of lessons."

Simply talk? Morgan sat beside her on the blanket, avoiding her level green gaze. He'd rather not "simply talk." Caroline had a disconcerting way of making even lessons about manners and protocol seem personal. Since their conversation in the music room, when she had so artlessly divulged the story of her life, he had been careful to keep their conversations as impersonal as possible. Caroline had made it clear to him, by words as well as actions, that she now considered him her friend, that she trusted him. It was difficult enough dealing with her innocence and generous friendship while remembering how he planned to use her. To become even more involved with her by speaking to each other as friends, to learn more about her by way of casual conversation—well, it just wasn't in his plans. The way kissing her had never entered his plans. The way wanting to kiss her again and hold her and teach her delights she couldn't possibly have ever dreamed of were all thoughts he was still determined to banish from his brain. And to love her? Ah, to love her was an impossibility!

"Morgan?" Caroline asked, leaning forward to gaze up into his face. "Don't you want to just talk?"

He stripped off his riding gloves and laid them at his side.

"I imagine we can do that, Caroline, as long as you don't try to drag me into another conversation about presenting Ferdie to London Society, as he wants me to do. I've already explained to you both that his father, Sir Joseph, might have something to say about the fact that I liberated Ferdie from Woodwere without his permission. I don't need any complications."

She shook her head. "No, I won't ask that again. Ferdie shall have to fight this battle on his own. I thought we would just talk of general things, the way I would in London. I may now know the names of all our queens and kings, but I doubt I will have much use for that sort of information if you succeed in procuring me a voucher to Almack's. So let's just talk. For instance," she began, drawing her legs up in front of her and hugging her knees, "how is the man doing—the soldier you visited this morning? You know, the one who served with you on the Peninsula."

Morgan turned to look at Caroline, immediately on the alert. "Bert broke his sole remaining leg, but should recover nicely in time, thank you. But please allow me to offer you my congratulations, imp. You have at last mastered a purely feminine wile—naked curiosity neatly cloaked in seemingly innocent inquiry. A lesser adversary would even now be relating his first bloody horror tale of his battles for king and country. Who informed you that I served on the Peninsula?"

She shrugged her slim shoulders. "What does that matter, Morgan? A more important question might be why, when you had me studying all those maps and things, you never mentioned that you were there. Was it very terrible?"

"It wasn't the most enjoyable interlude in my life," Morgan said, picking up a long, winter-brown blade of grass and twirling it between his fingers, "and it most certainly is not a subject I care to discuss. If it's conversational practice you're after, Caroline, I suggest you choose another topic."

"All right. Tell me about Jeremy, please. I had no idea that you had a brother. He was very handsome, or at least he seems so in his portrait, but I don't understand why—"

"Damn you!" Morgan sprang to his feet, glaring down at her. "What were you doing poking about in Jeremy's rooms? Was this a chance discovery, or have you been systematically searching every room of the house? While I have been complimenting myself on your progress, should I have also been searching *your* rooms for pilfered candy dishes and small articles of silver? I've dressed you in fine clothes and taught you how to hold your fork properly, but you're still a gutter-snipe at heart, aren't you, *Lady* Caroline? The illiterate, runny-nosed orphan whose greatest aspiration in life was to pass by a demented man's cell without being sprayed with urine! Peaches O'Hanlan's tutoring came first, and her seeds of thievery and low-bred boorishness obviously fell on fertile ground."

Morgan couldn't remember the last time he had been so unable to leash his anger. He prided himself on his control, his ability to keep his expression blank and his mind alert, confounding those around him, who never knew just what he was thinking—or when or where he would next strike. But Caroline Monday, a mere slip of a girl, had somehow found a way to crawl under his skin, to probe every hidden wound. *Damn her!*

Slowly, deliberately, he sat down once more.

"Morgan, I'm sorry," Caroline said, laying one small, gloved hand on his arm. He would have jerked his arm free of her hold, but that would only have proved that he was affected by her, that he did react to her touch. He'd spent three

long weeks convincing himself that their single kiss had been
no more than a temporary aberration and that his increasing
awareness of Caroline Monday as a woman, and not as a
means to an end, had been no more than the result of his
isolated circumstances at The Acres.

Not that he had gone to the Spotted Pony and the open
arms of any of the barmaids. Not that he had traveled to
London to spend a few sanity-restoring days with his mistress.
He hadn't succumbed to the first course of action because he
was by nature fastidious, and he had dismissed the latter
because he had no time to fritter away on self-indulgence
when Caroline still had so much to learn.

Or at least these were the excuses he had offered himself.

But now she had admitted to snooping into his private life,
into his father's private life—into Jeremy's rooms, for the love
of God! How he would enjoy putting a halt to the whole
thing, packing up Caroline and her ridiculous pair of eccentrics and hying them back to Woodwere so fast their heads
would spin. If it weren't for his plan, that is. He wasn't
keeping Caroline and her outrageous friends around because
he had grown fond of the young woman, that was for certain.
He wasn't going on with his plan, even if it seemed more farfetched, and perhaps even more dangerous, each day, simply
because the alternative would be to wave goodbye to Caroline
as she rode toward her promised cottage and out of his life.
His world held no open place for sentiment, for love. He had
a goal, damn it, and there was a method to his madness. And
madness it most certainly was.

"Sorry? Sorry for what, Caroline?" he asked at last, struggling to bring himself back under control. "Sorry that you
have betrayed my trust in you, my father's trust in you, by
snooping about like some housebreaker? Sorry that you were

curious about matters that are none of your concern? Or sorry that you admitted what you've done?"

"No, Morgan," he heard her say, although he had to lean slightly closer to her, for she was speaking barely above a whisper. "It's none of those. It's much, much more. I'm sorry that Jeremy is dead, Morgan. I'm sorry that you lost your brother, and that his grace lost one of his sons. But mostly I'm sorry that neither you nor your father will talk about it, talk about Jeremy. A pain has to be very deep if it hurts even to talk about it with your friends. I know I'm just a foundling brat dressed up in fine clothes, Morgan, but we have become friends, haven't we?"

"Oh, God," Morgan said, lowering his forehead into his hands. *Lovable.* Why did she have to be so damnably *lovable?* "Caro, forgive me. Please. I've grown so used to cynicism, to doubting motives—even my own, especially my own—that I forgot for a moment just how genuine, how honest, you are. What do you want to know?"

He felt her hand begin to stroke his arm, trying to comfort him, as if he were a child about to whimper, or that damn cat of hers, Muffie, who seemed to ascend to some purring heaven of ecstasy as Caroline stroked her long white fur. "I thought I wanted to know all about Jeremy and why his portrait isn't with the others, but hidden away in his rooms. I thought I wanted to know why neither you nor your father ever mention his name. But mostly I hoped that learning about Jeremy might tell me why you and your father seem almost like strangers and not at all as I have always supposed fathers and children should be. I have no knowledge of how families behave, of course, but only my dreams. I just thought…I hoped…" Caroline's words died away, and he felt her lay her head against his shoulder.

Her nearness was intoxicating, and her touch was driving him insane, but her words had poured cold water on his rising desire. "My father and I don't fit your fantasy of loving family life. That's what you mean, isn't it, imp?"

He felt her head move against his shoulder, nodding. "In Miss Austen's books, even when everyone in the family is running around trying to marry everybody else off to eligible *partis,* they all still seem to love each other. Your father is so solemn, staying to himself most of the time, and when you meet with him at the dinner table you both seem to be uncomfortable. His grace acts so sad, and you always seem to be angry with him."

"I am a bitter disappointment to my father, Caroline, I'm sorry to say," Morgan said, lifting his other hand to press his palm against her small cheek. "His grace and I were at odds almost from the time I was first let out of my leading strings. Jeremy was a much better son to him." He paused for a moment to wonder why he had admitted as much as he had, then continued, feeling curiously relieved to hear the words. "When Jeremy indulged himself in his single act of defiance by running off during the war to search me out, an impulsive rebellion against Father's authority that led to a hero's death, I was left alive to take the blame. Jeremy's things aren't all confined to his rooms because my father wishes evidence of his younger son hidden away, Caroline, if that's what you've been thinking. They have been placed there like holy relics, making it that much more convenient for my father to worship at the shrine he has erected to his son's memory."

She lifted her head, the movement making Morgan feel oddly bereft, then moved around on the blanket so that she was facing him. "His grace blames you? Oh, Morgan, that is so unfair. How can your father seem like such a godly man and yet be so unforgiving?"

Morgan smiled slightly, self-mockingly. "Ah, imp, but he has forgiven me. He even prays for my immortal soul. But you, my most observant little Caro, have seen what I know— that being forgiven and being loved are two exceedingly different things. I have accepted that fact, and there are now whole days when I can tell myself that his poor opinion of me doesn't matter, when I tell myself I am a man grown, and have built myself a full and satisfying life."

She shook her head, the sunlight glinting on her golden braid and tears standing bright in her usually laughing green eyes. "It's as if you are as much the orphan as I am, Morgan, although it is even worse for you. I at least have Aunt Leticia and Ferdie and Peaches."

"An orphan. An interesting, if unappealing thought." He cupped her face between his hands, his thumbs wiping at the tears on her cheeks. "But enough of such maudlin self-pity, Caroline. Just promise me that you won't mention Jeremy to his grace. It's enough that I've gotten him to agree to go to London with us. Fool that I am, I still harbor a faint hope that our trip to London and your introduction to Society might serve to lift him from the worst of his melancholy."

"You're such a good, loving son, Morgan," Caroline said, so that he was forced to close his eyes, to hide himself, hide his rapidly crumbling resolve to remain aloof from her open, trusting gaze. "I'm so happy to be able to help you." And then she leaned closer, and kissed him.

And with that kiss Morgan felt something snap deep inside him, the taut threads of civilization he had so carefully strung over his unexpectedly raw emotions ever since that night she had come to his room to return his peace offering because she had enjoyed his kiss. He needed her sweetness, her affection, the solace her warm body and warmer heart promised his bruised soul.

As Caroline moved to withdraw, Morgan opened his mouth slightly and pursued her, capturing her lips, laving them with his tongue, drinking in the honey of her mouth, devouring her innocence with a sensual assault born more of desire than of his considerable experience. If only he could steal some of that innocence, regain some of that sweetness that had abandoned his life so long ago. He held her tight against him, kneading her slim shoulders with his large hands, pulling her back with him as he fell onto the blanket, dragging her body across his hips.

"Caroline. Sweet Caro," he whispered hoarsely between assaults on her mouth, his hands going to the small buttons on her blouse, then to the larger buttons that held her jacket tight at her waist. He could feel her trembling against him, but her nervousness only excited him more, for if she was frightened, she wasn't resisting. Her hands were tangled in his hair, pressing his face against hers each time he tried to transfer his kisses from her mouth to her throat and the smooth, enticing skin that lay lower, exposed now that her buttons were freed of their moorings.

He felt so large, so clumsy, so damnably inept—and so unable to control himself that he knew he would later curse his actions and himself for what he wanted to do, what he needed to do, what he must do or else go mad. Rolling Caroline over, so that she lay on her back, he followed after her, their mouths still fused together, then slid his hand beneath the silk of her undergarment, to touch the even softer silk of her breast.

Stars exploded behind his tightly shut eyes as she moaned

softly into his mouth and he felt her nipple push against his palm. *Yes, Caro, yes. Let me do this. Let me give you pleasure.* His throat felt full, as if he were close to choking, and his manhood strained against the buttons of his breeches, the tension of the cloth no greater than the tension he felt building deep in his gut.

The smooth bud of her nipple felt like a small stone as he massaged it between his thumb and middle finger. He rubbed the callused pad of his index finger across her skin, urging her nipple into life so that he could catch it between his lips and suck it into full flower as his hand traveled to her other breast, to repeat his actions, touching her nowhere but on her nipples, teasing her with his lightly pinching fingers, his laving tongue.

He felt an insane urge—surely it was an insane urge!—to prove that lovemaking wasn't the dirty deed she had supposed, but something wondrous, something beautiful and infinitely pleasurable. He didn't know why, he didn't know how, but giving Caroline pleasure suddenly had become the most important mission he'd ever undertaken.

Caroline lay quite still for some moments, her body slack and unresponsive, nearly causing him to draw away, to return to sanity, to abandon his voyage of discovery, abort her lesson in what passed between a man and woman once they had traveled beyond kisses.

But then he felt her arms go around his back, and her own back arched, pushing her sweet breasts closer to him, ever closer. *Yes, Caro. Yes!*

He kissed both of her breasts in turn, then ran his tongue along the sweet valley that lay between. He lowered himself until his tongue reached her navel, where he lingered for some moments, probing the small indentation while gently kneading her flat belly, still hidden beneath the skirt of her riding habit. She was so small, so slight, so beautifully, perfectly formed. He could span her waist with his two hands, trace each slender bone of her rib cage, see the blue of her veins beneath her fragile translucent skin.

She didn't speak, didn't help him or stop him, but lay there quietly, her breaths rather shallow and rapid, allowing him his forays, granting him access to her even as his hand found its way beneath the hem of her divided skirt and began a slow climb up her calf, to the sensitive skin behind her knee, to the satin of her thigh—and beyond.

Only then did she move again, her legs falling open as if she no longer possessed the strength to hold them straight on the blanket, and he slipped his fingers beneath her undergarment and felt the warm moisture that had gathered like fresh morning dew at the apex of her thighs.

His mouth closed around one rosy nipple once more, and he began to suckle—like a child, like a supplicant, like an adoring servant bent only on serving his master, soothing her, exciting her, teaching her, learning from her. And still she held him, her small hands burning like hot brands through the fabric of his coat.

"Oh."

That was all she said. *"Oh."* It was a whisper, hardly more than a sigh, yet it held a world of wonderment, a universe of pleasure not unmingled with surprise.

He knew he should stop. At once. He should pull down her skirt, cover her breasts, take her back to The Acres. He should be ashamed of himself, disgusted by his actions, his desires, his unmitigated lust. She was an innocent. *An innocent!*

But she was flowering now. Beneath his lips. Beneath his stroking fingers. Her entire small body was blooming expressly for him. He could feel her fragile petals opening beneath the warming sun of his ministrations, lifting themselves upward, ever upward—toward his tongue as it slowly circled the small flower of her nipple, toward his fingers as he probed gently, separating each pink petal until the heart of her most secret flower, the small, hard center, was exposed to his touch.

"Oh!" Still she whispered, but with dawning knowledge coloring her voice, and he knew it wouldn't be fair—not to her, not to him—to turn back now.

He levered her thighs wider, then took the bud between his fingers, rotating it slowly, gently spreading the petals even more, his movements practiced yet faintly tentative, for he knew where he was leading her and she did not. He was taking her to a new land, a new universe, one filled with pleasure she could not imagine, had never before experienced. A dark, alien place that could be frightening the first time it was visited, yet a veritable paradise of sensation he longed to take her to again and again and again. *La petite mort.* The little death.

He cupped her breast in his hand, lifting it, molding it, holding it to his mouth so that he could flick at her nipple, faster, faster, perfectly matching the movement of his tongue with that of the finger that stroked the heated center of her being.

He was rewarded with her small gasp of astonishment, with the upward surge of her hips as she strained to be closer, ever closer, as even her innocence was no match for the ages-old, inborn reaction to pleasure.

This is for you, Caro, his brain screamed. *For you. For you. For seeing. For caring. For all I have planned for you. For my sins. Take it, sweet Caro. Take it. Steal a moment of pleasure from that sad little world you've lived in for so long. This is all I can give you. Glory in it!*

Faster. Faster. His tongue. His fingers. His straining manhood pressed against her leg. Her small body lifted to him, opened for him, and—at last, at last!—pulsated for him, clenching and convulsing and turning warm and wet and infinitely female.

And left him hanging on the precipice, mentally elated but physically unsatisfied, his body on fire, yet incapable of release, his gut a tightly clenched knot of driving desire.

She clung to him, her face buried against the side of his neck. He smoothed her skirt back into place and laid his head on her bared breasts as he took in great gulps of air, his inner tension threatening to unman him. He stared out over the fields, intent on the horizon, trying desperately to find the center of his world. He had to keep his eyes open, his mind on the future, on his plans, which included Caroline but did not include her. He had to keep his eyes open to his plans of revenge and not allow himself to be blinded by thoughts of love.

"Morgan?" he heard her whisper from somewhere above him, her voice clogged with happy tears. "I love you. I love you so very much."

He closed his eyes.

CHAPTER TEN

The heart has its reasons which reason knows nothing of.
                                                    Blaise Pascal

"DULCINEA, whatever are you doing?"

Caroline flung a satin slipper into the center of a small pile of clothing already heaped in the middle of the coverlet. "I'm packing, Aunt Leticia," she said, not looking at the woman but only pushing impatiently at the long braid that had come loose of its pins and now hung over her shoulder, getting in her way. "I'm not going to take everything the marquis bought for me, for that would be stealing, and I wouldn't give the bloomin' bastard the satisfaction of proving that you can't make a silk purse from a sow's ear. But I am taking enough to keep my belly full and coins in m'pocket until I can find some sort of work. I've earned that much. *More,* by God! Now, where is Muffie hiding? I'll not leave her behind."

"Dulcinea! Your appearance! Your diction! Your language! And your voice! It's too shrill, my dear. Too shrill by half."

"Yes, Aunt Leticia. Yes, it is—and I've barely got the bit between m'teeth, as Peaches would say. Wait till I really get going—I'll curse a hole straight through to China, and no mistake!" The second kid slipper joined its mate, and Caroline looked around wildly for something else to pack. She worked quickly, knowing she had to get herself quit of The Acres before she did something terrible. Like finding a long, sharp knife and plunging it straight into that insufferably smug Morgan Blakely's back. Like taking up the poker from the drawing room fireplace and splitting his thick skull.

Like crying.

"Call what he did part of my 'education,' will he?" Caroline said, grumbling, for if she could only keep on hating him with a white-hot passion she wouldn't have to think about what had happened beneath that tree at the far corner of the field and how she had made a complete gaby of herself by telling him she loved him. Loved him? She cursed the ground he dirtied when he walked on it! She hoped his backside would fall off and he'd have to shit through his ribs! His nose should run day and night, his eyes cross so that he could watch the drip, and his teeth come alive and scream curses at him until his mind turned to gibberish! Love him? She'd rather die a prune-faced old maid. She'd rather go back to Woodwere and become the bride of the Leopard Man. She'd rather throw herself down a poisoned well than love Morgan Blakely.

"Dulcinea, please sit down. You're making me quite dizzy. Are we going to London? I had thought we weren't to leave for another fortnight. Not all of Ferdie's fine new clothes have arrived as yet, now that the dear duke has agreed to allow him into Society. Although sewing them up shouldn't take too long, considering how small they are. Oh, pooh! I wasn't supposed to say anything about Ferdie's good news, was I? His grace wished it to remain a surprise."

Caroline's hands stilled in the act of drawing the edges of the coverlet together. Ferdie was going to be allowed into Society? And Morgan didn't know? Now, there was a thought to bring a smile to her face. But wait! Ferdie wouldn't be going to London. Not now, not if she left The Acres. Ferdie wouldn't go into Society, and Aunt Leticia wouldn't be able to sit with the dowagers at Almack's, fanning herself and preening and regaling the old ladies with her latest splendiferous notion.

"Aunt Leticia," Caroline began, at last turning to face the other woman—and then she stopped, her mouth hanging at half-mast, and simply stared.

"Do you like it?" the old woman asked, patting her two-inch-long bright pink hair. "Ferdie is in his rooms at this very moment composing a poem in honor of my new 'do.' He usually can make them up on the spot, but he told me I had left him speechless." Her smile was heartbreaking in its obvious pleasure. "I've never left Ferdie speechless before, you know. It will do him good to be humbled, the high-nosed pygmy."

Her own problems forgotten for the moment, Caroline advanced to where Leticia sat, then walked in a slow circle around her. No matter the angle, the view did not improve. "Aunt Leticia," she heard herself ask, "whyever did you dye your hair *pink?*"

The woman clapped her hands in delight. "Why, I should have thought you'd understand at once, Dulcinea. My turbans are all so horridly ill-fitting now that my hair is so short. I could have ordered more made, of course, but that does take so long, doesn't it? So I sat and I sat, and I thought and I thought—until I had the most *splendiferous* notion. And *voilà!* A living turban! Betts procured the ingredients for the dye at the apothecary in the village. And now everything is perfect, and so very easy. No muss, no fuss, no slippage. That's very important, you understand. No slippage! And now I match all my lovely new ensembles—excepting for the red taffeta—but a lady must be willing to make some small sacrifices in the name of fashion. Now, tell me again—what are you doing with that coverlet?"

Caroline's bottom lip began to quiver as she felt herself caught between her need to be gone and her worry for her friends. She had raced back from the stables, intent on nothing more than gathering up a few precious belongings and leaving The Acres so that she'd never have to face Morgan Blakely again after her great humiliation. She hadn't given a moment's thought to either Ferdie or Aunt Leticia. Damn Morgan Blakely for a Dutchman! He had ruined everything!

She collapsed onto her knees beside Aunt Leticia's chair. "Dear lady, does going to London mean so much to you?"

Leticia turned to Caroline, placing her hands on hers, her smile beatific. "Our quest, you mean? That's what London is, you know, Dulcinea—our glorious quest. We are to return you to the bosom of your family. And we shall do it, Dulcinea, for the kind duke and the brave marquis have promised me that it shall be so. 'No limits but the sky,' my dearest Don Quixote has said, and he is correct. We shall conquer the polite world!" She leaned closer to Caroline's face, to whisper, "And we might even be able to get ourselves some of those lovely Gunther ices while we are there. I had dozens and dozens once, a long time ago, and they are ever so delicious."

Caroline shook her head, sniffing, close to tears, yet even closer to laughter. "Gunther ices, Aunt Leticia? You'd like those?"

"Oh, dear, yes. The strawberry ones in particular. But that is just the least of it. You have no idea how prodigiously wonderful London is. I know I've told you how it will be when you make your come-out, but there is so much more. There is Astley's and the Tower and all those lovely shops on Bond Street, and—well, I can barely list everything, Dulcinea. My own Season was cut horridly short by the Infernal Laurence—and all because of that little trouble at Vauxhall Gardens." She gave a wave of her hand. "But we won't talk too much about that, of course."

"No, I suppose not. We never have before. It was shortly after he cut short your Season that Laurence first had you locked—um, that he first confined you to his estate, wasn't it?"

Leticia raised her chin and looked off into the distance. "We rubbed along fairly well together there for many a long year, Laurence and I. Until he married that red-haired hussy who was less than half his age, and she told Laurence I was dangerous, so he had me locked away at Woodwere. Yes, locked away! I will not tease myself anymore and pretend that I was only visiting at that horrible asylum, although it is only now—now that I am here at The Acres—that my mind seems so clear." She turned back to Caroline, her expression fearful, her fingers plucking at the skirt of her gown. "Do you think we'll have to go to Vauxhall, Dulcinea? I must confess I do not want to, even to show off my pretty hair. Terrible things happen there."

Dear Aunt Leticia! Did she know how her artless admission tore at Caroline's heart? "You have been happy since we came to The Acres, haven't you, Aunt Leticia? And you're correct. You have been very sensible since our arrival—not that you haven't always been extremely sensible." *Except, perhaps, for this business about pink hair,* Caroline thought, although she didn't mention it. "So, no—we will not even think about going to Vauxhall, no matter if it is the most fairy-tale-like place on earth."

Leticia smiled down at Caroline. "It is splendiferous, Dulcinea. We traveled there by water, Laurence and I, and always sat in one of the best booths, sipping cider and eating wafer-thin ham. Laurence always made me eat it all up, every last scrap, for it cost the earth. We dined there several times and watched the fireworks from our booth and viewed the Cascade, which was the loveliest waterfall. And then one night—"

Caroline shook her head again. "No, Aunt Leticia. You don't have to tell me, truly you don't." Leticia had never gotten this far in her description of her London Season while they were together at Woodwere, so there must have been some truth in her statement that her mind had been clearer since coming to The Acres. But Caroline didn't wish to push her into remembrances that might upset her. Besides, there was still the matter of the clothing heaped in the middle of the coverlet. Betts could come in at any time and discover it— and then there really would be the devil to pay!

"No, no, Dulcinea," Leticia protested, putting her hands together as if in prayer and tapping her fingertips on her thin lips. "I think it is time I did tell you. You are about to make your come-out, and I should perish if you were to have such an unfortunate occurrence befall you simply because I was lax in my duties and failed to inform you of all the pitfalls awaiting a young innocent set loose in London."

"Hardly a young innocent, Aunt Leticia," Caroline muttered, her cheeks flaming as she remembered her wanton behavior of only an hour earlier. Had she really allowed such liberties—indeed, aided and abetted them? Could that have been Caroline Monday lying back on the blanket, her legs splayed open like some penny-a-poke trollop, her breasts bared to the sun, her throat issuing soft moans and, at the end, one long, ecstatic cry of delight?

Dear God, Morgan's hands had been everywhere. His hands, his mouth—and she had gloried in them, raising herself up to him, seeking his touch, all but begging him to use her any way he wished, her most private parts on display, spread wide for his exploration, for his squeezing, teasing, madly stroking fingers.

Even now she could remember how she had arched her head backward into the blanket, her teeth clamped together, her breaths shallow and so unnaturally quick, her every fiber taut with a hunger that had no comparison in her memory. And as she held him close to her, some heretofore unknown craving had urged her on to further recklessness, to complete abandon—to hell or to heaven. It hadn't mattered where she was headed, as long as he didn't stop, didn't change, but stayed with her, driving her on, taking her higher. Always higher, until she had hovered weightless somewhere above the blanket, her body all but paralyzed with sensation, willingly held in thrall by the beauty of it all, by the rightness of it all.

And then, and then—oh, dear Christ and all the saints—and then had come the worst, the best. That wild explosion, those incredible, clutching, pulsating convulsions that had lifted her even higher until she could no longer bear them and had to press her legs together and stop his fingers, stop the involuntary clenching, stop him before he killed her with pleasure.

I love you, Morgan.

Stupid! Stupid! Would she never learn?

He didn't love her. What he had done had nothing whatsoever to do with love, with any tender emotion. Part of her education, he had called it as he turned away, holding his head in his hands, his breathing ragged, as if he might cast up his accounts all over the grass. As if touching her, pleasuring her, hearing her admission of love, had turned his stomach. Part of her education, he'd repeated; no more, no less. A necessary clinical demonstration of what she should not allow anyone to do to her.

But it had been much more than that, Caroline knew. She had told him that she'd never allow anyone to do the dirty deed with her, and he had gone out of his way—miles and miles out of his way—to prove that she wasn't immune to the baser cravings of the flesh. Morgan had done it to show her that lovemaking was different, better, between men and women of Society than it was for the inmates at Woodwere, and therefore even more dangerous.

He had been right about his way of making love being more dangerous to her than if Boxer had thrown her to the ground, as he had that poor, confused girl at Woodwere, to be ravished by the biting, slobbering buffoon who rutted like a dog. But Morgan had been wrong to say, as he had done when he helped her to mount Lady, that civilized humans had elevated lovemaking above the level of the dirty deed.

She had never felt more soiled in her life.

"…And so Laurence allowed him to escort me down the Grand Walk while he stayed behind to chat with his friends."

Caroline blinked twice, banishing the memory of the way Morgan had looked when she allowed him to help her dismount back at the stables, then turned away from her, his expression pained, as if today's instructions had been eminently distasteful to him. Aunt Leticia was speaking, and she hadn't heard a word of what the dear woman was saying.

"Yes, Aunt Leticia?" she improvised quickly when the woman fell silent. "You took a stroll down the Grand Walk with—um, with—"

"With Robert, my dear. Pay attention, do, for I have

decided you must know how to go on if you are to avoid the pitfall I tumbled into. We walked arm in arm for some minutes, admiring the scenery and nodding to acquaintances. Robert was very handsome, and I felt proud to be with him— even preened a bit when Lucille Hammond strolled by with her mother. Her face turned white with jealousy when she saw Robert with me. Silly girl. If she'd only known what a lucky escape she had!"

Caroline was paying strict attention now, for Leticia—the contrary evidence of her bright pink hair to one side—seemed unusually lucid. "Go on, Aunt," she urged quietly, taking the woman's hands in her own.

"There was another walk nearby. Lovers' Walk, I had heard it called, and some even termed it the Dark Walk. When Robert led me toward it I was sure he was about to propose, for many a young gentleman made his offer on that walk and then claimed a kiss as a reward. But Robert had other intentions, as I was soon to discover once we had moved some distance down the walk and out of sight of the other couples. Our steps slowed, then we halted altogether. I was so nervous with anticipation, so excited, so very much in love."

"Aunt Leticia, don't," Caroline begged tenderly, her own moments of disgrace not that far behind her. "I think I know what happened."

Leticia smiled brightly. "You do? How wonderful, Dulcinea. I really don't wish to speak of it. His hands, his mouth, his— Well, as you said, we won't speak of it, will we? Suffice it to say that Laurence was extremely put out when he learned that I was with child."

Caroline's head snapped up, her green eyes wide with shock. "With—with child? Oh, Aunt Leticia, I didn't know!"

Leticia patted Caroline's ashen cheek. "And why should you, my dear girl? But I was definitely increasing. That means pregnant, my dear, in case you haven't heard the term. Laurence—that infernal man—wouldn't even ask me how I had come to be that way, for fear he might have to defend my honor. Oh, no. Why should he chance spilling his precious blood over my shame? It was easier by far to whisk me away home, to lock me up until I was delivered of that shame some months later."

Her deep sigh nearly broke Caroline's heart. "I heard he was a lovely boy, my son. I never saw him, you see. Laurence had him taken away directly after the birth, saying he would not allow me to compound his shame by foisting my bastard on him for all the world to see. And I...well, I did not quite recover my strength after the birth. I cried most horribly for months and months until I at last resigned myself to Laurence's decision. He did it for the best, you know, Dulcinea. And then, one fine day, I awoke happy. I had been reading my dearest Cervantes, all about his heroic Don Quixote de la Mancha and his dreams of Good Triumphant. *I* was Don Quixote—I had recognized myself at once. All I needed was my Sancho, my horse, and my quest!"

"Your quest, Aunt Leticia? You mean you went off to find your son?" Caroline felt her heart breaking for this poor, befuddled, courageous woman.

Leticia nodded fiercely, her pink hair falling forward onto her forehead. "I set off again and again, only to have Laurence find me and bring me back. It became a most wonderful game, even after I learned that my dearest son had died years earlier. They don't last long in orphanages, Dulcinea, not the quality. I think our blood is thinner and our spleens not so hardy. You were the exception, my dear, I suppose. Then

Laurence married, and I took to calling his harridan of a wife Aldonza."

She turned to Caroline, grinning. "I thought it a master-stroke, but Laurence wasn't amused, and I was moved to Woodwere. I became almost happy when you came, for I had a quest again—my own Dulcinea. And the marquis agrees with me. You are to go to London. We are all to go to London. Laurence will be so incensed—he and his terrible Aldonza. So now you know it all.... Strange, isn't it? I had forgotten so much of it, and yet now it is all so clear once more. Promise me, Dulcinea—you must stay with your new, young, strong Don Quixote, with our dearest marquis, and never go anywhere without him—most especially to Vauxhall."

Or riding in the fields surrounding The Acres, Caroline added silently. "I promise, Aunt Leticia," she said, resigned to her fate. "But you must remember to call me Lady Caroline. Do you think you can do that?"

"Of course I can, Dulcinea. I told you—everything is eminently clear to me now. Just tell me, please, dear girl—what do you have wrapped up in that coverlet?"

PINK. PINK. Idiotic old bat! What rhymed with pink? Think? Ink? Link? Stink?

"That ought to do it. Stink. No, it would have to be plural. That wouldn't work. If she had to go and dye it, she could at least have thought of me. Red—that would have worked. Red, bed, led, said, *dead.* But pink—that's totally beyond me. Oh, the devil with it. She's so scrambled in her upper rooms that she'll probably forget I even promised her a verse."

So saying, Ferdie successfully banished thoughts of Leticia Twittingdon and her latest show of outrageous imbecility and curled up more comfortably on the wide drapery-

enclosed window seat that had long since become his favorite
refuge, a comfortable haven in the study, where he could contemplate the deliciousness of his upcoming meeting with Sir
Joseph Haswit, the self-proclaimed "childless" widower.

The duke's party would be traveling to London on the
second to last day of March, still a few months shy of the
seventh of June, but that too would work to Ferdie's favor.
There'd be time now to drag the business out, to prolong it,
to make Sir Bloody Joseph suffer for banishing his only son
to a madhouse. Ferdie's facial features—grotesque replicas
of his father's spread unevenly on the wide canvas of his
large head—contorted into a smile of gleeful anticipation.
He'd be so humiliated, his dearest papa would, and it would
be so delightful to watch the man scramble about, trying to
explain his misshapen heir.

Ferdie knew he had played the duke of Glynde like a fine-
tuned harp, plucking on the tender strings of his gullible
heart, running up and down the scales of the man's guilt for
being unable to meet Ferdie's eyes when he spoke to him,
strumming into awareness his inability to reconcile his vision
of God's mercy with the deformed freak of nature that was
Frederick Haswit.

And he had gotten his way. Morgan Blakely's arguments
had been shunted to one side, and Ferdie had gotten what he
wanted—-entrance into the Society his birth had entitled him
to and his father's horror and pride had denied him.

Ferdie had thought Morgan to be his friend, and still did.
Yet the marquis had not extended himself so far as to jeopar-
dize his private plans in order to accommodate this one simple
request—to allow Ferdie to go where he belonged. Ferdie was
not a bitter man—well, perhaps he was, just a little—but he
could not deny that his admiration for Morgan had slipped a

notch since that momentous day in the duke's study when Morgan had told him he was more of a man than he was.

Ferdie kept a mental ledger on anyone who had come into contact with him ever since going to Woodwere, toting up debits and credits and meting out rewards and punishments according to those calculations. He did not play favorites, rewarding the Rabbit Lady with one of his secret hoard of Leticia Twittingdon's pilfered sweetmeats when she allowed him to kiss her sagging breasts, and dumping one of the slop buckets in Boxer's cot after that man had caught him in a dark hallway one night and beaten him so savagely that he hadn't been able to walk for a week.

It was necessary to keep his accounts straight, his ledgers balanced. Especially when it came to sex—that lovely, barbarous animal act that was for the most part denied him. How he longed for a woman's tender touch, for kisses given without pity, for favors granted in the name of love, and not because the object of his desire was too demented to know she should be running from him, screaming.

But he loved only one. Caroline. His darling Caroline. From that first day, when he had found her backed into a corner on the public side, cursing and crying as she held off a hallucinating inmate with the business end of a snapped-off broom handle, he had devoted himself to her. She had such courage, such inner beauty, and she didn't laugh at him or pity him. She treated him as if he were as tall and handsome as the marquis, and talked to him as if he had a brain beneath the swollen melon of his skull. From the beginning—from that first day—she had behaved as if he were like anyone else, no better, no worse.

He would have died for Caroline Monday. He'd have killed for her. And now he'd go to London with her. Perhaps, once all his new finery was delivered and he had a snowy white neckcloth tied neatly beneath his chin, fine hose on his legs, and jackets without patches—perhaps, just perhaps, he'd have the courage to speak to her, to tell her how he loved her, how he…

But, no. He couldn't do that. It wouldn't be fair. Not to Caroline and not to him. She was destined for better things if Morgan succeeded in having her accepted as the real Lady Caroline, and Ferdie—well, he too had other plans. Carefully formulated plans, hopeful expectations. A day-by-day, year-by-year accumulation of pain that had to be balanced out, eradicated, expunged from the ledger.

> Hate for hate, pain for pain,
> Only death can erase the stain.
> Death for glory, death for fame,
> And everyone will remember my name!

Leaning back against the window embrasure, his short legs crossed in front of him, Ferdie repeated the verse in his head, smiling as he decided it was one of his better efforts. He'd have to write this one down in his journal. It was silly to waste his energies on finding words to rhyme with "pink," as if anything having to do with Leticia Twittingdon and her silliness should be immortalized for posterity.

He closed his eyes, for the sun had passed beyond the diamond-shaped stained-glass panes of the window, and his private rainbow of color had faded for the day. It would soon be time for dinner, he supposed, but it wouldn't hurt to tarry a while longer in this comfortable spot. At least then he wouldn't have to take the chance of meeting up with the duke before the dinner gong was rung. The duke, with his pitying eyes, his too-kind inquiries and prayerful remarks, always made him feel so inadequate, so personally responsible for his unusual body, so damnably *different*.

A small smile began to play around the corners of his mouth as a mental image of his father's horrified face floated behind his lids—Sir Joseph's mouth moving without really saying anything as he sweated and strained, trying to explain to the Prince Regent that he had somehow forgotten that he had a son. Perhaps Ferdie should have learned to juggle small red balls, just in case he was asked to perform during one of the informal parties so popular among the *ton*. Lady So-and-so would play the harp, Lord High-Instep would sing a tune for the assembled guests, Miss Lily-White would fracture a recitation of some epic poem—and Frederick Haswit would juggle, and perhaps execute a somersault or two, a rose stuck neatly between his teeth. Oh, yes. He was really going to enjoy moving about in Society.

"Step in here, please, Caroline. If you insist on speaking with me, I'd rather you did so in private."

That was Morgan's voice, and he sounded angry or, at the least, harassed. Ferdie opened his eyes and sat up straight, his ear against the velvet drapery.

"I'll just bet you want us to be private, Morgan Blakely! Not feeling especially proud of yourself at the moment, are you?"

Ferdie looked left and right, not for a way out from behind the drapery, but instinctively, just to assure himself that he was well hidden and not liable to be discovered. Something was up; he could tell it by the strained tone of Caroline's voice. He'd promised never to interrupt them again, never to walk in on them while they were in the study—but surely that promise didn't have anything to do with already being *in* the study, did it?

Ferdie leaned closer to the drapery, smiling at his inventive rationalization. Besides, Morgan didn't want him going to London with them. It might be useful to know what was going on between the marquis and Caroline, so that he could use it to his advantage, use it to secure the marquis's agreement to his father's invitation.

"All right, Caroline," he heard Morgan say wearily—or was it *worriedly?* "What do you want? I already explained that I was only attempting to further your education, to satisfy your obvious curiosity so that you would not feel tempted to indulge in dangerous experimentation with any of the young bucks who'll be banging down the knocker in Portman Square once my father has presented you. Ever since your mention of the 'dirty deed' that night you so foolishly came to my rooms, I have believed it my duty to replace the obviously distorted notions you must have picked up either from Peaches or from your experiences at Woodwere with some basic truths about this business of lovemaking. Your impetuous kiss this afternoon—the result of your childish infatuation with me— seemed a heaven-sent opportunity for initiating instruction."

"Liar!" Caroline exploded. "Filthy, miserable liar! What a crammer that is! I only kissed you because I felt *sorry* for you—because I foolishly believed that we had become friends."

"Friends? Really?"

Ferdie held his breath, for he could sense that Morgan was standing very near the window seat.

"An intriguing conclusion on your part, Miss Monday," he heard Morgan continue, his voice like black velvet sliding over ice. Whatever had been bothering the man, he seemed totally in control now. "Tell me, whatever made you suppose that we could ever be friends? Could it be our common background of breeding and gentility? Our mutual interest in literature, poetry, and the arts? Or perhaps you have mistaken simple courtesy for something more. If the latter is the case, please accept my most abject apologies. Your exterior renovations, your fine clothes, and your marginally improved manners must have combined to blind me to the realities of your limited capacity to recognize common courtesy."

"Oh, cut line, Morgan, because I don't believe a word of it." Caroline's tone had taken on a similarly cold edge, although Ferdie believed he could detect a hint of tears in her voice. Poor infant. She always cried when she became angry, and then her weak tears urged her to greater heights of indignation. "You knew just what you were about. You were out to humiliate me, pure and simple. I saw something you didn't want me to see—saw your pain over your father's poor opinion of you—and you couldn't abide that, could you? I didn't know just what you were doing—or even what I was doing, for that matter—but *you* did! And I'll never forgive you for it!"

What he did? What did he do? What did he do? Ferdie longed to peek out through the slight gap in the drapery, but he didn't, for fear of giving away his presence. In the mood Morgan Blakely was in, he'd probably snap him in half like a twig if he dared to show his face.

"You'll never forgive me. I suppose that means I should be a gentleman and forget I ever heard your sweetly juvenile declaration of undying love? Gracious me, Caroline, I believe I am crushed. Or is that relief I feel coursing through my veins? No matter. Consider your confession of love forgotten. Is this interview now concluded, my dear, or do you have more you feel you must say to me?"

"Oh, you think you're so bloody wonderful, don't you,

Morgan? Cock of the walk, that's you. I'd be out of here in a minute if it weren't for Ferdie and Aunt Leticia—and you know it. That's why you knew you could do what you did. It's probably why you allowed them to come to The Acres in the first place—just so you could hold their welfare over my head if I didn't do just as you bid me. Not that you went through with what you started this afternoon. What was the matter, Morgan? When you got right down to it, when you had me arsy-varsy like some drooling idiot—my legs spread like some willing whore—you couldn't do it, could you?"

"Now you're being vulgar, my dear."

Ferdie frowned as he heard a hint of sorrow enter Morgan's voice. Not censure, but sorrow.

"I thought," he heard Morgan continue, "that we had progressed beyond such coarse speech. I suppose it was overly optimistic to believe the lessons of years of low living could be undone by an introduction to the gentling refinements of civilization."

"Don't interrupt me! And I am not half so vulgar as you. I'm just not so damnably sophisticated that I back away from plain speech when it's needed. *You're* the one who pressed me onto the blanket and stripped off my clothing. I thought you were disgusted with yourself when you stopped, but you weren't, were you? You were disgusted with *me*. The foundling brat. The little madhouse drab who earned her bread emptying stinking chamber pots and binding up Mad Maggie's hands so she'd stop sticking everything she finds up inside her to rid herself of the billy goat living in her belly. You must have been without a willing woman for a long time, Morgan Blakely, that you thought you could sink to spilling your precious, titled seed inside someone so unworthy."

"Caroline, stop this at once!" Morgan roared, and Ferdie

sensed that he had taken a step forward, toward Caroline, then continued in a softer, soothing voice, "I made a mistake, I admit it. I wasn't trying to broaden your education. That was a lie I used to soothe my conscience, to protect you from my base desires. You were very appealing today, very kind, and I convinced myself that when you kissed me you knew what you were about, what you were tempting. But I didn't stop because you disgusted me. Far from it. I stopped because I was taking unfair advantage of you. I *have* been without a willing woman for a long time. And whether you wish to lie to yourself or not, you *were* a willing woman, Caroline. But it won't happen again. You have my word on it. I'm sorry that I hurt you. You were trying to be kind."

Caroline's disdainful sniff would have set Ferdie to laughing if he hadn't been so incensed, so outraged—so damnably, painfully jealous. "More lies!" she cried. "And these are worse than the first. You've had all afternoon to make up dozens of them, haven't you? You wouldn't know kindness, my lord Clayton, if it stepped up behind you and bit you on your lily-pure arse! You brought me here to do a job of work for you, and I'll do it. But don't you go thinking you broke my heart, because you didn't. As a matter of fact, I don't like you. I never did like you. All I really wanted to say to you, all I asked you in here to listen to, is that I intend to hold you to your promises."

"About the cottage and the allowance, Caroline?"

"No—about showering me with diamonds and escorting me to Rome to see the pope. *Of course* I mean the cottage and the allowance! But now I want more. Aunt Leticia told me that the duke has agreed to take Ferdie into Society. I know you don't want to do that, and you'll be out to persuade the duke to take back his offer now that you've heard of it. But you won't do that, Morgan. You'll take Ferdie to London, into Society, or the three of us will leave here tonight—and then what will happen to all your fine plans?"

Ferdie was sure he could hear his own heart beating beneath his chicken-boned breast. That angel! That dear, sweet angel! In the midst of her own trouble, her own undeserved ill treatment at the hands of this arrogant, boorish, *taking* man, she was thinking of *him,* thinking of her friend!

"I'd rather by far take you to Rome, imp," Morgan replied, his tone suddenly light, as if he had just gotten over some very rough ground and could now relax. "Truly I would. I wish for you to be conspicuous in London, but having Ferdie tripping along with us as we move through Society could prove awkward. His father denies his existence, you know, and won't appreciate the fact that I have unearthed his son from the 'grave' without his permission."

"Well, then, you'll just have to deal with Ferdie's father, won't you, my lord? You can be very persuasive—as I already know."

"Then you enjoyed yourself this afternoon, imp?" Morgan asked, moving away from the drapery, his voice low, seductive—so that as he listened Ferdie was amazed and disgusted to feel a responsive tightening in his crotch. "You were a most delightfully accommodating little minx, sweet Caro. So wet, so submissive, so pitifully eager to please. I believe you would have allowed me anything, any liberty, if only to prolong your very obvious pleasure. As you said, your legs fell open most willingly, inviting any and all exploration, and when you raised your hips and began grinding your sex against my roving hand—"

"*Bastard!* If you ever touch me again I'll take a knife to you!"

"Yes, well, I may be many things, but I can assure you—

I am not a bastard. Can you say the same for yourself, *Lady* Caroline? Or is this belated maidenly outrage evidence that you have begun to believe the fabric of lies I intend to string together to secure your place with the Wilburton family? Perhaps I ought to set you to emptying chamber pots for the duration of our time at The Acres, just to remind you of who you really are—and who you aren't?"

Ferdie heard Caroline's sharp intake of breath and then the sound of a slap. Overcome by curiosity, he peeped between the edges of the drapery in time to see Caroline's retreating back—and watch Morgan lift a hand to his reddened cheek.

As the door slammed behind Caroline, and as Ferdie prudently retreated behind the drapery, Morgan muttered, "Christ on a crutch, what have I sunk to? But it had to be done. Better her hate than her love. Nothing can stand in the way of my revenge—not Caroline's feelings, not my own. You were right, Uncle James. I am uncomfortably like you. Heartless. And cold to the bone." Morgan's sigh was barely audible. "But, unlike you, I can still feel the pain."

Ferdie waited until Morgan had poured himself a drink and quit the room, then waited even longer before he crawled out from behind the draper. He was so infuriated he could barely see straight, and so weak with sexual desire and self-pity that he had to hold on to the furniture in order to make his way to a nearby chair.

His Caroline. His sweet Caro. How could she have done it? How could she have kissed a man like Morgan Blakely, offered herself to him like some common slut? And how could he have taken up that offer? The Marquis of Clayton, a man who had it all—wealth, position, a tall straight body, a father who acknowledged him. And now he had Caroline—

had used her, and then tossed her away. Couldn't he have left something for Ferdie Haswit, who had nothing?

It wasn't fair. It simply wasn't fair!

He couldn't blame Caroline overmuch. She was an innocent, destroyed by a master. The bulk of the blame belonged to Morgan. The blame, yes. But it was Caroline who carried the shame. Caroline who had cried. Caroline who could only slap his face and then plead for her friend, use her pain to bargain for her friend's happiness.

Ferdie loved her. He loved her so. Why had she hurt him?

And that man—that ungrateful snake!—had touched her, had kissed her, had seen her sweet body. His hands had traveled all over her, learning her, using her, when he, Ferdie, would have worshiped her, wanting nothing but her pleasure and forgetting his own. To stroke her body, to watch her breasts flower beneath his small hands, to spread her legs wide and sink himself inside her, filling her, feeling her clutch him tightly, drawing him deeper, deeper.

No! Not Caroline. Caroline was to be worshiped from a distance. *Dulcinea.* Pure and chaste from afar. That was the way to love Caroline. His love for her had nothing to do with groping and sweating and grunting and rolling about like two wild beasts intent on nothing more than self-gratification. He never would have touched Caroline in that way, even if she had begged him. Caroline deserved a better love, a holy love.

Pure and chaste from afar.

But Morgan Blakely had crossed that line. He had taken Ferdie's most selfish fantasies and turned them into his own selfish realities. Morgan didn't love Caroline. *Really* love her. He didn't cherish her, adore her, long to protect her and cosset her for all of her days. He had used Caroline, debased her, humiliated her, and then lied to her to save himself the

embarrassment of admitting to his lust. He'd hurt her in order
to go on using her to his own ends, in order to wreak some
dark revenge, no matter how his plans might destroy Caroline.

And he'd pay for that. By God, he'd pay for that. Ferdie
Haswit would make sure of it. Morgan must be punished and
Caroline protected. It was time to balance out the ledger.

CHAPTER ELEVEN

Fate chooses our relatives, we choose our friends.
Jacques Delille

THE MANTEL CLOCK HAD just chimed out the hour of nine and Morgan knew he was already three parts drunk. He had been drinking steadily since shortly before dinner, hoping against hope that the fine aged brandy would dull his senses, blur his memories, soothe his conscience.

It wasn't working worth a tinker's dam.

He had to concentrate on the end—the end that justified the means he had chosen. He had to divorce himself from sentimentality, from pity—even from love. Jeremy was dead, damn it, and his death had to be revenged. Revenge is sweet, sayeth Lord Clayton. Retribution, destruction, social and monetary desolation, and perhaps—just perhaps, if Uncle James hadn't lied—confession and punishment.

The last thing he needed or wanted, the very last thing he had expected, was to feel anything for the instrument of his revenge. Caroline Monday. The orphaned guttersnipe with a convenient name and a mop of straight-as-straw blond hair. The former madhouse servant with the laughing green eyes and the fire and spirit—and remarkable honesty—of a true aristocrat.

And a sweet, soft body, and the most remarkable, kissable lips, and an inner fire that burned so bright it was no wonder he had reached out to see if it would burn his hand.

God, how he could love her.

Morgan took another sip of brandy, then placed the snifter on the table beside his chair. Perhaps it was time he rethought his plan. It wasn't too late to find another way. There was always another way, another avenue a patient man could take to seek out his revenge. Uncle James's deathbed confession— his last confounding confusion—had offered him an opportunity, but not the only answer.

He could pay Caroline off, remove her and her odd entourage to some bucolic thatched cottage at the other side of Sussex, and seek out another way to bring the Wilburtons low. Slipping a hand into his pocket, he withdrew the pendant Uncle James had given him that final night, holding it up to the light of the fireplace, watching the dull gold gleam as it spun around and around at the end of its chain.

His jaw tightened as he recognized yet again the ironic beauty of the plan he had formulated. Richard Wilburton had destroyed his family, and it was only fitting that he, Morgan Blakely, would destroy the Wilburtons. Let Richard's father suffer. Let Richard be stripped of all that mattered to him.

Any other revenge he had considered for the past years would be paltry compared to what he could accomplish with Caroline Monday's help. Caroline's help, and this pendant.

"May I join you, son?"

Morgan swung the chain upward, catching the pendant in his palm, then slipped it back into his pocket. "Of course, Father. This is your house, if you'll recall."

"While I live," the duke said, lowering himself into the mate of the chair in which Morgan sat. "Once I am gone, this house, all of my houses, all of my lands, will go to you. Even Hillcrest, which I had put aside for Jeremy. You'll have it all. It must make you very proud."

"Not particularly, Father," Morgan said, rising to refill his snifter from the decanter on the table. "I am content enough with Clayhill. A dukedom seems somewhat superfluous when I already have so much. For the moment I intend to drink myself into a stupor. Would you care to join me? But no. Forgive me. I forgot. You no longer partake, do you?"

"Morgan, please. Can't we have a single civilized conversation? Or is that asking too much?"

"It is when I already know the only reason you have sought me out is to ask me to allow Ferdie Haswit to enter Society when we travel to London. Your sympathetic heart—the one you have never seen fit to extend to me—has been misplaced again. Our elegant, cannibalistic *ton* will devour Ferdie in a moment. They always weed out the different, the unique, and destroy it, like hounds ripping at a cornered fox. That is, if his father doesn't get to him first and have him locked up at Woodwere once more. Woodwere, or some hellish pit seven times worse. Do you wish to see Ferdie confined to Bethlehem Hospital, Father? I don't."

"Surely you exaggerate, son," the duke protested, watching Morgan as he leaned against the mantelpiece, the refilled snifter cupped between his two hands. "You mustn't judge everyone by your own measure."

"No? Well, then, Father, let us judge by yours, shall we? You are Christian kindness itself to Ferdie—from a distance. I've watched you with him. You say all the correct things, gift him with your food, your shelter, your offers of assistance. But do you ever look directly into his eyes when you speak to him—when he speaks to you? Have you ever touched him, patted his hand, laid your arm on his shoulder? No. No, you haven't. Why not, Father? Are you afraid of acquiring some taint—the same sort of taint you must fear contracting from me, for the last time you touched me it was with a switch. Ferdie isn't any different from any of us, not on the inside. You pity the outside and neglect what lies within."

"That's not true!"

"Isn't it? Tell me, Father, has it occurred to you that Ferdie is nearly the same age Jeremy was when he left home?"

The duke sprang up from his chair, pointing a madly trembling finger at Morgan. "You take that back! Ferdie isn't anything like Jeremy. Jeremy was so perfect—God's vessel—strong and tall and totally without guile or sin."

"And Ferdie is sinful? Is that what you are saying, Father?" Morgan looked down at the brandy swirling in his snifter, wondering if he was seeing things more clearly because of it or if what he was thinking only seemed logical because of his partially drunken state. "Was Ferdie punished in the womb? Or is Ferdie living evidence of your God's meting out of punishment on the sons for the sins of the fathers? You don't blame your God for Jeremy's death, nor do you blame yourself. Yet you seem to believe that Ferdie is being punished by that same God. You can't have it both ways, Father. Either your God is loving or he is vengeful. He can't be both."

"Don't blaspheme! God is capable of offering great love and reward for good behavior and great retribution for transgressions. As well I know. *You* are God's punishment to me, Morgan!"

"Really, Father? How very interesting." Morgan lifted his hand, about to take another sip of brandy. Either that or he would have been forced to throw the contents of the snifter in the duke's face.

But before he could act, the duke shot out his hand, striking the snifter from Morgan's hand so that it splintered into a thousand pieces on the hearth. "Yes, you! *You* are God's punishment for the foolishness and excess of my youth, when James and I flouted the Lord's teachings by wenching and drinking and behaving worse than wild Indians. Poor, misguided James never learned, even when our parents died in that terrible fire. But I did. I came to my senses. But it was too late. God sent me you, and you have spent every day of your life holding up a mirror in front of me, showing me again and again with your defiance, your boldness, your mad pursuit of adventure, the sins I had committed. Your mother chose to cosset you, protect you, make excuses for you—but Jeremy was mine. *Mine!* Jeremy was to provide my chance for salvation, be my gift for mending my ways; his dedication to the church my thanks for the Lord's forgiveness. But in the end Jeremy became just another of your victims, another facet of my punishment."

Morgan stood very still, trying to absorb all the duke had said. "It's so simple. Why didn't I see it before this? All these years. All these years, you've seen me not as your son but as your penance. Why didn't you just drown me when I was small, Father, as you would an unwanted puppy? You must have wanted to be rid of such an unpleasant reminder of your checkered youth."

"I forgave you," the duke said, straightening his spine. "You were no more than the living representation of God's punishment, so I had no other choice but to forgive you."

"Forgive me, yes," Morgan replied, sniffing in disdain. "But love me? No, you never did that, did you? Fool that I am, I've been planning this revenge, this retribution, in the hope it would at last find me some favor in your eyes. You'll never know the half of what I have done to shield you from the truth, even to protect you from the consequences of James's treasonous folly. But I've been wasting my time, haven't I, Father? You've agreed to go along with my scheme, but only for Jeremy's sake. The only way I could *really* make you happy would be to die, wouldn't it? Then you could visit my grave, pray for me, and go away feeling holy and justified—and perhaps even redeemed. Having three lost souls under your roof can only add to your atonement, show your willingness to be God's willing servant. You make me sick!"

Morgan brushed past the duke, heading for the door. "Morgan! Where are you going?"

"Going?" Morgan turned on his heel and glared at his father. He had never been so angry, or felt so defeated, in all of his life, even during the darkest days of the war, those dark days when he'd had to make a choice that had cost him everything. Was it so much to ask for—a father's love? "I think it should be obvious. I'm going to London, to get revenge my own way—for *me*. I leave you to deal with our guests. Consider them my gift to you."

"Take your leave, sinner! Run away!
Neatly turn your back on what you've done today.
Sweet Caroline Monday you have seduced and debased,
Her innocence and chastity all but erased.
Have you no honor, no sense of what's right?
By man's law and God's law, she should be your bride tonight!

Morgan wheeled about, to see Frederick Haswit standing at the door that now stood open to the hallway, his face as red as Leticia Twittingdon's satin dress, his features a caricature of outraged fury.

"Seduced? Morgan, what is this boy saying? I knew you were godless, but to violate that poor, disadvantaged child while she is under my protection? Is nothing beneath you?"

"Obviously not," Morgan drawled, looking at Ferdie, who had hopped onto a chair and was standing on the cushion, his furious features somehow having transformed themselves into something else—something that looked very much like satisfaction. "I should have known she'd go running straight to you, her dear friend."

Ferdie continued to stare at him, a slight lopsided smile contorting his features. "If you say so, my lord Clayton."

His grace walked over to stand beside Ferdie, the two of them presenting a formidable, if oddly matched, pair of accusers. "Then you admit to these charges?"

"Of course. I wouldn't wish to add dishonesty to my accumulated sins, although I do believe I may have been accused of telling untruths earlier today. The list of my transgressions grows with such rapidity that I must confess to having somewhat lost track of its length."

The duke shook his head. "But this cannot be. I cannot allow this. Ferdie's correct. You and Caroline must marry—at once!"

Morgan felt a chuckle begin low in his throat, to escape his mouth as he contemplated the lunacy of his father's demand. "*Marry* Caroline Monday? Is that correct, Father? Make her my marchioness—the future Duchess of Glynde? Well, that ought to square you with your God. Although it would mean we'd have to give up our plan to present her in London. I mean, with a misalliance like that, we'd all have to hide out here in Sussex until another scandal raised its head. Perhaps Prinny will be good enough to divorce his wandering princess and marry the rat catcher's daughter." As he said the words, Morgan mentally apologized to Caroline, who at her worst was far more the lady than he had lately been playing the gentleman. And he would be the worst of scoundrels to allow her to be forced into a marriage with him, even if the thought appealed to him more with each passing moment—even now, knowing of her duplicity in speaking of their encounter with Ferdie.

The dwarf hopped down from the chair and began tugging at the duke's sleeve. "Remember your plans, your grace. I was listening outside the door, and I heard you talking. You can still have your revenge, for that is what you and Morgan want most, isn't it? I never for a moment believed you and Lord Clayton were acting strictly out of a wish to reunite Caroline with her family. None of us did. But revenge! Revenge is a good enough reason for anything. You can still have it—if we keep the marriage our little secret until Morgan has Caroline Monday declared a Wilburton. Then he will have wed the daughter of an earl. It would be even more important that you succeed in foisting Caroline on Society if she is to become a duchess. They can marry again at Saint George's, with all of Society weeping into their handkerchiefs, overcome by the romance of the thing. But they must marry *now*. Only think— Caro may already be carrying Morgan's heir. Your grandson."

"Hardly, Ferdie, although please allow me to commend you on the resourceful if twisted workings of your mind," Morgan said, walking over to where the two men stood, Ferdie looking so excited that he appeared in danger of jumping out of his own skin and the duke frowning fiercely, as if torn between disgust and righteous indignation. "For my sins, I can at least assure you, Father, that my interlude with Caroline earlier this afternoon will bear no fruit, no matter what she said to Ferdie. Although I would be interested in hearing exactly what she did say. I believe at least one of them harbors a slightly skewed idea of this business of pro-creation."

The duke's head came up and he glared at his son. "Don't compound your sin by attempting to have Caroline or Ferdie share in your shame. Gentlemen have taken their pleasure with willing women of the lower classes since time began. If you had done that, I would be disappointed in you, but not surprised. But I know this child. She is sweet and innocent, no matter how tawdry her background or unfortunate her birth. You will marry her, Morgan. You will marry her or I will disown you."

Morgan looked down at Ferdie, to see that the dwarf's triumphant smile had slipped a notch, almost as if he had gotten what he desired, only to realize that he no longer wished for it. "Why, Ferdie?" he asked, genuinely interested. "Did you wish to secure Caroline's future—or your own?"

Ferdie's small hands curled into white-knuckled fists. "You touched her! You said you wouldn't do it again, but you did. I never liked being a part of this game you want to play—this secretive attempt to use Caroline for your own ends. A cottage. An allowance. Paltry! A pittance! You've been teaching Caro to be a lady, and now she will be!"

"And you'll go into Society," Morgan said dully. "We shouldn't forget that, should we, Ferdie? That is a part of this, isn't it?"

Ferdie pulled three small red balls out of his pocket and ineptly juggled them for a moment before they bounced onto the floor. "If you say so, my lord. I know yours is the last word on such subjects."

Morgan bent to retrieve one of the balls, squeezing it in his hand. "I doubt that mine is the last word on any subject. Is it, Father?"

The duke all but collapsed into the chair he had been sitting in a few minutes earlier. "Your plan—our plan—does not have to be altered from the way it was when you first presented it to me the day you brought Caroline into this house. And it is not revenge we seek, Morgan, but righteous retribution. This marriage can be kept secret until we have accomplished our objective. But you will marry, Morgan. You will marry Caroline Monday, and you will be a model husband to her. For your sins."

FOR MY SINS. That was what his father had said. Morgan would marry Caroline Monday to atone for his sins. His father obviously believed that—or believed that the marriage was to take place because his son feared being disowned. It would probably never occur to his father that Morgan had agreed to the marriage in yet another weak, pathetic hope of gaining, if not his father's love, at least his respect. No, that would never occur to him.

Just as Morgan refused to acknowledge to himself that, even if she had used Ferdie to deliberately trap him into this marriage, he could not be sorry that Caroline Monday was to become his wife. Not that he loved her. He utterly refused to love her.

Morgan stood in front of the full-length mirror, watching as Simmons lifted an infinitesimal speck of lint from the dark blue superfine coat and stood back, admiring his handiwork.

"You look most handsome, my lord. A perfect bridegroom. May I take this opportunity to offer my congratulations and heartiest wishes for your happiness?"

Morgan swiveled his head slowly, to skewer the valet with his intent gaze. He could almost feel his well-laid plans beginning to unravel, thanks to this ill-timed marriage. "I thought you valued your position with me, Simmons."

The valet rubbed his thin hands together, then bowed twice. "But I do, my lord, I do!"

Morgan adjusted his shirt cuffs, stepping away from the mirror. "In that case, Simmons, it would be prudent of you to remember that knowledge of the upcoming ceremony is not to travel with us to London next week."

"Not a word of it will slip past my lips, sir, I promise. Would you like me to open the door for you now? I believe the ceremony is to begin in less than ten minutes."

Morgan nodded his agreement, then proceeded into the wide hallway and toward the staircase. The marriage would take place in the drawing room, with Leticia Twittingdon and Frederick Haswit serving as attendants. Morgan rather liked that—their presence, to his mind, lent precisely the correct farcical tone to the business.

He had not inquired after Caroline's opinion on the matter, just as he had not sought her out in these past ten days. In fact, they had not spoken at all since his father had proclaimed the upcoming nuptials at the dinner table the very day after their confrontation in the study. Morgan hadn't waited to hear Caroline's surprised, patently false response to the announcement, but had flung down his serviette and quit the room and, an hour later, The Acres itself, to return only this morning, three hours before the ceremony.

The ceremony. The burlesque was more like it! He still could not believe he had allowed himself to be a participant in such lunacy. But riding neck or nothing for Clayhill and burying himself there all this time had done nothing to make him see another solution. Was he so weak, so spineless, that even now, knowing how his father detested him, he would marry Caroline Monday in the hope of pleasing the man? Even worse, could he actually be looking forward to having the totally unsuitable Caroline Monday for his bride, looking forward to this evening, when they would be alone in his chambers and he could take what he had begun that day in the field and bring it to its logical conclusion?

What was it about this young woman, this infuriating little guttersnipe, that so intrigued him, so inflamed him? Her open honesty that bordered on brutal frankness? Her convoluted mixture of innocence and worldly knowledge? Her vulnerability? Her all-seeing green eyes? The way she had held him, shuddered beneath him, and whispered, "I love you. I love you so very much." Did he need love so much? Hadn't he done without it very well all these years?

"Pssst! Pssst!"

He turned toward the sound, to see Leticia Twittingdon poking her head out from behind the door of the chamber beside his—the one his conniving wife would sleep in tonight. If he allowed her to sleep tonight. "Miss Twittingdon," he said smoothly, taking in the fact that her hair was no longer pink.

Unfortunately it was now blue, a perfect match for her gown.

"Could I speak with you a moment, my lord?" she asked, opening the door wider and beckoning for him to follow her into the chamber.

"Of course." Sighing, Morgan followed after her. Anything to delay the inevitable. "What the devil…?" he asked a moment later. The room he had entered was filled with flowers. Roses. Lilies. Sprigs of lilac. Blues and reds and yellows and whites. Vases and urns of every imaginable shape and size were jammed atop each surface, and the perfume of the blooms permeated the air, all but suffocating him.

"Are you pleased, my lord?" Leticia asked, spreading her hands to encompass the room. "It's a heavenly bower. Betts helped me—and one of the gardeners, of course. A perfect setting for the beginning of your wonderful life together. My dearest Dulcinea and her Don Quixote."

"God's teeth," Morgan muttered under his breath in disgust, then quickly smiled at the woman. "Thank you, Miss Twittingdon. You have done a, um, a prodigiously splendiferous job. I am sure Caroline is well pleased."

"Oh, pooh! We won't speak of her. Caroline Monday is behaving like a stubborn minx. I cannot begin to tell you the trouble she has caused me these last days, refusing to listen to me while I told her of what a husband expects of his wife, and informing all who will listen that this marriage is none of her idea. But Dulcinea is different. She is dressing even now, Betts in attendance, and will be downstairs in a trice, to say her vows."

"Miss Twittingdon," Morgan pointed out carefully, worried that the woman had drifted even farther into her private world of illusions, "Caroline and Dulcinea are one and the same person."

She dismissed this statement with a wave of her hand. "I know that. But I much prefer Dulcinea. She is aeons more amenable. Caroline Monday appears less and less often now, and even her language is become much more ladylike—unless she is speaking of you, my lord, then it is atrocious and reeks of the influence of that terrible Irishwoman. Marriage will change all that. You will change all that. A sweet, perfect child to hold and love will change all that. Children are extremely important, you know. You must give Dulcinea a child—many children. Why, with children, with a child of one's own to love, one might never see Woodwere."

"I'm sure that's true, Miss Twittingdon," Morgan assured her, noticing that the woman had tears in her eyes. He might have judged her too quickly, believing her to be just another vague, harmless eccentric. Perhaps it would be worth his time to have his man of business in London discreetly delve into her background, and into the Infernal Laurence's background. "Shall we go downstairs now?"

"In a moment, my lord. I still need to procure a flower for my hair. A white one, don't you think? No, white is for purity. A pink one. I shall choose a pink one." She broke off a single showy bloom. "Oh, pooh! I have not enough hair in which to secure the blossom. Living turbans can be such a bother, don't you think?"

Morgan spread his hands helplessly, palms upward, incapable of making an intelligent reply to that particular question. "You could tuck it above your ear, I suppose," he offered at last, beginning to feel a headache gathering behind his eyes.

"There, or up her—"

"Ferdie!" Morgan cut in, wheeling about to see the dwarf leaning against the doorjamb, dressed in a dark superfine suit that looked eerily like Morgan's own, as if Ferdie, too, were a bridegroom, only in miniature. "I thought you'd have taken yourself off downstairs long since, to while away the moments before the ceremony begins by ogling the bride."

"Yes, I can see where you might think that, my lord," Ferdie said, pushing himself away from the doorjamb and sauntering into the room. "I say, Miss Twittingdon, you look quite a picture. Indeed, quite a picture. Don't she, my lord? Caroline wants you, Leticia—sent me to find you, as a matter of fact. Why don't you take yourself off now, while I escort his lordship down to the drawing room. Wouldn't want him getting lost, now would we?"

Miss Twittingdon, a hand to her mouth as if she had forgotten something important, curtsied quickly to Morgan and pushed past Ferdie, heading for the door. She turned at the last moment and, with a waggle of her head, informed them, "I'm going to weep buckets during the ceremony, you know. Won't it be the most splendiferous fun!" Then she headed out the doorway and turned toward Caroline's room, calling, "I'm coming, my dearest Dulcinea! I'm coming!"

"Her belfry's positively crawling with bats," Ferdie supplied dryly, selecting a bloom for himself and tucking it into the top buttonhole of his coat. "I still can't fathom how you've agreed to take her to London and yet cut up stiff over bringing me along as well. If anybody's going to give the game away, it will be good old Letty. Not that I'm complaining, my lord bridegroom, for I will be going to London now." He pushed out his chicken-boned chest, lifted his chin, and winked at Morgan. "I always knew I would—one way or the other."

"I'd offer you my congratulations, if you hadn't already congratulated yourself," Morgan said, wishing Ferdie were taller, so that he could invite him to square off with him and then pummel the man into insensibility. "You wanted to speak with me? Please don't tell me you wish to instruct me in my husbandly duties."

Ferdie smiled, but he didn't look happy. "I wouldn't presume to do so, even in my assigned role as your sole male witness and attendant. No, I have something else to say, although it pains me to have to compromise myself." As he stared up at Morgan, his smile faded, to be replaced by a curious stare. "You hate Caro right now, don't you? You hate her because she told me what you did to her that day you went out riding."

"I don't *hate* anybody, Ferdie," Morgan replied tightly as the dwarf's arrow pierced his pride. "It's unproductive. I merely do what I have to do."

"Yes, well, I suppose you can twist things around any way you want, you being a marquis and all. But I thought I ought to tell you something before the ceremony. You see, Caro didn't say a word to me about what you did to her. I was in the study when she came in before dinner that day to tear a strip off your hide."

Morgan bowed to the dwarf, tight-lipped. "My apologies, Ferdie, for my rather uncharitable private thoughts about you these past days. You *are* an honorable man."

"You don't believe me?" Ferdie abandoned his pose of leaning against the table to take a single step forward, his hands drawn up into tight fists. "How can you not believe me? I was there—I swear it! I hid behind the drapery in the window embrasure. I—I hide there all the time. I've been doing so ever since you said not to come into the study unannounced. I can't come in—if I'm already there. I'm telling the truth now. Caro didn't tell me *anything!*"

"Which of course explains why *you* felt it necessary to confront the duke and me with the knowledge that I had compromised Caroline, seeing as how you love her so dearly and have always wanted her for yourself. I, too, can be observant, Ferdie. And now Caroline, not to be outdone in the business, is proclaiming to all who will listen that she is totally against this marriage. This marriage, which brings with it a title and wealth beyond her most fervent dreams. And—oh, yes, lest we forget—this marriage also secures your livelihood, doesn't it, and your freedom from Woodwere? Surely she has promised you that in return for running to my father with tales of my brutal seduction of her unwilling body. What's the matter, Ferdie? Is Caro beginning to worry that I will exact my revenge on her body once she is legally mine to use as I wish? Surely that niggling thought will have crossed her mind by now. Is that why she sent you in here with that cock-and-bull story? Well, she left it a little too late. I don't believe, or trust, either of you."

Morgan was livid. Wasn't it enough that he was being coerced into this sham of a marriage? Did the girl have to compound everything by having the so loyal Ferdie try to fob him off by saying Caroline was innocent of trading their interlude in the field for the chance at a dukedom? And Morgan had been foolish enough to admire her honesty. *Honesty.* He should have known better than to think there might still be something left in this world to believe in, to admire. To love.

"I'm telling you that Caroline did not know what I'd done. She never would have seen the reason for doing it, for one thing. But I did. I heard what you said to her and what you said after she was gone. You want her, pure and simple, and you'll have her one way or the other. I only made sure it was the 'other.' It balances the ledger." Then Ferdie walked straight up to Morgan, not stopping until he was a mere foot away before intoning in a solemn voice:

"I speak the truth, but you won't believe.
Yet on a grander scale, a dark revenge you weave.
To use the girl is madness, yet to dishonor her is worse;
Now she is yours forever, and *I* end this discourse!"

His poem complete, Ferdie delivered a sharp kick to Morgan's left shin, then walked slowly out of the room, leaving the marquis to stare after him, feeling less honorable than he had ever known himself to be in his entire, not always so honorable life. What might have been even worse than Ferdie had hinted was that the dwarf's poem had also served to provide Morgan with an intriguing idea. An idea that had nothing to do with who had said what to whom about that momentous interlude in the field, but had a great deal to do with how he might be able to turn Ferdie's presence in London to his own distinct advantage.

It was, Morgan knew, beneath contempt to be thinking such things on his wedding day, but he had long since ceased to argue with his brain when it came to thoughts of revenge against the Wilburtons. If he believed himself to be a man who could be obsessed with anything, he knew his obsession had to lie with revenging Jeremy's death, his father's grief, and maybe, just maybe, some of his own guilt. Anything else, anyone else—including Caroline Monday, including himself—had to be secondary to that revenge.

However, he was about to become a married man, and whether his bride was willing or not, a conniving student of Peaches O'Hanlan or Ferdie's innocent dupe, it would not be gentlemanly of him to keep her waiting. He plucked a budding white rose from the vase beside him and, mimicking Ferdie's action of a few minutes earlier, tucked it into the top buttonhole of his coat, then quit the room to join his bride in the drawing room.

Caroline was already there waiting for him, or at least she was quick to turn her eyes toward the doorway when he appeared there, halting just inside the room to observe the scene. She was dressed in white, he noticed with some faint humor, although she was without veil or ornate train, and the small nosegay of white roses he had thought to have one of the gardeners prepare for her was lying abandoned on the table beside her. She looked pretty and virginal—and mad as hell.

His step faltered for a moment as he wondered if he *had* been wrong. She should be preening, happy to have brought him to the altar. His heart began to pound as he tried to push hope, that most defeating emotion, to the back of his brain.

Morgan nodded in her direction, but didn't speak to her, preferring to walk directly over to the duke, who was standing in front of the fireplace, and drawl, "Good day, Father. Your miscreant son has returned as ordered, to offer himself upon the altar of your misguided morality. Lovely weather for a forced marriage, isn't it?"

"A little less arrogance and at least a modicum of humility on your part would please me greatly, son," the duke said quietly, motioning for the minister to step forward, then indicating that Caroline should join them.

Morgan hadn't expected much in the way of wedding day pomp and formality, and his father's plans had not disabused him of his low expectations. The discreetly worded special license the duke's consequence had made available was already in the hands of the minister who had been called upon to perform the ceremony, so that there was little to do but say the vows and sign the register the minister had brought with him from the village church.

Morgan touched Caroline only when instructed to place the ring on her finger, and while Miss Twittingdon wept copiously in the background and Ferdie rocked back and forth on his heels beside him, the marquis uttered his vows in a voice totally bereft of emotion.

Five minutes later Caroline Monday, penniless orphan and the major character in Morgan's scheme for revenge, was legally—though apparently not happily—the Marchioness of Clayton.

The Marquis of Clayton declined to kiss his bride, and quit the room immediately, escaping to the fields to ride his hastily saddled mount nearly to a standstill.

CHAPTER TWELVE

Marriage has many pains, but celibacy has no pleasures.
                                        Samuel Johnson

CAROLINE WAS ALONE in the large chamber, with only her anger and her fears to keep her company. She'd also harbored some hopes—a few illusory, nebulous wishes—but those had disappeared earlier in the day when Morgan stood at the entrance to the drawing room and stared straight through her, as if she didn't exist.

How she hated Morgan Blakely.

How she loved him.

No! She did not love him. She couldn't love him. What she felt for him was gratitude, nothing more.

He had lifted her from the squalor and hopelessness of Woodwere. He had given her a name, even if it wasn't hers. He had taught her what it was like to go to bed with a full belly, and how wonderful it was to be clean from the skin out, with no uninvited guests taking up residence in her petticoats, to plague her with their bites.

He had introduced her to novels, to history, and to the glories of fine paintings and sculptures. He had shown her kindness, and some sympathy, and treated her as if she had been put on this earth for some reason other than to suffer.

He had even, through his strained relationship with his father, taught her that perhaps she hadn't missed so much as she'd thought, being an orphan. At least she could imagine that her parents had loved her.

Lastly, Morgan Blakely had introduced her to the indescribable joys of physical pleasure. The joys, and the shame that came later, once reason—which had flown high into the skies as his mouth captured hers—was belatedly restored.

And for that shattering indignity—for making her face the unspeakable realization that, no matter how much he'd tried to teach her about the part she was to play out in London, her low birth had provided her with all the ladylike demeanor of a common penny-a-poke whore—Caroline would never forgive him.

But now she was his marchioness. She had his ring on her finger to prove it—an odd ring, Morgan's own, that she had seen on the last finger of his right hand and asked him about early in their association, only to hear him tell her it was nothing but a trifle. Yet he had given it to her as a marriage ring, this plain gold band topped by a flattened circle of gold in which was carved the small figure of a unicorn. A trifle.

Oh, yes. She was his marchioness, and he was her marquis. He was hers to honor and obey and all those other things the minister had spoken of while she stood beside Morgan, mortified by his pointed neglect, her heart pounding, her hands aching to reach out and touch him, even to shake him into acknowledging her.

Caroline sat beneath the covers in the middle of the wide four-post bed, exactly where Leticia Twittingdon had left her—the virginal bride awaiting her groom. She felt like a Christmas goose, freshly washed, plucked, trussed up, and ready to be devoured, or a tethered goat, destined to be clawed to death in a bear baiting. Her high-necked white nightgown would be no defense against Morgan, now that he had a right as her legal husband to command her to strip it off while he watched, most probably smirking, from that chair in front of the fireplace.

Not that Morgan would stoop so low. Even while she had railed against him, against this absurd forced marriage, Caroline had quietly acknowledged to herself that Morgan Blakely was as much the victim as she—possibly more. The duke's announcement at dinner had taken her by surprise, but it had also taken only a single quick look at Ferdie to know that he had been up to his old tricks again.

Even as Morgan had pushed back his chair and stomped from the room in a very visible expression of his disgust, Caroline had remembered finding Ferdie tucked up in the study's window embrasure after one of her lessons with Morgan. Quiet as a mouse, and with more vices learned in the name of self-preservation than an Irishman living on his wits, Ferdie had always known how to secrete himself in places he didn't belong, to hear things he shouldn't hear, then use them to his advantage.

She couldn't blame Ferdie for running lickety-split for his grace the duke with his damning information. After all, she had even mentioned Ferdie's name during that humiliating argument with Morgan. Ferdie wanted to travel to London more than he wanted to be tall and straight, and he must have seen her marriage to Morgan as his sure entry to Society. His caring and attention to her these past days had proven his guilt as well as his belated remorse for what he had done.

Now she was left to face the consequences of Ferdie's mischief, and also to face Morgan's undoubted anger, born of what had to be his sure belief that *she* had been the one to

The Reader Service – Here's How it Works:

Accepting your 2 free books and 2 free gifts places you under no obligation to buy anything. You may keep the books and gifts and return the shipping statement marked "cancel". If you do not cancel, about a month later we'll send you 3 additional books and bill you just $5.49 each in the U.S. or $5.99 each in Canada, plus 25¢ shipping & handling per book and applicable taxes if any.* That's the complete price and – compared to cover prices starting from $6.99 each in the U.S. and $8.50 each in Canada – it's quite a bargain! You may cancel at any time, but if you choose to continue, every month we'll send you 3 more books, which you may either purchase at the discount price or return to us and cancel your subscription.

*Terms and prices subject to change without notice. Sales tax applicable in N.Y. Canadian residents will be charged applicable provincial taxes and GST. All orders subject to approval. Books received may vary. Credit or debit balances in a customer's account(s) may be offset by any other outstanding balance owed by or to the customer. Please allow 4 to 6 weeks for delivery.

If offer card is missing write to:

The Reader Service, 3010 Walden Ave., P.O. Box 1867, Buffalo, NY 14240-1867

BUSINESS REPLY MAIL
FIRST-CLASS MAIL   PERMIT NO. 717-003   BUFFALO, NY

POSTAGE WILL BE PAID BY ADDRESSEE

THE READER SERVICE
3010 WALDEN AVE
PO BOX 1341
BUFFALO NY 14240-8571

NO POSTAGE
NECESSARY
IF MAILED
IN THE
UNITED STATES

run tattling to the duke about his son's compromise of his houseguest.

She didn't know which she feared more—Morgan's arrival in this bedchamber or her reaction to that arrival. All she had to do was to close her eyes, and the memory of her behavior that day in the field—her rapturous delight in the sensations Morgan's mouth, Morgan's hands, had evoked, her brazen response to his lovemaking, her childish declaration of love— came rushing back to shame her, to make her wish she'd had the courage to leave rather than agree to this sham of a marriage.

But she had made her promises and had no choice but to live up to them. Promises to Ferdie and Aunt Leticia, to keep them safe and away from Woodwere. Promises to Morgan and the duke, to help them with their plan to introduce her to London as Lady Caroline Wilburton. Promises to herself, to never be poor or hungry or alone again.

If only her insides would stop shaking, making her feel as if she might faint, or be sick all over this lovely bedspread. If only Morgan would come now, while she still could cling to the hope that he might not be so angry after all, that he might grow to love her if he gave himself half a chance, and that her love for him would be enough to begin with.

As if in answer to her unspoken pleas, the door to the connecting dressing room opened and Morgan, clad in a dark blue banyan, slippers, and most obviously nothing else, entered. "Good evening, wife," he said in a tone that told her immediately that he was still in an ill humor. "How terribly accommodating of you to be where you belong. Foolishly, I had harbored some slight trepidation that you might have decided to thwart me, perhaps even going to such lengths as to arm yourself against me."

Caroline had believed she wanted him to come to her. That was a mistake. She didn't want him here. Not in his present mood. She wanted him gone, even if he hated her for it. She raised her chin, hoping she looked appropriately defiant, and said sweetly, "And why should I do that, my lord husband, when I now have everything I have ever wanted? Wealth, position—a name. Oh, I may have played the reluctant bride in order to gain your father's sympathy and that of the rest of this household, but I see no reason to feign reluctance now that I have what I want. Peaches always said it would be possible for me to make my living on my back. It appears that she was correct. Only come here, dear husband, and give me a child, so that I can secure my position as your marchioness."

She sat back, maintaining her smile only by the most intense concentration, desperately fighting against the urge to raise a hand to her mouth and worry at one of her short, rounded nails, and waited for a disgusted Morgan to explode in fury and then leave her alone. Alone and safe.

But he didn't leave. He stood very still for a long time, staring at her, saying nothing—until she thought she might scream.

"Should I utter my *'brava'* now, imp, or have you an encore planned?" he asked at last, approaching the bed, one hand going to the sash on his banyan. "Earlier, Ferdie swore to me that he was the little bird who whispered in my father's ear. I confess to having harbored a very real doubt as to his truthfulness—until you made that ridiculous speech just now, of course. But Ferdie was telling the truth—you had no plan to trap me into marriage."

"But I did, I did!" Caroline exclaimed quickly, her eyes on the knot in his sash. "I—I deliberately set out to seduce you, then had Ferdie blab everything to his grace. I *did!* I planned it from the very beginning. You need me too much to send me away until whatever you have planned to take place in London is completed. But once your scheme is over—and most especially if it fails—you will dismiss me as you would any employee. You might not even give me my cottage."

"Or your allowance. As Ferdie is not here to add that particular refrain, I shall do the honors for him. Unless he is hiding close by in another window embrasure. He has all the makings of a voyeur, our enterprising little friend Ferdie does. Shall I check?"

Morgan was now sitting on the side of the bed, not more than two feet away from her. And he was smiling.

Caroline felt her throat beginning to close. "You don't want me. I'm nothing, I'm no one. You only married me to please your father. You don't even want this marriage made public knowledge—and yes, Ferdie did tell me that much! You can't wish to stay married to me once this business you have planned for London is over. There can be a divorce— Aunt Leticia told me so—although they are very difficult to obtain. You're a marquis—you can petition the Prince Regent for a divorce. He'll understand. He wants a divorce himself— and you were the one who told me that, when we were discussing monarchs. But only think, Morgan! If you do— If we do— If there's a child—"

"If there's a child, my dear, it will become mine as a part of the divorce settlements," Morgan said, turning back the covers and rising once more, the sash to the banyan now nearly fallen open completely. And, damn him, he was *still* smiling!

"You wouldn't be so cruel." Caroline's breathing became ragged as she struggled to reconcile the seemingly heartless, ruthless man standing in front of her with the Morgan Blakely who had come to Woodwere all those months ago and sat with Aunt Leticia, sipping make-believe tea.

Morgan frowned, shaking his head. "No, infant, I wouldn't. We are married, for good or ill. I cannot pretend I do not desire you. It came to me while I was out riding this afternoon that I may be protesting too much. I need a wife. I need an heir. More than anything else, I enjoy having a willing woman in my bed. And you are that, Caro—you most definitely are that. I came here determined to overlook your duplicity in trapping me into wedlock, but now I don't even have that distasteful presumption to deter me, do I?"

"But you don't love me." Caroline knew she was close to tears, moments away from making an utter fool of herself.

She thought his eyes clouded over for a moment, but his next words told her she had been foolishly optimistic. "Ah, but there is the real beauty of the thing. You love me—or so you said before launching yourself into this evening's litany of lies. Loving me will keep you compliant and malleable once we are in London. My father is tolerably well pleased with me at the moment, although he will never love me as you do. Yes, Lady Caroline, I would say I have come off the victor all around in this particular battle."

A single tear coursed down Caroline's cheek, but she refused to wipe it away. "I don't want you, Morgan. Not like this," she said, feeling as if she had begun to die by inches. "I was stupid—a dreamer. I should have refused to do as your father bid. I should have run away. I don't want to be married to you. Not now. Not like this."

"*This* is all I can offer you now, imp," Morgan said as he discarded the banyan and lay down close to her, his naked body glowing golden in the light from the bedside candle, the illumination from the flames dancing in the fireplace. He laid a hand on her upper arm, the heat of him branding her through the thin material of her nightgown. "I promise you, Caroline, this time will be even better than before."

Her bottom lip began to quiver uncontrollably as he pulled her down beside him, her head and shoulders sinking into the soft down of the pillows, her body taut almost to rigidity as he began to loosen the dozen or so buttons that closed the front of her nightgown. She couldn't fight him, couldn't move. He was her husband, and she loved him.

"Don't cry, Caro," he whispered into her ear, his warm breath sending shivers down the side of her throat, down the length of her spine, all the way to her clenched toes. Her eyes closed as his hand slipped beneath the cloth, to cup her breast, to begin gently massaging her already taut nipple. "Yes, Caro, yes. You were born for this, my pretty girl. I knew it almost from the beginning, knew it and fought it. But not now, not anymore. You were fashioned for pleasure—your own and that of the man who brings you into the full flower of your womanhood."

"Morgan, I—"

"No, no, Caro. Don't talk. Just listen...just remember. Remember how you felt as I laid you back on the blanket. Remember the ache between your thighs, that tight, pleasurable torment that grew and grew until it exploded, until your very world shattered around you. Remember, Caro. Remember the feel of my mouth on your nipples, the touch of my hand as I slid it between your legs, finding the source of your pleasure, the wellspring of your desire. Come with me, sweet Caro, come back with me—back to the pleasure. We at least have this."

Caroline whimpered softly as she felt herself being divested of her nightgown, the memory of her brief glimpse at Morgan's body reminding her that this time it would be different. This time he would take his pleasure as well. Would she cry out in pain, as the girl had done at Woodwere, or would she be like those other poor demented fools, glorying in the act, writhing like some animal, biting and clawing and welcoming his alien presence inside her?

Morgan's body was so beautiful, nothing like those of the men she had seen naked and engorged with lust at Woodwere, nothing like Boxer, whose large body and larger paunch all but hid his manhood beneath a mountain of ugly flesh. Morgan's stomach was flat, and his legs were long and straight like those of the marble statues in the duke's gardens. Her cheeks burned as she realized she would like to see him again, even to memorize him, each leanly muscled inch of him.

Oh, God, it's true. I am decadent.

She shivered slightly once her skin was exposed to the cool night air, but Morgan's lower body soon covered her, warming her, as he slid one leg over hers, adjusting himself so that he could cup both her breasts at once, alternately teasing them with his tongue and his clever fingers.

He didn't speak now, which Caroline considered a blessing, for she was much too involved in trying to lift herself against his tongue without seeming to do so to begin to decipher anything he might say. The feelings had all come flooding back, well remembered and welcome, and her fears disappeared under rapidly building waves of desire.

And love. Whether he wanted it or not, whether he believed what she felt for him was honest or only the result of a silly, juvenile infatuation, she did not care. Caroline knew that she loved Morgan Blakely. She loved him when they sat, heads together, reading from one of the duke's books. She loved him when he discreetly cleared his throat at table, warning her that she was about to pick up the wrong fork. She loved him when he spoke kindly about Aunt Leticia's "splendiferous notions" and when he put up with Ferdie's misguided meddling and when his eyes clouded as his father treated him like an unpleasant but unavoidable guest in his house. She loved him when he taught her to ride, patiently keeping his horse to a boring walk until she learned to trust herself and her mount. She loved him for rescuing her from Woodwere, for giving her good food to eat and pretty clothes to wear and a safe, solid roof over her head.

But right now she loved him best when he drew her nipple into his mouth, holding it gently between his teeth as he flicked his tongue back and forth, back and forth, sending waves of desire along an invisible thread that ran from deep inside her breast down to her most intimate places, lighting small fires of desire, tying pleasurable knots that were alternately tautened and released, heaping sensation upon sensation until she began to moan, low in her throat, her head flung back against the pillows, her teeth clenched against the building ecstasy.

She didn't realize that she had grasped his head between her hands until he moved, sliding away from her, easing himself down her body the way he had done before, laving her navel, pressing lingering kisses on the sensitive skin of her rib cage, his hands gently kneading the soft flesh of her stomach.

But still his hand did not slip between her legs, where her body had begun to make itself ready for him. How she burned for him, unashamed by her building desire, uncaring that she had begun to move her hips invitingly, pleadingly, openly begging for his touch.

She sensed that he had raised his head, and looked down at him in question.

"Caro, listen to me. I don't want to hurt you more than I have to, do you understand? I'm going to be there for you, help you, so that when I have to give you pain I'll be able to kiss it away, to bring you back to the pleasure I want you to feel when I come inside you. Do you understand?"

"Yes—yes, I understand." But she didn't. She didn't understand at all. Not even when he lowered his head once more and his trail of kisses led him down, all the way down her belly, until he gently pushed open her legs and, and—

"*Oh*, oh, no. *Oh*—Morgan, what—" Caroline's eyes opened wide and she stared up at the material that spanned the top of the four-poster bed, seeing nothing, feeling everything. She would perish with embarrassment. She would die if he stopped.

His fingers spread her wide, so that she knew he could see her, see all of her, in the glow from the fireplace.

His fingers had spread her wide, and now his tongue quickly sought and found the small tight bud that had come to life, to awareness, for the first time only a short time ago but seemed now to know what was required of it, what reward lay ahead.

Morgan's tongue caressed...cajoled without words... prodded...and probed...and gave...and took. His fingers pressed and kneaded and then unexpectedly dipped, finding her aching openness, then slipping inside; first a single finger, then two.

She felt impaled, empowered, and his mouth now covered her budding center completely, the sweet suction of that mouth drawing her inside him, as if he might devour her.

His fingers still within her, he began to move, to open her, expand her, and she welcomed this new intimacy and the feeling of fullness it gave her. Until the pain began—a slow burning, a faint ripping, a strange, stinging pain that rapidly faded to inconsequentiality under the onslaught of Morgan's sucking mouth, his laving tongue, his gently nipping teeth. She felt a new wetness between her legs, but paid it no heed.

For it was beginning to build now. That pressure, experienced only once before yet never to be forgotten, that indescribable hunger, that overwhelming longing to give everything, take everything, *feel* everything there was to feel—and then die.

She felt Morgan's fingers leave her, and moaned at the loss. Then he withdrew his mouth as well. She was bereft, left to whimper and hold up her arms to him, begging him to come back. She was beyond shame, beyond pride. She needed Morgan, loved him so, wanted him close to her, his weight pressing down on her, his manhood sheathed deep inside her.

"Hush, imp, I'm here," she heard him say as if from miles above her, and she grasped him tightly, her arms going around his back, needing him to anchor her, to center her, before she was forever lost. "Let your legs fall open for me, Caro," he whispered from somewhere near her ear. "Don't be afraid. Don't be afraid."

She did as he bid, whimpering softly as she felt his body slide deep into hers with a single thrust that she was sure should hurt but didn't. He lay very still for a few moments, and she savored the unique sensation of completion, of wholeness. Then he began to withdraw—or so she believed. But he didn't leave her. He was only teasing, bless him, pulling back to the very edge of possession, then plunging into her once more, fast, then slower, deep, then—with exquisite torture— barely staying inside her at all.

"Wrap your legs around my back, Caro."

She heard his voice as if from another lifetime. What had he said? What did he want? She'd do anything. Anything so that he wouldn't stop, so that the sensations wouldn't stop, so that he'd never leave her, ever, ever again. But he was driving her mad with his games, with his teasing. She tightened her arms around his back, then daringly raised her legs, pinning them around him, holding him against her, rising with him when he seemed to withdraw, grinding herself against him when he plunged once more.

It was good; it was so very good.

But it got better.

Then even better.

Morgan increased the tempo of his thrusts, lunging deeper, staying longer, piling one on top of the other until she believed his violent motions would mean the death of her, the death of both of them.

The desire to move with him inexplicably faded as her passion spiraled higher, and all she wanted now was to hold on, her body open to all he wanted to take, all he wanted to give. She felt herself go limp as he buffeted her, his thrusts coming so quickly that they nearly blended into one. Her entire being became centered in that one highly sensitized area, the sensations building…building…turning white-hot with wanting…until she had to cry out, had to remember to breathe…had to give in to the throbbing, pulsating pleasure that coursed through her body.

Morgan went suddenly still inside her as she clung to him, dazed with all that had happened to her, and she became aware of a new throbbing, this time coming from him, and she gloried in the realization that he was spilling his seed deep inside her. The enjoyment was still physical, but now it was compounded by the dawning comprehension that Morgan, too, had gone beyond rationality, beyond control—and that she had been responsible for *his* pleasure, for *his* loss of control.

As he collapsed against her, as she stroked his perspiration-slick back and listened to his ragged breathing, a smile tickled the corners of Caroline's mouth, a smile of utter satisfaction that had nothing to do with the physical ecstasy he had given her. "I'll make you love me, Morgan Blakely," she whispered softly, so softly that she was sure he hadn't heard.

And she didn't cry until he had levered himself off her, slipped his banyan back around his body, and quit the bed chamber without saying another word.

BOOK THREE

In this assault I'm telling you of
there is no rescue outside of pity.

Thibaut de Champagne

CHAPTER THIRTEEN

Much malice mingled with a little wit.

John Dryden

RICHARD WILBURTON, Viscount Harlan and only child of the eighth earl of Witham, sat in the high-ceilinged dining room of the Montagu Square house along with his father and mother, torn between disgust for the former and pity for the latter.

Did his father—squeezed into his thronelike chair at the head of the long table—have to eat as if this were the last meal he would ever see on earth, and as if every scrap had to be consumed before the clock on the mantel struck eight? Did his mother have to sit at the foot of the table, a weak smile on her face, pretending to listen to her husband as if what the man was saying—his mouth full of chicken, his three chins shiny with grease—was actually of any consequence? Did he, Richard, have to sit here as well, midway between them, determinedly staring at the hideous, ornate silver epergne rather than get up, take the carving knife from the sideboard, and plunge it straight into Thomas Wilburton's black heart?

"And so I said to Lord Burnsey, I said to him, 'Burny, m'lad, if you can't aim any better than that, you may as well shove the barrel of that gun straight up your lily-pure ass and have an end to it.' An *end* to it! Hear that, Freddy, m'love? An *end* to it! Hah! Three brace of pheasants I brought home that day, and Burny nary a bird. Pitiful man. An Englishman ain't worth his salt if he can't bring down his prey, I say. Haven't spoken a word to him since. No, not Burny. Not worth his salt. Am I right, Richard?"

"Yes, Papa, you're correct. You're always correct," Richard heard himself answer, unpleasantly reminded of the single time he'd had the misfortune of going out hunting with his father. It was a fox hunt, and Richard was twelve. The day began pleasantly enough, and he was given a stirrup cup to drink before the riders headed off behind the hounds, their mounts throwing up large clods of fragrant earth as they galloped across the fields, the hounds baying, the morning air fresh and clear, with only thin threads of white mist rising from the streams tucked deep in the small valleys they rode through, following the sound of the horn.

How proud he had been of his father that day. His father, master of the hunt, even if his girth required that he be hoisted onto his hunter with a winch, even if his red coat strained at the seams like an overripe tomato about to burst. But that exhilaration hadn't lasted beyond the chase, the thrill of the ride; for once the fox had been cornered the frenzied pack had closed in, yelping and howling, to tear at the fox in front of Richard's horrified eyes.

And then, once his father and some of the others had beaten the hounds away, Richard was forced to watch as the tail was sliced from the fox's carcass and his father held it high, as if he had somehow seen an assault of twenty men and horses and thirty hounds winning out against one small fox to be a victory.

"Come here, boy," Richard remembered his father commanding him. "This is your first fox, and you know what that means."

Richard shook his head now as he had shaken it then, in mute denial of what was to come. It had taken four men to hold him down as his father laughed and cursed and roughly rubbed the bloody end of the tail across his son's forehead, down his cheeks, warm blood and urine-soaked clumps of fur finding their way into his nostrils…his mouth…

"Eh? What are you about, Richard, shaking your head like a hound ridding himself of a fly?" his father said now, and Richard blinked himself back to attention. "You trying to say you don't want to go tripping along to the theater with your sweet mama and me? Then why don't you say so? Speak up, boy! The hero of the Peninsula—and he can't find his tongue. If it weren't for the medals I wouldn't believe it! What's the matter with you, boy? Or do you have some other amusement afoot? Maybe one of those Covent Garden warblers has caught your eye, huh, and you don't want your mama and papa about when you're fixing to tumble some fine, pretty piece? Think that's it, Freddy? D'ya think our son's finally stickin' that thing somewheres other than between his own two pumping fists?"

"Thomas, please," Lady Witham began, but her voice faltered and she only looked at Richard pleadingly, as if begging him to understand that she was beyond helping him, had gone years past helping either one of them. "Perhaps Dickon simply has already formulated other plans for the evening?"

Other than that impossible fantasy of sinking the carving knife into his father's chest and then being hauled off to the guardhouse for his crime, Richard had no other real plans for this or any other evening. But he had long since realized the folly of admitting to such a lack of interest in the social activities of the Season. After all, he was Viscount Harlan, the hero of the Peninsula. He was the Unicorn, God help him, and there were obligations, certain things he must do, certain roles he must play out, certain appearances he must maintain at all costs.

He looked to his father, who had at least somewhat toned down his bullying these past few years, thanks to respect for his son's heroic accomplishments on the Peninsula. Richard wished he didn't still fear the man so, hate him so. Then he smiled at his mother, who loved her only child, but who didn't understand him, who refused to see that child for what he was—and what he wasn't. "In point of fact, Mama, you are correct. I have formulated other plans for the evening. I'm so sorry."

Frederica clapped her hands together, beaming at him. "I thought as much, as it is Wednesday, and Almack's first evening of the Season. The hero of the Peninsula will have his choice of all the lovely young debutantes. Won't he, Thomas?"

The earl extracted a bit of food from between his teeth and held it in front of his eyes, inspecting it, perhaps even trying to identify it, then wiped it on the fine linen tablecloth. "He had the pick of the litter last year, Freddy, not that he made anything of it. We came within an amesace of snaring that Pevensley chit—thirty thousand a year!—before your son announced to all who would listen that he couldn't abide her squint. For thirty thousand a year I would have divorced you and taken her myself, and I wouldn't have cared if she had two heads!"

"That is still an option, sir," Richard heard himself say before he could guard his tongue. If the man wouldn't die, at least a divorce would take him away and leave Richard free to protect his mother. The two of them could retire to the country, and—

"Hah!" The earl's laughter exploded in the room. "That's a rich one, boy. Divorce my Freddy! Did you catch that, my love?" he asked in a booming voice that Richard felt sure could be heard by the servants on the other side of the baize-covered door. "And why would I do such a thing? Couldn't find myself another so *unwilling* woman in my bed as your sweet mother if I was to hie myself all over this damp island looking. No, I'm happy as I am, thank you. Mounting a mistress, or two or three, is more than enough for me. Wouldn't know what to do with a willing wife under me, crying out like a bitch in heat instead of whimpering like some puling infant. Why, I might even end by not being up to my husbandly duties!"

Richard leaned his elbows on the table and rested his chin in his hands, watching as his mother fled the room, her serviette pressed to her mouth, then turned to his father. "My thanks to you, sir. These weekly family meals are always so comfortable in their predictability. I vow, I wouldn't know how to handle reaching the dessert course with Mama still at table."

Thomas leaned back in his chair, his corset creaking audibly, a heavy cut-crystal glass of his favorite gin—"the drink of a *real* Englishman, son, and not any of that watery French bilge you slop up"—clutched in his massive hands. "Yes, yes," he said in dismissal. "She would have flitted off soon enough anyway, trying to primp herself up some more for the theater. Feathers and turbans and all those god-awful fripperies women think we like. Give me a good whore any day, son—they know just what we men want on display, don't they?"

He leaned forward, slamming the glass down on the table top, nearly oversetting it. "Now tell me what I want to hear, boy. You going to marry me some money this Season, or ain't you? You may be the hero of the Peninsula, you may be the Unicorn—but that's today. The war's been over for damn near a year. How long d'ya think we can trade on your reputation and that pretty face of yours? I'll soon have duns cluttering up my drawing room, screaming for their money, and then no one will care if you're some blooming national treasure. We need some blunt, blast it!"

"I'm not ready for marriage, sir," Richard said quietly, toying with his fork and avoiding his father's eyes.

"Not ready? Not ready!" The earl's fist came down on the table, rattling the cutlery. "Christ, boy, nobody asked you to be *ready*. Just do it!" He stood abruptly, so that his chair toppled over with a loud crash, and shook his fist at Richard. "You don't know. You'll never know what I've done for you, what I've suffered to pass on the title that you deserve—that I deserved! And what do you do? You run off to war with that hell-raiser Morgan Blakely and get yourself wounded— nearly get yourself killed!"

"Morgan was very nearly killed, Papa, and his brother did die. I—I was fortunate."

"Don't try to fob me off with that sham show of modesty that has all the chits swooning at your feet. You're a *hero*— and don't you ever forget it! God knows it's the only thing that keeps me from wondering if you're some changeling your mama foisted on me. Won't hunt, won't shoot, won't put up your fives at Gentleman Jackson's, won't even go to the cockpits with me. Your own mother calls you Dickon, like you was still in leading strings. *My* son. Where's your spleen, boy? Now hie your pretty-girl self off to Willis's Rooms, like you told your mama, and find us a fortune!"

CAROLINE STOOD in front of the full-length mirror, nervously turning her wedding ring around and around her finger as Betts knelt beside her, fussing with the small flounce at the hem of the demure white gown.

"Almack's! The pinnacle of the polite world! The dream of every young girl and the social center of the universe! I vow, my heart pounds simply at the thought! Oh, dear. Oh, dear. Dulcinea, I may faint with anticipation of the pleasure we will find behind those sacred doors. Do you think the place is still so unremittingly ugly? And the food—dreadful, my child, simply dreadful! Although all that may have changed since my day."

"Thank you, Betts, I believe I am now as presentable as it is possible for you to make me," Caroline said as the maid gave a finishing pat to the flounce. She turned to smile at Miss Twittingdon, who looked most intriguing in her deep purple gown and gold turban, her long white kid gloves mercifully covering most of her bird-thin arms. "His Grace informed me just this morning at breakfast that Almack's is the most respectable ballroom in all of London, Aunt Leticia. Using that information as our guide, I would suppose we shall discover the place to be ugly, the food unappetizing, and the company unremittingly boring. But we will look nice, won't we?"

"Oh, pooh," Miss Twittingdon said, collapsing into a slipper chair. "With you already safely bracketed to his lordship, there is really nothing for us to do there, then, is there, Dulcinea?"

Caroline and Betts exchanged meaningful glances; then Caroline knelt beside the slipper chair and put her hand on Miss Twittingdon's arm. She had learned that the woman paid much closer attention to what was being said if the words were accompanied by physical contact. "Aunt Leticia, I know this has been extremely difficult for you to understand, but we must not speak of the marriage. We must not speak of Dulcinea. We cannot even speak of *Lady* Caroline. That was only at The Acres, and then only to help me begin to behave like that poor dead girl. Remember what Morgan told us this morning? My name is now Caroline Wilbur—Caroline Wilbur, Aunt Leticia—and I am no one else save the duke's ward until Morgan has played out his game. *Caroline Wilbur.* Nothing more. Nothing less. You will remember that, won't you?"

"Caroline Wilbur," Miss Twittingdon repeated dully. "Oh, my head! As if this scratchy turban weren't enough, especially when my golden, living turban was so perfect! Yellow hair was all the crack when I was a girl, you know. I owed many of my beaux to my blond hair. If you weren't already wed to the marquis, I vow you'd have half of London dangling at your shoestrings as well, begging for your hand, dazzled by your lovely blond locks. First the turban. Then I learn that Ferdie—that minuscule mountebank—is to go with us. Now you tell me I am to *think,* as well? I don't know if I shall survive this!"

"Perhaps a small glass of wine, miss?" Betts suggested to Caroline. "It worked wonders yesterday, when she got all to worryin' about seein' that infernal Laurence fella now we're in town."

Caroline sighed, then reluctantly nodded her agreement. Strange as it seemed, a slightly tipsy Leticia Twittingdon had proved to be a more placid, well-behaved Leticia Twittingdon. A few moments later Betts was leading the older woman out of the bedchamber, heading her toward the staircase and the drinks table in the drawing room, and Caroline was left alone—a condition she could not like, as she knew her husband was in the next room with his valet, likewise dressing for the evening's entertainment.

Morgan would be entering through the usually discreetly locked connecting door any time now, to inspect her appearance and judge for himself whether or not she had followed his orders as to her ensemble and the arrangement of her hair. He had been monitoring her appearance ever since the beginning of their association, but in this past week, since their marriage, she had grown to loathe these daily inspections.

Now he not only looked at her gown and her hair. Now he not only inspected her fingernails, searching for evidence of a return of her "unfortunate nervous habit."

Now he touched her as he adjusted her sash, stripped her to the buff with his eyes as he passed judgment on her choice of hair ribbons, gloves, and slippers. Now—now that he knew every inch of her, had seen and caressed and kissed and used every inch of her—his appraisals seemed like physical assaults, an invasion of the only privacy she had left to her. The only peace of mind she had left to her. The only strength of will she had left to her.

Not that he spent much time with her anymore, Caroline reasoned silently, peeking into the mirror once more and wondering if the low bodice of the silken gown might reveal an inch or two more of her than she might like. Morgan seemed to spend his days closeted in the study with the duke—and Ferdie, of all people!—discussing plans for her entrance to Society, while she was left to amuse herself the best she could. Why should he discuss his plans with her? After all, she was only the single person most centrally involved in the business, wasn't she?

He hadn't taken her riding. He hadn't given her any more lessons in history or helped her with her reading or offered any more hints as to how she should go on. She saw him only at meals—and, of course, after Betts had helped her to undress each night and then retired to her own bed in the servants' quarters.

Perhaps she shouldn't think that Morgan hadn't taught her anything in the past week. She had learned how to ride—and be ridden—their travels together taking them to the far corners of earthly delight. She had mastered the reading of his body, his every rippling muscle, and knew what that body was capable of, what pleasure it could evoke. And he had taught her more than manners. He had instructed her in the ever-changing sensations of lovemaking, the sharing of each new sublime pleasure.

Only it could hardly be considered polite or in the realm of correct manners for Morgan to come to her, take his pleasure and give her pleasure, and then leave her again—without a word of affection passing between them. Each night he came to her, each night he thrilled her beyond her wildest imaginings—and each night he left her alone again, to cry herself to sleep.

Except for last night, their first spent in the mansion in Portman Square.

Last night he had entered her beautiful bedchamber, this lovely room furnished in sweetly curving white furniture and hung with yellow draperies, and told her that, now that they had come to London, he would occupy his own rooms and not visit hers again.

Not all of the Portman Square servants could be relied upon to hold their tongues in the local taverns, even with Grisham brought along from The Acres, to ride herd on them. Word could get out, word that the Marquis of Clayton and the duke's ward were flouting the conventions, word that they were intimate. Such gossip, such speculation, would sweep through Mayfair with the speed of a falling star, and destroy her reputation.

And his plans, Caroline had thought to herself then as she thought to herself again now, but she had not voiced her conclusion aloud. Doing so would not help her, and she loved Morgan too much to complicate what, to him, seemed to be a very important mission.

Besides, she should have been glad that he wouldn't be coming to her at night anymore. Her willingness to lay aside her pride, to welcome him into her bed when he refused to acknowledge her as his wife during the day, was demeaning, insulting. She should be on her knees, thanking God that Morgan had ccascd using her, halted her willingness to be used by him, stopped encouraging her to hope that mutual physical pleasure, that intense desire that flared between them under cover of the night's darkness, could one day continue to blaze brightly in the morning sun.

She walked over to the dressing table and picked up a small crystal vial of perfume, removing the stopper in order to inhale the sweet fragrance. In another time, another place—a world that now seemed more alien to her than this world of comfort did now—the only perfume she had smelled was an absence of stench, during those times when there was no breeze wafting from the public side of Woodwere.

Would Morgan be pleased if she wore some of this French scent tonight? Or would he frown, saying nothing, and leave her torn between wanting to crawl away somewhere and die and longing to slip her hands around his starched-cravat-encased throat and choke him until his eyes popped like raisins from an overbaked tart?

"Are you ready, Miss Wilbur?" Morgan said, entering the

room. "The carriage should be brought around in a few minutes. I have timed our entrance so that we are neither too early nor too late. But if you still require your maid's services for your hair…"

Yes, choking him seemed like a reasonable alternative.

"And what's wrong with m'hair, I'm askin'?" Caroline questioned Morgan without turning around, having deliberately allowed her voice to drop nearly a full octave, to mimic Peaches at her most insulting. "Ye wanted yerself a blond, and it's blond I am. Now is it after makin' a fool of me ye'd be? Well, bad manners to ye, and no mistake!"

"Charming, my dear. Utterly charming," Morgan said, walking up to stand behind her so that she could see his handsome, expressionless face reflected in the dressing table mirror. "I cannot tell you how gratified I am to know that you must now employ that horrendous Irish cant on purpose and not out of any lack of knowledge that such low talk is definitely out of order. Your good habits learned these past few months have begun to undo a lifetime of atrocious speech and behavior. Now, turn around, please, so that I may see if the modiste followed my instructions."

Caroline closed her eyes and slowly turned, as he had ordered, feeling a kinship with those oppressed African natives stolen from their land and transported as slaves to the United States. "Would you wish to inspect my teeth as well, your lordship?" she dared to question him, remembering a drawing she had seen in one of the London newspapers just last week, a cartoon decrying slavery—not, as the duke had pointed out to her, that England had always been so aware of the injustices of the practice.

"That won't be necessary. I suppose you'll do. My mother's pearls add precisely the right touch. Sophisticated, no insipid milk-and-water puss, but you have retained enough of the look of the bewildered waif to suit our plans perfectly. Give me the ring now, if you please."

"My ring?" Caroline looked at Moran, really looked at him, for the first time since he had entered the room. He was magnificent! Dressed in the long-tailed coat and knee breeches that he had told her were *de rigueur* for Almack's, he had never before seemed quite so tall, his shoulders half so broad. Not that she'd tell him. She'd die before she'd compliment him. Her husband. Her lover. This handsome stranger who shared his body with her, but not his mind, his hopes, his dreams—his secrets. "Why do you want my ring?"

He held out his hand, and—hating herself, hating him— she laid the ring in his palm. "I should think that would be obvious, *Miss* Wilbur." He lifted her right hand and slipped the ring on her fourth finger. She felt the heat from his hands as he held hers, and looked up into his face as he began to speak again, dumbfounding her with his cool detachment as he detailed for the first time at least a part of what he had planned for her.

"There. You'll be wearing mitts tonight, rather than obscuring gloves. You've had this ring ever since you can remember, haven't you, Miss Wilbur, and are very proud of it? It is the only evidence, the only symbol of your origins, that you can claim. That and, of course, your name, which you told the charitable care-givers—now dead, alas—who reared you after discovering you sleeping on their doorstep one morning. As you were only a small child, and your command of language not fully developed, these unfortunately deceased care-givers, these temporary guardians, deduced your name to be Caroline Wilbur rather than Caroline Wilburton."

Caroline swallowed down hard on her nervousness and

pulled her hand free of his grasp. He looked so cold, so hard—
nothing like the man she loved. He was a stranger, issuing orders,
making statements, giving her a history of lies and willing her
to make them her truths. "But there was a wide search for the
real Caroline Wilburton, Morgan. Surely the searchers would
have stopped at her care-givers' house and discovered her."

Morgan's thin smile made her long to hit him. She should
have known he wouldn't be stymied by an introduction of
simple reason. Obviously this plan of his had been a long time
in the making. "Not at all. These dear people, a rather elderly
couple, were most reclusive and mistrusted almost everyone.
They were also childless, their only daughter having died in
childbirth a few months earlier, and they considered your
advent into their lives to be in the way of a heavenly blessing.
When the eighth earl of Witham—or whoever it was who
knocked at their door—asked if they had seen a small child,
they denied any knowledge of you."

"How was Lady Caroline—I mean, how was I finally discovered?" she asked. Morgan had begun to pace, and Caroline
watched in mingled awe and curiosity, for the first time in a
long time wondering what *really* lay behind his desire to have
her declared to be the long lost Lady Caroline. She gave an
unconscious shake of her head, willing herself not to think
about it again. After all, if she knew the whole of it, the truths
that lay behind his patently false explanations of altruistic
charity, she might have to hate him. She might even have to
hate herself for being a part of his plans—not caring why
Morgan wanted her to impersonate Lady Caroline, but interested only in her cottage, her allowance and, now, in Morgan
himself. She had already proved herself to be no better than
Peaches, and perhaps a whole lot worse.

"It was only by a stroke of simple, almost dumb luck,

actually. Some fifteen years passed before his grace, my most esteemed and believable father, stopped at the small, isolated farmhouse where you lived, begging a bit of refreshment and a rest from his travels," Morgan told her, having ceased his pacing to look at her intently, appraisingly, as if gauging her ability to commit what he said to memory.

"Ah, that was a stroke of good fortune, wasn't it?" Caroline felt herself beginning to grow angry. Why hadn't he been willing to keep at least some truth in his story? Was he so ashamed of her life at the orphanage, her years at Woodwere? *She* wasn't. She had worked hard, worked to grow, to survive, to become reasonably independent. She hadn't died, as so many of the orphans did, and that in itself was an accomplishment worthy of praise, of recognition. "Was I working a sampler when his grace arrived, my nails clean and my mind occupied with sermons and pure thoughts?"

Morgan's fierce look effectively silenced her, but added to her inner fury. "On the contrary. You were distraught, weeping. His providential arrival came just in time to rescue you from a life of penury as a servant at the local parish house after your reclusive care-givers fell victim to a mysterious fever. From the moment my father first saw you he was struck by your sweetness, your inborn air of gentility, and, mostly, your vague, haunting resemblance to Lady Gwendolyn."

Caroline frowned. Here was something she hadn't heard before. "I look like Lady Gwendolyn?"

"Not in the slightest. That is of no importance. Lady Gwendolyn has been dead these fifteen years. If our story is believable enough, if *you* are believable enough, we'll have Lady Jersey herself swearing to all who will listen that you're the image of your mother. It was Sally Jersey who provided your voucher to Almack's, if you'll remember. She has always been intrigued by the possibility of scandal."

"Scandal? How could returning Lady Caroline to her family be made into a scandal?"

"We'll leave that question for now, Caroline, if you don't mind. Now listen carefully. We don't have much time. It took his grace some hours to convince you of his sincerity and gain your agreement to return to The Acres with him, but in the end, once you had learned to trust him, you went with him. That same night you showed his grace this ring."

"Proving that I am Caroline Wilburton? Why?" She looked down at the ring, at the figure of a unicorn reared back on its hind legs, that was carved into the flat gold circle. She knew every line of the figure by heart, for it was the only part of Morgan that she believed to be hers. "This is all becoming most confusing. What does *your* ring have to do with Caroline Wilburton?"

His eyes became hooded, and Caroline knew he had told her all he was going to for now. "Nothing of real import will happen tonight. I am only laying some groundwork for you so that you can begin to prepare yourself for what is to come. For now you must remember only that you still do not believe you are truly Lady Caroline, even though the duke and now his son, the marquis, are certain of your identity. We went so far as to clothe you, house you, and feed you until you recovered from a debilitating bout of the same fever that struck down the people you considered your foster parents, and we helped you complete your scanty education—all so that you would feel more confident once we brought you to London to introduce you to your dear uncle, the earl, as well as to his wife and son. But you remain unconvinced, and would rather observe the earl and his family from a distance for a time, to ascertain whether or not you even wish to bring forward a claim. Kindly maintain that skepticism tonight and as we move through the Season, Caro. It will go a long way toward convincing the *ton* that you are truly who we say you are."

"No."

"No?" Morgan stepped closer and roughly grabbed her upper arms, his dark eyes flashing. "And pray tell me what is that supposed to mean? *No?*"

Caroline avoided looking at him, suddenly frightened by his vehemence. "I'm not sure, Morgan. I simply opened my mouth and the word slipped out." She raised her eyes to his, remembering how he had held her, how he had loved her—and how he always dismissed her when daylight and thoughts of his plan returned. Didn't he know, didn't he understand that she loved him, truly loved him? Didn't he realize that, if only he would trust her, love her in return—even just a little—she would do *anything* for him, without question? "Is it really still so important that you have me proclaimed Lady Caroline? Even now, Morgan?" she asked, hating the way her voice broke, the way her chin had begun to quiver. "Even now?"

He released her arms and turned his back to her, leaving her to close her eyes, fighting back tears. Leaving her alone. Empty. Peaches had been wrong, so terribly wrong. It wasn't enough to be rescued from Woodwere. She had to know the reason behind that rescue, the reason behind Morgan's plans. She could no longer hide behind her enjoyment of her new life, her clean body, her full belly, and the promise of a secure future for Miss Twittingdon, Ferdie, and herself.

She had to know.

"Morgan," she said, daring to close the gap between them, daring to lay her cheek and hands against the back of his lovely dark blue jacket, feeling the strength of him, the heat of him, through the smooth material, "please tell me why you are doing this. I know it's important to you, and I want to help you—I really do—but I have to know why."

He turned slowly, allowing her to step back, allowing her—for a moment, and a moment only—to see naked pain flicker in his dark eyes. "You are being presumptuous, Caroline, as well as ungrateful. You have long since agreed to this charade. You have benefited from and will continue to profit by that agreement. You have even ingratiated yourself to the point that my father believed you to be a gentle, innocent young woman capable of being compromised into marriage with his son."

"I *was* compromised, Morgan," Caroline retorted, slightly mollified that she had pushed him so far that he was forced to resort to bringing up an argument she already considered to have been settled in her favor. "And nobody should know that better than you, who gave me Miss Austen's novels in the first place. But the marriage was your father's idea, not mine—not that you've seemed too unhappy about your fate, for you've shown no great reluctance to share my bed each night."

Morgan smiled, and as he spoke she silently acknowledged that she should have savored her small victory of a moment ago, for yet again the battle had gone to her husband. "And why should I, imp?" he asked. "One woman is as good as another, you know, and all cats are gray in the dark."

She hit him square in the face—hit him with all her might, not standing on tiptoe and slapping his cheek the way she supposed fine ladies showed their anger, but with her balled fist, swinging from her heels—then stood there, shaking uncontrollably, as he turned on his heel and left the room.

It was only after he was gone that Caroline realized he had successfully avoided answering her questions.

CHAPTER FOURTEEN

He was a very good hater.

Samuel Johnson

MORGAN WATCHED as Caroline sat beside Miss Twittingdon, her gloved hands neatly folded in her lap, her intelligent green eyes surveying the large barnlike room with something akin to wonder as the beautifully dressed young ladies and their elegantly attired male partners whirled around and around the dance floor in the precisely orchestrated yet faintly decadent and subtly shocking steps of the waltz.

A small smile tugged at his mouth as he remembered the fury with which she had struck him, and his struggle not to reel back on his heels from the force of that blow. What a wonderful, vibrant, *headstrong* woman Caroline Monday was. And what a bastard *he* was to be using her in this way. In all the ways he had been using her, longed to continue to use her.

Morgan frowned, but only slightly, for he knew Ferdie was watching him closely. How wrathful, he wondered, was the God Uncle James seemed to have discovered in his last agony? How deep was the hell Uncle James had tumbled into when he at last fell out of this life? Would there be room enough for him beside the man once this was over? *Cold to the bone.* And he was.

Except when little Caroline Monday held him close. Little Caroline Monday, whom he longed to love and cherish and believe in. If only he could believe in himself again.

Morgan nodded to a passerby, a man he had met only twice before and could not quite like, then continued his surveillance of the room, mentally fitting himself back into the Society he had shunned for nearly three years, since his unheralded return from the Peninsula. He had gone directly to The Acres after leaving ship at Dover, his brother's battered remains ignominiously but of necessity pickled in a vat of cider vinegar, to face his father's grief, his father's denunciation, his father's damning "forgiveness."

For the first time since that return he felt truly alive again, in his element. Tonight London had become his personal arena of war, and Almack's the site of his first skirmish. His battle senses tingling, his brain all but percolating with plans, his entire being alert with the curious mix of nerves and nerve that preceded any military encounter, he put aside all thoughts of his continuing injustices to Caroline—his clandestine bride, God help her!—and scanned the room, an indifferent expression masking the fact that he was looking for his prey. His friend. His betrayer. *Richard.*

"Why is Caroline not dancing? She looks so sad, just sitting there, with only that looby Letty beside her, jabbering nineteen to the dozen and probably not saying a single thing of sense. She's been nipping at the wine again, you know. Wouldn't be surprised if she keeled over at Caro's feet any minute. Maybe then one of these perfumed asses will notice her."

Morgan peered down to where Ferdie Haswit stood beside him, dressed in the recognizable black velvet and snowy lace garb of a page—and looking like a particularly ugly child still stubbornly awake past his bedtime. "Caroline requires permission from one of the patronesses in order to dance. Are you willing to present yourself as her prospective partner in the next set?"

"Ha!" Ferdie exclaimed, drawing attention to himself from two dowagers seated nearby. "A perishing lot that would add to her consequence. Do you see them staring, my lord? Staring, then hiding their titters behind their hands. I should have brought my red balls, just as I told you I should have done. I'll stand on my head in the middle of the floor in a moment, just to give them a reason to look at me straight on, instead of peeping at me as if I wasn't supposed to know they're looking."

Morgan looked forward once more, delicately taking snuff, aware of his own finery and the impression his appearance was making on the other occupants of the room. "I told you this would happen, Ferdie. Although you may have as much right as any of us, possibly more, to be here this evening, your presence can only bring you pain. Unless—'

"Unless I do what you want?"

Morgan replaced his snuffbox in the pocket of his waistcoat and smiled down at the dwarf. "Precisely. These jackals can be vicious, but they are also depressingly predictable. For instance, right now they are all positively quivering with curiosity. Can you hear it? The air is buzzing, alive with their questions. What is that consummately eligible bachelor, Lord Clayton, doing here, when everyone knows he has always shunned with barely veiled derision this most pedestrian marriage mart? Who is that unknown girl he was seen escorting into the room, only to abandon her with the dowagers? Why on earth has his lordship, usually so sober, so detached from the whims of fashion, taken to traveling about with a costumed page—and such an unfortunately afflicted fellow into the bargain? Yes, Ferdie, the place fairly seethes with speculation, with question, with the unholy glee of stumbling onto a major *scandale* in this, the first flush of the new Season."

"I like you Morgan Blakely," Ferdie said passionately, his grin one of unholy delight. "I really, really like you. It's a shame I hate you so."

"Ah, Ferdie, but why? The liking and the hating balance out. As you've said, it's the balancing out that's important. And not to worry—your Caro is safe with me."

"Is she? Are any of us safe, excepting for his grace, hiding and praying in his Portman Square mansion, and that twit, Leticia, who wouldn't know danger if it came up to her dressed all in funeral black and introduced itself to her? This plan of yours—"

"Is about to commence," Morgan interrupted tersely, his pulses leaping, his slight nod indicating that Ferdie was to look toward the doorway. "Our luck is truly in this evening. Pay strict attention, my good and loyal page. The candles have been doused, the curtain is rising, and our little farce is about to commence. And, I pray you, remember, utter only those lines you have rehearsed. Extemporaneous speaking is not on the program this evening."

Morgan knew himself to be unusually lucky. He had secretly hoped for, but not really expected, Dickon to appear at Almack's tonight. The best he had bargained for was that word of the mysterious Miss Caroline Wilbur's entrance into polite society would reach his ears tomorrow. For Richard, like Morgan himself, had always shunned the asinine juvenility of Almack's. They'd always had better things to do, more exciting places to go, Dickon and he. Morgan, the dark angel, and Dickon, the blond god, alternately the terror and the titillation of all of London.

And such very good friends.

Now Morgan took a moment to assess the man, searching for alterations in his appearance since he had seen him last. He hadn't changed much in nearly three years, Morgan thought as Richard Wilburton, hero of the Peninsula, entered the room, stopping to raise his quizzing glass and survey the scene with a look that implied sophisticated boredom and a carefully cultivated lack of interest in his surroundings.

Tall and not particularly muscular, the Viscount was more beautiful than handsome, his blond locks glistening in the light of the chandeliers, his dark, expressive winged brows fitting accents to his startling blue, intelligent, even kind eyes. Morgan watched as Richard lifted one hand to the small diamond stickpin in his cravat, noting again how his long fingers tapered to perfect nails, his hands and fingers shaped to caress the keys of a piano, wield the fine sable brush of the artist, hold the quill of the poet.

Not like the hands of a hero at all.

Not, Morgan thought reflectively, even anything like the hands of a traitor, a betrayer, a murderer.

"That's him, huh?" Ferdie was all but leaning against Morgan, he stood that close, eyeing the viscount who was now walking toward them, skirting the perimeter of the crowded room, greeting acquaintances while deftly avoiding the whirling dancers. "That's the Unicorn?"

"The hero of the Peninsula," Morgan agreed through gritted teeth. "Come along, Ferdie, and I'll introduce you to one of England's most honored gentlemen."

FERDIE WAS CLOSE to jumping out of his skin with excitement. He could feel the tension in Morgan's tight control, his carefully measured steps, his nonchalant air. The marquis appeared outwardly polite, but he oozed a dangerous menace that the dwarf—who was already anticipating what was to happen—could see, smell, almost touch.

They were within ten feet of the handsome viscount now, and Ferdie would have sworn the air had begun to crackle.

Invisible bolts of lightning shot from Morgan's dark eyes, searing a passage through the milling dandies in their colorful silks and satins, past the feathered dowagers, their white, blubbery arms hanging over the tops of their tight above-the-elbow kid gloves. Ferdie followed in the earl's wake, not above elbowing his way through the crowd when he feared losing sight of the marquis. Finding his head to be at about crotch level to the rest of the world had long since served to keep Ferdie from being overly impressed with others, no matter how high their station, fat their purses, or fine their clothes. His world was filled with buttocks and crotches—and a good lot of them, even here, smelled no better than the barnyard or a three-days-dead fish.

Deafening thunderclaps that might only have been the sound of his own heart beating in his ears blotted out Ferdie's awareness of the musicians sawing away on their violins, and muffled the mind-numbing fall and rise of inane male and female chatter that permeated the overheated ballroom.

"Good evening, Richard. What have we come to, you and I, that we should find ourselves within these stultifying, tedious walls?"

Ferdie stopped dead, careful to remain two paces behind Morgan, as a good page should, but not so far away that he could not see everything, hear everything. And the first he saw was Richard Wilburton's handsome smile disappearing behind an expression of startled recognition mingled with fear. Yes, fear. It was a look the dwarf knew well, for it was the one his "loving" father had worn the day Ferdie had dared to stroll into the drawing room while his dear papa was entertaining a small gathering of gentlemen, and demand to be introduced. A fear that announced to all who cared to look deeply, who understood, that the man's personal world was threatening to come to a horrifying end.

What Ferdie did not see was that fear changing, hardening into a tight mask of hatred, the way his father's had. Instead, Richard Wilburton's fear remained embarrassingly visible, exposed, as his blue eyes darkened with pain, perhaps even with affection.

"Morgan," Richard said at last, extending his hand. "How good you look. It—it has been a long time, hasn't it?"

Ferdie held his breath.

"Long enough, Richard," Morgan answered at last, taking the man's hand in his own, but only briefly, as though he knew that if he held on any longer the sparks flying between the two men might become visible. "How is your dear father? Well, I trust."

"I left him only a short while ago, gnawing on a bone and coloring the air with his curses. All in all, I'd say he's as he was when you last saw him, Morgan. Only more so."

Ah! Ferdie recognized that expression as well—the quick flash of disgust, the slight tightening of lips, the small, weak joke at the absent man's expense. Richard didn't honor his papa any more than Ferdie loved his. Of the three of them, standing together on this small isolated island in the middle of this great sea of Almack's, only Morgan loved his father. Only Morgan, whose father despised him. Once more the world was out of balance.

"It's good to have you back in London. Do—um—have you seen many of our old comrades-in-arms, Morgan?"

"Hardly, Dickon," Morgan answered in a lazy drawl that sent icy fingers of anticipation crawling up Ferdie's spine. "As you might recall, there were precious few of our little group still aboveground when last you saw them. A baker's dozen, I believe. Other than myself, only Bert still survives, as a matter of fact, and he's not quite in plump currant at the moment. You missed Jeremy's funeral service, although I can appreciate how busy you were here in London, what with having to deal with being paraded about as a hero. The fetes, the balls, the celebratory speeches."

"Morgan—look, I know this is difficult for you. It's difficult for me. I wanted to come, to—"

"Snuff?" Morgan interrupted, offering his enamel-lidded box. "It's my own sort, specially mixed for me by an exceedingly expensive little man near Piccadilly."

The viscount shook his head, whether to decline Morgan's offer or to clear the air of tension Ferdie couldn't be sure. "You're right, old friend. I shouldn't have said anything. What's past is past, isn't it, and can't be undone? For a time I thought, I even hoped, that you would search me out, denounce me, challenge me. But you never did. You kept silent. Why, Morgan? Why?"

Ferdie leaned forward and peeked up at Morgan, also wanting to hear the answer to that question.

"Ah, my poor Dickon, have you been living in abject fear of me these past years, quaking at every sound, wondering when I might strike, how I might strike?" Morgan asked, smoothly stepping forward to slip his arm through the viscount's and begin to steer him down the length of the room—toward the chair where Caroline sat primly, her hands still folded in her lap. "Please accept my apologies. I should have known. Perhaps I should have penned you a note, to ease your fears. How would I have worded it, do you suppose? 'My dearest Dickon— Do not fear me. I forgive you for what you did.' My, that makes me sound almost godlike, doesn't it, or it would, if I didn't have firsthand knowledge of the lack of comfort one man's forgiveness holds for another." He looked back at Ferdie. "Come along, Frederick—don't dawdle. I wouldn't wish to lose you in this crush."

Richard stopped abruptly, so that Ferdie, who was following close behind, cannoned into him. The viscount's buttocks smelled clean, of soap and good habits.

"This page is yours, Morgan?" Richard asked, turning to look down at Ferdie, who grinned widely and waved up at him with both hands, happy to at last be noticed. The viscount must have been the only person in the entire ballroom *not* to have seen him until now—an oversight Ferdie knew could only be laid at Morgan's door. Who could afford to look at the floor when his greatest enemy in the world was smiling at him?

"Yes, for my sins, Frederick is mine," Morgan answered, dropping his arm, then carefully adjusting his shirt cuffs.

"I don't believe it. You've never been the sort who would stoop to exploiting the disadvantaged for your own consequence, Morgan. You're much too subtle."

"There are degrees of subtlety, Dickon," Morgan answered obliquely, so that Ferdie was hard-pressed not to giggle. It was a pleasure to be in this man's company, to be a part of such delicious deviousness.

Now was the moment, Ferdie was sure, to give his first recitation. He took a single step backward and pressed his splayed hands to his bowed chest, tilting his chin upward— the pose of the thespian about to deliver a soliloquy—and said importantly:

"What is small, I ask of you?
Is it how you look *or what you do?*
Do you look with your eyes or see with your
heart?
Good m'lord, what a man is, is only a part
Of what he can do, of who he is—what he
feels.
Look not with your eyes, think not with
your vices,
For a man is a man, no matter what his
size is!"

A small but appreciative smattering of applause punctuated the finish of Ferdie's poem. He took four lavish bows, one in each direction of the compass, and ended by kissing Morgan's hand. His heart was pounding again, but this time it was with exhilaration, with the sure knowledge that, at last, he had found his niche in this world, the single place where he truly belonged. He fought back grateful tears as Morgan withdrew his hand and turned to the viscount, saying, "Happy now, Dickon? As you can see, Frederick is much more than my page. He is my conscience, reminding me daily—and, alas, at times hourly—that no matter what mask we wear, we are all alike. Isn't that right, Frederick?"

"What a droll, amusing little creature!"

Ferdie turned to see an enormous woman, nearly as tall as Morgan and Richard and twice as broad, grinning down at him. He felt that if she opened her mouth only a fraction more, she would be able to swallow him in a single gulp. But she had enjoyed his poetry, and for that Ferdie loved her. He adored her! He longed to embrace everyone in this entire room! His people, his peers, his equals! At last, at last—he was where he belonged!

"My lord Clayton," she announced, eyeing Ferdie hungrily, "how wonderfully clever of you to have discovered him. You must, you simply *must* bring this little man with you to my soiree next Tuesday. I insist, dear boy—I utterly insist!"

Morgan bowed over the woman's obscenely puffed, beringed knuckles. "I would be charmed, Lady Waterstone."

Lady Waterstone's mud-brown eyes narrowed as she continued to look at Ferdie. "And he will perform for me, won't he? Percy, that naughty boy, brought me a monkey last Season, vowing the beast could sing, but it all came to naught. Not a note did that filthy creature utter, and then he climbed my draperies and wouldn't come down for two days. I was not best pleased, and lost the use of my music room for a week, until it was fumigated, you understand. Is yours trained?"

Would Ferdie relieve himself on her fine imported carpets? That was what Lady Waterstone wanted to know. She had understood nothing of his poem other than that most of it rhymed! Ferdie's heart dropped. What a fool he had been! Morgan had been right all along. These people were no better than his condemning father, who looked at him and saw only his own failings, and not his son. These people were no better than Boxer or any of those drooling imbeciles at Woodwere. They only dressed better.

"Frederick is a human being, Lady Waterstone, and an obviously intelligent, talented one into the bargain. I doubt highly that he will disappoint your guests."

Ferdie's head snapped up to hear the viscount defending him with such passion, such kindness. He cocked his head to one side, attempting to look beyond the man's beautiful face, beyond his understandable fear of Morgan, and into the man's mind, his heart.

"Yes, yes, Richard, of course you're correct," Lady Waterstone trilled, opening her fan and beginning to rapidly wave it in front of her, creating a breeze that ruffled Ferdie's hair. "When word gets round that the Unicorn has championed this little fellow, why the entire *ton* will be agog to see him! You will come to my soiree as well, won't you, Richard? And bring your dear mama. I vow, it has been an age, simply an age, since I last saw Frederica. Well, I really must be going. I'm popping off Arabella—my youngest, you know—and I must see to it she doesn't fritter the evening away talking to some half-pay officer."

Richard and Morgan bowed their farewells, and Lady Waterstone sailed away in a puff of French scent and English sweat, leaving Ferdie to look up at Morgan questioningly. "I believe your lordship may have been about to make an introduction?" he prompted as he saw that Morgan, like Ferdie himself, appeared impressed by the viscount's defense of "the page."

"Ah, Dickon," Morgan said, his smile so apparently genuine that Ferdie was convinced it was false, "do you now see why I keep Frederick? Not only does he serve me well with his immense wit, but he reminds me of my duties. I was, in fact, about to introduce you to someone. My father's ward, one Miss Caroline Wilbur. The moment I saw you I was struck by inspiration! Do you think you could do me the favor of petitioning Sally Jersey's permission for the dear child to dance? I fear that if she sits alone much longer she will wilt."

CHAPTER FIFTEEN

Whistling to keep myself from being afraid.

John Dryden

CAROLINE HAD NEVER BEEN so afraid in her life.

Not as a child of five, when she had tripped over her dragging hem and spilled her breakfast bowl in front of the headmistress at the orphanage, some of the thin gruel splashing onto the volatile woman's rusty black skirts.

Not at seventeen, when one of the attendants at Woodwere had told her she was to assist him with one of the public side inmates and then tried to back her into a corner, his hands working to loose the buttons of his breeches.

Not even on that most embarrassing day when she had stupidly stepped entirely into the linen closet at Woodwere and the heavy door had slammed shut behind her, leaving her locked up alone in the small windowless cubicle.

She shivered slightly, correcting herself. Perhaps she was not as frightened now as she had been in that closet. By the time some of the other attendants had found her, led to the door by her screams, she had been cowering on the rough wooden floor, her knees drawn up and her arms tightly wrapped about her head, reduced to babbling like a hysterical child terrified beyond reason by the red-eyed demons of the dark.

But that did not mean that she was not frightened now, sitting with a slightly tipsy Leticia Twittingdon while Morgan, damn his black soul to the deepest, most everlasting hell, was off somewhere with Ferdie, just as if she no longer existed.

How could he have brought her to this lovely if rather oppressive fairyland, then rudely dumped her on this terribly hard straight-backed chair, leaving her to twiddle her thumbs and smile at passersby like some pie-faced looby who didn't know enough to understand that she was being stared at, talked about, and pitied? Yes, pitied! She could see it in their faces—these pampered and painted dowagers, these fresh young beauties, these starched, simpering dandies, these pot-bellied belching old men.

And yet here she sat, and had sat for this past hour or more. She could perish from thirst, or keel over in a dead faint thanks to the crushing heat of the near-stagnant air—and would Morgan care? Ha! Would he even know? Her husband. Her protector. She'd get more protection from a good, loyal dog. She knew what she should do. She should stand up, haul Aunt Leticia to her unsteady feet, and walk straight out of here. *That's* what she should do. Yes. That's what she should do, all right. She should get herself up and then herself out. Then what would happen to Morgan's precious plan?

Caroline allowed her shoulders to slump momentarily in defeat. She wasn't going anywhere. She was going to sit here until Morgan came for her, until Morgan showed her what he wanted of her, what terrible scheme he had fashioned that was so important to him that he had gone so far as to marry her rather than abandon it. And then, God and all his saints forgive her, she was going to do her best to see that his plan succeeded.

"Dul— I mean, Miss Wilbur! Oh, pooh, I shall never remember, never! *Wil-burr*—it sounds like something that gets caught on your cloak when you walk through the woods. I'll simply call you Miss Caroline. Is that all right, Dul—Miss Caroline?"

Sighing, Caroline turned to smile at Miss Twittingdon. "Call me anything you wish, Aunt Leticia. Call me silly, call me stupid. But mostly, I believe, you should call me *bored*. I never knew it could be so tiring, watching other people enjoy themselves."

"Yes, yes, of course, dear child," Miss Twittingdon answered quickly. "I too was suffering from ennui—but no longer. Only look, Caro, for his lordship is coming back to us, and he is bringing Lady Jersey and the most delightfully well favored gentleman with him. Do I look all right, Caro?" she asked, pushing at her turban so that it tipped forward over her left eye. "As you are already spoken for, dear Lord Clayton must be bringing him to me. I do hope the musicians strike up a Scottish reel. I cannot be certain to remember the steps to anything more modern."

Caroline looked at Miss Twittingdon owlishly, determining that the woman genuinely believed she was about to be introduced to a dance partner, then peered beyond her to see that it was true, Morgan was heading in their direction. She deliberately raised her chin a fraction as she lowered her lashes, then pointedly turned away, hoping she appeared sufficiently aristocratic as she gave him what Aunt Leticia had called "the cut direct."

But then, only a moment later, she abandoned her pose, anxious to see whom he had brought with him. She dismissed the woman as inconsequential, for she had seen her flitting about the ballroom all evening, hands fluttering, her mouth flapping at a furious pace, her entire demeanor telling Caroline that the woman had the wit of a sparrow. It was the gentleman beside Morgan who caught and held her attention.

He was well favored, as Aunt Leticia had said. Extremely well favored. He was also tall, nearly as tall as Morgan himself, although he was assembled on a more delicate frame, his shoulders not quite so broad, his legs, although straight, not quite so muscular, his even features not nearly so impressively male, so threatening, so appealing to her senses. Walking as they were, side by side, he and Morgan looked like summer and winter, day and night—good and evil? Now why had she thought that?

And then, seeing that she was looking at him, the stranger smiled warmly, his startlingly blue eyes sparkling, and Caroline knew she had at last found a friend within these alternately pitying, ignoring, and hostile walls.

"ARE YOU ENJOYING your first evening at Almack's, Miss Wilbur?" Richard asked, handing her one of the glasses of warm lemonade he had procured from Henry Chomprey, the young man ridiculously, embarrassingly thrilled to have been noticed by the Unicorn. If he only knew. If the world, his father, if they all only knew...

Caroline nodded, accepting the glass with a smile as she sat on the stone bench located on a small balcony just outside the ballroom, then drank down its contents in a single gulp, so that he offered her his own glass, which she also disposed of with dispatch. "Oh, thank you, my lord. I had no idea dancing could make me so thirsty. I don't think I even mind that the lemonade was horrid." She grimaced, wrinkling her delightfully retroussé nose, then added, "I wasn't supposed to mention that, was I? That the lemonade was horrid, I mean.

Why is it, do you suppose, that ladies aren't encouraged to say the obvious?"

Richard smiled, liking this strange child more with each passing moment. He'd concentrate on her for the moment. It was safer than thinking about Morgan's friendly greeting, Morgan's motives. "I imagine, dear lady, that it is because females are purposely raised to ignore the obvious. Otherwise, none of you extremely bright creatures would ever condescend to speak to us men—all of whom can be inordinately *horrid* from time to time."

"That's true enough," she answered, nodding, obviously taking his words to heart. "Mor—I mean, Lord Clayton has elevated horridness to an art form, as I believe it is called. Do you know that he left me entirely *alone* in that room for over an hour? I had begun to wish I had brought a book with me, to occupy my time."

Richard leaned back against the stone balustrade that ringed the balcony, feeling the soft night breeze caress his skin, still heated from his romp around the dance floor with the lovely, vaguely mysterious Miss Wilbur. "Ah," he said, looking down at her upturned face, "then you are a bluestocking, Miss Wilbur. That too must be carefully hidden—along with your penchant for honesty—or else the gentlemen of the *ton* will flee from you in a veritable stampede, leveling everyone and everything in their path in their terror. You do know that a woman's worst curse is the possession of a brain that is stuffed with anything weightier than feathers?"

She grinned up at him. "You're not running, my lord," she pointed out, once more employing that same honesty that had led her first to warn him of her beginner's status as a dancer and then to comment on the sad state of Almack's refreshments. "Are you, then, an uncommon man?"

Richard pushed himself away from the balustrade and sat down beside her. "More than you know, Miss Wilbur," he said, looking through the open doorway to where the dancers swept around the floor in yet another dizzying waltz. He saw Morgan whirl by, a dazzlingly gowned young creature of—if Richard remembered the chit correctly—great fortune and little common sense, gazing up at him in obvious adoration, and repeated dully, "More than you know."

What was Blakely doing here? Morgan loathed Almack's. Richard smiled sadly, remembering Morgan's sometimes scathing, always hilarious references to this place, which he'd said bore all the earmarks of a second-rate horse sale. Why, before leaving for the war, the two of them had shown up just minutes before the doors closed to new arrivals at eleven—both of them three parts drunk—and announced to all the frantic latecomers that they would never be so silly as to waste *their* time squiring horse-toothed inbred nags around the dance floor while everyone knew the best rides were to be had on the fillies from Covent Garden.

Yet Morgan had agreed to squire his father's young ward to this insipid marriage mart. Poor Morgan. Wasn't it time the man outgrew his overwhelming need to gain the duke's affection? And yet who was Richard to judge, as he had not yet outgrown his fear, his loathing, of his own father? More important at the moment—what was this girl doing here, this girl with the truly fascinating, patently false name? She seemed so out of place, so frightened, and yet so challenging, and he had caught her looking at him, assessing him, as if she knew something about him that he himself did not. How had she come to be with Morgan, of all people?

Why had Morgan breached a silence of nearly three years, when Richard knew his old friend had long since ceased to be anything even vaguely resembling a friend? In order to introduce his father's ward to him? That didn't make sense. And if there was one thing Richard knew about Morgan, it was that everything the man did, every move he made, always had a purpose—even if it took some time for that purpose to be revealed to those around him.

"What do we do now?"

Richard turned and smiled at Caroline, who was sitting very primly on the edge of the stone bench, looking about as happy as he had been the day he was forced to admit to his pain and give up a molar to the tooth drawer in Piccadilly. "I beg your pardon?"

Caroline shrugged. "We've danced—although I must apologize again for stepping on your toes—and now we've sampled some refreshments. Do we dance again, or will you return me to Aunt Leticia, bow over my hand, and then run away to someplace more congenial? You look very uncomfortable out here, you know, almost as if you don't know what to do, either."

"Are you always so brutally frank, Miss Wilbur?" Richard asked. She blushed and averted her eyes, as if belatedly realizing that she had erred on the side of honesty again. He held out his hand to wave away her answer. "No—don't spoil it. I'm enjoying myself. Truly I am. And to answer your question, I believe we are expected to talk for a few moments—a simple exchange of pleasantries and perhaps a dollop or two of gossip—and then I am most definitely to return you to your chaperon."

She nodded, as if accepting his instructions, almost as if she had spent every moment of her life in the schoolroom and was accustomed to taking orders, to following rules. "What shall we talk about? I really don't know anyone important, so I can't gossip the way I heard a few of the young ladies going on about some poor man who has to marry to keep his estate from falling into the hands of his creditors and has therefore just thrown himself away on some spotty miss with twenty thousand a year and a lingering smell of the shop. I consider that to be most poor-sporting of the young ladies, for they will most probably never have to know what they are capable of doing for money, for shelter, for security, seeing that both of them were positively *dripping* jewels. I don't think I'd care to gossip even if I did know something. It all seems so useless, don't you think, when there are slaves in America and English soldiers starving in the streets and weavers being tossed out of their livelihood because of the new looms. Am I talking too much?"

Yes, she seemed very fresh from the schoolroom, and a unique schoolroom at that. "Not at all. Morgan has been serving as your mentor, hasn't he, Miss Wilbur? Your interests in the moral trials of mankind and the evils of injustice remind me very much of him. Tell me—how did you come to be the duke's ward?"

Richard watched as Caroline's fingers twisted together in her lap. "It's a very long story, my lord, and probably not mine to tell," she said, her voice so low he had to lean closer in order to hear her. "Besides," she added, lifting her head, so that it nearly collided with his chin, "I don't believe half of it anyway. Would you like to take me out driving tomorrow afternoon?"

"Would I like—*ha!* Miss Wilbur, I assure you that I should be delighted beyond words if you would drive out with me tomorrow afternoon. I can see it now, Miss Wilbur," Richard told her, helping her to rise, "you are going to be the most startlingly *original* Original ever to slay male hearts across

Mayfair. It will do my consequence no end of good to be seen with you." Holding on to her right hand, he bowed over it most formally, his lips lightly touching her skin before he rose to look deep into her rather confused yet lively green eyes, deliberately holding his smile in place as his personal world tilted on its axis. *The ring. She's wearing Morgan's ring. My ring.*

"Oh, but I don't have the least desire to slay anyone, my lord," Caroline protested hotly, startling him back to the moment at hand. "I have no intention of doing anything of the kind. I'm only here because...because..." Her voice trailed off, and she bit on a corner of her lower lip, eyeing him guiltily. "I think I'd like to go back to my aunt now, if you please, my lord."

Richard tried to decide whether he was looking into the eyes of a true innocent or was staring down the mouth of a pistol that had been personally loaded by Morgan Blakely, then aimed in his direction. The child was too ingenuous to be believed, too honest to be telling the truth, too guileless to be without ulterior motives. And the ring she wore, the ring he had very nearly kissed—what of that? Dear God, what of that?

"Of course," he said, slipping her arm through his and turning back toward the ballroom. It was time he was shed of her and left alone to think about Morgan's new friendliness in the face of all that had happened between them, to think about the ring. "I have kept you away too long as it is, haven't I? Your aunt must be worried half out of her wits."

Caroline's giggle at his last words had him raising one eyebrow, wondering what he had said that she found amusing, but then he continued, hoping his interest sounded casual: "Tell me, please, of your connection to Miss Twittingdon, as

I believe I heard Morgan refer to her. How are you connected to her?"

He felt Caroline draw in a long breath, and sensed that she was about to lie to him. "His grace the duke hired her to be my chaperon in their male household, my lord," she said, as if reciting the words by rote, "and as she is so kind, I have taken to calling her 'aunt'—merely as a term of affection." Then she smiled at him again, and he forgot that he had momentarily doubted her honesty. "She is no relation to me at all, my lord, I fear. I am really quite alone in the world, except for the duke of Glynde, of course."

"And the marquis," Richard amended, seeing Morgan approaching now that the waltz had ended. He felt suddenly cold, as if a goose had just walked over his grave, as if Death were approaching, and smiling as he came. "You also have your guardian's son to assist you as you enter Society."

"Oh—him," Caroline answered, sniffing. "I suppose so, if you call leaving me alone tonight assisting me. Why, if it hadn't been for you, my lord, I would have soon slit my wrists with one of the ivory sticks from my fan, just to alleviate the boredom. Thank you very much for being nice to me."

Richard knew he had to say something, and he decided to take the offensive again, just to see Morgan's reaction. What did he have to lose, now that he had lost everything? "In that case, you are most welcome. I am happy to have been of service, thus helping to avoid the loss of one so beautiful, so vastly entertaining as you. Are we crying friends, Miss Wilbur, do you suppose? Then you might call me Richard, you know, and I could have the honor of addressing you as Caroline, just as good friends do."

She beamed up at him, and he felt instantly protective and

most fiercely dedicated to making her entry into Society a smooth, successful one. Morgan might be using this sweet child to his own advantage, but that did not mean that he, Richard, would be so boorish. He had always been the gentler of the two, the one who saw the beauty along the path, rather than only looking forward, to the destination. Had that gentleness made him more human than the coldly calculating Morgan, more sensitive—or was it only another sign of his fatal flaw, his debilitating weakness?

"Oh, yes, please, Richard," he heard her answer. "I should like that above everything, truly I would. You're *nothing* like Morgan."

Richard's smile faded, along with a good deal of his hastily summoned bravado. "No one is, Miss Wilbur, no one is," he said as Morgan stopped in front of them. "Morgan! You have done me a great service tonight. Your Miss Wilbur is fascinating—utterly fascinating—and has even been so condescending as to agree to drive out with me tomorrow afternoon. If you believe that will be all right with his grace?"

"I should think that my father will perform handsprings in his delight, Dickon," Morgan drawled, inclining his head in a motion that swiftly brought Caroline to his side, like a well-trained dog coming to heel. "After all, to have Miss Wilbur seen with the Unicorn can only add to her consequence—as long as you promise to bring her back to us. You do have some slight problem with returning to where you have been, as I recall. I should think you'd wish to collect her shortly before five o'clock—in time for Caroline to enjoy the Promenade?"

Richard ignored the veiled insult, Morgan's artfully couched reminder. He bowed to Caroline and Morgan in turn, then bid them both a good night. As he turned away he heard Morgan say to Caroline, "Miss Twittingdon is suffering with the headache, imp. It is time for us to return to Portman Square and allow her the comfort of removing that most abominable turban."

"Yes, Morgan," Richard then heard Caroline answer, her voice devoid of the life and fire that had colored it while she spoke of "horrid lemonade" and themes of social injustice. But she went willingly, which meant that Miss Caroline Wilbur loved Morgan Blakely. People who loved Morgan Blakely would follow him anywhere, into hell if he asked it of them. Was Morgan as oblivious to Caroline's love as he had been of…

But, no. He wouldn't think of such things now. Instead, he propped himself against a nearby pillar, watching as Morgan collected Miss Twittingdon—Twittingdon, Twittingdon, where had he heard that name before?—and all three said their good-nights to the patronesses before departing the hall.

Morgan hadn't changed much in the years since Richard had last seen him, those long years since the Peninsula. Maybe he was a little harder, a little older, a little more intense—if that was possible. But nothing Richard hadn't seen before. Morgan had always been deep, almost secretive, which had made him a perfect— No, he wouldn't think of that now, either. He never thought about that nowadays. Or nearly never. It was only at night, when he lay alone in his bed, racked alternately by nameless fears and an unceasing loneliness, that he remembered, and the faces floated in front of his eyes. Terrible faces, with even more terrible eyes, mouths moving in mute appeal, in wordless confusion, in silent accusation. And that most wonderful, most beloved face of all, turned away from him in despair, in disgust, in disillusionment, in defeat.

But he wouldn't think of that now. He couldn't think of that now. He couldn't afford to remember the past, not when

Morgan had suddenly reappeared in his present. Not when that pretty child who called herself Miss Caroline Wilbur was wearing his ring…that damnable, damning ring.

What had he said when Morgan stepped in front of him unexpectedly, like some terrifying specter from the past? Oh, yes. "It has been a long time, hasn't it?" That's what he had said. And Morgan had answered, "Long enough, Richard."

Long enough. Richard leaned against the post for a long time, wondering what devious, dangerous game Morgan had set in motion this evening, trying to understand exactly what role Caroline Wilbur played in that game—and how long it would be before Morgan made his next move. He could make that move tomorrow, or not for months and months. Yet if nothing else was certain, it was certain that, after three long years, Morgan was preparing to take his revenge.

God help me, Richard prayed, closing his eyes, wishing he weren't still a coward, too much the coward to tell the truth. Morgan's hatred was preferable to his disgust. Jeremy's memory must be protected at all costs. No matter what that cost…to Morgan…to himself.

"Beware the fury of a patient man," John Dryden had written, and Richard knew that Morgan Blakely was a patient man.

Patient—and dangerous.

CAROLINE HELD MUFFIE close against her cheek, seeking warmth and comfort in the kitten's soft fur. She was very much in need of both, for the ride home from Almack's had been cold and prodigiously uncomfortable, with Morgan sitting rigidly at her side, his lips drawn together in a thin line, his fury held tightly in check, his dark mood reminding her of a lit fuse, steadily burning down to ignite the bomb of his temper.

Not that Aunt Leticia had noticed, chattering happily all the way back to Portman Square, gaily informing Morgan of the wondrous sights she had seen, the many people she had recognized from her long-ago London Season, the effects of too much heat on hair stuffed beneath silly turbans, even the thrill of meeting the Unicorn—who, according to the woman, "I vow to you, my lord, has to be absolutely the most handsome, the *bravest* gentleman in all of England since dear Lord Nelson was lost to us. Or at least that's what I heard tonight. How fortunate Caro is that you have had the pleasure of knowing him. His kind attention to her this evening will be the making of her Season! Did you have some of the lemonade? I did. Horrid—simply horrid!"

Ferdie, who hardly ever passed over an opportunity to make a May game of Miss Twittingdon, had remained as silent as Morgan, sitting in a dark corner of the carriage, his index finger stuck in his mouth, as if lost in his own unappealing thoughts. Poor Ferdie. How he must have hated playing the role of Morgan's page. When at last Miss Twittingdon succumbed to a yawn, effectively cutting off her garbled recital, Caroline had asked Ferdie if he had enjoyed mingling with Society—a mistake she immediately regretted, as the dwarf had sat up very straight and recited importantly:

If I stabbed their hearts, they would not bleed.
If I looked in their minds, I would see only greed.
They dress like kings and behave like jackals.
All I hear are their laughs, their twitterings, their
cackles.
As they point and giggle, posture and preen
Not my equals, not my peers; simply loathsome,
and *mean*."

"Why, I do believe that Ferdie—unlike you, Caroline—was not as easily impressed with everyone he encountered tonight," Morgan had then pronounced unnecessarily, which was the last thing anyone said as the carriage wended its way back to Portman Square.

But now they were home once more, and had been for over an hour. The duke had remained awake to hear firsthand how the evening had gone, and seemed pleased to learn that she was to go out driving with Viscount Harlan, although his pleasure appeared to abate somewhat under the heat of Morgan's black stare.

Aunt Leticia, her headache seemingly forgotten, had gone off happily enough with Betts, to regale the maid with details of everything she had seen and heard.

Ferdie, his neckcloth stripped off while he was still in the carriage, had moments later caught up a decanter of brandy and stomped off to his rooms, leaving the duke to frown after him and ask Morgan's opinion as to whether or not "the child" should be drinking strong spirits.

That had left Caroline and Morgan standing in opposite ends of the smaller drawing room, the duke between them, and a silence as loud as cannon fire charging the air with tension.

Caroline had looked from one man to the other, wondering what on earth could be wrong, and then quickly said her good-nights and headed for her bedchamber, wishing she could understand Morgan. He had introduced Richard Wilburton to her, hadn't he? He had all but pushed her into the man's arms, so that the viscount had no choice but to lead her onto the dance floor. She had been clever enough to arrange for them to meet again tomorrow—a move she had believed to border on the brilliant at the time.

Caroline lifted Muffie in front of her face and stared into the kitten's sleepy green eyes. "So why is Morgan angry with me, Muffie? Can you answer me that? Anyone would think he'd be grateful that I did half so well. Grateful? He should be delirious with joy! Richard is curious, very curious, and I believe he even might like me a little."

"Richard, is it, Caroline? My, my. You do learn quickly, don't you? Or did you revert to your earlier teachings and behave in the best traditions of your former teacher and twopenny trollop, Peaches O'Hanlan, inviting intimacies no young woman of good breeding would ever entertain?"

"Morgan!"

Muffie hissed and scratched at her as Caroline involuntarily squeezed her fingers tight around the small animal, and she quickly set the cat down on the bedspread. Then Caroline closed her eyes, upset with herself for being startled. When was she going to cease reacting nervously to Morgan's penchant for silent entries, his footsteps making no more noise than Muffie's cushioned feet as the kitten padded her way across the width of the satin bedspread?

Her eyes popped open wide once more as she felt the weight of Morgan's body depressing one side of the mattress, and she saw him sitting on the edge of the bed, still dressed in his evening clothes, although he had discarded his satin coat, his neckcloth, and his evening shoes. Muffie had seen him, too, and daintily picked her way up onto his right thigh, to begin kneading at the fine silk, her contented purr the only sound in the quiet room.

"Stop that, you destructive little beast," Caroline commanded, quickly pulling Muffie away before the kitten's claws could ruin the fine material of Morgan's midnight blue breeches. "Morgan, you shouldn't let Muffie do that, or else soon your entire wardrobe will be in tatters."

After settling Muffie on a pillow, Caroline lifted her eyes to look at her husband. *Her husband.* The man who had just as good as called her a trollop for doing what he had told her to do. Anyone would think he was jealous, a circumstance which was entirely out of the question, for the man had made no secret of his lack of interest in her except as a convenient recipient of his physical desire. Muffie might be a beautiful white kitten, but even she looked gray in the dark, just as Morgan had said. Her husband? Morgan was many things, but he was not her husband. Not really.

"What did you say as you burst into my bedchamber without knocking, my lord?" she asked, deciding to feign ignorance, since he seemed to have so little confidence in her intelligence. Besides, her vagueness might anger him, and right now she preferred him to be angry. "I'm afraid I wasn't really paying strict attention."

"As I recall it, imp, I commented on your use of Viscount Harlan's Christian name," Morgan answered, his thin smile telling her that she hadn't fooled him for an instant. What a miserable failure she was. She couldn't keep him in her bed, and now she couldn't even hold his anger. "I believe I also may have insulted you."

Caroline rolled her eyes. Once again he had thwarted her, confounded her, then neatly backed her into a corner. She couldn't agree or disagree with his assessment without admitting that she *had* heard what he said about two-penny trollops. When was she going to learn that she couldn't outwit the man?

Nevertheless, she tried again, latching on to his first statement. Stubbornness had kept her alive all those years in the orphanage, after all, and sustained her through all those months at Woodwere. "His Christian name? You're angry that the viscount has asked that we be informal? Why, Morgan? If you didn't want me to make any new friends, why did you introduce him to me in the first place? Richard is Viscount Harlan—but he's also Lady Caroline's cousin, isn't he? The son of her uncle, the Earl of Witham?"

"*Your* cousin, Caroline. *Your* uncle."

She waved her hands in dismissal. "Yes, yes, I understand that you want me to think as if I am truly the long lost Lady Caroline. But we're alone now, Morgan. Can't we speak freely?"

He moved slightly on the mattress, and she wondered how he could sit there so stiffly and not want to come closer...kiss her...hold her...take them both back to that ecstasy they had shared. She could hear his voice, low, and raspy with desire as he had whispered to her that last night at The Acres, when he had come to her and stayed almost until dawn. "Open yourself to me, Caro," he had said. "Let me taste you...let me feel you melt again beneath the heat of my mouth. Ah, sweet. So sweet. Yes, Caro, yes—purr for me, little kitten... Purr while I drink your sweet cream. Ah! Yes. Yes! Now hold me. Caro! Hold me!"

Caroline felt her body going warm at the memory, and hated herself for desiring a man who had taught her to feel desire and then refused to love her. She hated Morgan even more for making her love him. Damn him. *Damn him!* Why wasn't he hurting the way she hurt? Didn't he miss that closeness? Didn't he find his bed lonely? She did. The past two nights had been the loneliest of her life.

"And did you, Caro—speak freely, that is? Did you tell Richard the story I told you tonight?"

She averted her eyes, sure he could see her desire for him, her love for him, in their depths. Taking a deep breath, she forced a light tone into her voice, asking, "You mean that fara-diddle about your father discovering me living on some secluded farm?" Caroline shook her head. "I didn't know if I should. You didn't say I could, if you'll remember. You really should have been more forthcoming, Morgan, you know, if you expect me to be of any great help to you. That's why I asked him to take me driving tomorrow afternoon. I figured that I could ask your permission to repeat the lie, then tell it tomorrow. Wasn't that brilliant of me?"

Morgan propped his elbow on his thigh, then dropped his chin in his hand. He looked so weary. She hoped he had the headache as well. It would serve him right. "*You* asked Richard? Well, that must have given him pause. Yes, I believe you should allow him to pry all of that particular information out of you as you drive through Hyde Park. Only be careful, imp, in case he loses his wits entirely and runs his equipage into a tree. One more thing. Did he see the ring, or were you too busy flirting with him to notice?"

Caroline deliberately pushed her temper closer to the boiling point, believing that hating Morgan would do more to preserve her sanity than loving him would ever do. "I did *not* flirt with Richard, Morgan. What would be the point? I'm his *cousin,* remember? And yes," she told him honestly, although she wished she could get away with a fib, "Richard did notice the ring. When he kissed my hand. His face went very pale for a moment, but he recovered quickly, just the way *you* do when your father asks you to give the prayer before we eat. You knew he'd be upset, didn't you?"

"A simple yes or no would have sufficed, Caroline," Morgan shot back, pushing himself away from the mattress, to stand glowering down at her, and she knew he was about to leave the room, about to leave her lonely again, beset by unanswered questions again. Yet she felt a small thrill of satisfaction at having ruffled his feathers. If she could make him uncomfortable her evening would not have been a total disappointment. "Did he ask you about the ring—where you got it, who gave it to you?"

"No."

"Well, then, what did he say?"

Caroline stubbornly refused to speak.

"Caroline," Morgan prodded after a moment. "What did Richard say after he saw the ring?"

She smiled up at him, smugly, with her lips closed over her teeth, then said, "I'm terribly sorry, but I'm afraid I can't answer that question, Morgan. It can't be disposed of with a simple yes or no."

"Imp," Morgan countered tiredly, "it has been a long, rather intense evening. If I hurt your feelings by leaving you alone with Miss Twittingdon while I circulated, on the off chance Richard would appear, I can only offer you my apologies. But some things in this life are more important than your recently discovered feminine sensibilities. Now answer the question—what did Richard say after seeing the ring?"

Caroline capitulated, for she could see new lines of strain around Morgan's mouth. He was so very smart to have made her love him. She couldn't refuse him anything, even when he deserved noting more than to be thrown into a deep pit and covered with writhing snakes.

"He didn't say anything, Morgan, so I suggested he return me to Aunt Leticia," she said, then frowned, trying to remember everything that had happened. "Richard did ask me how I had met Miss Twittingdon. And he asked me if we could cry friends, so that he could call me Caroline and I could call him Richard. And then...and then he agreed that he was nothing like you. He said *nobody* is anything like you. I think, Morgan, that Richard greatly admires you. Oh—and he said that I am an Original, and sure to be the sensation of the Season. I really like Lady Caroline's cousin, Morgan. He's very nice."

"Christ on a crutch! Caro— Oh, never mind!" Morgan spread his hands, then balled them into tight fists, as if squeezing his uncharacteristically visible display of temper back into hiding. "Just never mind. This won't work. I don't know why I ever thought it would. I've taken an impressionable young girl into a lion's den and all she can see is that Richard Wilburton is 'nice.'"

Caroline bristled. "Well, isn't he? Almack's might be your idea of a lion's den—I know I certainly didn't find it to be the most *splendiferous* place I have ever seen—but you'll never convince me that Richard is dangerous. You're capable of a lot of things, Morgan, as I more than anyone should know, but I can't make myself believe you would purposely introduce me to someone who might hurt me."

Morgan looked at her, his expression bleak. "No, you wouldn't believe that, would you, imp? But then, you've been wrong before, haven't you?"

CHAPTER SIXTEEN

Oh God! I could be bounded in a nutshell and count myself a king of infinite space, were it not that I have bad dreams.

William Shakespeare

THE DREAM BEGAN as it always did…with Morgan. In the beginning, in the end. Always Morgan.

Morgan, riding out of the pitch dark night and into the light of the single campfire. Morgan, his strong body clad all in black, his face covered in black silk, his cloak billowing in the sharp wind, his hulking great stallion a powerful, stamping, ebony beast breathing steam like a dragon ready to send a blast of white-hot flame searing across the land, clearing his way.

So dramatic, so inspiring, so unattainable. *My friend. My friend. Always my friend. Only my friend.*

The dozen or more weary foot soldiers were frozen in shock, maggoty food halfway to their mouths, their weapons lying useless at their sides, the sentries posted on the perimeter still innocently, stupidly staring in the other direction, not aware their lines had been breached by the master of deception, the wizard of stealth, the sorcerer who could appear and disappear in a puff of smoke—the Unicorn.

It was he, Richard, who had given Morgan that name, his name and the ring he wore on the last finger of his right hand, its flat gold center flashing in the light from the campfire—flashing as Morgan's dark eyes glittered, seeing everywhere, understanding everything. Knowing nothing.

The dream took Richard back in time, as dreams had a way of skipping about, alighting on important memories, critical turning points that had seemed at the time to be nothing more than innocent moments, benign interludes of no real import. A token of friendship. To Morgan. A token of love. From Richard. A curse. Courtesy of Dame Fate.

Morgan and Richard had volunteered for the dangerous work of spying on Napoleon's armies—and, even worse, spying on Napoleon's spies—and Morgan, whose natural abilities and bent for adventure had marked him for the superior role, had been in need of a code name. It was *de rigueur* for spies to have a code name, or so Richard had told Morgan as the two of them did their best to drink themselves into insensibility, knowing they had embarked on a dangerous, probably deadly game.

Richard had looked down at his ring, looked down at his family symbol, the unicorn, and then slipped the ring from his hand. He gave it over to his beloved all-unknowing friend as they sat around a campfire much like this one, three years in the past. "Here you go, Morgan. I hereby dub thee Unicorn. Just keep a keen eye out for those virgins, all right?"

With this ring I thee wed…with this ring I pledge my… No!

The scene changed, returning once more to the night Morgan had ridden into the mountain camp.

Richard watched as Morgan dismounted in a single graceful move, swinging one leg forward over the stallion's head, his booted feet hitting the frozen ground together, the movement again unaccompanied by sound. How could there be sound, when the stallion was not saddled, his simple bridle fashioned only of black leather, with no metal bit, no chains or loops of steel to clank and chink and alert the thousands of enemies who listened in the dark, rifles at the ready. Morgan wore no spurs, carried no whip. He didn't need either, for he and his fleet-footed stallion melded into one whenever he straddled his back, the two moving together swiftly, silently, through the darkest nights, the most dangerous countryside.

"Sorry to be so delayed, Dickon. I would have thought I'd be here a week ago, but you know how it is. The enemy sometimes refuses to be cooperative. This isn't the most pleasant camp you've ever had to wait in, is it?"

"We've had better." Richard motioned for the soldiers to go back to their meal. After all, the only reason they were here was to await Morgan's arrival, their small camp serving as a way station for the most important, most secretive, most successful agent in Wellington's army. They were there only to supply him with a meal, to guard his tent while he rested— then look the other way again when he slipped back into the night once more. Yet only they, only these few loyal soldiers, were aware of the true identity of the Unicorn. Not even Wellington knew which of his two volunteers, Morgan or Richard, carried out the dangerous missions and which played the supporting role. That had been Morgan's idea, Morgan's decision. Morgan, who valued secrecy over everything. Morgan, who trusted his good friend without question.

How could such a brilliant man have been so blind?

Richard escorted Morgan toward the single tent, putting a hand on his arm at the last minute, to keep him from bowing his head and stepping inside, to delay the inevitable. "Anything?"

"Now, Dickon, you know I can't tell you anything. What if you were captured?" Morgan laughed quietly. He was clearly excited. "Oh, all right, as it's good news. Dickon—good friend—we are no longer the only Englishmen to have at last made it into France," he whispered softly as Richard leaned close. "If we take Leipzig, Napoleon will be running. Wellington should move troops toward Bordeaux now—before the French can pull back behind the Rhine—and have the Austrians cut down through Switzerland. It would be perfect, and Napoleon would never suspect it. We'll have him in a pincer once we can move. Once this damnable unexpected freeze lets up. I have it all here, in my notes to Wellington," he said, pressing one gloved hand to his chest. "After I have delivered them, after our dear Iron Duke acts as I know he will, this war will be over—at least for us."

"Thank God!" Richard closed his eyes, sending up a silent prayer of rejoicing. It was almost over. Morgan would be safe. They could go home. Three long years, and soon they could go home, go back to the way it had been. Or could they? Could anything be the same again, now that—

"Have those sentries replaced, Dickon. I could have ridden in here blowing a horn and banging a drum, and they still wouldn't have heard me. They must be too frozen to care about anything but keeping their blankets wrapped tightly about their ears. We haven't come this far to be captured by the few French who are still lurking about, looking for someone to kill. Now, come along inside and let's have a drink. I'm so cold I can barely feel my own bloody feet."

"Morgan—wait." Richard didn't know how to tell him, what words to use, but he could not allow his friend to go, unprepared, into the tent. "There's something you should know."

Morgan's eyes flashed, his body tensed, as if his every sense was alert to a hint of danger, and he cast an assessing gaze toward the soldiers, as if looking for something. "What is it? You haven't had any encounters, have you? Are there any injured? Our numbers look about the same."

Richard licked his chapped, cold-cracked lips and nervously cleared his throat.

And the dream began its downward spiral—toward the nightmare.

"It's Jeremy."

"Jeremy? Dickon, what are you talking about. Jeremy is in Sussex."

"No, Morgan. No, he's not. He's here. Here, inside this tent. He's been here for over a fortnight, having talked the men into allowing him to join them when they returned from picking up new supplies at headquarters. I don't know how he managed it, how he got so far, how he found me—found us, but—*wait!*" Richard grabbed his friend's arm as Morgan swore under his breath and turned once more toward the tent flap.

"Wait? For what, Dickon? The idiot should be horse-whipped!"

"Morgan, you can't let him see how worried you are, how angry you are. He's not much more than a boy. And he's sick, Morgan. He's got that damnable dysentery, and has had it for the last four or five days. It doesn't help that we've barely got any rations left, or clean water, either. Several groups of French troops have passed through the valley below us these last days. The men couldn't go out to hunt without chancing giving away our position."

"Christ on a crutch!" Morgan's exhaled breath was visible, even with the silk mask still covering his mouth. It was as if his curse, like his breath, had frozen in the frigid air, to hang between them. "I've always wanted him to rebel, to show some spleen—but did the idiot have to pick this time, this place? God, Dickon, we're miles behind our lines, miles from help."

Richard bowed his head. Morgan wasn't telling him anything he didn't already know. He'd been sitting next to Jeremy for the past four days, looking into those beautiful, trusting blue eyes, kissing his hand, stroking his brow, his heart breaking for the courageous, foolish young man he had last seen at that secluded inn near The Acres. Richard remembered when he had last held him, when he had last loved him—

Oh, God, oh, God, oh God! Jeremy. Jeremy. The only one who knew. The only one who understood. The only one who ever loved me.

The dream shifted, moving ahead, mercifully blocking out the next few days, days that Morgan lingered at the camp, his mission forgotten as he struggled to nurse his brother back to health.

Pictures flashed before Richard's tightly closed eyes, scattered images, fragments of memory, all of them half hidden behind the swirling snow that had begun that same night and never stopped for three days, making it impossible for anyone to leave the small encampment.

Morgan encouraging his brother to eat, denying his own hunger to give his portion to Jeremy...

Jeremy, still sick, but forcing a weak smile, mouthing jokes, squeezing Richard's hand when Morgan at last gave in to fatigue and slept on the dirt floor, his blanket beneath him...

Richard himself, acting the concerned friend, hiding his

tearing grief, his mushrooming fears—the fear of losing his beloved Jeremy, the heart-shattering fear of discovery, the fear of seeing Morgan's disgust...

Morgan wouldn't understand.

Not Morgan.

Not the man Richard had worshiped since first they had met as schoolboys, his new friend the antithesis of everything Richard's father was, yet twice—no, three times the man his father was. Not crude but strong. Not brutal but fair. Not vulgar and crass and filthy-minded but the epitome of everything Richard himself ever had wanted to be, prayed to be, but knew he could never become.

Not Morgan, who had invited him along when he went wenching—and, loving him, wanting to be with him, be like him, Richard had gone.

Not Morgan, for whom Richard had tried his best to be like other men.

Not Morgan, whom Richard had loved too much to ever reveal that love, that desire.

He wouldn't have understood.

He would have turned away in disbelief, in disgust.

Only Jeremy had understood. From the first. Even before Richard had known that this beautiful, pure young man was Morgan Blakely's brother. With Jeremy he had at last felt whole, complete—normal.

Oh, God! Jeremy! Don't die. Don't die!

The nightmare had Richard tight in its deathlike grip now and wouldn't let go.

The scene shifted yet again, and Richard and Morgan were standing outside the tent. The snow had finally abated, and the sun was visible once more.

"Jeremy's much better, but we can't move him yet,

Dickon—and now half the men are sick," Morgan was saying. "I won't leave Jeremy. But any further delay could destroy everything. Holland may have fallen to us by now, please God. Napoleon will be on the move again. You'll have to go in my place. Tonight. Ride straight for Wellington's camp, then send us help. It's time you shared a little of the excitement, my good friend, a little of the glory—on this, the Unicorn's final mission. Here—take this."

Richard felt his hand being filled by a flat oilskin pouch, the pouch containing Morgan's precise notes, Morgan's incisive recommendations, Morgan's well thought out plans for the final push against Napoleon. "No—no, you go. I'll stay."

I'll stay. I'll stay. Don't make me leave you... leave Jeremy. How can I leave either of you? You're all I have! You don't know, Morgan. You don't know!

"Morgan!" Richard sat up straight in bed, his hands pressed to his mouth, his cheeks wet with tears, his entire body drenched in sweat. "Oh, God," he groaned, looking about his darkened bedchamber, feeling physically ill. "Oh, God, Morgan. You have to leave it alone. You have to forget. I'm already a dead man. You can't hurt me. What are you going to do now? What are you going to do now?"

"I BELIEVE WE SHOULD GIVE a party."

Morgan looked around the drawing room, at the faces of the other occupants of the Portman Square mansion. His cohorts, his companions in the mission. His none too loyal allies. Had any general been forced to deal with such a ragtag, potentially dangerous group of foot soldiers?

He looked first at his father, who had become increasingly nervous as the days went on, increasingly prone to fits of prayer, expressions of misgivings, apprehensions about the wisdom of Morgan's plans.

He looked at Ferdie, who had become a minor sensation after the soiree at Lady Waterstone's and whose prearranged "spontaneous" poetry dealing with the frailties of society and the meanness of man's inhumanity to man was being repeated—and lamentably written off as no more than simple entertainment. Ferdie was champing at the bit, eager to be on with it, eager to get Morgan's business behind him so that he could concentrate on Sir Joseph, his condemning, dismissing father. Morgan was sure of this, for if Society was only parroting Ferdie's poems, Morgan was listening carefully, especially since the dwarf had lately taken to improvising new verses.

Yes, Ferdie and his personal vendetta were on the brink of becoming expendable to the mission.

Then there was Miss Twittingdon, who had begun to exhibit some anxiety about a possible encounter with her brother, the Infernal Laurence, who had unexpectedly come to the metropolis last week, his wife and marriageable daughter in tow. Miss Twittingdon had refused to go into Society since reading about Laurence's arrival in the newspapers, an unlooked-for mutiny which had limited severely Caroline's appearances, Morgan's opportunities.

Lastly, he concentrated his gaze on Caroline, his wife, his instrument, his most unwilling conspirator of all. He looked at her hands, saw that her nails were once again bitten nearly to the quick, and knew that he was responsible. She hadn't challenged him again since that night he had come to her chamber after their return from Almack's, but he was aware of her unhappiness, her confusion, even as she followed his orders, even as she drove out with Richard Wilburton, feeding him the information Morgan had authored.

She looked so guilty. So sad.

"What sort of party, Morgan?" his father asked, calling his attention back to the matter at hand. It didn't pay to think about Caroline, to think about her riding out with Richard, liking Richard, growing closer to the man Morgan knew he was about to destroy—and farther, even farther from him. Did she even remember that she was his wife? Or had Caroline's "love" for him evaporated due to his neglect, his determination, his most damnable, damning obsession for revenge?

Morgan took a seat on the sofa, next to Caroline, close to her, but more distant, more removed from her than he had been since their first meeting. "I thought a small family gathering—a reunion of sorts—would be appropriate," he answered at last, looking to each of them in turn.

THEY ALL LOOKED LIKE the footmen in the duke's entrance hall, the servants she saw carrying trays and shouldering the cloaks and gloves of visitors who deposited their belongings with them and then moved on, into glittering ballrooms, intimate drawing rooms, formal dining rooms.

Only they weren't servants, these strangely dressed men, clad in wasp-waisted satin coats fashioned in every color of the rainbow, their heads topped by curled powdered wigs. And there were women with them, lovely women who wore decorative patches on their cheeks, small patches shaped like stars or moons or even roses, and whose hair was piled high on their heads and powdered to look like snow, their stiff taffeta gowns rustling as they walked, their skirts wider, their bodices lower—and many with thin scarlet ribbons tied around their necks.

Many of them, men and women both, held feathered masks to their faces, each mask supported by a single gilt stick, their owner's eyes peering out from behind cleverly cut slits as they laughed and talked and danced and glittered beneath the light of a thousand candles twinkling from their holders in two dozen crystal chandeliers.

Such a lovely scene, such beautiful, happy people. And Caroline saw them all as if she were situated high above them, looking down at them from some hidden lair, some secret place where she could see and not be seen, listen and not be heard, enjoy and not be scolded.

But then one of the lovely ladies threw back her head, laughing at something her companion said—and Caroline knew she had been discovered. She watched, not in fear, but in happy anticipation, as the lady excused herself and headed toward the staircase, that long, wide, winding stairway that led to where Caroline had secreted herself, peeking out through the balustrades, watching the ball.

She suppressed an excited giggle as the lady hiked up her skirts while still trying to keep her mask in place, and began the walk up the staircase, shaking her head in loving disapproval even as she called to a nearby servant to fetch a small plate of party treats for the "naughty, naughty child" before taking her back to her bed.

But then, just as the beautiful lady was about to reach her, kiss her, tell her she loved her—the scene faded, then changed.

It was dark. So very dark. Above her. Below her. All around her. Everywhere. Caroline could barely move. She could scarcely breathe. And there was thunder, loud, and frightening. Then voices raised in anger, shrill with fear.

She had to get out, get out! Her fingers hurt, all her fingernails ripped to the quick as she struggled and fought and clawed to get out. Get out! She had to get out! She had to find the beautiful lady!

And at last, at last, there she was. But the beautiful lady wasn't beautiful anymore. She wasn't laughing. She was lying very still, although the echoes of her screams still rang in Caroline's head. She shook her, hit her, begging her to open her eyes. Wake up, beautiful lady. You have to wake up. Wake up. *Wake up!*

"Wake up! Caro! Listen to me—wake up! You're having a nightmare. Caro! For the love of heaven, wake up!"

Caroline fought her way back from the nightmare, back from the terror, responding to the one voice that wielded more power over her than the thrall in which the nightmare had held her.

She opened her eyes.

"Morgan," she said, knowing his name had come out in a half sob, a remnant of the tears she had shed in the dream. She felt his hands on her upper arms, could see the outline of his head and shoulders as he bent over the bed. She struggled to sit up, wiping away her tears with the heels of her hands. "I—I'm sorry."

"As well you should be," Morgan retorted not unkindly, sitting down next to her on the mattress, "calling out 'Wake up!' at the top of your lungs, so that I came bursting in here, believing the mansion to be on fire at the very least. Was it a bad dream, imp?"

She pushed herself into a sitting position against the pillows, feeling rather ashamed of herself. "It wasn't particularly jolly, or at least I can't imagine that it could have been. I—I never remember anything about it, except hearing myself calling out 'Wake up.' My bedmates at the orphanage used to pummel me with their clogs, thinking I was calling them to breakfast. But I haven't had the nightmare in years."

"How would you know? You've already said you never

remember it," Morgan pointed out, probably reasonably, although she didn't need his rationalizations at the moment. She needed him to hold her, to comfort her while she brought her emotions back under control, until she didn't feel so lost, so alone. *So cheated.*

Muffie hopped up onto the foot of the bed to begin kneading the bedspread with her splayed claws, holding a small piece of the material between her teeth, her purrs rumbling like benevolent thunder. Thunder? Caroline stuck out her tongue to moisten her suddenly dry lips. "Morgan," she said, avoiding his eyes, "you can leave now. I promise not to disturb you again, especially as I know how much it must have cost you to come to my rooms like this after you've been avoiding me this past week."

"Can't wait to be shed of me, can you, imp?" Morgan's tone didn't convey anger. If anything, it sounded bleak, almost sad. "Our dear, mutual friend Richard has been keeping you very happily occupied, hasn't he, taking you driving in the park, escorting you to the theater with his mother? For the love of heaven—his mother!"

"Lady Witham's very nice, Morgan," she told him, bristling, the lingering traces of melancholy caused by the nightmare rapidly being replaced by anger. "As Aunt Leticia steadfastly refuses to budge from this house, it was the only way I could go to the theater. And I'd wait a long time before you took me anywhere again, wouldn't I? Not that you were very nice to me last week at Almack's. Why, if it hadn't been for Richard's kindness, I would have been miserable."

"Richard. Always Richard." Morgan shifted on the mattress, leaning closer to her, so that she could see his dark eyes glittering. "Do I sense a shift in your affections? Correct me if I'm wrong, but wasn't it not that very long ago that you swore you loved me?"

Caroline shook her head. "Don't be an ass, Morgan," she said, angered past watching her words, bitterly learned lessons of self-preservation coming to the fore, lending her courage. "Richard is no more than a very good friend. Anyone would think you were showing signs of being a jealous husband. Husband. *Husband?* Do I have a husband? I seem to remember someone, something, but no, that must have been another dream. Or another nightmare. Go away, Morgan. I'll need my rest if I am to play your game for you again tomorrow night at this party you have planned."

"Little witch! I'll teach you to remember! I'll dare you to forget!"

Suddenly, gloriously, Morgan's hands were on her arms once more, gripping tightly, and his mouth claimed hers in a hard, plundering kiss as he drew her down, down onto the mattress.

Yes! Yes! Caroline's brain screamed to her even as she opened her mouth to him, as her tongue began dueling with Morgan's, as her body melted beneath his fevered touch, the weight of his body.

Morgan's mouth left hers, to begin traveling down the side of her throat, each kiss searing her skin with its feverish heat, and he buried his face in the folds of her nightgown, nuzzling her breasts through the sheer material. "So long…too long… Caro, my sweet, sweet Caro."

She roughly pushed him away with a burst of strength born of passion, so that he stood beside the bed, seemingly caught off guard by her refusal.

But she wasn't refusing him, and soon, very soon, he would know it.

Her breathing ragged, her body on fire, and miles past shame, she eagerly removed her nightgown, and threw it toward the bottom of the bed, where a belligerent Muffie began tearing at the material with her teeth and claws. Caroline didn't notice, didn't care. She had been too impatient with the barriers that had kept her from the ultimate closeness, her most longed-for intimacy.

She moved to the side of the bed, her blond hair hanging free down her back almost to her waist, approaching Morgan on her knees, her hands going to the sash on his banyan even as she claimed his mouth in a short, singeing kiss, pushing her bare breasts against him as the banyan slid away to the floor. She had taken on the role of the aggressor, the seducer, the wanton, demanding what was hers, offering him what was his. What had always been his. What would always be his, beyond death.

"Love me, Morgan," she whispered against his chest, using the tip of her tongue to lave one tight male nipple, then running her tongue in a line across his chest, to minister to the other. "I'm your wife, Morgan," she said, placing her hands on his tightly muscled buttocks, pulling him closer as she trailed wet kisses down the length of him. "And you're my husband."

She felt his hands on her shoulders, attempting to push her backward. "Caro, this is insane. Do you think me some green boy, to be taken in by your soft body, this clumsy attempt at seduction? I don't want this. I don't want any part of this."

Caroline looked up at him, hearing the lies in his voice, seeing the truth in his eyes, the pain that this lie and all his lies were costing him. "Really, Morgan? Have I upset you? Good! I'll make you angry, if that's what it takes. Angry enough to come to me. To love me. Remember, Morgan? Remember my love? Take what I can give you, my darling. Give me whatever part of yourself you can. We can do anything, fight any enemy, as long as we're together. I want to help you. I want to see the shadows leave your eyes. I want to put the past behind us. It's the future that matters. *Only our future...*"

Time hung suspended as he returned her stare, long seconds during which Caroline suffered the agonies of the damned. Had she gambled everything, only to lose? *Dear God, don't let me lose. If I lose now, Morgan will have lost everything.*

And then Morgan's hands no longer held her away, but began to draw her to him.

Heady with the rush of renewed power, nearly drunk on her love for him, Caroline dipped the tip of her tongue into Morgan's navel, sliding her hands forward to skim the taut skin of his belly, to lift his engorged manhood, to cradle the soft, velvety coolness of him as he shifted slightly, spreading his legs. For her. *For her.* Because he could do nothing else.

Because she had the power now.

It was her turn now.

Her game to play.

Her victory to be won.

Caroline heard Morgan's low moan as she opened her mouth wide, feeling strangely feral, oddly fierce, then claimed what was hers. As she closed her lips around him, she began moving her tongue in slow circles, measuring his arousal, alternately flicking at the satiny underside of his shaft, his most vulnerable, excitable area. He had taught her, taught her well, but now she was the teacher.

She was all-powerful.

She was the giver of ecstasy.

Of release.

Of blessed forgetfulness.

No more nightmares. No more pain. Nothing but each other. Nothing but their love.

She gave herself over to ministering to him, worshiping his body with her hands, her mouth, her mind screaming to him, begging him to understand.

"Caro! Christ, Caro, I can't take any more!" Morgan's exclamation came an instant before he pushed her away from him, so that she tumbled back on the mattress.

"What of Richard now, Morgan?" she teased, feeling strangely feline, infinitely feminine, exquisitely powerful. "What of Lady Caroline? Well…what of them? They are nothing. *Nothing*. You, Morgan—*you* are everything. *I* am everything. Here. Now. *Forever*. Together we can be everything, have everything, fear nothing, want for nothing. Revenge is empty, bitter, a slayer of love. Let it go, Morgan. Let the game go. Let the hate go. I don't understand it, I don't want to know it. I only want you. Little Caro Monday longs only for you, Morgan. I want to love you, cherish you, bear your children, die with you, spend eternity with you. Let it go, my darling. Let it all go."

"Little Caro," he said, leaning toward her. "My Caro. My sweet wife—who talks too much." He took hold of her legs, pulling her toward him as she grinned up at him. He stood between her thighs as she hung nearly half off the bed, as she felt him slide into her, filling her, beginning to move inside her, becoming the aggressor.

And still the power was hers. The victory was hers. For she loved this man, loved him with all her heart, all her being, and he could take only because she freely gave.

She looked up at him through the near darkness broken only by the light of one small candle, the light of the moon as it spilled across their bodies, the light of her love as it shone, unashamed, from her eyes. She pushed out the tip of her tongue, to slide it across her moist, swollen lips, to taste the salty evidence of his arousal, his capitulation. Their eyes locked as he continued to thrust into her, his deep lunges and his position combining to fill her until she believed he could touch the mouth of her womb, deposit his seed deep within her where it could not help but bear fruit.

He leaned forward, bracing his arms on either side of her head, his fingers tangled in her hair, his breath hot as it fanned her already heated flesh, his chest heaving as she reached up to press her palms against him, to slide her arms around him, pull him down to her, capture him forever within the circle of those arms, within the grip of her legs that had somehow found their way around his hips.

"You're mine, Caro," she heard him vow fervently as the tempo of his thrusts increased, driving her toward the completion that he had taught her to expect, encouraged her to enjoy.

"Yes, Morgan, yes. I'm yours," she told him, closing her eyes, doing her best to separate the passion from the love, the sensation from the emotion. "Always yours. Always and forever yours. And now, my stubborn darling, you are mine."

And then the heat took over, the spiraling phenomenon that had so surprised her the first time, that still awed her with its intensity, its ability to set her afloat, free of herself, of any lingering inhibitions, any thoughts of maidenly reserve. The varied hues of passion colored the darkness behind her eyelids, turning her world deepest blue, then sunrise red, then shining white. White-hot and pulsing and flowing and gripping and—

"Yes, Caro! Yes! Take all of me. God help me—I can't fight anymore!"

And then…when it was over…when their passion was finally spent…then Caroline held him, sheltered him, soothed him…while Morgan Blakely cried.

LATER, MUCH LATER, as she lay in his arms, her head tucked into the hollow below his shoulder, one slim leg draped across his thigh beneath the sheet he had thrown over them, her breathing even with the weight of sleep, Morgan faced the truth.

He had begun something three years ago, begun a mission—or a quest, as Leticia Twittingdon had termed it—that he had no choice but to finish now that he had set its wheels in motion at Almack's, no option left to him other than to bring the ugly business to its inevitable conclusion.

But his heart wasn't really in it anymore.

His heart—the part of him that he had always believed to be invulnerable, cold, and detached—was now and ever would be irrevocably in the small, nail-bitten hands of Caroline Monday.

CHAPTER SEVENTEEN

*Depend upon it, sir, when a man knows he is to be
hanged in a fortnight, it concentrates his mind
wonderfully.*

Samuel Johnson

"ARE YOU FEELING ALL RIGHT this evening, Dickon? You seem
somewhat distracted, and I vow I cannot like your color.
You're too pale by half. Perhaps it is time you gave up this
unnecessary business of living on your own and came home
to us."

"*Hah!* Here we go again, don't we, Freddy?" Thomas
Wilburton slammed his hamlike fists down on the dining
room table, the blow setting the crystal to chattering. "Why
not put him back in short coats, and have done with it?
Mayhap you'd like to suckle him again, put him to one of
your sagging teats, and—"

"Oh, Mother, do sit down," Richard said wearily as Lady
Witham began to rise, ready once more to flee the dining
room and her husband's crudeness. He felt numb, beyond
pain, beyond embarrassment, and most certainly beyond fear.
"Please, Mama," he added, summoning a small smile.

Richard looked to his father, who was sitting, open-
mouthed and appearing rather elated at his son's outburst.

He'd soon prick that small bubble of approval. "Papa, I believe we are obliged to have a small talk before the party this evening."

"Are you planning to offer for Miss Wilbur, Dickon? Is that why our invitation—so last-minute, so slapdash—said that there was something important to be discussed?" his mother asked quickly, so that Richard was for the first time in his life totally put out with the woman. "Oh, I realize that this is all rather sudden, but she is a lovely child, or at least she seemed so when we had her as our guest at the theater last week. Such pleasant manners, so very amenable, and quite a pretty little thing. Thomas, isn't this above all things wonderful? Our Dickon, betrothed to the ward of a duke! It's all you have hoped for, surely, and more."

"She's well dowered, then, Richard?" the earl asked, leaning his elbows on the table as he looked piercingly at his son. "Are the chit's hips wide enough to give me grandsons? I will not have my blood die out! There's no title there, but—"

"I am not going to wed Caroline Wilbur," Richard cut in forcefully, angrily, so that the earl, his avaricious grin fading, dropped back in his thronelike chair, scowling. How lovely it was to have at last traveled beyond fear of his father, fear of discovery, fear of living, of dying. "I believe there are laws prohibiting marriage between first cousins."

"Cousins? You and Caroline Wilbur? But that's impossible. Dickon, I don't understand!" Lady Witham stood—but instead of fleeing from the room she came around the end of the table to stand beside her son. "You have no first cousins, Dickon, not since Henry and Gwen were murdered by those terrible highwaymen, and dear little Caro—Caro? Oh, my gracious!" She looked to her husband. "*Thomas!* Do you think— Do you even suppose—"

"Shut up, Freddy," Thomas Wilburton ordered, glaring at Richard, who was eyeing his father carefully, piercingly, watching for some sign of understanding. But he saw nothing—save anger, and perhaps a small measure of cunning. "And take your hands off his shoulders, blast it! For the love of God, he's a man grown, and past such womanish coddling. Richard, I believe you had better explain yourself."

Several sleepless nights of thinking, supposing, and attempting to penetrate Morgan's always convoluted yet always frighteningly sane thinking processes had taken their toll on Richard, but he believed he had at last come up with a single workable theory. The duke's invitation to an "intimate gathering of a few close friends" had put the seal on that theory.

And now, now that they were due at the duke's Portman Square mansion in less than three hours, he had no choice but to confront his father with the end result of his deductions, even if it exposed him to the man's complete contempt. After all, his father already disliked him. To be despised by the man might not be so terribly difficult to handle.

It was because of his mother that he had decided to say anything at all. She had to be prepared, had to be alerted against Morgan's chosen method of revenge. If wreaking havoc on the entire Wilburton family was Morgan's price for Richard's betrayal, Richard's sin, then his mother had to be warned, so that she could remove herself from the line of fire. Otherwise he might have been tempted—no, he most definitely would have been more than tempted—to stand back and watch as Morgan enacted his vengeance.

He could not find it within himself to care about the earldom, about his inheritance. Both could be gone tomorrow, along with his good name, his position as the hero of the Peninsula, the respect and admiration of his peers. He hadn't wanted any of it in the first place, would have traded it all long since for some peace of mind, a few nights of untroubled sleep. It was his father who gloried in the name, the fame, the idea that his only son—in most ways a bitter disappointment to him—was a national hero. The single thing Richard could not bring himself to do was to hurt Jeremy's memory. Hurt Morgan any more than he had been hurt. He would allow Morgan his pound of flesh. All he had to do now was to give his father a plausible reason to believe the man wanted that revenge.

And if Morgan's revenge ended by destroying Thomas Wilburton? Well, there were always benefits to be gained from any tragedy, if one only looked for them.

"I agree, Papa," he said at last, turning to kiss his mother's hand as it lay on his shoulder; she was trying to protect him now as she had tried, and failed, to protect him from her husband for more than thirty years. "It is time I explained *myself*, for *you* have never understood me. I suggest we begin by dispelling this absurd notion of continuing what you believe to be your precious bloodline. My dear, *dear* sire, it is both my distinct pleasure and my greatest relief to inform you that I have no intention of every marrying, of ever providing you with any grandsons. You see, I have had and vow to have only one lover—and he died three years ago."

MORGAN STOOD at the doorway to the drawing room, smiling, as he watched Caroline speaking animatedly with his father, her beauty so breathtaking, her sweetness and loyalty and good nature so very visible that he wanted to grab hold of her hand, rush out into the streets, and proclaim to all who would listen that *this* was his wife—his Caro!

He had left her at dawn this morning, reluctantly, returning to her bed three times for a last kiss, a final embrace, and had finally gone only because he had a long day ahead of him.

He had so much to tell her, so many secrets that had lain in his heart for so long, for too long. But last night hadn't been the time. Last night had been a time for coming together, for pledging undying love, for setting the first of the stones that would make up the solid foundation of the life they would build together.

Now more than ever he wanted it over, all over. He wanted the past behind him—now that he had a future, now that Caroline had given him reason to look forward to that future with heady anticipation, with hope for an unexpected chance at happiness.

But taking on Ferdie and Miss Twittingdon in order to keep Caroline in line—keep her pliable, beholden—had not only complicated matters, it had given him more problems to solve before he could finish this business with Richard, end it. And he had to end it, distasteful as it all now seemed. He had already begun a chain of events that had to be measured out to their conclusions, had already lit a dangerous fuse that would burn down to the flash point whether he wished it or not. Richard wasn't a stupid man. He had to suspect; he most probably already knew more than half of it.

It was too late to turn back now, too late to avert the inevitable.

He had no choice. It was dangerous to go on; it was more dangerous to quit now.

"Like to the Pontick sea,
Whose icy current and compulsive course
Ne'er feels retiring ebb, but keeps due on
To the Propontic and the Hellespont,

Even so my bloody thoughts, with violent pace,
Shall ne'er look back, ne'er ebb to humble love,
Till that a capable and wide *revenge*
Swallow them up."

Morgan looked down at Ferdie, who was for once not
dressed in his velvet suit, but clad in the dark blue superfine he
had worn at the wedding. *The wedding.* That pitiful farce of a
wedding. Caroline deserved better. He'd have to do something
about that once this mess was over. "That was very nice,
Ferdie," he said, smiling. "However, I believe I would be
shirking my duty if I did not point out that it is also plagiar-
ism."

Ferdie's wide grin reduced him to a naughty child with the
eyes of a dead man—an extremely disconcerting image.
"Shakespeare. Yes, I know. But when it comes to expressing
thoughts on revenge, I am not too proud to bow to the master
poet. 'Bloody thoughts, with violent pace'—lovely, simply
lovely, don't you think? So exact, so *balanced*."

"As I believe I have mentioned before, my friend—you can
be a remarkably maudlin little beast."

"Thank you, my lord, you flatter me," Ferdie answered,
bowing formally. "Have you told the Twitt? Oh, my—I see
that we're puce this evening! Do you think any of those dyes
have bled into her brain?"

Morgan looked across the room, to where Miss Twittingdon, clad all in puce satin, her hair—as Ferdie had already
pointed out—matching perfectly in hue. She was sitting
quietly, staring into space, her features more than usually
vacant.

Morgan hoped she would soon be back to her nattering,
silly self, which would make Caroline happy. Besides, he, too,

had become fond of the old woman and her tales of Don Quixote and quests and Gunther ices. And he had rather enjoyed his interlude with Laurence Twittingdon earlier that afternoon. "No, Ferdie, I haven't said anything to her. I'm leaving that to the Infernal Laurence, once he arrives with his wife and daughter in tow. As I told you earlier, my man of business was very helpful on that head. It is amazing how the mere mention of Laurence's wife's parentage has proved to completely reconcile the man with the notion that his dearest sister might have every right to live her life as she pleases— and to live it *outside* the walls of Woodwere Asylum."

"It's a joy to be around you sometimes, Morgan Blakely," the dwarf said, contorting his features as he tried without much success to make use of the quizzing glass he'd bought with some of the allowance the marquis had bestowed on him, "although you let him off too easily, if you ask me. A fishmonger's daughter! You could have had him laughed straight out of London with that piece of news. Why, even I—the misshapen, disowned son of a peer—would have turned up my nose at a fishmonger's granddaughter."

"One week in Society, a small flurry of popularity, and a quizzing glass. So that's all it takes to fashion a snob? I had always wondered." Morgan caught Caroline's eye, and she blew him a kiss. Cheeky miss! "But we have other things to speak about right now. I want you to be on your best behavior tonight when you meet with your father. I only invited him in order to clear the air, to make him aware that we know who he is, and to promise him that we won't say a word if he agrees to keep quiet himself. I need Twittingdon and Sir Joseph settled, settled with Lord Witham watching, so that we can get on with—"

"My lord?"

Morgan turned to see Grisham standing beside him, his expression troubled. "What is it?" he asked, unhappy to be interrupted, wishing he felt more secure in Ferdie's avowals that he would not cause a scene, thus jeopardizing Morgan's plans for the Earl of Witham and his son.

"I hesitate to inform you of an unlooked-for development, but I believe I must ask you to come to the kitchens with me."

Morgan suppressed an exasperated curse. The butler was a good man, but he did, at times, tend to overreact to problems. "What is it, Grisham? Has the cook set fire to the place?"

The butler opened his mouth to reply but was interrupted by a loud voice emanating from the other side of the baize-covered door. "Keep yer filthy dabblers off o' me, ye bloody Englisher! It's m'Caro I've come ta see, and it's m'Caro I'll be seein', iffen I has ta blacken both yer daylights first. Caro? *Caro!* And where are ye hidin' yerself, girl? Yer lovin' Peaches is here ta see ye."

"Forgive me, sir," Grisham said quietly as Peaches O'Hanlan burst through the door and into the entry hall, her greasy red hair flying, her ragtag clothing instantly telling Morgan that life had not been treating the Irishwoman kindly since last he saw her.

"Och! There ye be, yer worship!" she exclaimed happily, flashing him her near toothless grin in obvious satisfaction as she braced her body against the door, which was moving slightly, most probably as one of the servants tried to burst through it and recapture her. "Top o'the evenin' ta ye. That there pantler of yer da's tried ta fob me off—the divil mend 'im—sayin' m'Caro ain't here. But Peaches O'Hanlan is fly ta all that and don't get fobbed off so easy, don't ye know."

"Yes," Morgan answered easily, surprised to find himself

almost pleased to see the enterprising woman who had sought them out in Portman Square. "I believe we all know quite well how very talented you are, Miss O'Hanlan. And how are my father's candlesticks? Have you succeeded in finding them a pleasant new home?"

She pushed herself away from the door, leaving it to fly open, and Grisham motioned for the footman who immediately cannoned through it, falling to the floor, to rise and return to his duties, then bowed and excused himself from the scene as well. "Now, don't ye beat the divil fer roguery, yer worship? Ye ain't gonna cut up stiff over a few bits of silver, are ye? It's stifled I was in that big house, perishin' by inches, iffen ye gets m'drift. I had ta push on—and needed m'self a bit of the ready ta push on with." Her grin widened even farther. "But I be back now, don't yer know, ta see m'Caro girl. Ye looked at her a little queer, I got m'self ta thinkin', and I wouldna be a good mither iffen I didn't make sure ye ain't tumbled her or nothin'."

"Mother?" Morgan deliberately kept his expression blank. And he had believed himself pleased to see the woman? Was he settling two of his problems tonight only to have another complication raise its ugly head? "What rig are you running now, Miss O'Hanlan?"

Peaches sashayed closer, her hands plunked down hard on her hips, eyeing Ferdie with distaste as she came. "No, and it's the truth I'm speakin' now, don't ye know, yer worship. I did a bad thing, lettin' ye take m'Caro, feedin' ye lies ye was pantin' ta hear—takin' bits and pieces of what that rum cove said all those years ago when he come sniffin' around fer a Caroline of his own ta take away with him, and even addin' some new ones I made up while I went along. But salvation seized m'soul these last months and, by the hokey, I had ta bring m'self here and ease m'mind that ye're doin' right by m'sweet baby."

Morgan sensed that Caroline and his father were standing behind him in the doorway, still out of sight of the Irishwoman. "I see. So what you're telling me now is that you lied to me that day at the orphanage. You didn't discover Caroline on the doorstep when she was three years old. Caroline is *your* child, and in order to improve your daughter's lot in life, you used information from the gentleman who had preceded me by fifteen years. Have I understood you correctly, Miss O'Hanlan?"

"Right as the fact that there little fella is the ugliest, scariest piece o'work God ever botched, yer worship! Ye speak the plain truth, I say, and shame the divil. Now, where's m'sweet *aingeal,* my angel baby?"

"She's standing right here, Peaches," Caro announced coldly, brushing past Morgan to step into the hallway. Dressed all in palest pink, her hair gleaming like sunshine in the light of the chandelier, she looked nothing like the Caroline who had enthusiastically embraced Peaches O'Hanlan that long-ago day at Woodwere. And yet, beneath the fine clothing and newly acquired polish, Morgan knew there would always be a bit of the grateful waif in his wife, a part of her that harbored a frightened child's affection for the crafty Irishwoman. "And is it an autem mort ye're up ta playin' this day?"

Ferdie tugged on Morgan's jacket. "What's an autem mort? And even more to the point—why haven't you thrown that toothless bitch out by now? Not two minutes in the house and she's got Caro talking just like her."

"Be quiet, Ferdie. Let Caroline handle this." The woman was lying. She had to be lying. Personally, Morgan knew it didn't matter to him if his wife was the product of a union between a two-penny whore and a chimney sweep, but knowledge of her true parentage undoubtedly meant a good deal to Caroline.

Caroline smiled down at Ferdie, and Morgan, following her lead, allowed himself the luxury of relaxing fractionally. "An autem mort, my friend," she informed him, "is an extremely vile beggar woman who stoops so low as to hire children in order to excite more charity as she solicits money. Isn't that right, Peaches?"

Peaches winked at Morgan. "Sharp as a tack, ain't she? Taught her all I know, ever since she was no higher than m'knee. Not that I taught her any of those jawbreaker words. Yc did that, didn't ye, yer worship? And it's a fine job ye did!" She pressed her hands to her scrawny breast, blinking rapidly as if to fight back happy tears. "And ain't she dressed up smart, with all those pretty shingerleens? Those real pearls, yer worship? Must be, and worth a tolerable mess o'blunt. *Go méadaí Dia duit.* May God bless ye, Caro. Now come kiss yer poor old ma who's loved ye truly all these years."

Caroline stood very still, shaking her head, saying nothing. Perhaps she wasn't so sure that the Irishwoman was lying. Morgan fought an insane urge to choke Peaches O'Hanlan.

"Morgan? Do you think she's speaking the truth?" The duke was extremely pale, his arms wrapped tightly around his frail body as he peered from Peaches to Caroline, as if looking for some hint of a family resemblance. "I had almost begun to forget, even dared to hope, but—"

"I don't know, Father," Morgan interrupted tersely, "and frankly, I don't really care. We all have enough on our plate right now without dealing with this at the moment. *Grisham!*" he called out, then waited for the butler to appear—which he did most promptly, probably because he had not retreated more than a single step beyond the baize-covered door. "Kindly procure a pistol for yourself from the study, load it, and then escort Miss O'Hanlan upstairs to the servants' quarters. If she attempts to leave—shoot her."

"The divil ye say!" Peaches swiftly looked right and left, as if measuring the shortest route to the street, through either the baize-covered door or the front entrance, then smiled ingratiatingly at Morgan. "Now, yer worship, ye can't go puttin' a hole through a lady fer tellin' the truth, can ye? Bring me a Bible, why don't ye? I'll swear it there, and it won't be no calfskin fiddle neither when I kiss that holy book. Not me! I'll kiss the book, not m'finger, and may I be damned to everlastin' hellfire if I—"

"Very good, sir!" Grisham replied, cutting off Peaches in mid-appeal, smartly snapping his heels together in the way of a soldier. "It would be my distinct pleasure."

"Morgan—"

He turned to Caroline, who was looking at him imploringly, as if reluctant to believe what Peaches had said, yet fearful—or relieved?—that it might be true. "Later, imp, I promise," he said, lifting her hand to his lips. "For now we shall content ourselves with introducing you to another *relative,* your uncle."

"And Sir Joseph," Ferdie piped up as Grisham, looking oddly competent with a pistol in his hand, marched a still bitterly complaining Peaches toward the back stairs. The dwarf's words reminded Morgan yet again, unhappily, that his path to revenge—and beyond, to his future with Caroline— still contained more than a few stumbling blocks.

At that, the knocker banged loudly, and a footman raced to open the door. The evening, already off to a shaky start, had to be faced without further delay.

As the duke quickly shooed all of them into the drawing room, so that they wouldn't look to be hovering at the doorway, awaiting their guests, Morgan felt Caroline's small hand slip into his and he squeezed it, hoping to lend her some of his courage, his resolve.

RICHARD STOOD beside the mantelpiece, cradling his drink in his palm, astonished at his cool composure, actually pleased with himself for the first time in many long years, and content to stand back and watch Morgan's revenge unfold—with a few alterations, of course.

The drawing room was elegant, just as Richard remembered it, with high stuccoed ceilings, tall windows looking out over the square, and well-proportioned furniture upholstered in grass greens and softest yellows. A lovely room, a comforting room, a place where guests could relax, be at their ease—be taken off guard. Hardly an imposing setting for a denunciation, but it had been Morgan's choice, not Richard's, and he supposed it must be preferable to some of the other venues his old friend might have chosen.

Like the ballroom at Almack's.

And what an odd assortment of guests he had assembled. The tall, beak-nosed, chinless Laurence Twittingdon for one—who seemed to be as much or more of an ass than any man Richard could recall ever having met—although he, his wife, and his sallow-faced daughter seemed well pleased to have been invited and were even now fawning over an obviously disapproving Miss Leticia Twittingdon, who appeared rather ashamed of her relatives.

Richard looked to where his mother was sitting beside Caroline, twisting her handkerchief between her hands, a sickly smile on her face, her eyes still red-rimmed from weeping. He would much rather that she had remained at home, but she had insisted upon coming along, saying she had to "be a supporting prop to my son in this time of trial." Richard didn't believe she understood the half of what had gone on in his father's dining room. All she had really seemed to absorb was the distressing noting that she might never have a grandchild to dandle on her knee. And she wouldn't, poor lady. Richard refused to marry, to inflict himself on some sacrificial virgin longing to be a countess. He had lived a lie for too many years. He would not live that same lie again. Not even for his mother.

The Earl of Witham was another matter. He had understood everything he was told, and Richard believed that his father—this man who enjoyed being the Earl of Witham, the father of the Unicorn—more than most men feared death, would be willing to give in to Morgan's "blackmail" in order to preserve his position.

It must have taken Morgan a long time to think up this scheme, locate the soft underbelly of the Withams, and then produce a young woman credible enough to present as Lady Caroline. Now, Richard felt sure, Morgan would demand that his father acknowledge the so-called Caroline Wilbur as his long lost niece, bestowing upon her the inheritance she had been denied. Morgan would do this, of course, in exchange for his silence about his, Richard's, "unnatural, even illegal proclivities."

Or so Richard had purposely allowed his father to believe.

Only that wouldn't be quite true. Morgan would demand that Caroline be recognized, all right, but only to punish Richard for Jeremy's death, although Richard felt confident that Morgan would never say so. He would say only that he planned to expose Richard as a coward who had abandoned his fellow soldiers, then set himself up as the hero of the Peninsula.

Richard's father had taken a chair beside his grace, and was downing tumblers full of gin nearly as fast as he could pour them from the decanter he had rudely lifted from the drinks table moments after entering the drawing room. His complexion was cherry red; perspiration beaded his forehead. He only nodded by way of answering the duke's excruciatingly civil remarks as to the weather, the sad condition of the king's health, and the possibility that England would have a pleasant spring. For once, his normally bombastic, overbearing father had been rendered speechless.

Richard truly believed Morgan should thank him, for he had made his old friend's work that much easier by reducing Thomas Wilburton to a point where he would agree to anything.

He wondered if he should feel guilty for his father's discomfiture, and then quickly decided he could not compound his sins, his failings, by becoming a hypocrite. *Learning that his only son is a man-milliner, as dear Father so delicately refers to such persons as myself,* he decided, smiling, *seems to have succeeded where all Mother's "Please, Thomases" have failed.*

"Ah, you're smiling, Richard. How nice that you are enjoying yourself, even if I cannot say the same for your father, who is looking almost distracted," Morgan said from just beside him, so that Richard was hard-pressed not to flinch, so startled was he by the man's appearance when he hadn't heard him approach.

"Still the master of stealth, I see, appearing without a sound, without a hint that you are about to pounce," Richard answered, looking deep into Morgan's dark eyes, searching them for some sign that he remembered how it had been, how they had been before. "Do you remember Keating, Morgan? He took to wearing an amulet to keep him safe from your sorcery."

"Keating died in the first volley, his body sprawled alongside those of Jones and Waters. I watched as they beat Pippin to death."

Richard closed his eyes, fighting a wave of nausea, remembering Pippin, the youngest of the soldiers, the most prone to asking him to please write letters to his ma for him. "Morgan, I…"

Morgan held up his hands, smiling. "No, Richard. Please don't spoil it now by apologizing. You're three years too late. For Jeremy. For Pippin. And most definitely for me. Have you seen Frederick? His father should be here any moment."

Fighting through his misery, Richard struggled to understand Morgan's last statement. "His father? You've invited your page's father? In God's name, man, why? I've already alerted my father to what I believe to be your plan, as I supposed you wished me to do. But I have to tell you, Morgan, you've selected odd witnesses for this revenge you're playing out tonight. First Twittingdon, and now Frederick's *father?* I don't understand."

Morgan's smile sent a chill down Richard's spine. "Revenge? You do seem to harp on that theme, don't you? My dear friend, whatever are you babbling about? I have no revenge planned. Only a family reunion of sorts. Ah, here is Sir Joseph now. Please excuse me, Richard, as I have taken over the duty of host at my father's request."

Richard looked toward the doorway, to see that Sir Joseph Haswit had entered the drawing room, his aging yet still handsome face a thundercloud. Haswit—Frederick's father?

Unbelievable! Inconceivable! And most ludicrously funny, considering that Haswit was a supercilious bastard. Richard leaned against the mantelpiece, a slight smile tugging at the corners of his mouth as he watched Morgan walk across the room to greet the man. First Twittingdon, acting as if the greatest pleasure in the world was to claim a puce-headed old biddy as his beloved sister, and now Haswit—father to a dwarf. *Ah, Morgan, old friend, you are a pleasure to watch, even if I know that tonight I, too, will become your victim.*

"Where is he? Damn you, Clayton, where are you hiding him? I heard about your damnable dwarf, but I never believed—I never dreamed… And then this afternoon, when I opened that miserable invitation… Where is he, blast it!"

"Sir Joseph!" Morgan exclaimed genially, his hand held out in greeting. Richard listened intently, knowing that a genial Morgan was Morgan at his most dangerous. "What a delight to see you again. When was the last time? Could it have been at White's? No, that's right, you were blackballed, weren't you? Something to do with your lucky streak that had entirely too much to do with extra trumps, as I recall. Forgive me for mentioning it. But to answer your question, I believe Ferdie—the 'damnable dwarf' you spoke of—is about somewhere, most probably primping for his long-awaited reunion with his beloved father—the man who disowned him, locked him away in a madhouse, then proclaimed himself childless."

There came a collective gasp of disbelief from many of the occupants of the drawing room. *Yes,* Richard reflected, taking a sip of his drink, *this is almost better than a play.*

Sir Joseph's eyes narrowed dangerously as he glared at Morgan. "Why are you doing this? What possible reason could you have to do this?"

That's an extremely good question, Sir Joseph, Richard

answered the man silently, *although I do believe I am beginning to understand precisely why Morgan is doing this. It's brilliant, actually. Deceptively convoluted, yet amazingly simple. Subtle. Deadly.*

He cast his gaze about the room, gauging the varying responses to Sir Joseph's angry outburst. Everyone was staring at Sir Joseph, some in confusion, some in dawning knowledge, some in open disgust. And Sir Joseph was staring back at them, seeing a miniature of Society's reaction, knowing he was being judged—and condemned.

"Lies! All lies!" Sir Joseph exploded as Morgan stepped back, leaving the man very much alone in the center of the large room. Spreading his hands, Sir Joseph looked first toward a glaring Caroline, then to the sad-faced duke, to Richard's weeping mother, to a clearly confused yet slightly guilty-looking Laurence Twittingdon, and lastly, to the earl of Witham, who was gnawing on one fleshy knuckle, watching with less enthusiasm than he would normally have shown in such a situation, as Sir Joseph's remaining composure disintegrated before his eyes.

Sir Joseph half ran across the room, stumbling, to approach Richard, pressing both hands on his forearm. Did the pathetic man really think he had found an ally? "You—help me. You can—you're the Unicorn, for the love of God! Help me! Somebody has to believe me! I mean it! I swear it! I have no son!" He shook Richard's arm in his fury, in his fear. "*I...have...no...son!*"

Richard Wilburton looked down at Sir Joseph's hands, so that the man quickly removed them. "My dear sir," he said smoothly, "I quite sympathize. Many of us would exchange our relatives if we could. I imagine, for instance, that Frederick is equally unhappy about acknowledging an ignorant fool like you as his sire."

"Hate for hate, pain for pain,
Only death can erase the stain.
Death for glory, death for fame,
And everyone will remember my name!"

Richard looked toward the doorway, to see Frederick Haswit standing there, clad not in the dandified velvet and lace of a page but in the fine, understated tailoring reminiscent of Morgan's own severe fashions. He made an odd picture, rather as if Richard were looking at the young man through the wrong end of a spyglass—his short, bowed legs and too-short arms overshadowed by his painfully prominent chest and large, melonlike head, his stubby child's hands visibly trembling as he used them to grasp a pair of heavy, long-barreled dueling pistols.

Richard's gaze shifted to Morgan, who was standing very still, halfway between Frederick and Sir Joseph, his expression more pained than perturbed. "More poetry, Ferdie? I thought we had agreed to do away with cryptic verse, as it has had precious little effect to date. Hence this gathering—remember? It's unfortunate, yet true, that some people have to be tapped on the head with a red brick in order to see what is before their eyes. Those pistols, however—I think they're overdone."

"Shut up, Morgan," Frederick—Ferdie—Haswit bit out, causing Richard to admire the odd young man more than a little. Of course, being armed to the teeth did make his bravery less than it might otherwise have been. "You've done your part. You've brought him to this house. Now it's my turn."

"You're going to shoot him, I suppose," Morgan drawled with maddening calm, reaching into his waistcoat pocket and extracting his snuffbox. "Would you mind terribly if I removed myself out of range of those evil-looking pistols? Your hands are shaking in a most alarming way, my little friend, and I shouldn't like to think one of those things could go off while I am still blocking your target. Richard? You might also wish to consider a prudent retreat. This is Ferdie's revenge, not mine."

Ferdie's eyes, intent on his father, shifted quickly to Morgan. "You—you're not going to try to stop me? I made up that verse just for this moment. Made it up, memorized it, just for this. I am going to kill him, you know. He descrves it."

"He most certainly does, Ferdie. Go ahead—have at it. Now, while he's standing near the hearth. I wouldn't want the housemaids trying to scrub Sir Joseph's claret out of this fine carpet."

"*No—wait!* I had to do it," Sir Joseph cried out, dropping to his knees at Richard's feet, looking up at him pleadingly. "Don't you see? Everyone would laugh—stare! I couldn't even marry again, produce another child. What if that child were like *him?*" he asked, pointing an accusing finger toward Ferdie. "Then it would have been *my* fault, not hers. I couldn't risk it. I couldn't take the chance. All I could do was hide him away, try to forget. Do you understand? You *have* to understand!"

"No. I hesitate to point this out, but I don't have to understand. You could have applied for my father, however, for he might have been able to offer you sympathy. Now please excuse me. This is a new jacket, and I wouldn't wish to see it ruined when the bullet explodes your brain."

Richard stepped away from the cowering, cringing Sir Joseph, caught between admiring Morgan's coolness at what had to be an unlooked-for development, and a niggling fear that this time Morgan might have misjudged his man. Ferdie looked angry enough to actually shoot down his father in cold blood. And what of that poem? That second pistol? Once Sir Joseph was dead, Richard felt certain Ferdie planned to turn the second pistol on himself. Did Morgan realize that?

"Well, what are you waiting for, Ferdie?" Morgan's voice was softly goading. "It's not yet the seventh of June—your twenty-first birthday, Ferdie—but surely it's close enough. Balance it out, Ferdie. Balance out the pain, the hurt, the denial. The world ends, not on June seventh, but now, tonight—or does it? Why, you know what, Ferdie? I don't believe it does. It couldn't. I, for one, have plans for tomorrow. I think I'll take Caro out for a drive. Perhaps Leticia and my father will come along as well. To Richmond Park, I believe. Lovely place. It's a shame you won't be with us. But you can't be with us. You'll be dead, won't you? Pity."

Ferdie began jumping up and down in place like a spoiled child denied a long-promised treat. "Shut up! Shut up! *Shut up!* He has to die, Morgan. He has always had to die!"

Morgan didn't answer, so that Richard once more became aware of the others, who had all gone as still as statues the moment Ferdie entered the room. The only sound that could be heard was Sir Joseph's weak sobbing—and the earl of Witham's hiccups, the curse of too much gin combined with what had to be one more in a small series of nasty frights.

But then, just as the silence, the tension, grew to almost impossible proportions, Caroline stood up and walked to Ferdie's side. "You don't have to do this, Ferdie," Richard heard her say reasonably as she knelt down beside him, her innocent beauty a startling contrast to the dwarf's homeliness. She was speaking softly, intimately, so that Richard had to listen closely to hear her. "I know your father has hurt you, but if you kill him he will have won. Don't you see? The best revenge is the one Morgan has already gotten for you, just as he has done for Aunt Leticia. Your life—free of your father, free of Boxer, free of Woodwere. The only reason Sir Joseph is here tonight is to promise that he will not try to hurt you— in return for our promise not to expose him as your father. And why would we be doin' that, I'm askin' you, Ferdie?" she added, her voice taking on a delightful Irish lilt. "It's not as like you'd ever be wantin' to claim the miserable bugger."

"As I may have mentioned before, Ferdie," Morgan said softly, "you are twice the man I'll ever be."

Ferdie's lips twitched, even as tears coursed down his chubby cheeks. "Thank you, Morgan. I'll try to be. And my father is pitiful, ain't he, Caro? Hardly worth the killing. Here—you'd better take these before they go off. Pistols are dangerous, you know. And—and it wasn't a very good poem anyway, was it?"

Richard looked at Sir Joseph, who was on his knees in front of the fireplace, covering his head with his hands, and silently agreed with Ferdie's assessment of the man. He most definitely wasn't worth the killing. He also understood. At last. He understood the reason behind this party. Laurence Twittingdon and Sir Joseph were not much more than examples, proof of what Morgan—Morgan the all powerful, Morgan the *Unicorn*—was capable of if people did not cooperate with him. He had gathered them all here to make demands of them, to watch as they acceded to his demands—all in this public, yet not quite public, venue. He had given them a taste of humiliation, of what he could do to them if they dared to cross him, of how he could destroy them, and both Sir Joseph and Twittingdon had capitulated. And soon now—now that Caroline had possession of the dueling pistols and Ferdie was smiling—Morgan would tell Lord Witham and his son what he demanded of them.

Very civilized. Very subtle. Extremely effective.

Richard walked over to where Morgan was standing and said in genuine delight, "All in all, my onetime friend, I'd say this is one of the better parties I've attended in many a Season."

Miss Twittingdon, showing her firm misunderstanding of all that had gone on, immediately clapped her hands and piped up: "Oh, good. Will we be serving tea now that Ferdie has done with playing the fool? Minuscule moron! Tea, you know—Dulcinea! Please get up, dear, it is not polite to sit on the floor—is always served at the best parties."

CHAPTER EIGHTEEN

*Only the brave know how to forgive.... A coward
never forgave; it is not in his nature.*

Laurence Sterne

CAROLINE WAS SO FURIOUS with Morgan that she did not at first
really take in what happened after he relieved her of the
dueling pistols and helped her to her feet. Hadn't he realized
what a chance he had taken by goading—yes, goading—
Ferdie into shooting Sir Joseph? It must be above everything
wonderful, she thought angrily, to act the puppeteer, to pull
the strings and watch while everyone danced, but there were
limits to what a man should take it upon himself to do!

She retreated to her original set, to sit glowering at her
beloved, still trembling with nerves after Ferdie's near
disaster. Morgan was arrogant. He had been arrogant since the
first time they'd met—arrogant even before she had known
the definition of the word. He might be her husband, and she
might love him beyond her own life, but he could be maddeningly, infuriatingly, *insufferably* arrogant.

And depressingly *obvious*.

He was showing his power, that was what he was doing.
It was as plain as the beaklike nose on Laurence Twittingdon's
pinched face. Morgan had set out to prove that he could

destroy those who did not go along with whatever he asked of them. She shouldn't have been surprised. Hadn't he done the same to her—dangling a new life for Ferdie, Aunt Leticia, and herself in front of her, if only she would do what he wished, while the horror of Woodwere was the only alternative? He could be very cold, Morgan could. Cold, hard, and single-minded.

All right. So he had been successful with Laurence Twittingdon. That was no great feat. It wasn't as if Aunt Leticia's brother was a *dangerous* sort. He wasn't about to slap Morgan's face and demand satisfaction on the dueling field. No. Laurence Twittingdon possessed all the spine of a jellyfish, and besting the man, bending him to his will, had entailed little more than the introduction of a helpful piece of information and a veiled threat. Anybody could have taken care of Laurence Twittingdon. Given the same information Morgan had enlisted his man of business to ferret out as ammunition, *she* could have taken care of Laurence Twittingdon.

But Ferdie and Sir Joseph—ah, that had been a different kettle of fish entirely. What could Morgan have been thinking, to even allow both men under the same roof? Ferdie could have killed the man! Ferdie could have been hauled away to jail and then hanged for his crime!

All this to impress the earl of Witham with his power? Surely there could have been another way?

Once this evening was over, and it had better be over soon, before Caroline exploded with her suppressed rage, she was going to have a long, long talk with her husband. She would learn once and for all why he wanted revenge against the Wilburtons, and she wouldn't be put off by her love for him. She would demand that he— But what was this? Morgan was speaking again, once more from his position in the very center of the room. Ferdie was gone, as were Sir Joseph, Aunt Leticia, and all the depressing Twittingdons.

How could she have missed their departure?

How? In her present state, she most probably wouldn't have noticed if the Prince Regent himself had come riding through the door, perched atop an elephant! Shaking her head to clear it of her lingering nervousness and anger, she leaned forward in her chair to listen to her husband.

"...and so, my lord Witham, Lady Witham, I apologize again for the theatrics. I hadn't planned for them to be quite so dramatic. However, I believe our two *reunions* tonight, along with Sir Joseph's agreement to accede to my wishes concerning his son and Mr. Twittingdon's decision to restrain himself from any further interference in his sister's life, prove the point I am about to make."

"What do they prove, you arrogant bastard?" Lord Witham demanded. "That you're nothing more than a filthy black-mailer, trying to force this unknown chit Richard told us about down our throats? That you could destroy all of us if the whim took you? That you're so *superior* to the rest of us?"

I may not particularly like you, Lord Witham, Caroline thought, looking at the red-faced man with distaste, *but I can't say that you don't seem to have a good understanding of my dearest husband.*

"If I might interrupt?"

Caroline looked toward Viscount Harlan as he stepped forward, his demeanor much as it had been that night at Almack's—friendly, open, and oddly comforting. It was dif-ficult to believe that he could have been fathered by anyone so grossly barbaric as Thomas Wilburton. In truth, he reminded her much more of her own husband. Her own husband, who suddenly didn't look quite so sure of himself.

"Thank you," the viscount continued when Morgan bowed his agreement. "First, my friend, I must congratulate you on your finesse. You have a remarkable and most original way of making your point. However, as there are ladies present, I believe I should step in now so that we do not have to endure an explanation of your reasons for presenting Miss Wilbur to Society. I have already informed my father of my very real, my very deplorable *sin,* and in return for your silence he has agreed to acknowledge her as his long lost niece. Isn't that what you were attempting to convey, Papa?"

"*Bastards.* You're all bastards! My *son*—I should have strangled you in your cot! Your *friend!* Miserable, backstabbing, blackmailing whoreson!"

Caroline looked to Lady Witham, who was sniffling into her handkerchief, and then to the earl, who had turned even more red-faced, his large, beefy hands closed into white-knuckled fists. She didn't understand. She knew, had guessed, that Morgan wanted revenge against the Wilburtons. But what was the "sin" that had set Morgan on this course?

"May I take it from that outburst that you are admitting your culpability, your guilt? That your father agrees?" Morgan asked, one eyebrow raised inquisitively.

"It does."

"And you're not going to fight this? You aren't going to call me out?"

"Again, Morgan, you are correct. I could never do that."

The duke, whose presence Caroline had nearly forgotten, pushed himself slowly to his feet, then held out his hands as if to call a halt to the proceedings. "I don't want to hear any more, Morgan. You were wrong to do this, and I was wrong to agree to it. Hearing the man admit his guilt doesn't help. I had thought, I had hoped…but it doesn't change anything. I can't listen to any more. All this time, and for what?" Caroline watched silently as, without saying another word, the man quit the room.

And Morgan. She saw that he was watching his father as well, his expression painful to see, his love—always offered, never requited—burning in his eyes. Caroline averted her own eyes, knowing he wouldn't wish her to serve as witness to this latest rebuff, this new disappointment.

Instead, she brought her thoughts back to the moment at hand. The earl had agreed to what? What had Richard confessed to doing? It was as if Morgan and Richard had spoken in a secret language known only to the two of them. They had conversed in the way of very good friends, who understood each other, who could look into each other's mind, reach each other's thoughts, and finish sentences the other had begun.

After a few moments Richard exhaled his breath on a sigh, then continued: "Did my father—did we—have any other choice but to agree? You are not particularly transparent, Morgan, to most people. But we have known each other well, haven't we? This has to stop here, for everyone's sake. I will tell you what we've decided, and then, if you agree, I should appreciate your consideration in allowing me to escort my mother home. You have no quarrel with her, certainly?"

"My apologies to you, ma'am," Morgan said sincerely, inclining his head to Lady Witham, "but, as is the way of war, there are always unavoidable casualties among the innocent. I could have applied to my father for confirmation, but as you have seen, he has already gone off to nurse his own wounds. Richard?"

"Thank you, Morgan. Now, to tell you what my father and I have agreed to do. We will host a rather large party next week, during which we will introduce your discovery, your Miss Wilbur, as Lady Caroline Wilburton. We will smile, we will appear overjoyed to welcome her back into our family. And we will see that she receives all the estates and funds originally bequeathed to her by her father, the seventh earl. It will nearly beggar us, but we will do it. That is what you wanted, isn't it, Morgan, what this travesty has been about? To see the Wilburtons brought low?"

Morgan smiled weakly, and Caroline bit her lip. "No, Richard," she heard him say quietly, honestly. "Actually, I wanted you dead." Morgan appeared confused, at sea, and perhaps even somewhat ashamed, and Caroline suddenly wasn't angry with him anymore. As he spoke, he looked toward the doorway through which his father had left the room. "I had always thought so, at least…but now I know that wasn't what I really wanted at all."

MORGAN OPENED the connecting door between his chamber and Caroline's, wondering if he should be prepared to duck as she launched a porcelain figurine at his head. Earlier she had looked incensed enough to use one of the dueling pistols on him, even as she stood beside him when Richard and his parents hastily took their leave, her chin held high, as if she totally agreed with what he had done.

What he had done. And he had done it, hadn't he? He had passed off the orphanage brat, the asylum servant—passed off Caroline Monday—as Lady Caroline Wilburton.

Stupid. *Stupid. Stupid!*

This wasn't over. This was far from over. He had known that Richard would see through so obvious an appellation as Caroline Wilbur. He had actually counted on it. But he had badly misjudged Richard's reaction, hadn't counted on his easy capitulation—which had taken the power from Morgan's hands and placed it in Lord Witham's.

Caroline was, now that the earl was about to acknowledge her, the ward of the one man in England who would most benefit if she were to die. Even now, although she was married to Morgan. For she was underage, and the marriage could be, would most definitely be, ruled invalid. Witham was still Caroline's legal guardian, her closest male relative and beneficiary. Of course Witham had claimed her. Of course Caroline, his well-loved niece, lamentably would perish in a sad accident within six months of the grand party the earl had said was already in the planning stages.

Why hadn't he seen that possibility? Why had he been so sure his plan would unfold the way he had envisioned it?

Morgan had always known that his planned revenge would put Caroline in danger if anything went wrong. Always, in the back of his head, buried nearly as deep as his conscience, he had known that. But only now, now that Richard had trumped his ace, as it were, by agreeing to Morgan's terms, was he willing to take out what he had done, the way he would take a shirt from a drawer, and examine it.

"Ah, here you are at last, my lord idiot," Caroline said as Morgan entered her room. "Tell me, are you happy now? You have at last gotten just what you wanted, haven't you? I'm actually to be named as the real Lady Caroline. Unless, of course, we decide to believe Peaches, which only a mutton-headed idiot would ever do, as the woman would swear she was the devil's sister if she thought there was a profit to be made from it. But let us return to this business about my recognition as the long missing Lady Caroline, shall we? My goodness, does that mean I shall be presented at court? I suppose I should thank you for all those lessons, for the Prince

Regent won't be serving turbot every night, will he? Will I
have my own carriage and three houses to live in, when I can
only live in one at a time anyway, and new gowns every other
week, and shall I go to Almack's and sip tepid lemonade? And
where will you be, my dearest husband? Will you ask me to
dance, become one of my many beaux? If I'm not dead, that
is. You have thought of that, haven't you? I have. I've been
doing quite a lot of thinking these past hours—something I
should have started doing a good deal sooner. Lord Witham
didn't exactly fall weeping on my neck, happy to have his
niece returned from the grave, did he? Perhaps that's because
he is already preparing a new one for her?"

Morgan looked at his wife, who was sitting in the middle
of the wide bed, Muffie on her lap. Dressed as she was in a
snow-white dressing gown, she looked as soft and touchable
as the kitten, but her biting, incisive arguments had made her
unattainable. She had gone straight to the heart of the matter,
even discounting Peaches O'Hanlan's claims, as he'd hoped
she would. He wasn't surprised. Hadn't he always known that
she was an intelligent minx, sopping up information like a
sponge? But did she have to disseminate that information so
well, see the rest of it so plainly? Did she have to make it
obvious to him that she knew he had lost control of the situation?

"I never believed he would acknowledge you," Morgan
heard himself admit as he spread his hands helplessly. "I had
it all worked out. I did everything tonight save threatening to
hire a town crier to broadcast my supposed discovery of the
missing Wilburton infant to the whole of London. I thought
the earl would publicly deny your claim—my claim—and
Richard would then be forced to call me out. He certainly
would have had enough reason, and he could hardly have

refused to seek satisfaction if he wanted to remain the hero of all those silly, simpering idiots in Society. But Richard turned the tables on me. They've agreed to recognize you, and there will be no duel. None of this makes any sense, Caro. Why didn't they deny you?"

"You're asking me? Morgan, much as I hesitate to point this out—you haven't told me enough to know why *any* of this has happened! I'm only the lowly servant you hired, the one who wasn't supposed to ask any questions. I was simply ordered to do what you said, earning myself a cottage and an allowance, remember? I didn't ask questions. Although, in hindsight, it appears that I certainly should have, doesn't it?"

Morgan held out a hand to silence her and, bless her, she immediately subsided. He had to think. He had to push his disappointment over his father's reaction, his own bitter disappointment in himself, out of his mind—and *think*.

He began to pace, his gaze concentrated on the floor, his mind reeling as he considered the impossible. "Uncle James said it, but I didn't really believe him. The man never told the truth in his life, never did anything unless it benefited him. But what if he was right? What if— My God! What if the earl really *did* have something to do with the murder of his brother and his wife? What if he believes I have somehow stumbled onto proof of his guilt? The fear of *that* disclosure would go far beyond anything I might have said about Richard, would cut immeasurably deeper than having to acknowledge you as Lady Caroline. Witham—a murderer? I mean, I've thought about it, entertained the possibility, but I've never *really*..."

He ran a hand through his hair, trying to cudgel his brain into remembering more of what his uncle had said. He could recall only the man's curses and his very real fear, his overly dramatic entreaties for Morgan to save his soul, save both their souls.

Abandoning that line of thinking, he concentrated on the events of the evening just concluded. "Thanks to Richard's unexpected intervention, I never did get to say what I wanted to say tonight, missed the opportunity to explain my reasons for doing what I've done. And even if I had spoken, none of what I know to be true can ever be proved. Not really. To the world, Richard is the Unicorn. Richard is a hero. Even Wellington believes it! It would only be Richard's word against mine. That's what has always stopped me before—I couldn't *prove* anything. It would have been my word against that of the Unicorn. I would have been despised, and laughed out of England.

"Then Uncle James handed me a gift, a way, the seed of a plan. It seemed perfect, and it would force Richard onto the dueling field, where I could finally take my revenge, leave the earl to mourn the loss of *his* son. But if the earl actually believes I know something about the murders themselves— if he thinks I could expose *him,* and the devil with what I know about Richard—then he might be frightened enough to give in to my demands, at least until he can think of a way to get himself shed of me. The party isn't until next week. That gives him plenty of time. With me gone, and my father already abandoning the field, he'd have nothing to fear from you, Caro. Maybe he's not protecting Richard—maybe he's protecting himself!"

Caroline must have slipped from the bed, for suddenly she was standing in front of him, blocking his way, so that he had to stop his pacing. "I'm going to count very slowly to ten, Morgan, and then you're going to sit down and tell me everything. Everything about your uncle. Everything about Richard. Everything about this damnable revenge that has consumed you to the point where you don't even notice that your wife is looking extremely fetching in her new dressing gown. Is that understood?"

Morgan smiled, taking hold of Caroline's slim shoulders. His head was pounding, and he wanted nothing more than to return to the study and think about what had happened tonight, but she was right. "I've been babbling, haven't I, darling? I'm sorry. And you're correct. You deserve an explanation. Come with me, you might as well be comfortable while I tell you what a fool I've been. But I warn you, it isn't a particularly pretty story."

"I never supposed that it was. Secrets usually aren't."

He led her back to the bed, dropping a kiss on her forehead as he tucked her legs beneath the coverlet, then joined her, sitting with his back against the headboard. "I'll begin at the beginning, I suppose," he said, not without pain, knowing he was going to put into words events that he had kept silent about for three years, events he had tried his utmost to forget, to expunge, along with his desire for revenge against Richard. He would tell Caroline everything, not leaving out the worst of it, as he had with his father the day he brought Caro to The Acres. "I'll begin with Jeremy."

Caroline slipped one small hand into his, but as he began to speak he forgot her, forgot where he was, and saw only the campsite, felt only the stinging bite of the frigid wind as it swirled on the mountainside, remembered only the frustration he had felt as he watched his men fall sick, one by one— waiting. Waiting for help. Waiting for Richard.

Three days and nights, then four, then a week, he told her, until he was forced to acknowledge the fact that Richard must have been captured. Jeremy had already broached the subject, had asked if Morgan believed that Richard was dead, then retreated into a silence he hadn't broken for two more days.

Jeremy, who wasn't a soldier, who never should have been in that godforsaken camp in the first place, had yet to learn how to deal with death, how to bury the pain, how to grieve, yet still carry on.

They were isolated, alone, cut off from the rest of the world, thanks to Morgan's desire for secrecy. Only Richard knew where they were. Only Richard knew that they actually existed. Only Richard could have saved them from the elements, from hunger, from the French. Hancock had already succumbed to dysentery, and Bert, a man from The Acres, would die soon as well if the wound in his leg wasn't attended to by someone with more surgical training than Morgan possessed.

And they couldn't leave. The retreating, regrouping French were all around them now, and moving the sick and injured men would be impossible. He would have a better chance of slipping a camel through the eye of a needle than of threading his men through the troops ringing the countryside below the camp.

Even worse, if Richard had been captured, if Richard was dead, then Morgan's coded messages concerning troop strength and movements had fallen into enemy hands. Richard, whom Morgan had stupidly told things he shouldn't know, might have broken under torture, exposing thousands of Englishmen to danger.

There was nothing else for it—Morgan would have to leave the camp. Leave his men. Leave Jeremy. He would have to abandon them to their own devices, their own resources, and possibly sacrifice them—sacrifice his own brother—in order to save thousands of lives.

It was the most difficult decision Morgan had made in his life, the most personally painful, but he had made it. He'd had no other choice. He would set out on foot as soon as it grew dark, locate friendly troops, deliver his information, and then bring help to the stranded camp. If it wasn't already too late. If his return wouldn't be too late.

But as it had turned out, it was his decision that had been left too late.

He had traveled less than a mile before he heard the sharp crack of rifle fire behind him. Running, scrabbling for footholds on the slippery hillside, he had retraced his steps, at last throwing himself onto the frozen ground of an outcropping above the small English camp to watch as two French soldiers held Jeremy between them, his brother frantically struggling to break free. Three of Morgan's men lay quite dead in grotesque sprawls around the campfire one of them must have built, against his express orders, the moment he left the camp.

Morgan's hands had drawn into fists, and he had longed to race into the center of the camp, to rescue Jeremy, who was wearing the distinctive, damning jacket of an officer. But he couldn't. He had only a single pistol. He couldn't risk his information, the information that might save a thousand lives, for the honorable, yet suicidal gesture of going to his brother's aid.

All he could do was stay where he was. Stay where he was, and watch.

He knew it wouldn't take long.

And then it had begun. The questions. The torture. Jeremy's bravery as the desperate French beat him, demanding information in exchange for his life and the lives of his fellow soldiers, had not been without its effect.

But Morgan remained silent.

This was war at its most raw, its most brutal. His countrymen's cause was nearly lost and, obviously believing that he had stumbled onto a secret operative, an English spy, the officer in command was willing to try anything, dare any brutality in order to learn what he could about Wellington's movements.

Jones was shot early on, as he tried to crawl away into the underbrush.

McDonald, already sick, was kicked to death so that Jones's attempt might not be repeated.

Pippin died next, calling for his ma.

After that, Morgan had lost track of the dying.

But Morgan had watched. He'd watched as the French once more concentrated on Jeremy. He'd watched as Jeremy bled. He'd listened as Jeremy screamed. In the end, just as dawn was breaking, when the French had left the camp, he'd scrabbled down the frozen hillside and taken Jeremy's broken body in his arms. He held his brother as Jeremy breathed his last, his final words not for his brother…or for his father…but a wretched cry to Richard Wilburton, to the bastard who had left them behind.

"Only Bert," he ended, "who was unconscious inside the tent, and I were still alive an hour later, when we were rescued by a small troop of Austrian soldiers. I brought my brother's remains home with me—to give him the hero's burial he deserved, to face my father's damning 'forgiveness.'"

"And Richard?" Caroline's question was hardly more than a whisper as she lay against his chest, her beautiful green eyes awash with tears, eloquent with pity. "What happened to Richard?"

Morgan gave a short, self deprecating laugh. "Why, imp, Richard had indeed somehow succeeded in getting through to our troops. My information had been delivered. Consider this, Caro. I thought I couldn't fight for Jeremy's life because of the information I held. I couldn't attempt to save him, or even die with him. Or so I thought. But I was wrong. Richard *had* done it. He'd gotten the notebook through. He had simply neglected to return for his comrades-in-arms, a reasonable omission, I suppose, for a man so instantly famous. He made England before me, to be hailed as the Unicorn, England's greatest, most successful, bravest of spies, and was being feted at Carlton House even as I was driving a hired farm wagon from Dover to The Acres, with Jeremy's body stuffed in a barrel of vinegar, to present to his father for burial. I was home for about six months before I rejoined the troops, and have been back at Clayhill again ever since Waterloo. Richard has never tried to contact me, never offered an explanation for his desertion. When I saw him at Almack's last week it was the first time I had laid eyes on him since he rode out of camp on my horse, wearing my cloak and mask, carrying my messages—and vowing to return as soon as possible."

"No wonder you've wanted revenge, Morgan," Caroline said, sitting up, looking at him tenderly, nearly unmanning him with her quick understanding, her caring heart. "And no wonder the duke agreed to help you, even if you only told him that Richard left you and Jeremy to die after promising to return to camp. You were right not to tell him everything, for he never would have survived hearing that Jeremy died after being tortured. But I never would have waited three years for my revenge! I would have ridden straight to London and denounced Richard, then shot him—squarely between the eyes! How could you have waited to long?"

"A good question, imp," Morgan replied, pulling her down beside him once more. He felt drained, yet oddly calm, after telling his story. It was as if he had exorcised some deeply rooted anger, perhaps even some well-hidden guilt. Guilt because he should have known, should have acted differently in some way, somehow saved his men, saved his brother.

"I had more than a few old scores to settle relating to my service during the war, not the least of which was one that included my esteemed uncle James. I preferred to get those out of the way before going after Richard. I believe, evil as it sounds, that I wanted Richard to suffer, to feel the fear, to know that I would be coming for him someday—but he'd never know when, he'd never know how."

Caroline pulled away from him, and he looked up at her questioningly. "You disapprove obviously. You think I'm as my uncle painted me—cold, and heartless. Perhaps even godless."

She shook her head. "No, Morgan. I wouldn't presume to pass judgment. I never had a younger brother. I don't know how I would have reacted if I had suffered what you've suffered. I haven't wanted a father's love enough to risk everything to gain a single word of affection. But I do know one thing. Your revenge hasn't gone as planned, has it? Richard hasn't called you out. He told his father all about his desertion before you could reveal it, and now his father has agreed to acknowledge me rather than chance having you kill his son. Richard, it would seem, is acting the coward again, hiding behind his father—except that I don't believe that. And, from what you were babbling about when you first came here tonight, neither do you."

Muffie padded her way up Morgan's chest, to rub her face against his chin. Impatiently lifting the cat away from him, Morgan left the bed, to begin pacing once more. So, Caroline had seen what he had only now begun to admit to himself— that he hadn't really wanted revenge. Even he hadn't recognized that fact until a few hours ago, when his father left the drawing room. Punishing Richard was not what all this mess had been about. What he had wanted, what he still craved, what he now recognized as an impossible dream he would never possess, was his father's approval, his father's love. Had Cervantes ever explored this sad theme? What would Miss Twittingdon's Don Quixote have to say about Morgan's unachievable quest?

"Well? Do you still think Richard is a glory-hungry coward—that he deserted you and Jeremy and your men?"

Morgan called himself back to attention. He had faced disappointment before, had learned to live with the unalterable, and would handle this latest frustration as well. "If only he had come to me, if he had made so much as a single attempt to contact me, to explain…" He shook his head. "To answer your question, imp, no, I don't believe that Richard deliberately left us to die. Perhaps my anger, my grief, made me believe it once, but now, having seen him again, I keep remembering his bravery, his loyalty during all those years of playing at spies. Which brings us back to Uncle James, I'm afraid—and to *this*." He reached into the pocket of his banyan and removed the pendant his uncle had given him.

Caroline scrambled off the bed to take the pendant in her hand. "Why, Morgan, it's a unicorn! How beautiful! It's almost like the one on my ring—on your ring—only much more intricate, and so beautifully colorful." She frowned. "But how—"

"The pendant is a replica of the Wilburton family crest. Richard gave me his own ring when he decided that my code name should be the Unicorn—a romantic indulgence I granted out of friendship. My uncle swore that, after watching the Earl of Witham murder his brother and the countess, he removed this pendant from the neck of the real Lady Caroline before depositing her at the orphanage in Glynde. You see, again according to my uncle, he had extracted payment in exchange for his silence for many years before Lord Witham demanded he produce you. When he couldn't, when Peaches judged him and found him wanting, Uncle James was left to dabble in espionage in order to supplement his income. A particularly unlovely man, my uncle."

Caroline squeezed the pendant in her fist. "Then it's obvious, Morgan. No one could have invented such an unbelievable story. The Earl of Witham murdered his brother! Why did you ever question it?"

Morgan smiled, opening Caroline's hand before the delicate golden pendant could come to grief in her death grip. "You'd have to know a great deal more about my uncle before you'd understand, I suppose. At the time, I believed he had commissioned the pendant himself after learning my code name, only to watch from hell as I ran myself in circles trying to gain my revenge by proving his lies. It wouldn't have been a particularly formidable task, you understand, duplicating the pendant, and it was an obvious choice of 'proof.' Everyone knew Lady Gwendolyn always wore the pendant. Ah, Caro. Even now I'm having difficulty believing any of this is true. The real pendant is most probably buried along with the countess, not that I'm planning to violate her grave—again, something my uncle would have counted on."

"May I have it, Morgan? May I have the pendant?"

He stared at her piercingly, surprised by her request, looking for the reason behind the question.

"It—it's pretty," she said, then bit her bottom lip. "I don't care if it's real or not, although I think we both are beginning to believe that it is. And I know I'm not Lady Caroline. At least a dozen new orphans are brought to Glynde every year, and the real Lady Caroline probably was one of the unlucky ones who died within weeks of their arrival. But I could have known her, Morgan, I might even have shared a bed with her. It is possible, you know. I know the pendant doesn't belong to me, but... Oh, maybe I don't know why I'm asking, what I'm really feeling at this moment. I just feel so *sorry* for Lady Gwendolyn, for the real Caroline. I almost feel that in a small way, I *do* know them. Am I being silly?"

Morgan lowered the chain over Caroline's head, watching as the pendant slid down her chest, to hang just below her breasts. "Considering the fact that—if the impossible is true, and the Earl of Witham did murder his brother in order to inherit the title—my attempt to force Richard into a duel has resulted instead in placing my most beloved wife in danger, I would say that you deserve anything you want, my love."

Caroline smiled, then laid her head against his chest. "But the Wilburtons won't hurt me, will they, Morgan? You won't let them. You are the Unicorn, the best and bravest hero England has ever known. Even if England *still* doesn't really know it, will never know it! Even more importantly, I am your wife, and you love me. You would never let anyone hurt the woman you love, now, would you?"

"Your logic is faulty, even if your sentiments are flattering," he told her, burying his mouth in her hair. "But you are right in one thing. I love you more than life itself, and I will not let anything happen to you. I promise you, Caro—no one will touch you!"

Her grin, as she looked up at him, was positively wicked. "No one, Morgan? Now you have disappointed me, as I do believe I very much would enjoy being touched tonight."

"Oh, really, imp?" he answered, slipping an arm beneath her knees and lifting her high against his chest. She knew him so well. Knew that he no longer wanted to think about what had happened tonight, think about what he would have to do tomorrow. She was offering him herself, as sweetly as she had that first day under the trees, but now not with the naiveté of innocent infatuation but with the intriguing knowledge and sweet promise of a well-loved and loving woman. "And what sort of touching do you have in mind, if you don't mind reversing our roles and taking on that of my teacher?"

She nibbled on the underside of his chin, her moist tongue drawing small circles on his evening-beard-roughened skin as he carried her over to the hearthrug in front of the dying fire, then giggled as he laid her down. "I think, my lord husband," she said, drawing him close, "I should prefer to begin with the touch of your fingers on these ridiculous buttons I have closed so carefully, in anticipation of your slipping them free of their moorings…one by one…by one."

He released the last button, then slid his hand inside the gaping bodice of her dressing gown, capturing one perfect, well-remembered breast in his hand. "Ah, yes, Morgan—you are an apt student." He felt her thigh against his leg, for she had already opened herself to him. "But you do have *two* hands—don't you, my lord? Surely you can find some occupation for the other one?"

"Minx," he growled low in his throat, already pushing her gown aside in anticipation of her next instruction. He moved his hand slowly, lingering over the satiny smooth skin of her inner thighs, skimming her flat belly, tracing the curls from side to side, hinting at but not really dipping lower—to where she would have to tell him to go.

"Morgan. *Morgan,* please," she whispered, her arms around him now, her body lifting from the hearthrug, her breath warm against his ear as she nibbled at him, tugging his earlobe with her small white teeth, prodding him with the tip of her tongue. "*Please,* Morgan."

He pushed her down once more, moving his mouth to within inches of hers, staring deep into her eyes. "Tell me, Caro," he said, intently searching her face, and seeing her arousal as it dueled with her sensibilities. He continued to play with one engorged nipple, rubbing it between his fingers, while his other hand lay flat against her abdomen, spanning her from hipbone to hipbone, applying gentle pressure, his fingers kneading her soft skin. "You are the teacher, remember? You must tell me what you want."

"I want—I want you to love me," she said evasively, pressing kisses against his chin even as she moved her hips invitingly, her body speaking most eloquently even as her mind seemed unable to put her desires into words. After her boldness, her overt seduction of him last night, her sudden shyness was proving to be wildly provocative. She was showing him more of her endless variety, more of the Caroline he knew he would love forever, even if he would never really know her.

"I'll always love you, imp. Always." He lifted his head out of her reach and smiled down at her, silently thanking her for the lifelong gift of her love, this momentary miracle of forgetfulness. He inched his hand lower, tangling his fingers in her warm living silk. "Now, my wise and beautiful mentor, please—tell your most devoted student what you want."

CHAPTER NINETEEN

'Tis strange—but true; for truth is always strange;
Stranger than fiction.

George Noel Gordon, Lord Byron

CAROLINE WORE her pale blue muslin walking gown, because Morgan had told her that he considered blue her best color and she was feeling extremely charitable toward her husband this morning. Betts had brushed her long hair over the curling stick, so that there was a hint of a wave in its normally straight length as it was held back from her face by a wide watered-silk ribbon. Her soft kid slippers were white, as was the reticule she carried, although she had no intention of leaving the mansion. She simply liked the reticule. Surely that was reason enough to carry it.

And, suspended around her throat, its delicate gold filigree and lovely colors contrasting well with her gown, was the Unicorn pendant.

There were still problems to be faced, and Morgan still had to go to the earl and retract his claim that she was the missing Lady Caroline, but she felt fairly confident that at last she and Morgan were on the road to a lasting happiness. He had even promised to talk to Richard, and to *listen* while Richard talked to him. Why, if she weren't an entirely silly, empty-headed miss, she might even believe that finding love had made Morgan a better, more accepting, more forgiving man.

"Good morning, your grace," she said happily, slipping into the drawing room, although that smile faded fractionally when she saw that the duke, sitting in his usual chair, already had his prayerbook lying open on his lap, his usual frown accentuating the lines of sorrow etched into his face.

She didn't know what she felt more—pity for the man who had lost his younger son or anger for the stiff-backed fool who refused to recognize how much his remaining son loved him. "I trust you are feeling more the thing today," she continued, hoping to lighten his mood. "We had quite an unusual evening last night, didn't we? Aunt Leticia is already teasing Betts into locating a dye to match her purple gown, for her next foray into Society you understand, and Ferdie should be very pleased with himself. I know I'm extremely proud of him."

The duke looked up from his prayerbook. "Frederick forgave his father. Forgiveness is our duty as good Christians." He nodded twice, as if agreeing with his own words, then frowned. "Forgiveness is also, unfortunately, not a natural precursor to forgetting. No matter how I try, no matter how much I pray, there is still no forgetfulness. Morgan has failed me yet again. I should have known. He has always been a disappointment."

Caroline mimicked the duke's frown, struggling to decipher the word "precursor," but quickly abandoned the exercise as her temper, which seemed to reach the flashing point very quickly where her husband was concerned, took control over her better judgment. "Do you know something, your grace?" she said, walking across the room to stand directly in front of him. "There are times when I wonder why

Morgan even cares what you think of him, why he went to such lengths to try to win your love."

"Morgan?" The duke looked at her blankly, as if she had suddenly spouted Greek to him. "My dear girl, I don't know what you're talking about, truly I don't. Of course I love Morgan. He is my son."

"No, your grace," Caroline asserted, jamming her fists onto her hips, deciding she would just as happily hang for a sheep as a lamb. "Morgan is not your son. Jeremy was your son. Morgan, your grace, is your *victim.*"

The duke's chin quivered as tears sparkled in his faded eyes. "Jeremy? What has Morgan told you about Jeremy?"

"Has he told me about how Jeremy ran away, how he followed Morgan to France—how he died? Yes, your grace. I know it all—more than you'll ever know."

"I know enough! Jeremy was sacrificed because of his misguided devotion to his brother! He died because of Morgan, because of Morgan's selfish, single-minded foolishness, Morgan's godless pursuit of excitement, Morgan's wicked determination to steal Jeremy's affections!"

"Really?" Caroline gripped the strap of her reticule, longing to use it as a weapon with which to beat some long overdue sense into the duke's head. "If you feel that way, your grace, why did you go along with Morgan's plans for revenge against Richard, against Lord Witham?"

The duke bent his head, rubbing at his forehead. "Foolishness. Simple foolishness. I wanted to believe it would help to see Richard branded a coward who deserted his friends in order to save his own life, to watch him brought low, to watch as the Earl of Witham suffered some of what I am suffering.'

"And to watch your son go off to duel with the viscount?" Caroline suggested, her blood cold, at last seeing everything so clearly, so impossibly logically. "To hope that Morgan would die?"

William Blakely, Duke of Glynde, and God-fearing Christian, pushed himself slowly to his feet to look directly into Caroline's eyes. "Yes, my child. To hope that Morgan would die. To pray that they would both die, that he and Richard would succeed in killing each other. To banish Morgan from my sight, from my conscience, from my memory. He should have been the one to die. Not Jeremy. Never Jeremy. God took the wrong one."

Caroline squeezed the reticule's straps until her fingertips dug into her palms. Perhaps being an orphan, never knowing her parents, had been a blessing she hadn't really fully appreciated until this moment. "Yes, your grace," she whispered hoarsely at last, when the silence, and the tension, had become almost unbearable. "God did take the wrong one. He should have taken *you*. Then maybe he could have explained to you how the world *really* works!"

And then she turned on her heel and walked out, wondering what sort of maggots could reside in her head that she had thought the morning to be so fine.

"GIVE ME A FEW MOMENTS, and then you may show him in. Oh, and Hatcher, please see that we are not interrupted, even if you should hear—ah—any *disturbance*. Thank you, Hatcher."

Richard sat sprawled in the black leather chair, already dressed for the day although it had only just gone ten, and looked longingly toward the decanter on the drinks table, its amber liquid contents beckoning.

"Claret is the liquor for boys; port for men; but he who aspires to be a hero must drink brandy."

Who had said that? Oh, yes. Sam Johnson. The dear, dead Samuel Johnson. Richard shook his head. No, he'd leave the brandy where it was. After all, he had tried Johnson's prescription three years ago. Crawled inside a decanter and dedicatedly remained there for nearly four months. Just long enough to get him through those first fetes, those first speeches, those first award ceremonies—those interminable evenings when, his beefy arm draped around his son's shoulders, weighing Richard down like an anchor, the Earl of Witham had bragged to all who would listen about his hero son. The brandy hadn't worked then; it had neither dulled the pain nor lessened the memories.

There was no reason to believe it would work now.

Now, with Morgan at the door, Morgan on his way to the study, Morgan, looking for answers.

Richard picked up his teacup, then thought better of it when he felt his hand trembling, and replaced it on the tray beside him. He had to keep his composure, had to forget how much he loved Morgan Blakely, remember that he had to protect him, protect Jeremy's memory. Protect himself. Protect himself? Was that what he had been doing? He eyed the decanter once more. Perhaps just three fingers of the mind-numbing stuff?

"You've been expecting me."

Richard turned his eyes to the doorway to see Morgan's tall, wide-shouldered body nearly blocking the light from the window in the hallway. Morgan hadn't asked a question; he had stated a fact.

"Actually, old friend, I expected you hours ago. Was it so very difficult—leaving her bed?"

Why had he asked that? Wasn't it enough that he had seen the love in Morgan's eyes last night when he looked at

Caroline Wilbur? Had seen the look he once longed to see in Morgan's eyes as he looked at *him?*

Morgan walked into the room to take a chair across from Richard's. "I am through with the idea of calling you out, Dickon," he said quietly, almost conversationally. "Actually, I am almost relieved that you didn't take up my clumsy challenge—a ragtag scheme that you so successfully and, may I add, most confoundedly thwarted last night. However, my onetime friend, if you insult my wife again I shall have no compunction about horsewhipping you."

Richard thought the pain, so unexpected, so fierce, might kill him. Marriage. It was so final. Hope he hadn't known still flickered in his heart sputtered and died. "I didn't know," he said honestly.

"Ah, that is a comfort, as you've always seemed to know everything about me, ever since we were boys in school. But I shouldn't be surprised, for even I didn't know how much I loved Caroline until after we were married. That marriage, in case you were about to ask, was my father's idea. He thought, I believed at the time, to make a man of me. Now, however, I believe he had hoped to punish me for my wicked way. Caro is my first and last gift from the man, who must now be sorry he forced the union, which I shall make public the moment I have untangled this web I have so inexpertly woven about her being Lady Caroline. Strange, isn't it?"

"Your father has never appreciated you, Morgan. He's been your one weakness, as my dearest papa has been the greatest of mine. You would do anything to have your father love you, and I would do everything to have my sire forget I exist. Have I yet thanked you for making my father uncomfortable last night? For a few moments there I hoped he would suffer an apoplexy, but I shouldn't be greedy, should I?"

Morgan sighed. "Yes, last night. It's so strange. My mission—the one you already know about, the one that would have revenged Jeremy's death—was nearly ruined last week when you danced with Caro at Almack's, when you charmed her, when she smiled up into your face. When she told me you had asked her to call you Richard I nearly gave up the game entirely. I didn't know I was capable of such fierce jealousy. All in all, these past months have been extremely educational. But I allowed the game to be played to its unexpected conclusion. I had to, as I already knew you suspected something. I should have let it go, shouldn't I? I'm not usually so sloppy. As it has fallen out, I've succeeded only in placing Caroline in a dangerous position, while still earning my father's contempt. Again."

Richard rose from the chair, to begin pacing in front of the fireplace. "Your father is an ass, Morgan, and carries more blame in this than anyone will ever know," he said feelingly. "He never really knew either of his sons."

The moment the words were out, to hang in the air like a confession Morgan still didn't realize he'd heard, Richard knew he had made a mistake. Or had he? Morgan had come here this morning to talk, but perhaps it was time he listened. Perhaps it was time it was over. That was what he wanted, wasn't it? What both he and Morgan wanted? So why didn't he just do it? After spending yet another near sleepless night, thinking, wishing, planning—why couldn't he find the words?

"Morgan," he said, turning to face the man he had loved since the age of fifteen, the day they had escaped their classes to go swimming together in a nearby pond. Since that glorious, damnable day, when Morgan had unselfconsciously stripped to the buff and dived cleanly into the pond, then surfaced, grinning, shaking water from his dark hair like a spaniel, and called for Richard to join him.

Until that moment Richard had wondered, had questioned, had denied. Until that moment, as he stood on the bank, holding his clothes in front of him, hiding his revealing, condemning arousal, he hadn't really known. Hadn't really understood. *Oh, God. Oh, God. Why did you make me this way? Wouldn't it have been easier if I had never been born?*

Morgan's voice reached him through the pain. "Yes, Dickon, you were saying…? Never mind. I didn't realize you knew Jeremy that well. You were only together that single Christmas when I brought you home to The Acres, and Jeremy couldn't have been more than, what—twelve? You must have had several long talks while waiting for me to ride into camp."

Richard wet suddenly dry lips. Morgan had given him one last chance, one last escape. But he couldn't take it. He couldn't even turn his back. He had to face Morgan while he said this, see his shock, his disgust. "Morgan—" His voice broke and he closed his eyes for a moment, then began again. "Morgan, I barely remember Jeremy at twelve. I—my mind was otherwise occupied. But you must know this—I knew Jeremy before he came to the camp. I knew him well. I knew him intimately. You see, Morgan, Jeremy and I were—"

"Otherwise occupied?" Morgan broke in abruptly, smiling. "We were fifteen, Dickon. We weren't occupied with anything—unless, of course, you mean that upstairs maid. What was her name? Mary? Margaret? We both had her, as I recall—or did you? I forget. I do remember how you stood guard outside when I tumbled her in my father's bed. God, Dickon, I was a handful, wasn't I? No wonder he beat me so much. Sometimes I think I went out of my way to aggravate him."

Richard rubbed the back of his neck. He didn't need reminders of the times he had abetted Morgan, standing by, dying inside, while his friend took his pleasure with a willing woman. "Morgan, I would greatly appreciate it if you didn't interrupt, for I'm trying to tell you something."

Morgan stood and walked to the drinks table, his back to Richard, although Richard could see a muscle twitching in his friend's throat. "Yes, Dickon. I know you are. But you see, I don't want to hear it." A snifter of brandy in his hand, he faced Richard. "All right, we'll talk about Jeremy for a minute. I loved him. Loved him very much. Jeremy…well, Jeremy wasn't anything like me, Dickon. Jeremy was obedient, loving, and gentle. Our father saw this as a sign that Jeremy was destined to enter the church. I—I guess you could say I saw it another way."

Morgan took a drink of the brandy, then cradled the snifter in both hands. "At first, in the beginning, I attributed it to Jeremy's attempts to please our father." His smile was self-deprecating. "I think I've almost always measured things according to how they might please or displease our father. I pushed Jeremy into riding, shooting, even boxing, whether because I was his older brother and thought he should know such things, or because I was jealous of his hold on our father's affections I'm still not sure. Jeremy, God love him, played along, tried his best to keep up with me, but, God forgive me, I *wanted* to keep winning.

"But then, as Jeremy grew older, as I invited him to join me in the village or, later, in visits to a discreet house I knew in London, and he steadfastly declined…"

Morgan's voice trailed off and he downed the remainder of his brandy before looking levelly at Richard. "So you see, Dickon, I know. I've always known. But I don't want to hear that you also knew. I don't want you to tell me that what I saw in the one I failed to recognize in the other. We've been together forever. We've wenched together, drunk together, fought side by side—"

He slammed the snifter onto the table. "I don't want you to tell me that you and Jeremy— *Christ!* My brother and my best friend." He turned away and poured himself another drink. "I don't want to hear that, Dickon," he ended quietly. "Please."

Richard found his way to the chair, collapsing into it. All these years. All these years he had tried to protect Jeremy, protect Morgan. *And Morgan had known.* Morgan, who had never been able to hide anything from his best friend, had hidden the most important thing very, very well. He *was* the Unicorn, the master of deception. They *both* had been great keepers of secrets. "Why—why didn't you tell me? Were you ashamed of Jeremy?"

Morgan also returned to his chair. He looked hurt, vulnerable, and Richard longed to reach out to him. "Ashamed? Christ, no. He was my brother. Can we drop this subject now, Dickon? As a matter of fact, let's drop all of it. I'll admit it. I did come here this morning hoping to clear the air, planning to allow you to tell me—or even *force* you to tell me—what happened out there after you rode out of camp. But now— now I don't think I want to hear. I think I just want to forget. I want to forget everything. It won't change anything, after all. Jeremy's still dead, I've lost my best friend—perhaps for the second time—and my father despises me." He laughed weakly. "Well, I never did hold out much hope in that quarter, now, did I?"

Richard lifted a hand to massage his forehead, and surreptitiously wiped at the tears in his eyes. "I don't think we can do that, Morgan. I think you have to hear it all now. I loved Jeremy, that's true, but in the beginning he was only a substitute for my first love."

Morgan's head snapped up. "A *substitute?* What in bloody hell is that supposed to mean?"

I want some brandy. I need some brandy. "It *means,* my good, trusting, and so blind friend, that Jeremy had your eyes, a certain look of you about his chin, a trace of your voice in his laugh— God, Morgan! Don't you understand yet?"

As Morgan sat very still, staring at him, incredulous, uncomprehending, Richard bolted from his chair, heading for the drinks table, unable to continue. With shaking hands he splashed a quantity of brandy into a snifter, downed half of it before pouring more, leaving the snifter where it sat, then turned, bracing his hips against the table edge. "At first, only at first, Jeremy was a substitute for you, Morgan—a substitute for the love I couldn't ask, would *never* ask you to give me."

There was silence in the room for a long time, a silence that was filled with memories. Memories of their years together. Memories of pranks they played while at school, of evenings spent on the town in London, of battles fought side by side, of long weeks when they had shared a campfire and a tent and their meager rations. Memories of a friendship based on two very different definitions of love.

"Tell me what happened, Dickon," Morgan said at last, still seated in his chair, still with his back to Richard. "You loved Jeremy. You say you loved me. I can't believe you deserted us. I've tried all these years, and I can't. You would have come back for us if you could. You wouldn't have left us to die. Tell me what happened after you rode out of camp. It's time."

Richard shook his head, denying Morgan's request, thought about the full snifter, then opened his mouth, and the words came tumbling out, almost faster than his mind could form them.

"I stopped to rest. Only for a moment, you understand, no longer than it would take to get my bearings. I *had* to get my bearings. It was dark, it was snowing, and I was having trouble. That damnable mask of yours, Morgan— it kept the snow away, but it also made it plaguey difficult to see. I slipped it off, along with that black cloak. I never should have had either in the first place. On you they looked wonderful, they were a part of you, of what you are, what you are capable of. On me they were only a costume covering the truth, hiding my incompetence. I wasn't the bloody Unicorn. I was a follower, not a leader. I was only Thomas Wilburton's mistake, his spineless son who lost himself in the home wood while trying not to hunt down the hare he'd been sent to trap and kill."

He saw himself as he had cowered in the cover of the trees, snow swirling everywhere, his heart pounding with confusion, his mouth rusty with fear. He kept speaking, but now he was speaking to himself, for himself, and Morgan only happened to be there, to listen.

"But I had a mission. I had to get vital information to our troops. I had to rescue my lover and my best friend. God! How could I have left them together, left them with Jeremy still weak, still prone to talking out of turn? What if he said something? What if he confided in Morgan? What if he told him how he had found his way to the campsite, not to see his brother, but to be with *me?*

"I was in a panic. Morgan couldn't know. I had been so careful—all those years, so careful. I had been so afraid, those days and nights when Jeremy was ill, afraid that he would call out for me, say something that would reveal our secret. I had barely slept. I had given most of my rations to the other men, and my stomach was cramping with hunger. And I was so frightened. I held Morgan's mask, thinking of him, remembering him as he stood at the edge of the camp and slapped the stallion's rump, sending me out into the night.

"He shouldn't have done that, he shouldn't have put his trust in me. All those years, I had pretended so well, following where he led, doing what he did, even volunteering to help him with this reckless insanity of the Unicorn, just so that I could be near him. He never knew. He thought I was like him.

"But I wasn't. *I'm not!* I shouldn't be out here. I should be back at the camp, still playing my part, still helping but not called upon to help.

"I'll have to wait for morning. I'm not the Unicorn. I need stars to guide me. I'm no omnipotent sorcerer. I need the rising sun to show the way west. I'll stay where I am, Morgan's cloak spread over me, the stallion well hidden. Just for a little while. Just until the snow stops and the stars come back. Just until dawn. And then I'll ride. I'll ride for help. I'll ride through hell itself for help. I can't fail them. Not Morgan. Dear God, not Morgan.

"Damned horse! Willful, ignorant beast! Where have you gone? I only slept for a moment. No more than an hour. *Damn you!* What's that? Horses. French soldiers. Three of them. Ragged, their uniforms barely recognizable, beards obscuring their faces, their eyes narrow, mean, hungry. And Morgan's stallion with them!"

Richard slid slowly to the floor, cowering as he knelt there, the nightmare that had robbed him of sleep for three long years somehow being played out while he was awake. Seeing the men approach, feeling the fear of discovery, he heard again his father's voice: "*Sweet Christ!* You can't do anything right, can you? Always a disappointment. I'd think your mother played me false, only she doesn't like being poked enough to spread her legs for anyone else."

He sat back on his haunches, as if hiding behind the same tree that had given him inadequate shelter that night, and closed his eyes.

"Shut up! Vile, coarse, ignorant *brute!* I can do this. I can do this! Bury the notebook in the snow. Quickly, quickly. Then stay very still. They're coming closer. Don't move. Don't breathe. *Closer.* For the love of Christ—*don't think!*"

Richard kept his eyes closed, the visions behind his lids no worse, no better, than those he would see if he opened his eyes. And the visions wouldn't stop. They kept on and on, as they did in his dreams. The men were on him now, pulling him from the safety of his tree, tugging roughly at his arms, his legs, laughing at his predicament, their foul breath turning his already delicate stomach queasy.

"What? Get away from me. I don't know anything. No, I don't have any food for you. I'm a deserter. Yes, we're all deserters. Damnable, stupid war! And I'm as lost as you are. No, stop tearing at me. I told you I haven't any money for you. God, man—I'm lost in the woods!

"What are you doing? I told you—I have nothing for you. Let go of my boots! Oh, all right. Take them, and be damned to you! No. Stop that! Take your hands off me. You're soldiers! Give me back my clothing. You can't do that. What do you mean, that's all I have to give you? What's all I have to give you? Don't touch me! We're all soldiers! Not animals! Let me up! Oh, sweet Jesus, no. Let me up! Get off me! *Get off me!* No. *No!* We're…not…*animals!*"

Richard flinched when two hands came down on his shoulders, then swallowed hard as he looked up, all the way up, and into Morgan's solemn face. Why was Morgan so tall? How had he come to be sitting on the floor?

"Leave it, Dickon, leave it. Forget it. What happened next—afterward?"

Richard coughed, clearing his clogged throat as Morgan stepped away from him, then clasped his hands in his lap. He thought once more of the snifter sitting on the table just beside him, then dismissed it. He didn't need the brandy anymore. He had gotten through the worst of it.

"I didn't know men could be like that, Morgan. Desperate, vile, degenerate. They were no more than animals, less than animals. I don't know how long they—they *used* me—hours...days. Hours, I think. It only seemed like days. Rape. I thought it only happened to women. It never occurred to me that—"

Morgan's voice was tense as he barked out the order. "I said leave it, Dickon. War does strange things to men. Reduces them to what you called them. Animals. You're to concentrate on what happened next."

Richard nodded, obeying him, as always, automatically agreeing to go wherever Morgan led. "I killed them. I killed all three of them...with their own knives...after they fell asleep. I killed them the way I'd always wanted to kill my father, by slitting their throats from ear to ear, so that they couldn't scream, couldn't curse me, couldn't call me what I am, what I never wanted to be. How could I face either of you after what had happened? I was shattered, used. Over and over and over.

"I could barely think rationally enough to remember where I'd buried the notebook. It took a century to find it. Then I pulled on my clothing and took one of their horses. I hugged your cloak to me, covered my shame with your mask—trying to feel you near me, trying to rid myself of their stench. I left that damned stallion to starve! I rode out, in the daylight, not caring if more soldiers found me, hoping to die, hoping to be rid of my shame. I remember that much. I remember our troops finding me, remember one of them holding your notebook. They were very pleased and promised to have it delivered to Wellington."

He pulled himself to his feet, then looked at Morgan, barely seeing him through tears that, once begun, refused to dry. "The soldiers saw the cloak, the mask. They saw the blood on my hands, the bruises on my face, They called me the Unicorn. I knew I had to tell them about you, about the camp. I had to lead them back—only I couldn't remember where the camp was. I didn't know where I was. I couldn't face you, face Jeremy. I'd never felt shame with Jeremy, but now I was so ashamed, so sick. I was dirty. I'd been violated. I panicked. I couldn't think anymore! I had to be by myself, just for a few minutes. I had to *think,* clear my head, organize my thoughts. I had to wash myself, clean myself, lose the taste of them, get the memory of their hands on me out of my mind before I could face you. But when I stripped off my clothing in the tent; when I looked down at my body, remembered what they'd done, how they'd—I don't know what happened to me then, Morgan!"

He averted his eyes, concentrating on the flames dancing in the fireplace. "Yes, yes. I do know. I fell apart. Like a weak woman having a fit of the vapors, I simply and completely fell apart. Two weeks or more passed before I spoke again— or so they told me, for I have no memory of any of it—and by the time I became aware of my surroundings I was aboard ship, heading back to England. You were dead, as far as I knew, although I prayed that you'd found some way to save Jeremy, to save the men. But I doubted it. I was sure you had all died, caught as I had been, by retreating enemy soldiers.

"When I disembarked, when they hailed me as the Unicorn, when they believed that I was the one who had worked for Wellington all those years, I didn't contradict them. After all, it was a way of keeping your memory alive—and a way of earning my father's approval. I'll not pretend that I didn't see the benefits. No one questioned me. Why would they? The Unicorn was my family symbol. I stepped into the role you had played, and I played it as best I could until word came that you had returned to England. I'd never been so happy—or so frightened. I thought about suicide, but I couldn't do that. I couldn't deprive you of your revenge. You'd earned it."

His eyes shifted to his friend, to the man he had left to die. "I've been waiting for you ever since. And now you're here. Now, at last, you know how very badly I failed you, failed Jeremy—in *every* way."

Morgan didn't say anything, but only stood directly in front of him once more, then extended his right hand, palm up.

"Morgan? What—what are you doing?"

Morgan's voice was very low, almost a whisper. "It's very simple, Dickon. I'm offering you my hand. That's what friends do when they meet each other again after a long separation."

CHAPTER TWENTY

I have found you an argument; I am not obliged to find you an understanding.

Samuel Johnson

"DULCINEA, I have just had the most splendiferous notion! I believe I should like to be addressed as Miss Cervantes. Miss Leticia *Cervantes*." Miss Twittingdon leaned forward and added in a serious near-whisper: "I have given this matter considerable thought, my dear, and I have decided that it would not do my chances at matrimony a whisker's worth of good if it became public knowledge that I am even distantly related to the inferior Laurence."

Caroline, who had been sitting alone in the morning room, contemplating the notion of asking Morgan if they could retire at once to Clayhill and simply forget that London and Richard and Lord Witham and even the Duke of Glynde— most *especially* the Duke of Glynde—even existed, looked up at the older woman and smiled weakly. "I thought that was the *Infernal* Laurence?"

Miss Twittingdon sniffed in what she had always lectured Caroline was an unladylike way. "It was, until he told me how dear Lord Clayton got him to agree to be nice to me. A fishmonger's daughter? Hah! I always knew there was some-

KASEY MICHAELS 371

thing fishy about that woman! To have called her Aldonza was an insult to Mr. Cervantes's fine creation. Now, with that settled—which of these many kind requests will we be honoring with an affirmative response? We've been woefully out of touch since our debut, you know. I do *not*, I must inform you, consider last night's affair to have been anything in the way of an official party. Did you notice how quickly the earl and his dear wife departed after Ferdie's melodramatic outburst? Although I will say that seeing Sir Joseph take to his heels added greatly to my enjoyment of the evening. What a thoroughly obnoxious man. With Sir Joseph as his sire, it's no great wonder Ferdie is such a pocket-size pickle-head."

Saying that, Miss Twittingdon collapsed into a facing chair, fanning herself with the small sheaf of invitations that had lately resided on the mantel in the drawing room.

Why did so many people seem to have labels affixed to them, as if they were products in a greengrocer's case? Infernal Laurence. Unicorn. Orphan brat. Unloved son. When had they stopped being people and begun being descriptions? Caroline looked at the woman inquiringly. "Aunt Leticia, do you really dislike Ferdie—because he's small, I mean?"

"Dislike him?" Miss Twittingdon stopped fanning herself to stare at Caroline in alarm, as if she had just blasphemed. "Whatever gave you that idea, Dulcinea?"

Caroline shrugged. "I don't know, Aunt Leticia. Perhaps because you are always calling him names. Like abbreviated little snot and pernicious pygmy and half-pint half-wit, and—what was that last one?"

Aunt Leticia laid the invitations in her lap. "Dulcinea, I thought I had taught you better than this. I refer to Ferdie's size only because I know that *he* knows that I like him well enough. I would *never* be so mean-spirited as to do so if I *didn't* like him. Just as Ferdie would not *dare* to poke his pitiful poetry into what *some* people are so silly as to believe to be my little eccentricities. If we did not *like* each other, if we did not have the common bond of wanting you, my dear, to be happy, we would most probably be very civil to each other—when we were not ignoring each other, that is. That is how intelligent, civilized persons of the *true* quality behave. Only the very *lowest* of people would deliberately persecute a person, a person they don't happen to know very well or like overmuch, for something that person cannot possibly change. I thought that would be *perfectly* obvious! Do you understand now?"

Caroline nodded, feeling the beginnings of a headache behind her eyes. She understood so little of Society. How could it be that Sir Joseph Haswit and the Duke of Glynde were both accepted as members of the quality, while Miss Twittingdon and Ferdie, who had also been born into the same Society, were hidden away as unacceptable? "I think life was simpler at Woodwere, Aunt Leticia," she said after a moment. "At least it was easier to figure out who the real lunatics were."

"Yes, yes, yes," Miss Twittingdon said quickly, picking up the invitations once more, her lesson for the day obviously completed to her satisfaction. "Now we must get back to the important business of deciding whether we shall grace Lady Hereford's ball or sit through an interminable evening at Lady Sheffield's, listening as her prune-faced daughter saws a violin in half with her cow-handed playing. Sally Sheffield has several daughters, you know, all equally prune-faced, although I would never tell her that, you see, as I didn't like her above half when we were girls together, so that I am *ex-*

tremely civil to her—just in case you were going to ask another depressing question, Dulcinea. Now, what are we to do? It's my Clarence blue if we go to Lady Hereford's, and my Jonquil if we visit Lady Sheffield, and I must be sure Betts is prepared with the correct tint for my hair. By the by, Dulcinea, have you noticed that my hair is beginning to fall out in the most *alarming* way? I think it is all the soot from these dreadfully dirty London chimneys."

Did she dare to point out the obvious? "Aunt Leticia, do you suppose it's at all possible that your continual tinting of your hair could be injurious in some way?" she asked, wondering why she was bothering to inject any sort of sense into the woman's happy chatter.

"Oh, pooh! That's what Betts said," Aunt Leticia answered, pulling a face, so that her long, thin nose wrinkled alarmingly. "I suppose you may be right. And just when I was about to bring living turbans into fashion. Isn't that the way of all my splendiferous notions, Dulcinea? They begin with such brilliance, only to fritter away into nothingness. Ah, well. I shall have another splendiferous notion before noon. I always do, you know."

Caroline hid a smile behind her hand, then sobered. If only the world were as simple as Miss Twittingdon made it seem. "May I tell you something?" she asked, blinking back unexpected tears as she slipped off her chair to kneel beside the woman who had given her so much without ever asking a single thing in return. She and Ferdie both. Peaches, the woman she had trusted implicitly, had tried to feather her own nest through her. The duke had suffered her presence only to use her to his own twisted ends. Even Morgan, much as she loved him, had wanted something from her. But not Leticia Twittingdon. Not Ferdie Haswit. They hadn't asked anything from her; they had only given. "I love you, Miss Leticia Cervantes. I love you very, *very* much. Have I ever told you that?"

"Why, no, I don't think…but aren't you kind!" Miss Twittingdon began furiously fanning herself with the invitations. "Oh, my, is it warm in here? Soon there will be no need for fires, morning or evening, and I shall absolutely *perish* in those depressing turbans, and— Oh, pooh! Come here child, and give me a kiss!"

Caroline rose on her knees, to be enveloped in Miss Twittingdon's perfumed embrace, the first she had ever had from a woman, the first that felt even vaguely maternal, if maternal was the correct word. Caroline wasn't sure, as she had so seldom experienced any human contact beyond a cuff on her ear when she didn't move fast enough to suit someone, or Morgan's passionate embraces. This was nice. Comfortable. Rather protective. And Caroline wanted nothing more than to bury her head against Leticia Twittingdon's breast and sob.

She wanted to cry out all the years of being alone, of taking care of herself. She wanted her tears to wash away the last of the bad memories so that she could feel free to open herself entirely to Morgan's love. She wanted this day to be over, her husband reconciled to both Richard's actions and the duke's horrible mangling of his son's affections, the slate wiped completely clean so that she and Morgan could build their future with no shadows of the past hanging over their heads. But mostly, right now, she wanted to be held…and sheltered…and rocked…and told that everything was gong to be all right.

"Three souls from drear Woodwere departed,
One man and two maids, still downhearted.

But the turn of the days
Has changed all their ways,
And ne'er again will this *family* be parted."

"Ferdie!" Caroline pushed back from her fierce embrace of Miss Twittingdon and, wiping at her tears with the backs of her hands, turned about in time to see the dwarf execute a perfect somersault as he entered the room. "That was beautiful!"

Ferdie landed on his rump, his stubby legs stuck out straight in front of him, and grinned. "Thank you, my dear watering-pot marchioness. Are you complimenting my poem or my trick? What ho—is that the fair Miss Twitt wiping her beaky nose in that handkerchief? I do believe she is in looks today. I did tell you that it is a wondrously glorious day, didn't I? Yes, I believe I mentioned that. A totally, wondrously glorious day—especially since I hadn't thought I'd live to see it. Remind me to thank Morgan when I see him, won't you? Where is he, anyway?"

"And isn't that wot I wants ter know? Where's he hidin' himself, that filthy Englisher? Put his pantler on me like a fox guardin' the henhouse. Why, iffen I hadn't tapped him over the head with me bootheel once he'd finally nodded off, then lifted his locksmith's daughter ta dub the jigger, there's no tellin' how I woulda escaped with m'virtue. Mornin', m'darlin'—I see yer still rollin' 'round the floor with these two freaks o'nature. Do ye think it's a cuppa tea I could be havin' before I'll be takin' m'self off?'"

"You!" Ferdie exclaimed, looking up at the woman. "You get out of here—you're not wanted!"

Peaches O'Hanlan looked down at Ferdie and grinned. "Och, me knees is rattlin' like bones in a sack, just ta think about what ye might do ta me, ye bitty worship, and ain't that a fact? And it must be thinkin' it's one o'the little people ye are, able to put a foul curse on me or somethin'. But ye ain't— ye're just a loony, let outta his bin. So why don't ye shut yer potato trap and give yer tongue a holiday?"

"I'll handle this, Ferdie," Caroline said quickly, motioning for Ferdie to be silent. She scrambled to her feet, eyeing the Irishwoman balefully. Did Peaches have any idea how badly she'd shaken her last night, until she had taken a moment to think, and seen through the tissue of lies to the woman's greed? Not that she would have been ashamed to have Peaches for a mother—but to have the woman keep the relationship secret? *That* had smacked of a certain lack of motherly love.

"Did you really hit Grisham over the head and steal his key, Peaches, or is it just that you're so greasy that you could slide your sneaking, thieving self under the door? My *mother!* I'd rather my father's intended mother died an old maid, than to know I'd have to claim such a nasty piece as you as my kin. And to think—I trusted you! I *believed* in you!"

Peaches jammed her fists onto her hips and sashayed toward Caroline, carefully skirting Ferdie, who had begun to juggle three red wooden balls he'd taken from his pocket. "Ah, ducks," she quipped, winking, "believe me and who'll be believin' ye, I'm askin'? I was good ta ye in m'own way fer many a year, and not just 'cause ye reminded me o'the little one I'd birthed and lost not three weeks afore ye showed up."

"Really?" Caroline questioned her, trying her best not to be taken in yet again by the Irishwoman's blarney. "So then, why did you champion me?"

Peaches's eyes slid away from Caroline's steady gaze, to survey the room as if inventorying its contents. "I had me reasons, ducks. Ye was different, like I always told ye—spunkier. Had all the makin's of a fine lady—small, good bones, the promise of a bonny face. Whoever planted ye at the orphanage wanted ye ta disappear, I figured, so there was no reason ta give ye back. Finders keepers, that's what I says, and what I thought when that flash cove with the boomin' voice and red face came lookin' for ye when ye hadn't been at Glynde more'an week—while ye was still tucked up in m'own cot with that fever I told ye about."

Caroline shivered, as if a goose had just walked over her grave. "A week, Peaches? Are you saying that someone came looking for me only a week after you found me?"

Peaches shrugged. "Maybe more. Maybe less. And he only *coulda* been lookin' fer ye. Coulda just as easy been lookin' fer somebody else. It's not like the cove was offerin' any blunt fer answers ta his questions, so that I didn't listen with more than half m'ears. *My* little treasure you were by then. It was m'future I saw winkin' in yer lively green eyes, don't you know. And ye didn't disappoint me. By the time ye was ten or so, I coulda sold ye fer a pretty penny or even hired ye out as a virgin—there's ways, ye see, ta do that over and over. It's my salvation from that pesthole at Glynde that ye were to be. Only, when the time came, I couldn't bring m'self ta do the deed. It's a winnin' way ye have about ye, Caro, so that I ended by cuttin' m'losses and sendin' ye off ta Woodwere instead."

Caroline shook her head. "For all the ways you have of turning a profit, Peaches, I'm astonished that you don't have your own fine town house and carriage."

Peaches used the back of her hand to wipe at her nose. "Now, Caro, don't go cuttin' up stiff. Ye wouldn't go lookin' down on a poor soul fer tryin' her best to yank herself up a notch or two in the world, now, would ye? Anyways, it all worked out fer ye. So it's on me way I'll be now, off ta starve in the gutters, lessen mayhap ye'd be wantin' ta give me a silver glimstick or two ta take along with me. It's not proud I am, and will take most anythin'—exceptin' that silly bit o' nothin' ye've got hangin' about yer neck, of course. Aye, and it's candlesticks I'll be takin' fer sure, for that poor thing won't do me a lick o'good, and no mistake."

Caroline lifted the pendant from its resting place against her bodice and looked down at it. "You're losing your touch, Peaches, if you think this pendant is worthless. It's a very beautiful, very expensive piece of jewelry."

"...Nor shall they have my beautiful pendant. There are some things that simply cannot be replaced."

Caroline shook her head. Her headache must have grown worse than she thought if she was beginning to hear voices inside her skull.

Peaches held out a hand, touching the pendant. "Is it after makin' a fool o'me ye'd be? There's a whole world of sense outside yer head, little girl, iffen ye be thinkin' that. Clap yer peepers on it fer a minute, Caro. Look at it good. Up on its hind legs, like a dog beggin' fer scraps. But it's a horse, or so I'm thinkin'. Now, tell me—what good's a horse with a bloody pole pokin' out from between his ears, I wants ta know? Sure and the gold's real sparkly-like, but the rest of it? Pure ugly. I thought so then, and I thinks so now."

Caroline's heart was pounding; her throat had gone suddenly dry. "You've seen this before, Peaches?" she asked, pushing the pendant closer to the Irishwoman's face. "Where?"

Peaches pushed the pendant away before spying the tray of cakes beside Miss Twittingdon. Shoving one of the confections into her mouth while pocketing two more inside her bodice, she nodded, then spoke around the mouthful of cake. "Ah, fairy cakes. Lovely things. Now, what was it ye was askin'? Oh, yeah, the horses. They was in the gown ye was wearin', and don't ye know. All around the hem, marchin' like soldiers, all done up in pretty threads. All those prancing horses—with bloody poles stickin' out from between their ears. Tried pickin' out the threads—ta sell 'em—but it weren't no use. It was a real mess ye were, Caro, all bloody and mud ta ye ears. Threw it all away in the end, slip and all, only cuttin' off the buttons. Brought me three pence, the buttons did, and a fistful of questions I didn't want ta answer. Bloody waste." She popped another cake into her mouth, wiping her hands on her tattered skirt. "Forgot about that. Three bloody pence. Couldn't even get no one ta lay down some blunt on yer shoes—seein' as how there was only the one."

"The blanket from the coach was located a good mile away, one small slipper wrapped inside it...." Caroline pressed her hands to her cheeks, remembering the duke's words. She closed her eyes, seeing a little girl dressed all in white, kicking her chubby legs so that the pretty red, blue, yellow, and even green horses moved, galloping and galloping along the hem of her gown, 'round and 'round and 'round—until the carriage blanket came down, covering them, tucking them into bed for the night.

She moaned aloud.

"Caro? Are you all right?" Ferdie asked, tugging on the skirt of her gown, his voice seeming to come from very far away. "You don't look very well."

The scene inside her head shifted. The little girl was frightened, clutching the carriage blanket to her and looking up at the handsome man with her eyes wide, her bottom lip trembling as she tried to be a big girl and not cry any more.

"Henry, no! For the love of heaven, don't leave us."

"She's crying. The beautiful lady is crying. I should be able to cry too. Can't I cry, beautiful lady?"

"Here, my darling. You hide in here for now, until Papa comes back."

Caroline shook her head, looking into the dark compartment, seeing spiderwebs in the corners, seeing the rough wood that would snag at her pretty gown.

Caroline's lips began to move once more, but she still didn't know she was speaking, her voice high, childlike, as she begged the beautiful lady. "Don't put me in there. Please. It's dark in there. Caro says no."

"Caro play a game? Yes, darling! What a good girl you are. You are my sweet, darling Caro. Now give Mama a kiss."

"Mama?" Caroline kept her eyes tightly closed, trying to hold on to the picture of the beautiful lady, the lady who was so soft and smelled so good and kissed her and smiled at her and loved her so very much.

But everything was dark and small, and the little girl was so afraid. She couldn't breathe, couldn't see, and the beautiful lady was screaming...asking "Why? *Why?*"

"Let met out. Let me out!" Caroline's hands came away from her face, to begin beating against the air above her head, her fingers curved into claws, scratching and tearing and trying to push the darkness away.

Noise, like thunder splitting the night. Rain everywhere. Horses—not pretty like her horses, but dark and breathing steam; rearing, then riding off, leaving her alone.

Alone.

But not really alone.

"Papa? Papa, get up. Play a game, Papa? Caro play a game? Caro sing for you, Papa? Mama? Mama, wake up. Wake up, mama. *Wake up. Wake up!*"

Caroline felt the sting of the slap Miss Twittingdon delivered to her cheek, then opened her eyes at last, staring at the woman, who appeared confused yet caring; looking to Ferdie, who was staring back at her with such eloquent pity twisting his features; looking to Peaches, who had just finished blessing herself, then backed it up by making the sign against the evil eye.

She could barely see them, because the tears were falling now, falling so hard and so fast that no one could stop them, nothing could stop them. Tears of confusion…tears of overwhelming terror…tears for the horror she had seen…the horror she had lived…the lifetime she had forgotten.

How had she forgotten? All these years. All these long, cold, *cheated* years.

"Dulcinea?" Miss Twittingdon was leading her to the settee, helping her to sit down, dabbing at her cheeks with a small white lace handkerchief. "My dear girl, what is it? Please forgive me for striking you. Ferdie, quickly! Fetch my vinaigrette. I think dear Dulcinea is about to swoon!"

"Vinaigrette? Damn your vinaigrette, Letty! Where's Morgan? He should be here. His grace will be no good to us— we need Morgan!"

"Yes, well, I must be goin', don't ye know? I'll just be takin' this here little silver box—pretty little thing, ain't it?— and mayhap these candlesticks. And the cakes. And the tray they're sittin' on. Good day ta ye, now. Better a good run than a bad stand, I say. The good Lord's blessin' on ye, Caro—it's needin' it I think ye be."

Caroline looked down at her hands, surprised to see that

they were free of blood—*her father's blood, her mother's blood*—surprised to see her nails short, but nicely rounded, and not ripped nearly to the quick. She was shaking so badly, her feet unable to stay flat on the floor, her teeth chattering, her hands trembling almost uncontrollably.

And she was cold.

So cold.

She was alone.

So very, very alone.

So *cheated!*

Her trembling hands slowly reformed themselves into trembling fists...

CHAPTER TWENTY-ONE

To see you I lose my life.

Maurice Sceve

MORGAN WATCHED as the servant placed a glass of Burgundy in front of him, then lifted it toward Richard, toward his friend. "To Jeremy."

"To Jeremy," Richard echoed. "And to good memories."

Morgan took a sip of the Burgundy, then replaced the glass on the table. They had quit Richard's rooms and adjourned to White's, to sit at a small table in the corner of the room. It was better this way, removed from the depressing atmosphere in Half Moon Street, away from the echoes of the confession Richard had made, away from the horrors of a remembered war, away from the uncomfortable silence that had fallen as they had stood in the middle of the room, hands clasped, souls bared.

"I like your Caroline, you know," Richard said after putting down his own glass. "She's very frank, very forthcoming, uncommonly innocent—the total opposite of her husband, as a matter of fact. I only wonder how you talked her into assuming the role of my cousin in the first place."

"A cottage for her and her friends, an allowance, some white kittens, and a yellow dog. Those were her conditions as I recall them. And, vile bastard that I am, I agreed. Then, dear friend, I proceeded to seduce her." He picked up his glass once more, slowly turning it by the stem. "Of course, she then seduced me. Caro is a very quick learner, you see. All in all, I'd say we both got more than we bargained for. And, strangely, I have you to thank for my happiness. Without my insane plan for revenge I would never have met her. God, Dickon, what a terrible waste that would have been—my life without Caroline in it."

Morgan felt a faint flush of embarrassment. "I'm sorry."

"Morgan, before anything else, I was your friend. After everything that has happened—and perhaps even because of everything that has happened—I still wish to be your friend. If you can accept that, so can I. I have with very little effort taken on the role of celibate since Jeremy's death—since the incident—and have gained myself a measure of peace. Your friendship completes my life. So, my friend, what happens now? You said you're going to go to my father and retract your claim that Caroline is my cousin and heir to all the money and lands that weren't entailed. He'll probably fall weeping on your neck, thanking you."

Morgan wished it were that simple. And perhaps it was. But he doubted it. Somehow he doubted it. He learned forward, placing both forearms on the table. "Dickon, what did you say to your father? He came to Portman Square last night seemingly prepared to do whatever I asked. He—both of you—really caught me off my guard with your ready acceptance of terms I'd never believed enforceable. I don't wish to harp on the subject, but after what you've told me today, I have to be sure. Did you tell him that I was going to expose you as a coward, and not the Unicorn after all?"

Richard finished off his Burgundy in one long swallow,

then shook his head. "I couldn't be sure that would be enough to make him agree to your blackmail. 'Caroline *Wilbur?*' That was unusually heavy-handed of you, Morgan—or perhaps your heart has never truly been in this revenge business. Either way, I knew you were up to something. But enough of that. You wanted me punished, and I wanted to be punished—and the idea of hurting my father in the process? Well, that was irresistible. Being handed a white feather would have embarrassed me, but no one could ever call my father a coward. The scandal would hurt him, touch him, but not destroy him. But I knew what would."

"Richard, that I should have pushed you to—"

"Don't apologize, my friend. I rather enjoyed myself. But to get back to my story. I told my father—I told him about Jeremy, about how I loved him, about how we'd been together. It was a crushing insult to my dear sire's overweening masculinity that he could not bear to have made public—much like Sir Joseph's horror of Society's reaction to his dwarf son. Your unwitting parallels of last evening amused me very much, by the way. But it is true. Each man has his own vanity, and I knew where to aim my dart where my father was concerned. I've always known. It just took your return to London for me to find the courage to fit the arrow into the bow and send it winging toward its target."

He took a deep breath, then smiled sadly. "I didn't use Jeremy's name, Morgan. I had to protect Jeremy's memory, even from you, which is why I couldn't simply go to you in the first place, tell you the truth, and have done with it. Jeremy, and my shame, kept us apart for three long years. But, to get back to the subject—to learn that I'd loved another man was enough to get my father's agreement, enough to give you your revenge. After all, if you had succeeded in forcing me to the dueling ground I would only have shot into the air, and you—gentlemen that you are—couldn't have killed me in cold blood. I couldn't thwart you that way. So I told my father you were prepared to announce my disgraceful liaison to the world. Dearest Papa could have his only son branded a coward, but he could never live with the idea that Society would know *he'd* sired such a…a—"

"Why, Dickon? It must have been a terrible scene. Why go through that?"

Richard sighed. "Look, Morgan—you wanted to provoke me into a duel, using my father to do so. To prove I wasn't the coward you were going to paint me, my father might have forced the duel on me. But he would never let his family name be defended by a man-milliner, a deviate, a—"

"All the same, you took a terrible chance. And I'd appreciate it greatly if you would not persist in demeaning yourself. You are what God made you, Dickon, just as I long ago came to grips with the fact that Jeremy was as God made him. Ferdie, after all, doesn't apologize for his size."

Richard smiled yet again, and suddenly he was the old Richard, the man Morgan had always known. "That's two things we all have in common, then, isn't it, my friend? Ferdie, Jeremy—even *you*—and I. God, and our fathers. Your dear wife should consider herself fortunate to have been raised in an orphanage, and thus having escaped at least some of the taint."

Morgan looked about the room, assuring himself that he couldn't be overheard, then at last broached the subject that had been plaguing him since last night. "Dickon, what do you remember about the murders?"

"The murders?" Richard frowned, clearly confused. "Oh, you mean the robbery, don't you? Damned highwaymen!

Butchers! To kill my aunt and uncle was bad enough, but to carry off a child and most probably kill her as well, then hide the body?" He shook his head. "Yet to tell you the truth, I don't remember much. I was at school with you, remember? I can recall my mother crying, my father blustering about in his usual way, the funerals, and then the move to our new estate. Nothing much. We drove to the funeral with the paint still wet on the crest Papa had commissioned painted on our coach. He could barely contain his glee at being the earl." He took another sip of wine. "God, how I've always detested that man."

Morgan placed his hands on the arms of his chair and hitched it forward, closer to the table. "Your father was a younger son, Dickon, with few prospects. It must have galled him no end when your uncle married so late in life. I mean, he must have thought that he would inherit, mustn't he?"

Richard motioned for the servant to refill their glasses, waiting until the man had left before replying. "Are you suggesting that my father had something to do with my uncle's death? Morgan, that's absurd! He's a bombastic, mean, ignorant bastard—but a *murderer?* Why, that would mean that my confession meant nothing to him, and your unspoken claim that I had acted the coward would have meant even *less* than nothing to him. It would mean, Morgan, that my father capitulated to your terms so quickly last night because your wife could actually *be* Lady Caroline—because my father *knew* that the real Lady Caroline did not die that night! That's almost depressing, and it means I would have confessed for nothing. Jesus, Morgan, what made you even summon up such a farfetched notion?"

Morgan reached into his pocket and pulled out a cheroot, lit it in the flame of the candle that burned on the table, then exhaled a thin stream of blue smoke. "Dickon, old friend, do you remember my uncle James?"

Fifteen minutes later the two men were on the flagway in front of White's, having decided to confront the earl of Witham with what they supposed, what neither of them completely believed yet did not doubt enough to dismiss. Now. Today. Before the earl could act, if he was planning to act.

"Morgan!"

Morgan turned to see Ferdie Haswit's head sticking out of the window of the duke's town coach as the equipage drew up to the curb. "Ferdie? Where the devil are you going? I know I promised everyone a ride to Richmond Park, but I asked Caro to explain that I had some unfinished business—"

"The devil with Richmond Park! I've been all over London looking for you!" The dwarf flung open the door and leapt lightly to the pavement, his face red with exertion, his expression alarmingly solemn. "It's Caro, Morgan," he said in a voice heavy with portent. "She's gone to Witham, crying and cursing a blue streak. I tried to stop her. We all tried to stop her, even the Twitt. But you know Caro—when she gets the bit clamped between her teeth there's no talking to her. Damn that Irishwoman for a fool!" He took hold of Morgan's arm. "It's wonderful! It's terrible! Our Caro is Lady Caroline, Morgan! She's *really* Lady Caroline!"

"What?" Morgan's blood ran cold. He felt as if all his worst dreams were coming true at once. The impossible was becoming possible. The unbelievable was gaining credibility. The unthinkable was suddenly conceivable. His uncle James must be chortling with glee as he looked up from hell to see how his most hated nephew had bungled things. Stupid. *Stupid!* What had he done? "How? What happened, Ferdie?"

Morgan and Richard exchanged looks; then Richard pulled open the door to the coach. "We'll talk on the way, Morgan. No matter what, Caroline could be in danger. Come on, man—move!"

"ONCE AGAIN, I cannot tell you how very *delighted* I am that you have been found! It's a miracle! Dear sweet little Caroline." Lady Witham dabbed at her moist eyes with the tip of her handkerchief, then sighed. "I was nearly demented with happiness by the news, which is why I could not find my voice last night. What a to-do! My husband—your uncle—rushed me out so quickly that I barely had time to kiss your cheek, didn't I? But now you've come to me, and I—I'm all but *overcome!* Poor Henry, poor dear Gwen—that they did not live to see this glorious day!"

Caroline kept her hands clenched in her lap, torn between pity for this unknown, obviously unknowing woman and an almost uncontrollable urge to leap up from her seat, to go tearing through the house willy-nilly, calling for the earl to show himself. "I know, Aunt Frederica," she replied, attempting a smile. "You did say Uncle Thomas will be joining us shortly?"

Caroline had been sitting in the drawing room for more than a half hour, waiting for the man to appear. Coward! He couldn't even face her! But what could she expect of a man who did murder under cover of a highwayman's mask? Every word Morgan had told her about his uncle James's accusations was still ringing in her head. Every feeling that had come bubbling to the surface after Peaches's reminiscences broke through the ice covering her memories of the past, of that terrible night, still boiled inside her, keeping her suspended partway between unbelievable grief and overwhelming anger.

Coming here was stupid, dangerous, but she could not have stayed away, could not have waited for Morgan to return, could not have remained in Portman Square, seeing the looks of pity and concern from Aunt Leticia and Ferdie. She had to be on the move, she had to focus on the moment, she had to concentrate on her uncle, on hearing the words from his own mouth, on listening to his explanation for what he had done. She had to be certain that he was the one.

"I have not yet discussed this with your uncle, Caroline, but I am convinced that we should have a come-out ball for you as soon as possible. You will be moving in with us here, won't you, my dear? I have always so longed for a daughter. And now, now that Richard has said— Well, never mind about what Richard has said. *You* will be my daughter now, not that I could ever dream to replace Gwendolyn in your affections. Do you remember her at all, my dear? Such a lovely girl. You look nothing like her. Oh—not that you aren't very beautiful, for you are, you are. It's only that you favor your dear father more in your coloring, being blond and all. Perhaps you have Gwen's eyes. Yes. Yes, I do believe you have our mother's eyes. Although hers were brown…"

Caroline smiled weakly, wishing her aunt Frederica would shut up, then slid her hand to the pocket in her gown to feel the dagger she had secreted there before running out of the mansion in Portman Square. She had no real knowledge of pistols, but Peaches had taught her a trick or two with a knife that should stand her in good stead. She was angry, her hatred burning white-hot, but she wasn't stupid. Her plan might have been hastily formulated, but it was clear in her head.

The Earl of Witham had murdered her parents, murdered her life for the past fifteen years and more. The man deserved to be punished. Morgan would not be the one to handle this.

Morgan might kill him, thus becoming a criminal himself. She couldn't chance that possibility. So it had to be done her way.

Today, and for the first time in her life, Caroline Dulcinea Monday Wilburton Blakely, orphanage brat, madhouse servant, Marchioness of Clayton, would take responsibility for that life into her own two hands!

Today she would hear the truth from the man's own lips. She had to hear it, hear it all. Then and only then could she completely believe, and be the captain of her own destiny.

And then, when she had tricked her vile, murderous uncle into revealing the extent of his crimes, she would march him, at knife point, to the nearest guardhouse.

All those years! All those terrible wasted years. The orphanage. The drudgery. The not knowing, the never knowing. Woodwere. That night in the common room. Boxer. The Leopard Man. All the pain, the fear, the heartache, the loneliness, the despair. All the waste. That terrible, terrible *waste*.

Cheated!

She had been cheated—cheated of her parents, cheated of the carefree childhood she should have led, the security she should have known, the warm, golden days, the comfort of a soft, perfumed embrace, the guidance of the strong hand of her father, the good-night kisses at bedtime. *The love.*

"Caroline? What is it, dear? I've been speaking for close to five minutes—rambling on most terribly, actually—and you haven't said a word. Have I been taking things too fast for you? I do that, you know. Your cousin Richard always says so. Richard says I have been planning his life since before he was born—although he also says that I have always had his best interests at heart. And I did, you know, I really did. Which is why I should have been more firm, I suppose, and should have taken him and gone when I first thought of it, when Thomas first hurt him, first made him cry...oh, dear. Please forgive me. I sustained two rather large shocks less than twenty-four hours ago, and it would appear that I have not yet recovered from either of them. Would you mind waiting here alone, Caroline? I believe I need to lie down on my bed for a space and collect myself."

"First sensible thing you've said in thirty years, Freddy. Take your usual flit—you know the way. Me and m'niece here have things to say to each other, and I don't need you sniffling into your handkerchief while we're trying to get them said. Go—get yourself gone—and if you're a good gel I'll trip upstairs later and give you a tumble. That's what you need— a good tip-over. Been needing it for years. Too bad you're too ancient to give me a son, but then, you never did give me a *real* son, did you, Freddy? *A real man.*"

Caroline watched, fascinated, as her Aunt Frederica scrambled to her feet and fled the room, her handkerchief pressed to her mouth, stifling her sobs. Then she directed her gaze at the man she had seen for the first time last night. Seen and dismissed as nothing more than a coarse, crude Boxer dressed up in fine clothing. That had been stupid, for Boxer could not be dismissed; dismissing such a beast was not only reckless, it could be downright dangerous. The Earl of Witham even had the look of Boxer about his eyes—so close-set against his nose, and never still, but always darting about, as if looking for trouble or hunting up some way to cause it.

She had to remember that he didn't know. He couldn't be sure. As long as he couldn't be sure, she held the power. Morgan had laid the groundwork, now all she had to do was build on that foundation. As long as she controlled herself, said the right things, asked the earl the right questions, listened carefully to his answers, and didn't betray herself, she would be the one in charge. She had to give him enough rope, had to reel it out to him bit by bit—until he had taken enough with which to hang himself.

And she'd begin as she planned to go on.

"Thanks, ducks," she said brightly, rising to cross over to the drinks table and pour herself a glass of canary, purposely presenting her back to the earl. "One more bleedin' tick-tock o'havin' m'wattles banged on by that waterin' pot an' I'da flashed m'hash." She turned about smartly, holding the decanter high. "Would ye be wantin' a nip o'the creature yerself, yer worship? Doin' business is such dry work, don't ye know, and it's business we two will be doin', iffen I've read ye right."

The earl's grin gladdened her heart, and she watched as he visibly relaxed, lowering his bulk into a nearby chair. "Ah, so the veneer of civilization slips away, does it? I had thought as much. You wouldn't be here today if Clayton's plans were holding together. Where did he find you, m'lovely? Which bawdy house were you working? I know round heels when I see them, and you've been on your back more than once, haven't you?"

Caroline handed him the drink she had poured for him, then perched against the arm of the chair across from his, steadying her own glass with both hands, so that she wouldn't spill the contents she had no intention of drinking. "I'll not be insultin' that great hulkin' corporation ye're wearin' about yer middle, yer worship, and ye won't be taking the sharp side o'yer tongue ta me—you ken what I'm sayin'? It makes no never mind where I been. It's where I'm goin' ta that we're talkin' about this day."

The earl nodded, then downed his drink in one long gulp. "And where would that be, Miss— What shall I call you?"

"Monday," Caroline said quickly, longing to hit the man. His very lack of shock was already telling her that he was guilty. "Caroline Monday. And I'll tell ye where I'm *not* goin'—and that's back ta those mucky cribs. I went along with the high-and-mighty Clayton's rig, learnin' how ta eat, how ta talk, how ta dress like some proper milk-and-water puss, but now he's gone and went back on his word. Lady Caroline m'sweet arse! All the clean sheets and sugarplums I could want fer the rest o'me days! A hulkin' great gravy boat o'me own ta swim in! Lies—all filthy crammers!"

Thomas Wilburton placed his empty glass on the table beside him and shifted in his chair, looking at her piercingly. "Let me see if I'm clear on this, Miss Monday. You're saying that Lord Clayton promised you recognition as Lady Caroline Wilburton and all the money and estates that recognition would bring you, and now he has reneged on his promise? How do you know that?"

"There's a great lot of knowledge outside yer head, ain't there, yer worship?" Caroline countered, beginning to pace the length of carpet behind the chair. "Cried friends, they have, yer son and his worship. Clayton ain't makin' no claims fer me now. He plans ta shunt me off, send me packin' ta some cottage. And what would I be doin' with a bleedin' cottage, I ask ye? Diggin' turnips and tendin' cats? Not bloody likely! So I said ta m'self, I said, Caro, ye've got other fish ta fry, other cows ta milk."

"I see," the earl said, his eyes narrowed to small slits, so that he resembled nothing more than an overfed ferret. "And you believed that *I* will help you? How?"

Caroline's heart was beating so quickly that she was finding it difficult to breathe, but she walked around to the back of the earl's chair anyway, standing just behind him as she said lightly, "Ah, come on now, ducks, don't go all silly on me now. We're peas in a pod, ye and me. I was there last night, remember? I can smell fear as well as the next one, and ye was all but wallowin' in the stuff. His worship didn't smell it, but *I* did. He still doesn't believe it, neither, but *I* does. His worship only wanted ta watch ye squirm, ta get some o'his own back on yer sprout what betrayed him. He doesn't ken what's right afore his peepers. Ye didn't go sayin' yes to his worship ta save yer kiddie's hide—ye were coverin' yer *own* skin. Ye didn't want all that there business about yer brother dragged up again fer a new airin'."

She leaned over the back of the chair, so that her mouth was just beside his ear, so close that she could see the coarse hairs on his earlobe, smell the kippers he'd had for breakfast. "Ye did it, didn't ye? His worship didn't believe the fella what told him ye did, how he bled ye fer it, but ye did it plain. Ye had ta, else ye wouldna been scared spitless ta hear that yer blackmailer was tellin' ye straight all along and that yer little niece was alive. She saw ye, didn't she? Saw ye clear. Ah, ducks, but does she remember? Can she point a finger at ye? That's what had ye sweatin' like a pig, ain't it? I coulda been her—ye didn't know. I coulda been her!"

The earl turned so quickly that Caroline's senses were assaulted by his vile breath before she could back away, the canary splashing overtop the glass to stain her gown. "Who told you? I worried that he might have stumbled onto— But Clayton couldn't *know.* Not really. Not for certain. *Nobody* knew. But you said somebody told him. But there was no one. Unless—" He slammed a fist into his facing palm. *"James?"*

Oh, God, oh, God, oh, God! It was true. It was all true!

"That'd be Lord James Blakely, yer worship? His holy autembawlin' grace's brother? The one what gave Clayton *this?"*

She flung the glass to the floor and reached up to her throat to pull the pendant from its hiding place beneath her gown.

"*Christ!* Where did you get that? She wasn't wearing it! The bitch wasn't wearing it!"

Caroline watched as the earl's face went deathly white, then flushed almost purple with rage. He all but leapt from his chair, a piece of furniture Caroline prudently kept between herself and the man who had murdered her parents.

"Why didn't I make the connection?" the earl raged. "Why didn't I see that Clayton had to have gotten his information from someone who knew, someone who set him on this road. We talked—we both talked—but James never hinted, I never suspected. He made no move. He had as much of a grievance as I, maybe more, being a twin. Accidents of birth. Nothing but accidents of birth. But I was the only one with the spleen, the *bottom* to do as I'd said. I laughed at James—laughed! Living in the hellhole while his brother had it all. But not me. I *acted!*" He raised a fist toward the ceiling. "Damn you, James! *Damn you!*"

All right. Now she knew. Now she was certain. There could be no doubt. Lord Witham had murdered his brother, her parents. He had done it to inherit the title. Lord James Blakely had been telling the truth all along. She reached into her pocket, her hand closing around the hilt of the knife. But then she hesitated.

"Iffen yer goin' ta climb into the alts, yer worship, ye go right ahead. I'll be waitin' when ye comes slidin' back down again," she said, watching as he ran both hands through his hair like a man trying to rid himself of thoughts he didn't wish to face. "Then, when ye have done with yer bawlin', we'll talk about what yer goin' to do fer Caroline Monday."

That caught his attention, and he stared at her, his raisin-pudding black eyes spitting fire. "You ignorant bitch. Do you really think I'm going to feather your nest now that Clayton has dropped you—that I'm going to be blackmailed *again?*"

Caroline took a deep breath, exhaling slowly. She'd heard enough. It was time to stop playing games. More than time.

"No, Uncle Thomas," she said slowly, distinctly, "I never believed you would willingly open yourself to blackmail a second time. I did, however, wish to hear from your own lips that you were the one I saw that night, the one who laughed as he reached for me, who cursed me as I bit him, then flung me to the ground against my dying mother's body when shots rang out and he had to abandon the area or else risk capture. Some things are still muzzy, but I'm remembering now. I'm remembering more of it every minute. You haven't aged well, Uncle, but then, I was only a very small child, wasn't I, and couldn't be counted upon to recognize your features fifteen years later. But, as I've already said, you couldn't be sure, could you, Uncle? You couldn't be certain I wasn't Lady Caroline, that I wouldn't remember some of it one day. Just enough to hang you. Isn't that right, *Uncle?*"

"How? You're lying—guessing! How in bloody blazes could you know any of what happened? Who told you? I killed the man who rode with me—killed and buried him that same night. No one saw. We got away before anyone else came into the roadway. James couldn't have been close enough to see it all, to see the brat bite me. You couldn't know—you can't really be her. *You're dead!*"

Caroline was crying. Why did she always have to cry when she became angry? Like a child. Just like a stupid idiot child! Yet her tears only made her angrier, served only to feed her fury, reinforce her hate. "You slimy bastard! You whoreson! You *murderer!*" Her passions exploding, she raised her clenched fists to him, shaking them, longing to fly across the room and pummel him, beat him into a quivering jelly, have him at her knees, begging for a mercy she would never show him—the mercy he had not shown either her or her parents. *"Did the title mean so much?"*

The earl turned his back to her for a moment, and when he whirled around to face her he held a pistol in his hand, a pistol that must have been in the drawer of the table behind him.

She flinched, not so much in fear as in frustration at her own stupidity, then stood very still as he said calmly, almost conversationally, as if having the pistol in his hand had lent him a modicum of composure as well as control, "The title meant everything, you idiot child. It was to be mine. Mine, and then Richard's." He sniffed in what could only be disgust. "My *son*. I'll have to do something about him, won't I? A carriage accident, I suppose, ridding me of both the mother and the abortion she brought to term, the abomination she foisted on me."

He shook his head, then smiled without humor. "Accidents of birth. Henry before me. William before James. My lying brother taking himself a wife long after he'd declared he never would. Waiting out the birth, waiting to learn if it was a boy child. Once was a terror. I couldn't bear it a second time. But he took me aside, told me she was gong to whelp again. *Again!* The bitch was capable of breeding like a bloody rabbit! I kill rabbits. Vermin, filling their bellies in fields that should never be theirs. Listed them in my game book the next morning, you know. A good sportsman always records his kills. A brace of pheasants, a half-dozen grouse, a hedge-hog—*two rabbits*."

Caroline was falling apart. She could feel herself literally fragmenting into tiny pieces. She shouldn't have come. She should have waited for Morgan, should have realized that hearing the truth would destroy her composure. The earl's pistol didn't worry her. He wouldn't shoot her, not here, not in his own house. But he could destroy her with his words, his taunts, his horrendous, obscene truths.

Her mother had been with child. She'd lost not only her parents but a brother or sister as well. What sort of monster could cold-bloodedly murder a pregnant woman? What sort of world was this that such horrors could happen and then go unpunished for fifteen years?

Forgetting the earl, forgetting his pistol, forgetting her knife and Morgan and where she was, who she was, Caroline dropped to her knees, wrapped her arms protectively about her own stomach, her own womb, and began to rock. She was overcome with pain, devastated by grief, isolated from life as it went on around her.

Until she heard a voice. Not any voice, but that one particular voice, the one belonging to the man who had brought her back to the world of the living, back to where she belonged. The man who loved her.

"Caro! Are you all right? My God, I thought I might be too late!"

She looked up to see that Morgan had somehow appeared in front of her, his beloved face distorted with fear, his hand clutching a carriage pistol much like the one her father had refused to use that fateful night. *"Morgan,"* she breathed on a sob, reaching up to him, allowing him to gather her to him, hold her tightly against his chest, share her pain. "He did it. He murdered my parents."

"We know, darling. We all know, and we're sorry. We're so very, *very* sorry."

Suddenly the drawing room was crowded with people.

From her position, her cheek pressed against Morgan's chest, Caroline saw Ferdie, her cousin Richard, and even Lady Witham. They were all there somehow, she didn't quite know how, and they were all looking at her, sympathizing with her, caring for her.

Her chin began to quiver, and she turned her face against her husband's chest, deep sobs racking her from head to toe, tearing at her lungs, clawing at her constricted throat, welling up from deep inside her, from her bruised soul, her battered heart. She was a child of three again, crying for her beautiful mama, for her dear papa; frightened, alone, begging for comfort.

She felt the rumble of Morgan's chest before she heard the words he was saying, only composing herself enough to hear him addressing her uncle. "And so, my lord, as you can see, there is no reason for you to continue holding that pistol. Richard and I are both armed, as is Ferdie. You have but a single bullet. It's over. Give it up."

"The devil claims his own, it's said,
Marks them out and slays them dead.
The knife, the noose, the blade, the gun;
Hell's flames await when the race is done.
He builds them up just to lay them low,
With envy and greed and—"

"Ferdie, not now!" Morgan commanded tersely, so that the dwarf instantly fell silent.

Caroline turned to look at the earl, who was standing very still in the middle of the room, the pistol pointed directly at her, at Morgan. And then—very strangely, she thought, for a man in his position—the earl smiled.

"One bullet, you said. And you are correct, Clayton," the earl remarked at last, slowly raising his arm, so that Caroline could feel Morgan tensing as he cocked his own pistol. "I do have but a single bullet. I could shoot you, I suppose, or that interfering chit there, or even my worthless son. My son. Fruit of my loins, heir to all I killed to get. Damme, it's almost funny! Not Freddy, though. I couldn't shoot her. That would only be a waste of good ammunition."

"Papa," Richard interjected as his mother stood very still beside him, for once not crying. Caroline actually believed the woman to be smiling with real pleasure. "Put down the pistol, Papa. We can't stand here all day, frozen in this absurd tableau."

"Ah, so speaks the heir, the last of the line. My God—the last of the line. You make me sick!"

"That will be enough, my lord," Morgan said tersely.

"Just about, Clayton. Just about. But not yet." The earl indicated Caroline with an imperative toss of his head. "You—*Caroline*. I just want you to know something. I'd do it again—only I'd do it better. Much better. See that you tell them to mark this kill as 'Various,'" he told her, and then—

…before anyone could move,

…before Morgan could do more than push Caroline's face against his chest so that she would not see the worst of it,

…Thomas Wilburton, the man who had murdered his own brother in order to become the Earl of Witham, stuck the muzzle of his pistol into his mouth and pulled the trigger.

EPILOGUE

Summer 1818

It is a true saying, that a man must eat a peck of salt with his friends, before he knows him.
Miguel de Cervantes

On the wings of Time grief flies away.
Jean de La Fontaine

THE ACRES WAS ALWAYS at its most beautiful in the summertime, the grass lushly green, the leafy trees giving shade from the noonday sun, the formal gardens a riot of fragrant roses. Caroline had long since decided that the small stream running along the bottom of the garden, its banks shaded by weeping willows, was her favorite spot on the entire estate. Here, dabbling her bare toes in the cool water, the skirt of her muslin gown spread out on the mossy bank, her hair loosed to catch each soft breeze, she felt like a child—as much of a child as her daughter, Gwen, who was napping quietly on a nearby blanket.

There would be another child soon after Christmas, and this time Caroline hoped for a son. A black-haired little demon with flashing dark eyes and the wicked, wonderful smile of her husband, the Duke of Glynde.

What a good father her husband was, kind but firm, loving yet not overly indulgent—although Gwen did have a way of wrapping the man around her chubby little finger just by smiling up into his face.

Caroline smiled now, looking toward her daughter, seeing

her hair turned to gold by the sunlight that filtered down through the trees. Muffie, having escaped from her nearly three-month-old kittens, slept beside the baby, her head tucked against Gwen's knees. It was wonderful to see Gwen so still, when she was such a bundle of motion when awake. The child had just begun to toddle this past week, tightly clutching Ferdie's hands as he walked behind her, encouraging her to step out on her own.

Poor Ferdie. He mustn't have known what he had started, for now Gwen squealed and held up her hands to him each time she saw him, demanding that he perform the office of hand-holder. The dwarf had just this morning composed a nonsense verse he'd titled "Gwenny's Slave."

Dear Ferdie. He had recited such a lovely poem at the late duke's funeral last summer, speaking of love that cannot be friendship yet persists because it has to, because love and forgiveness and understanding must be granted if anyone is ever to move on, to live his own life free of the shadows of the past.

Morgan had wept that day, and Caroline had held him, thankful that he understood, thankful that he had made his peace with himself even if he could never have the fatherly affection he had struggled most of his life to gain. The duke had died with a prayer on his lips and his "forgiveness" lying like a rock on his chest, squeezing out the last beat of his heart—without ever really accepting Morgan's love.

But William Blakely's pitifully twisted conceptions of life, love, and punishment didn't matter anymore. Morgan had accepted his own love for his father, and that had been enough. He had forgiven, and he had moved on. He was the duke now, and Caroline was his duchess. Life was good. Very, very good.

"What's that smile about, Caro? You look like a cat with canary feathers sticking out of its mouth."

Caroline pulled her feet from the water and turned to see Richard standing beside her. "Dickon—I was woolgathering and didn't hear you approach. How wonderful to see you! Morgan didn't tell me you were back! Is Aunt Frederica with you? How did you both like Italy? Morgan says he will take me soon—if I ever stop having babies long enough for him to trust me aboard ship." She smiled as he bent to kiss her cheek. "Did you bring me anything?"

"Morgan doesn't know I'm back. Mama is sitting on the terrace with Aunt Leticia, telling her about the latest fashions, which, by the by, bear precious little resemblance to whatever the dear lady is wearing around her head. I cannot believe how big Gwen has grown. Do you mean to tell me, my dearest cousin, that you're increasing *again?* As for your last, most impertinent question, minx—leather gloves from Florence, a portrait of some martyred saint from Rome, and an obscenely expensive cameo from Capri. Now, may I wake my godchild or am I going to be forced to sit here and watch her sleep?"

Caroline's delighted laugh floated lightly over the air, like music, and the child stirred on the blanket, stretching her chubby limbs. Then she opened fetchingly slanted vivid green eyes. "Mama?" she pronounced questioningly, looking toward Richard.

"Oh, dear, I don't think she remembers you, Dickon," Caroline said as Gwen rapidly crawled toward her, to press against her mother's lap. "That will teach you to go away for months on end."

The Earl of Witham went down onto his haunches, a lock of blond hair falling forward over his forehead. "Perhaps this will help. Here, little Gwenny—look what I've brought for you," he said, pulling a small, porcelain-headed doll from where it had been tucked inside his frock coat and holding it in front of him.

Caroline blinked back unexpected tears. "Dickon! Its little face looks just like my mother. And the clothing! The ensemble is exactly the same as she is wearing in the portrait you gave me last Christmas—even the pearl drops in her ears. Gwenny has her namesake, her dearest grandmother, after all! Oh, how beautiful, how perfectly wonderful! How—however did you manage such an ingenious present?"

"Why, by being a genius, of course." He smiled as Gwen cocked her head to one side, as if deciding whether the doll was worth crawling closer to the unfamiliar man, then held out her hands eagerly, so that he lifted her into his arms as he stood. "I had an artist in Florence copy the face and clothing from a miniature of my aunt that I discovered when last Mother and I were at home. My goodness—either this child has grown or I'm getting older. What are you feeding her?"

"Sugarplums mostly, Dickon," Morgan said as he made his way down the path, the big yellow dog, Don Quixote, trailing at his heels, "or at least Aunt Leticia is, whenever we turn our backs. I saw your mother on the terrace and knew I'd find you here. Caro always comes here when she wants to play, don't you, my darling? Welcome home, my friend."

Caroline watched as the two men shook hands—her husband, so tall, so dark; her cousin, equally tall, day to Morgan's night. And the child, her baby, her beautiful Gwen, one arm tightly wrapped around Richard's neck as she leaned forward, pink lips puckered comically, to kiss her father.

Caroline's eyes stung with happy tears, and she smiled, her heart all but overflowing with love. Love for her husband, her child, the family she had found—the life she had discovered upon becoming the bride of the Unicorn.

REQUEST YOUR FREE BOOKS!

2 FREE NOVELS
FROM THE ROMANCE/SUSPENSE
COLLECTION PLUS 2 FREE GIFTS!

YES! Please send me 2 FREE novels from the Romance/Suspense Collection and my 2 FREE gifts. After receiving them, if I don't wish to receive any more books, I can return the shipping statement marked "cancel." If I don't cancel, I will receive 4 brand-new novels every month and be billed just $5.49 per book in the U.S., or $5.99 per book in Canada, plus 25¢ shipping and handling per book plus applicable taxes, if any*. That's a savings of at least 20% off the cover price! I understand that accepting the 2 free books and gifts places me under no obligation to buy anything. I can always return a shipment and cancel at any time. Even if I never buy another book from the Reader Service, the two free books and gifts are mine to keep forever.

185 MDN EF5Y   385 MDN EF6C

Name _____ (PLEASE PRINT)

Address _____ Apt. #

City _____ State/Prov. _____ Zip/Postal Code

Signature (if under 18, a parent or guardian must sign)

Mail to **The Reader Service:**
IN U.S.A.: P.O. Box 1867, Buffalo, NY 14240-1867
IN CANADA: P.O. Box 609, Fort Erie, Ontario L2A 5X3

Not valid to current subscribers to the Romance Collection,
the Suspense Collection or the Romance/Suspense Collection.

Want to try two free books from another line?
Call 1-800-873-8635 or visit www.morefreebooks.com.

* Terms and prices subject to change without notice. NY residents add applicable sales tax. Canadian residents will be charged applicable provincial taxes and GST. This offer is limited to one order per household. All orders subject to approval. Credit or debit balances in a customer's account(s) may be offset by any other outstanding balance owed by or to the customer. Please allow 4 to 6 weeks for delivery.

Your Privacy: Harlequin is committed to protecting your privacy. Our Privacy Policy is available online at www.eHarlequin.com or upon request from the Reader Service. From time to time we make our lists of customers available to reputable firms who may have a product or service of interest to you. If you would prefer we not share your name and address, please check here. ☐

BOB07

KASEY MICHAELS